ONLY THEO

A. K. STEEL

Copyright ©2021 by A. K. Steel

All rights reserved. No part of this book may be reproduced or transmitted in either electronic, paper hard copy, photocopying, recorded, or any other form of reproduction without the written permission of the author. No part of this book either in part or whole may be reproduced into or stored in a retrieval system or distributed without the written permission of the author.

This book is a work of fiction. Characters, names, places and incidents are products of the author's imagination. Any resemblances to actual events, locations, or persons living or dead is purely coincidental.

The author acknowledges the trademark status and owners of products referred to in this fiction which have been used without permission. The publication and use of these trademarks is not authorised, associated with, or sponsored by the trademark owners.

Published by A.K. Steel

Edited by Contagious Edits

Blurb by Contagious Edits

Cover Design by Opium House Creatives

ABOUT THE BOOK

As if raising a child on my own isn't hard enough...

I'm Ivy Anderson, and there is nothing special about me. Plain as they come, really.

A t-shirt-and-jeans-wearing, eternally single yoga teacher whose social life consists of her child and her two besties.

Until Detective Theo Walker, charming single dad, who looks like a god. And he has a story just as heart-breaking as my own.

Theo makes his intentions clear--he wants to have a little fun. He convinces me to put my anxiety aside, give in to temptation and live a little. The chemistry between us is off the charts! I fall for him hard and fast, even though I know I shouldn't.

I can't.

I'm too damaged for him, too messed-up emotionally to start anything new. I live in constant fear, and I haven't been totally honest with him either... I'm scared my past is about to catch up with me.

We're both single parents with heart-wrenching pasts. If anyone deserves true love with a happily ever after it's us... right?

But is it really possible for us to heal each other's hearts and learn to love again?

Or will all my fears come true, destroying our chances at happiness forever?

CHAPTER ONE

THEO

This wedding has been a long time coming. Today, our family finally gets to witness my younger sister, Elena—or Elly, as we all call her—marry Fraser, the man she has been in love with since she was a kid. They have been engaged for four years, but since they both run thriving businesses and have a kid, life kept on getting in the way. They just haven't found the time to plan a wedding. Mum and Indie, Elly's best friend, finally talked them into settling on a date.

So here we are on a boiling day in the middle of summer, at the beach not too far from my parents' house where we grew up, watching them recite their vows. I'm sitting in the front row with our two little boys—my son, Jasper, and Elly and Fraser's little boy, Cooper. They make for very cute page boys in their little navy suits. My brother, Elly's twin, Drew, is one of the groomsmen, along with Fraser's two business partners, Blake and Ash. Indie, Elly's best friend, and Janie, Elly's assistant, stand by her side.

Mum and Dad are sitting proudly in the front row next to us. Mum is radiating happiness in a burgundy off-the-shoulder cocktail dress, a beautiful woman for her age. Dad, like me, is in a suit. We have both ditched our jackets because of the heat, and they now hang off the back of our seats. Lucky for the groomsmen, Elly opted for crisp white shirts and tan tailored shorts; she figured it would be hot, and she was right.

Elly looks magnificent, of course, in a slinky silk gown that Mum said cost her a small fortune, but knowing Elly, it's designer and she just had to have it. The way she and Fraser look at each other could melt my frozen heart, and for a split second, I think I want what they have. Someone to cuddle up to at night, to share my hopes and dreams with, to experience being a parent with. But then I remember love is a motherfucking bitch, and I don't need that shit in my life.

With love comes the worst type of misery when it's ripped from you, the type that prevents you from getting out of bed for days on end. You lose your appetite and motivation to do anything; you don't care what happens to you. I'm not whinging like a pussy, swearing off love forever because some girl dumped me for another guy or some shit like that. Nope, I wish that were the case. My life was literally ripped to shreds when my beautiful fiancée, Fiona, was killed in a horrific car accident at eight months pregnant with our first child. Somehow, they saved Jasper, and I'm eternally grateful every day that they did. It gave me something to live for in those dark days when I thought I couldn't go on without her. He needed me, so I had no choice but to live for him.

As I said, I'm lucky I had my family there to pick me back up and help me get on with my life. But I'm not the same man I was. She died that day. And so did any possibility for me to love another woman, and I am okay with that. Between the long hours I have to put in with my job as a detective and being the best single parent I can be to Jasper, I don't have time for anything else anyway.

I went for the promotion to join the detectives about six months after Fi was taken from me. The driver that killed her was high as a kite and on the run when he barrelled into their car head-on, and if I have to move forward with my life without her in it, I am going to make damn sure that won't happen to someone else's family. I know we can't get everyone, but it's my life's mission to clean up this town as best I can.

And when I have time off, I party hard—even more now Drew's back home with an injury. It's just like when we were younger, a line-up of hot-as-fuck girls ready for some fun for the night. They know with the Walker boys it will be nothing more than that. Just a fun distraction from reality for the night. Yeah, they all say I'm cold-hearted, but I don't care. Better that than a broken heart.

Coop tugs on my hand, snapping me from my thoughts. "Uncle Theo, can I run over to them now? They did the kiss."

Shit, I missed the whole reciting of the vows, trapped in my own thoughts. "Yeah, buddy, go for it." I release his hand, and he takes off running to his mum and dad, pushing his way between them. Fraser reaches down and picks him up, and the three of them nuzzle their faces together. I'm happy for them, I really am. Jasper comes to sit on my lap, and I hug him into my chest, messing up his hair.

Mum looks over at me with a sympathetic smile. "You okay, love?"

I plaster on my best fake smile. This smile is so well practiced over the last few years, I don't even have to try anymore. "Why wouldn't I be? It's a wedding, we're celebrating."

"I know, love, but it can't be easy." She gives my hand a squeeze.

"You can be happy for your sister and still be hurting, Theo," adds Dad. I know it's just because they care so much, and it must have been hard for them to watch their son go through losing someone they love, but I hate the pity in their eyes. I don't want them to see me as weak—I'm not, and I don't need any pity from anyone.

"It's fine, guys, really. I'm all good." I stand, taking Jasper's hand. "Let's go congratulate the happy couple, Jas." We head towards where the bridal party has gathered in some shade under a large Pandanus tree. Guests line up and fuss over Elly and Fraser, offering hugs of congratulations and well-wishes for the future.

I love my mum, but since the accident, she has been trying to fix me. And I don't need fixing, I'm not broken. This is who I am now, and nothing is going to change that.

We reach the front of the line. Which is lucky, because Jasper can't stand still any longer, he's so excited to see Elly. She's his favourite adult; he spends a lot of time with her, and he adores her. He runs to her first. "Auntie Elly, you look like a princess."

"Thank you, sweetie, you look like a little prince in your suit." He smiles shyly.

"Congratulations, sis," I say, throwing my arms around her in an embrace. She beams with happiness, and I kiss her on the cheek.

"Thank you, big brother. I really appreciate you taking care of Cooper today. Hope you didn't teach him any bad habits."

"Just all my good ones," I say with a wink.

"Great, so I'm in for hell over the next few weeks, am I?" She laughs.

"I think I need to be more worried about what he is teaching Jas." I laugh back.

"I know," she says, burying her head in her hand and shaking it. "What am I going to do with him?"

Fraser returns from talking to one of the other guests. I pat him on the back, and he pulls me in for a hug. "Congratulations, mate, finally made it official."

"I would have done it years ago, but it was this one that kept putting it off."

Elly shrugs then weaves her arm around his waist, gazing up at him lovingly. "I was in no rush, I had everything I needed." She smiles.

Another couple comes to steal away their attention. "Let's go find Uncle Drew," I say to Jasper, and he nods.

We walk into the reception area to find him already at the bar with Blake and a very-pregnant Indie. She and Blake have three kids already, so this will be number four. Blake is Fraser's business partner, and Indy is Elly's best friend—that's how they got together. They've only been together for four years, but they have made the most of that time.

"Don't you guys have to get your photos done or something before you drink?" I call out to him.

Drew turns from his place at the bar. "Just grabbing a quick water before we start. You'd better too. Elly says she wants you there for it, and it's bloody hot out there."

"How are you holding up in the heat, Indie?" Poor Indie looks hot. Standing up on the beach for an hour in the middle of summer wouldn't have been much fun at seven months pregnant.

She fans herself with her hand. "I'm okay. I'm just happy to have the night off from my crazy children." She laughs.

"I bet they are full of energy, those boys of yours especially. I don't know how you keep up with them."

"Why do you think I came straight for the bar?" laughs Blake, beer in hand. "I'm making the most of it while I can."

"I would die for a proper drink right now too. It feels like it's been years," says Indie. Blake wraps his arm around her, giving her a squeeze.

"That's because you keep having babies. Don't you two know how to use protection?" says Drew. I give him a look to be careful what he says in front of Jas.

"We wanted a big family, and with twins in the mix, well, we got extra lucky," says Blake, shrugging.

Indie gives him a look. "But we're done now. Four is definitely enough."

"We haven't decided that," grumbles Blake, and Indie gives him a serious look. I'd say she has had enough, especially now, in her state.

"Hey, Jas, you want a water?" asks Drew, pouring him a water and handing it to him. "It's so hot out there today, isn't it."

"Yes, please, Uncle Drew," he says sweetly.

I turn my attention to Drew, leaving the lovers to have their tiff. "What're the plans for tonight? After the photos, I'll take the boys back to the house with the sitter Elly organised."

"See those two chicks over there? Sisters." He tilts his head subtly toward where they're standing.

The girls are just outside the marquee on the grass, champagne in hand, chatting away. "Nice." They're hot, both blonde with pretty faces, kind of young, probably in their mid-twenties.

"They recognised me from some article the paper did on top Aussie surfers and wanted to know if I had a friend looking to party tonight as well."

I shake my head. Of course they did, everyone knows Drew.

Mum enters the marquee to call us back to the beach to have photos taken. Taking Jasper's hand, I plaster on my best fake smile and do my brotherly duties.

An hour later, after a very long photo session with hundreds of photos of us all sweating our arses off, we're walking up the beach to what the photographer described as the most romantic spot. Don't know how romantic it was for Elly and Fraser who seem oblivious to the heat, but for the rest of us—especially the men in suits—it was fucking sweltering. By the end, the kids had stripped off their suits and were paddling in the shallow waves.

I have now driven Jas and Coop back to Mum and Dad's place, the sitter will have them until Mum and Dad get home at eleven. Mum has given me the night off to have some *fun*, her words. I enter the marquee looking for Drew. His back is to me as he sits at the bar. I take a seat beside him and order a beer.

"This place looks epic," I say, admiring the girls' handiwork.

"The girls have outdone themselves this time," he agrees, turning to the room to take it all in.

For a marquee, this place looks amazing with a timber hanging install attached to the ceiling of the marquee with draped eucalyptus and pepperberry cascading down. The cocktail-type tables are scattered with vases of native Australian flowers in pale pinks and burgundies. They might have waited four years to get married, but Elly has certainly gone to a lot of effort to have the wedding of her dreams. Janie, Elly's assistant, did all the floral arrangements. Janie has branched their styling business into weddings and just completed her florist degree, so this would have been all her doing. There's no seating plan here. They wanted a more casual cocktail vibe so people could mingle and dance all night, not be stuck at a table. We grab a drink and make our way to one of the rattan lounge seating areas down the back of the marquee.

"How are you holding up, man?" Drew asks, that same look on his face as our parents had.

I give him a warning look. He's the last person I expect to be throwing a question like that at me today. "Why do people keep asking me that today? It's my sister's wedding, I'm happy for her."

"You know what I mean. It's the first family wedding since—"

I cut him off. "Not talking about the past today," I say with a look that says *drop it now*.

"Got it. So, how about we find those girls?" He smiles, and right on cue they come walking through the groups of guests mingling around the venue towards us.

"Looks like we won't have to, they have found us." They make eye contact as they sway through the crowd. They're confident, the kind of girls that always get what they want, and lucky for us, tonight it looks like that's us.

"Drew," purrs the taller one, "we thought we had lost you. Where did you get to?"

"Bridal party duties, but we're all done with that now, so we're not going anywhere."

"Who's your friend?" says the other one, wearing a silky ice-blue dress that matches her eyes. She hasn't taken her eyes off me since she walked over here.

"Theo, his brother," I say, holding my hand out for her to

shake and offering my most charming smile. She places her hand in mine and smiles sweetly, batting her eyelashes. You can tell she has done this many times before. She's pretty and just the distraction I need for tonight.

"Brothers, how convenient. I'm Roxy, and this is Lalla, my sister. Can we sit with you? We're Fraser's cousins from out of town and don't know anyone else."

We both shuffle over to make space for them as they slide in next to us. And that's where we stay for the rest of the wedding. Drinking, laughing, telling stories, every so often dancing when a song comes on that the girls like. They're young and fun and the perfect entertainment to get me through the night.

When it comes time for the night to end, Roxy suggests we take the party back to her hotel room, and how could I turn down such a promising offer? This is what I do, right? Pick up a girl, have a fun night of fucking, then never see her again. But that twinge I've been getting lately is there again. That empty feeling that I can't seem to fill, no matter how many girls I sleep with, and lately it feels like it's getting worse. I scull the rest of my drink and decide to take her up on her offer anyway.

We barely make it through the door of her hotel room before she launches herself at me, her lips locked with mine. She's like a wild beast trying to devour me. I back her up towards the wall and press her against it as I kiss her back, hurried lips going everywhere. I run my hands up her arms, slipping the thin straps of her dress down her shoulders; it drops to her waist, exposing her breasts. They're perky and perfect, and I cup them in my hands, massaging, trying to enjoy this moment with the hot-as-fuck chick standing in front of me. My head is all over the place, though, anywhere but here in this moment. I'm back at the wedding ceremony seeing the way Elly and Fraser looked at each other, the way Mum and Dad looked at me with pity.

Get out of your head, Theo!

I must be drunker than I thought, because my body's not quite catching up with the program and I'm only semi-hard. I pull her breast to me and suck hard, hoping to kick myself into gear. She drops her hand, palming me through my suit pants, and my cock twitches, springing to life.

She moans loudly as I suck on the other breast. I pull back, and she fumbles with my shirt, pulling at the buttons trying to get them undone. I shrug out of my shirt then start on my pants, and she shimmies out of her dress and underwear. I pull a condom from my pocket before I toss the wrapper on the floor and roll it on. My hands are back on her, kissing her again, pulling her into me.

But that pain is there again, that dull ache in my chest.

I try to push it away and concentrate on what I'm doing, ignoring the pain. I push her back onto the bed and spread her legs as wide as they will go. She is laid out in front of me; how could I not want this, she's gorgeous. Stop thinking, Theo, just do. I scrabble up the bed to where she is, and in one fast thrust, push straight in.

I'm buried deep inside of her, moving back and forth, trying desperately to fuck this feeling away. But it's no use. She looks up at me, her eyes blinking back with lust, and all I feel is that fucking pain as my heart thumps loudly in my chest.

I'm fucking dead inside, empty, and the pain just gets worse. I feel dizzy.

I pull out. "I can't do this, I'm sorry."

She looks at me as if I'm joking or something. I scramble off the bed quickly, grabbing for my suit, pulling it on as fast as I can.

"What are you talking about, do you have a girlfriend or something?" she says, confused, pulling the sheets up to cover her body.

"No, I just... I have to go, I'm sorry." I grab my shoes and hurry out of there with them in my hand, not stopping to put them on. When I get out the front of the room, I try to catch my breath. My heart is hammering in my chest, I feel like I can't breathe. What is wrong with me? I feel terrible for the poor girl. I just ran out on a one-night stand because I feel like I'm about to have a panic attack. What the actual fuck is wrong with me.

CHAPTER TWO

IVY

I HEAR THE PITTER PATTER OF HER LITTLE FOOTSTEPS as she runs down the hall, and I know the chance for any more sleep is over.

Her warm little hands clutch my arms, shaking me. "Wake up, Mummy, wake up! Come on, lazy bones, wake up, it's a very important day!"

My eyes flutter open to see a very excited Harmony, standing beside my bed trying to wake her poor sleep-deprived mother. She's already dressed herself for the day in an eclectic outfit, fairy wings and all. Her platinum-blonde hair is a mass of unruly curls tucked into a sparkly plastic tiara. I roll over, blinking my eyes, wiping the sleep away. I must have eventually fallen asleep last night, but I feel like it was only an hour ago. I'll never get used to the early mornings that come with being a parent, and when you sleep as poorly as I do, the morning always comes too soon.

"Oh, Harmy, can't Mummy have just five more minutes?" I pick her up, pulling her up into the bed with me, tickling her tummy then cuddling her into me. "Happy birthday, baby girl. I can't believe you're five."

She tries to wiggle out of my grip, giggling. It's the cutest sound ever, and even though I'm tired, it's all worth it to have these precious moments with her.

She gets free of my grip, jumping out of bed, her little hand tugging on mine to do the same. "That's why you have to get up right now, Mummy, we have lots of things to do today."

"Okay, baby, let's get started," I say reluctantly, sitting up and searching around the bottom of my bed for my dressing gown. I drop my legs off the edge of the bed, my feet finding my warm, cosy slippers, slowly making my way down the stairs behind an overexcited birthday girl. It's Sunday morning, and we have a tradition of pancakes every Sunday, so I get to work on our special treat, a stack of pancakes with blueberries and maple syrup together. Yum.

Breakfast made, we sit at the breakfast bar scoffing it down. As I dig into the delicious stack of pancakes in front of me, the doorbell rings.

Harmony runs excitedly over to the door. "It's Auntie Jen, and she has presents!"

Jenna—also known as, "Auntie Jen" —is our neighbour and my best friend. She has been my rock since I moved to Broken Point five years ago to start a new life. I honestly don't know what I would have done without her. She's family to us, my voice of reason, and even though she's a couple of years younger than me, she is definitely more mature. She always knows just what to do when I'm having a moment of freak out!

She beams at Harmony, all excited, and hands her the rather large present wrapped in rainbow-coloured paper she has in her hands. Harmony wraps her arms around Jenna's legs, nearly throwing her off balance since she's holding a tray with two coffees in it as well.

Harmony sits on the plush rug, holding the present up to her ear, giving it a little shake. Her tongue is out to the side, and I know she's dying to know what's inside. "Can I open it?"

"Sure, why not," I reply.

Jenna slides the tray with the two coffees onto the breakfast bar in front of me. She is stunning even at this time of the morning, looking all glam in faded skinny jeans teamed with a black-and-white-stripe, off-the-shoulder top that highlights her tanned shoulders. Her long chestnut-brown hair in a high ponytail sways as she walks towards me, kissing my cheek.

I give her a squeeze back. "You're the best, Jenna, what would I do without you?"

"Not a lot, probably, without your morning coffee." She grabs my fork that was sitting on the edge of my plate and digs into my pancakes.

I bump her arm. "Hey, I wasn't done with those."

She smiles. "But what would you do without me?" she mumbles with her mouth full, spitting pancakes everywhere as she talks. I push the plate across to her.

"They're all yours. I've lost my appetite."

She smiles happily, now getting the rest of my breakfast to herself. She's lucky I love her.

I watch Harmony as she tears apart the present, wrapping paper flying everywhere so she can get to the goodies inside.

She squeals excitedly. "Oh yeah, I love these!" Everything is rainbows, glitter, and unicorns, and I can see by the little smirk on Jenna's face that she is very pleased with herself for just how well she knows Harmony.

Harmy jumps up, the unicorn toy under her, and rushes toward Jenna. "Oh wow, thank you, Auntie Jen! This is the best birthday ever!" She throws her arms around her legs, hugging her. Jenna plays with her curls, untangling them in a motherly way. She will make such a wonderful mother one day.

"You haven't even gotten your surprise from me yet, baby girl."

Her eyes rise excitedly to me. "What is it, Mummy, what have you got for me? Can I have it now?"

"Well, if you want to know, you're going to have to finish your breakfast so we can get a move on. We have to go for a drive to pick it up!" Before we know it, she's back in her seat, shovelling the pancakes in as fast as she can.

"Careful, you're going to choke," I scold. She looks at me but continues at the same speed.

Jenna whispers to me, so Harmony can't hear, "Are you ready for this? A cat is an enormous responsibility."

"Thanks, *Mum*, I'm sure we can handle it," I whisper back.

Harmony drinks her juice and grabs me by the hand, pulling me toward the door. "So, I guess we're going to see what the surprise is then?"

"Yes, come on, let's go."

"Let me get out of my pyjamas first, then we'll go." I throw on a pair of faded ripped jeans and a tee with a sunflower on it. I run a quick brush through my hair then brush my teeth, and I'm ready.

We all jump in the car and take off on our special adventure to our surprise location. It's just a short drive up the road in Mullumbimby, but Harmony can't contain her excitement and is singing in the back, "Happy birthday to me," on repeat.

As we pull up outside, I look in the rear-view mirror to see her reaction. Her eyes widen as she sees the blue-and-white sign with a cat and dog on it and realises we're at the animal shelter.

"I'm getting a pet," she sings from the back seat with excitement, and I know this is the right decision. She has been pestering me for a cat all year. She loves animals, and I'm ready to add to our little family.

When we enter the shelter there is a lot of noise from all the animals, and Harmony clings to Jenna's leg while I go talk to the lady on the front counter.

"We're here to pick up a kitten under the name of Ivy Anderson." I smile.

"Oh yes, dear." She looks me over, pushing her glasses back up her nose. "I won't be a second," says the lady as she disappears through a door to the side of the counter. She returns moments later with the cutest little fluffy ginger-striped cat you have ever seen. Harmony comes running over to take her from me, and the cat squirms in her arms as she cuddles her in close. This poor cat is going to be loved to death.

"Oh, Mummy, she's just the cutest. Do I get to keep her?"

"She's all yours, baby girl, but you're going to have to learn how to take care of her. She is just a kitten so she will be a bit of work for a while."

"What are you going to call her?" Jenna asks Harmony.

"Oh, I don't know." She thinks for a while, stroking the kitten's soft fur and bringing her face up to hers close so she can look her in the eyes. "Her name is Tiger," she announces, pleased with herself.

"Sounds like a perfect name for a little ginger fluffball," says Jenna. We gather up all the things we need to care for the new addition to our family and make our way home.

Back at home, I'm finishing the last details of icing on Harmony's unicorn cake, while Jenna and Harmony play in the yard with Tiger. We're just having a few friends over for cake and a little party in the backyard of our townhouse. Harmony has only just started school, and she doesn't have a lot of friends her age yet, so we only invited our Broken Point family, Penny, Jenna, and Fay.

We're a funny mismatched group. We all kind of found each other because we moved here from out of town at about the same time.

Penny is 25, and we work together at the yoga studio. She was on the run from some ex that had broken her heart, and she has been sworn off anything serious ever since.

Jenna moved into the house next to me about six months before me. She's an aspiring writer but never really had the self-confidence to do anything with it, so for now, she works at the local library, trying to gather the courage to do something about her dream. I'm not sure what her family situation is; she refuses to talk about it, and I'm okay with that because I'm the same. I think that's why we became friends so quickly—we both have a shitty past we would prefer to forget and never talk about.

Fay, our next-door neighbour, is in her 60s. She lives alone, never having been married or having kids of her own, so has kind of adopted us all, especially Harmony. She's like a grandmother to her, and we're so blessed to have Fay in our lives.

Since none of us has any family of our own to speak of, this is our family. Just us girls.

Fay and Penny arrive, and we sing Happy Birthday to Harmony, who is too busy playing with Tiger to notice all the fuss over her—but she's first in line once I cut the cake! It's a unicorn, of course, with glittery sparkles all over it and a number-five candle. This house is going to be covered in glitter by the end of today.

Fay grabs my hand. "Thank you for the cake, honey, but it's getting late, and I better be going. I'm teaching a pour art class tomorrow, and I need to get organised for it."

I give her a kiss on the cheek. "I'll walk you to the door. Thank you so much for coming and the lovely present you bought for Harmony; she loves to create, and the art set is perfect."

"You'll have to send her over for art lessons next week so we can use it together."

"Oh, she would love that, thank you, Fay." I give her a big hug goodbye at the front door. I'm so grateful for her.

Just as I go to close the door, Tiger makes a run for it, squeezing through my legs. She's through the front door then the security gate so quickly, I can't catch her before she's through. I have to punch my code into the gate for it to open before I can run around and save her from the oncoming traffic. I look back to make sure Harmy's not following me, but she watches in horror from the house as a white Jeep screeches on its brakes in an attempt not to hit Tiger. Jenna picks Harmony up and is hugging her close to stop her from chasing after me.

I make it out the gate and to the car as fast as I can as it screeches to a stop. There's no sign of Tiger. *Please let her be okay.* The man in the car turns to say something to a little boy in the backseat then opens his door, bending down and collecting our small ball of fluff from the road. He cradles her in his arms, and she cuddles in, probably scared as hell.

She's alright, though. He rounds the front of his car, and I get a better look at him. He's gorgeous. And as he walks towards me, it's as if time stands still. I can feel the thump of my heart in my chest from running down the drive, and the adrenaline is racing.

"I'm assuming this is your fluffball?" says the g*od* standing in front of me. Man, he looks like one of those action heroes—I think it's Thor, with long dirty blond hair all messy and piercing Nordic-blue eyes that are fixed on me. It's making me feel self-conscious.

I swallow the lump in my throat as he closes the gap between us. I know I'm staring at him, unable to take my eyes away or speak. What I must look like to him. He stands in front of me, a cheeky smile crossing his face. He knows the effect he has on women, how could he not. He's tall; he towers over me, and I'm pretty tall for a girl, but he's got to be way over six feet, and it's clear from the size of his arms that he works out too. And I mean like he must spend all his time working out, like some professional athlete or something.

He hands the trembling kitten to me, and our hands brush, leaving a strange tingling behind. What was that? I go to open my mouth to say something, but nothing comes out. The man looks like a god, and I have no words.

CHAPTER THREE

THEO

That's it, I'm done for the day. I'm not getting anywhere, anyway. I remove my glasses and throw them down on my makeshift desk I have set up on my dining table and close my laptop, running my hands through my hair. It's getting long, and I make a mental note to get a cut soon.

I'm tired. I've had a long week. It's now Sunday, and I'm still working on this case. There's more work on at the moment than we can finish at the station with my normal Monday to Friday, so I've been bringing my paperwork home to finish whenever I can. This case is getting to me. Our team has been working on it for close to three years now, which is normal with narcotics cases, but it feels like we're going round in circles. We're missing something, but I can't work out what it is, and it seems whenever we get close, key evidence disappears.

The afternoon sun is streaming in my dining room, and by the looks of it, I'm missing out on a cracker of a day. Normally on the weekend I try to spend as much time with Jasper as I can, but today I needed to get this done. I check my watch; I need to pick up Jas and get going to Drew's. He'll be pissed if I'm late for our surf lesson.

DRIVING THROUGH THE SMALL BEACHSIDE SUBURBS, I always feel so lucky to have called this place home my entire life. I grew up in the main township of Byron Bay itself. My parents still live there; they love being a part of all the action that takes place, but that wasn't for me. I get enough of that with my job as a detective, so I've moved just outside to Mullumbimby. It's close enough that I can still surf on my days off but far enough away that I can relax and get away from it all when I need to.

I stop in at Elly's and pick up Jasper. He's been there since last night for a sleepover, something we try to do at least once a month so the kids can have some time together and I have time to go out with the boys and catch up on work. Truth be told, I know Elly does it for me. It's the way she feels like she's helping, and I love her for it.

My phone rings and I see Drew's name flash up on the car screen. "I'm on my way, mate, just picked up Jas.

"Good. I've been waiting all arvo for you. I'm heading over to the beach now. I need to get in the water. Elly will be here soon, you can catch me up."

"Yeah, I know, see you soon, chill out." I end the call.

He's so impatient. I said I would be there by three, and I will. I don't know what his hurry is; he's probably been out surfing already today, anyway. He's surfing obsessed and has been since he was a little kid. Luckily for him, all the practice has paid off, and he's been on the world surfing tour since he was 18. This year he's out with an injury, so he's more of a pain than usual, with nothing better to do. He's a lucky bastard. Must be nice to get paid to do something you're passionate about.

When I first started in the police force, that was how I felt, like my passion for helping people could somehow change the world one case at a time. But after nearly 15 years on the force, and now working in the narcotics unit, I've seen too much. The shit that messes with your head and keeps you up at night. If we solve the case, you feel you're making a difference, getting these lowlifes off the street and saving innocent lives, but it's never for long. There's always some new drug lord ready to take the place of the last.

Sometimes I wish I had chosen a different career path, not to follow in my dad's footsteps, so I wouldn't carry so many demons with me. My dad was always such a hero to me when I was a kid, and I couldn't think of anything I wanted to do more than be just like him. So, when I finished school, it was a no-brainer for me. I got accepted into the academy and didn't look back. So much has changed since then, my perspective on life, and with every fresh case we get, I have to solve it. Someone has to keep these pieces of shit off the streets before they destroy someone else's family. That's the only reason I keep going to work every day.

What the fuck?

Out of the corner of my eye, I see a slight flash of ginger fur run across in front of me, and I slam on the brakes. My wheels screech to a stop, and I hope to God I stopped in time. I take a second to settle my hammering heart and turn to Jas.

"You okay, mate."

"I'm fine, Dad, but you better get the kitten before she runs again." His face is pressed against the window looking for the cat.

I open my door, searching for the culprit. A small ginger

furball sits just in front of my tyre, and I scoop it up, cuddling it into my chest. It's shaking, so I stroke it. "It's alright, you're okay, you silly thing." Jasper is watching us through the window and smiles when he sees it's okay.

I round the front of my car, ready to have a go at the woman running out of the gate for not taking better care of her pet, but I stop when I see her. My heart is still hammering, but it's for a different reason now. She's hot as fuck with honey-blonde hair down to her waist, sun-kissed at the ends, fanning out behind her as she runs. Her skin is tanned, her body fucking perfection. I can see even through the skinny jeans and tee she's wearing that her body is toned and muscular, so casual, but she makes it look hot. She stops just in front of me, panting from running after the cat. Her eyes lock with mine and she waits, not saying anything. I blink back at her, a little lost for words myself. I have never seen anyone quite like her.

Seconds pass, minutes maybe, with us just like this until I snap out of my daze. "I'm assuming this is your ball of fluff?" I smile at her cheekily as I hand her back her kitten, our hands brushing.

She blushes when she realises she's been staring for quite some time without talking and finally finds her voice. "Oh, I'm so sorry, it's my daughter's kitten, she got her for her birthday today, so we're still getting her used to the rules, she just escaped when we opened the door, she's way too quick for me. I'm so sorry to have scared you. Thank you for saving her." She talks quickly without taking a breath, then pats the little fluffball on the head, and it wiggles in her arms. "Little Tiger here is a naughty girl."

Oh, she's got a daughter. Of course someone as hot as her is married with a kid. I glance down at her hand holding the cat. There are many rings on her hand, but not on the right finger.

She looks over to where a group of women have gathered along the fence. They must be having a party. I get a wave from the rest of the crowd standing at the fence, and the stunner walks over and hands the cat to her daughter who has clearly been crying. She looks about the same age as Jasper. She cuddles the cat close to her chest.

"Take her inside, I'll be in a minute." Her friends whisper something to her and give me another wave, then help the little girl back inside with the cat. The woman heads back to me. "Thanks again. I'm so sorry to have caused such a fuss, we'll be more careful now."

I scan her face, taking in every detail. She's beautiful, her eyes a bright cobalt blue, outlined with long dark lashes, looking up to me shyly. She twists her hands and plays with the many rings on her fingers. I can't help but notice she's got a daughter but no wedding band—interesting. Might still be in with a chance. I can't take my eyes off her, and I'm racking my brain to think of something else to say to keep her here longer. Drew won't like it because I'm going to be late, but he can wait!

I'm not normally like this. Charming women comes naturally to me. As soon as I hit high school, the attention I was getting from girls was enough to give me all the confidence I needed to flirt with whoever I wanted to, and it's been that easy ever since. But this chick seems different.

"No trouble at all." I put my hand out to shake hers. "Sorry, I didn't catch your name?"

"Oh, I'm Ivy." She looks down at the ground as she talks, then puts her hand in mine. Her skin feels nice under mine, and I don't want to let her go, so I don't. I look into her eyes, still holding her hand.

"I'm Theodore, but my friends call me Theo. Looks like you're having a bit of a party. You could always invite me and my son in for some cake to repay me for my good deed. That's if your husband won't mind?" I say with a mischievous smile. That should work; I'm sure she can't resist my charm, no girl can.

"No husband," she says quietly.

"Boyfriend?"

She just shakes her head. Wow! So, she's single, I almost can't believe it. How is it possible? I'm about to ask, but our attention is drawn back to the front door as it opens and her little daughter comes out with some birthday cake. I realise I'm still holding the woman's hand as she pulls out of my grip. Heading over to the fence, to the little girl, I kneel to her so I can see her better.

She puts her hand through the fence. "This is for you, mister, to say thank you for being my hero and saving Tiger."

"Oh, thank you, how thoughtful," I say with a smile, taking the cake from her. "Now, let me guess, you must be turning five?"

She smiles broadly. "How did you know?"

"My son is the same age and about your size," I say, pointing to the car where Jasper sits.

"Maybe he could come and have a play with me one day. I don't really have many friends, I only just started school."

"I'm sure he would like that. He might even be at the same school as you. He goes to Broken Point Primary."

"Yes, that's where I go to school." She looks towards the car. "I don't really know him, he's in the other kindy class."

Ivy stands behind me. "Harmy, head back up to the

house, I'll be there in a sec. I'm sure this man is very busy and needs to get on with his day."

"Okay, Mummy. Eat the cake, mister, there is enough for your son as well. It's so yummy. My mum made it, and she's the best at making cakes." With that, she skips back to the house calling, "Are you coming, Mummy?" There goes that plan of inviting us to the party.

"Be right there, baby girl," she calls to her daughter. "Sorry, she can talk all day if you get her started."

"That's okay, she's a cute kid."

"Thank you again, Theo, you have saved the day." She puts her hand on her heart and says, "Our hero," with a little laugh.

"No worries, Ivy, but you're not getting away that easily. You owe me a coffee, you know, payback for saving your cat, and it sounds like your daughter would like a play date with my son as well."

I go to my car, handing the cake to Jasper. "Won't be a sec, mate." The cake is straight into his mouth. There will be none left for me, that's for sure. I use the napkin to write my number on it, then jog back to Ivy, handing it to her because I can't help myself. I'm not done here. "Whenever you need someone to save the day." She looks at the napkin and shakes her head with a small smile.

"So, you're a single parent as well?" She looks over to my car again, where Jasper is watching us through the window from his car seat.

"Since the day he was born, yes."

"I know what that's like."

"Then we already have something to talk about."

Her brows furrow. "Are you always this forward in asking someone out?"

"Yes, I don't have any trouble going after what I want,

Ivy." She's blushing again, and it's the cutest that I have this effect over her.

She looks back to the house. "Oh, okay, thanks for your number, I better go," she says, looking down like she's lost her voice again. "Bye, Theo. Thanks again." She turns, walking away, and punches numbers into the security gate before running back into the complex. Oh well, the ball's in her court now, I guess.

I jump in the car and watch as she goes inside. "That was interesting," I say out loud.

"Who was she? Why were you talking for so long?" comes a small voice from the back. I turn to look at him. His face is covered in frosting.

"Did you enjoy that cake?"

He nods, licking his lips.

"Her daughter goes to your school."

"Yeah, I know her. She's in the other class with Cooper. She sits by herself at lunchtime."

"She said she doesn't have many friends yet. Maybe you can fix that and sit with her for lunch so she's not alone."

"I sit with Cooper."

"Well, you could both sit with her."

I turn on the car and see the time is 3:30; Drew is going to be pissed. He will be waiting for us at the beach right around the corner from his house with Elly and Cooper. It's only a few streets from here so it don't take long to arrive in the beach car park.

I get Jasper out of the car, and I pull his board off the roof racks. Jas and Cooper have been in the water since they were born, and they both started surfing lessons with Drew when he came home this time. He said it's never too early to start, and they're both loving it. Jas is a natural in the water, just like his uncles.

I walk up the sandy path to where we normally meet, Jasper's surfboard under my arm. As soon as Jasper sees them, he takes off running.

I'm slower to make my way over, still going over what just happened in my head. I get to where the other two stand and drop his board to the sand and sit down, running my hands through my hair.

"What's going on with you?" asks Drew.

"Nothing, we were just running late," I huff, not ready to share whatever that all was with my siblings.

"Yeah, and? You look weird," says Elly, giving me her knowing look.

These two don't miss a beat. "And nothing. Just been an interesting afternoon. Sorry we're late."

Drew shrugs and takes after the kids to the water. Elly sits down beside me, tapping me on the knee. "Been a big week, hey, bro?"

Ivy

I stroll back into my house holding the little pink napkin with Theo's number on it. Still shaking my head in disbelief at the events that just took place. That cat is going to be trouble.

I can feel Theo still watching me from his car. I can't believe he gave me his number. Does he really want me to call him? Surely, I couldn't look that appealing. A single mother, her hair a mess from the busy day, icing spilt down my T-shirt. Why on earth would he want to give me his number? Maybe it was for the play date for the kids? It wouldn't be such a bad idea; Harmony hasn't really made many friends since starting school, mainly because I don't know any of the other parents, so this would be good for her.

My beautiful friends have cleaned up the mass of wrapping paper that was spread all over the house from the party and are now in the kitchen stacking the dishwasher, chatting away. They turn to look at me as soon as I walk through the door, their eyes wide.

"What?" I say, unable to hide the smile on my face. They drop what they're doing and come over to me with grins like Cheshire cats.

"What was that all about, missy? Long chat with the man that nearly ran over your cat."

I collapse down onto the couch. "It was nothing, just saying thank you." If I'm being honest with myself, I don't know what to make of it. It was strange, that's what it was. I look down at my hands and remember how his touch felt. What was that? Has it been so long that a simple touch of my hand has me all giddy like a schoolgirl? Pull yourself together, Ivy. This isn't some rom-com where a man nearly runs over your cat, you work out you're both struggling single parents, and you're the missing part to each other's life. You fall deeply in love, living happily ever after.

This is real life, and shit like that doesn't happen to us.

Penny comes to sit next to me, tucking her legs up underneath, getting comfy. "Did you get his number? He was probably the hottest guy I have ever seen in real life, and that's saying something. I have pretty good taste and I date a lot, so you know I see a lot of hot men."

I show her the napkin with his number on it. "I'm not sure how, I barely said two words to him."

"Oh my God," Penny squeals excitedly, "are you going to call him?"

I can't believe she even thinks I'm going to go out with him. "Um, Pen, I don't think his type is a single mum who's not had sex in five years! Do you think a god like that wants to go out with plain old me? He was probably just being nice or something with the awkward weirdo staring at him with her mouth wide open. He's a single dad, so I think he was just trying to organise a play for the kids, since they're at the same school."

Jenna gives me a look, her nose scrunching up like she's not convinced. "I don't know, Ivy, he was staring at you as much as you were at him, and that's super cute if you're both single parents."

"I don't know about all of that. Besides, my life's too complicated to be running around town on dates. I've got more baggage than an airport, and to be honest, the last thing I need is more complications. I like this safe, comfortable life where I don't have to worry about any of that."

They both roll their eyes at me. They have heard it all before. Every time they try to convince me it must be time to get out there and meet someone, my answer is always the same. And for good reason. What I have now is safe, and that's the way I like it.

"You don't always have to be a saint just because you're a single mum, you know, Ivy. You can live a little too," Penny says as she walks away. Her face is more than disappointed. I'm sure she's right, but it's taken me years to build this safe little fort for myself, one brick at a time, and these walls aren't coming down for anyone. I don't care how dreamy he is.

I let out a massive sigh. "You're probably right, Pen, but it's not just me I have to think about. I tell you what, though, my battery-operated friend will get a workout tonight. He was really hot, hey?" They both laugh at me and shake their heads.

"Too much information, Ivy!" says Jenna. She's a bloody little miss goody-two shoes. I'm not even sure if she's ever had sex, by the way she acts. If we bring up anything to do with it, she's disgusted by it.

CHAPTER FOUR

THEO

It's Wednesday morning, and the sun isn't quite up yet. It's early, but I need to get a workout in before I get Jasper sorted for school and head to the station for the day.

I've been feeling off since Elly's wedding. That night shifted something in me, and I've felt off-balance ever since. Then there is that chick I met on Sunday afternoon, with the kid and the cat. We had a pleasant chat, established she was single. There was a definite attraction there. But she hasn't called, and I can't help but feel a little disappointed. It was obvious she was shy, but I was forward and made it clear I was interested—I was sure she would have called by now. They always call. Shit, if it was anyone else around here, I'd have already fucked her out of my system and been over it. Now I'm sounding like some needy chick, waiting for the phone to ring. This isn't like me, I need to snap out of it!

I just need a good workout, then I'll stop whining like a pussy. I heard Talon's car arrive 20 minutes ago. He's keen today. When Fraser and Blake built this place for me, we had a gym installed downstairs, knowing I wouldn't be able to leave the house early in the morning like I was used to. It was the perfect idea.

Talon joins me most of the time. It saves him on gym membership, and we both have company. He lives out this way as well, on a block with some land, so it's easier for him to come here than into town. We work out most days before we start at the station; I find it's the best way to start the day, especially with some of the shit we see in our line of work. It clears the mind. I know my dad was always the same, and that's how he coped on the force for 40 years.

I grab a towel from the linen cupboard and head downstairs to join him. He's on the treadmill warming up, and I take his lead, heading straight to the treadmill next to him to warm up. Talon's already worked up quite a sweat. He just gives me a nod to acknowledge my presence. Good, I don't feel like talking this morning. I glance over and can see he's already run three kilometres, and my competitive side kicks in. "Beat you to ten," I say, keen for the distraction.

"You've got no chance, man," he says as he picks up the pace.

That'll make me feel better, a little friendly competition. I'll kick his arse on the treadmill and all balance will be restored in the universe. I was a long-distance runner in high school, and I've kept it up most days, so I'm pretty quick. I'll beat him for sure.

I get to nine kilometres, and I glance over again and can see he's just in front of me. I'm going to have to sprint this last kilometre to beat him. I pick up the pace as much as I can when my legs are already burning. This is the fastest I've run in years, but it feels good, and I haven't thought of Ivy once... until now.

I've nearly caught him. We have 100 metres to go, and we're both sprinting. I'm nearly out of breath, but I've got to win for bragging rights. Head down, I sprint the last 100 and look up to see him finish just before me.

"You had a head start," is all I can get out between trying to suck in air. I sound like a whiny bitch, but I hate losing.

"You're a sore loser!" he says between heavy breaths. He's right, I am, always have been. I'm super competitive, and when I want something, I get it. This was probably a bad idea, and we're both going to pay for this today. I slow to a walk, trying to cool down and get my breath back.

"What's your problem anyway? You've been in a mood all week!" He looks at me, kind of pissed that I made him run so hard. He didn't have to accept the challenge, but that's something I've learned about working with Talon for so long—he'll never say no to a challenge, just like me.

"No, I haven't," I huff.

He throws me a look. "You can't lie to me. I see you every day, man, I can tell when something's off."

I have known Talon for eight years now, since he was a junior training at the station. Then about three years ago, he was promoted to detective and became my partner, and we have been mates ever since. We spend a fair bit of time together between work and the gym, and he's always up for a night out. There are hardly any of us left now in the station who aren't married with families, especially at my age. Talon's only 27, so he's happy to have a bit of fun without having to settle down with anyone. He's the perfect wingman.

"It's nothing, just some chick I met on the weekend. She hasn't called, that's all."

He clutches his chest dramatically. "Oh, has she wounded your ego, poor Theo? The first time a girl doesn't fall for your shitty pickup lines."

"Hey, you're supposed to be my wingman. Those shitty pickup lines have worked out well for you more than once."

"Whatever you say, man. You need to get out of the bad mood is all I'm saying." We make our way over to the weights station.

"She's just different. I met her when I nearly ran over her cat. She's a single mum, and it was her daughter's fifth birthday party."

He raises a brow. "MILF, hey. Not really your style."

"What even is my style? I'm a single dad, and she was fucking hot, like out-of-this-world stunner."

He nods as if understanding exactly what I'm talking about. "Well, what are you going to do about it? Not like you to back down from a challenge."

"I don't know yet. I know her first name and address, but that's about it."

"I'm sure you'll work it out. If I know you, Theo, you'll see it as a challenge to find her and win her over. She'll be in your bed by the end of the week." He thinks he knows me so well. I could track her down, but then what? I come across as a total creep, stalking her. Not the best first impression. Probably not worth it anyway, since she's got a kid. It's probably all a bit too complicated for a quick fuck. But that feeling is in my chest again, that one that says I don't want this life anymore. I want more, and Ivy, she was perfect.

"Yeah, maybe. Maybe I just need a night out and I'll forget about her. Are you still up for Saturday night, the usual?"

"Always."

It's probably just what I need to take my mind off her and get out of this mood.

Ivy

I'm walking to school with Harmony, her little hand in mine, unicorn backpack slung over my shoulder. She's beaming with excitement and pulling me along so we can arrive at school faster. This is the first time since she started school three weeks ago that she has been excited to go. Yesterday, she made a friend when her teacher Mrs Meriwether sat her at a desk next to another quiet little girl, Quinn, who she hasn't stopped talking about ever since.

She drags me along, pulling my hand as hard as she can. "Come on, Mummy, hurry. Quinn is going to wait for me by the gate."

"I'm going as fast as I can, baby girl. I'm sure if she said she would wait for you, she will still be there once we arrive." We round the corner and can see the front gate of Broken Point Primary.

She turns to me grinning. "That's her, Mum, she waited for me."

Just inside the gate waits a small girl with long, light brown hair pulled into two braids. She wears pale-pink glasses, and her smile matches Harmony's. My baby girl has made a friend, and it warms my heart.

"See you after school, Mum," she says, dismissing me.

"Okay, have a nice day," I say, bending to hug her. She quickly hugs me back, then takes her backpack and runs off to join her friend. They happily walk towards their classroom, and just like that, I'm not needed anymore. No more clinging onto my leg as we stand and wait outside for her teacher to pry her off me. She has a friend, and she's happy.

I start the short walk home. We only live two streets over from the school. It was one reason I picked our house. I don't have a class to teach until 12, so I have the morning to catch up around the house. And think way too much.

That guy Theo has been on my mind all week. I wish I had the guts to message him, but I don't. I'll do nothing with his number. I know I should, even if it is just to help Harmy make some more friends, but I'm sure a guy like him has already moved on to the next cute thing to look his way and has forgotten about me entirely.

It makes me question myself a bit for the first time in years, though. I thought I was happy just plodding along, making do with the work I get at the yoga studio and spending my free time with Harmony, Jenna, and Penny. I didn't think I wanted anything more. But somehow, meeting Theo has got my mind racing again with possibilities of what life could have looked like if I wasn't too scared to even try something new. How nice it would be for Harmony to have a male role model in her life. At the moment, she doesn't have any, with my dad being gone and her dad locked up, and he would never be allowed to see her even if he found us one day. She just has us girls, and until now, that has been enough—but what if it's not enough?

I would love her to have some sort of normal family one day when we're both ready. At the moment, I still don't feel strong enough to even try with someone. I have no trust in the opposite sex, and honestly, who would want a single mum anyway? It's just all too complicated, especially when he has a child of his own. That sounds like all types of messy. He probably has some awful ex wife he's still dealing with.

I type in the pin code and the gate buzzes open. I wait for it to close behind me, then I make my way up to my house and let myself in. Bloody Tiger, she pounces at me, scaring me half to death as I walk in the door. Jenna might have been right about this cat; she's already driving me nuts. She's pulled holes in the curtains because she likes to run and jump from the coffee table and hang from them. She rounds me up by stalking me then chasing me up the stairs trying to tap my feet. She jumps all over the furniture with muddy little footprints after being in the yard. She is a naughty little ball of energy, but Harmony loves her, and it's nice to see her so happy. Hopefully, Tiger will settle down soon.

I do a quick tidy of the kitchen then decide to head in to the yoga studio early so I can fit in a hot yoga class before I teach my beginners class. If I hang around here much longer, I'm going to drive myself insane overthinking my life. I chuck on my burgundy yoga tights with the flower pattern up the leg, a magenta-coloured crop top, and a loose singlet. I throw my hair up into a high ponytail and grab my gym bag and a change of clothes in case I need to change before my class, and head out to the studio.

Our studio is owned by a brother and sister team, Jameson and Kyla. They're both in their late 30s and have been yogis their entire lives, taking over their business from their mum a few years back. The studio sits in the hinterland, surrounded by tropical rainforest. It's on the same property as their mother's house that sits on 50 acres of land just over the other side, so it's pretty secluded from society, which is why I think people love to come here. It's close enough to town, being only a 15-minute drive, but far enough away from the hustle and bustle of everyday life that you feel you're having a mini-break every time you come out here.

I slide open the door to the studio to see Jameson setting up the mats. He smiles when he sees me. "What are you doing here so early?"

I shrug, putting my bag in a locker. "Thought I might take your class, it's been a while."

"Maybe I'll stick around and take yours as well. After class, I can take you out for a nice lunch?"

I offer a smile. "Sorry, Jameson, I'll have to head home. It won't be too long until I will need to get Harmony from school."

He covers his chest to feign a heart attack. "You're a heartbreaker, Ivy."

"You know I don't have time to date. Besides, I'm too old for you anyway; isn't your usual style no older than 25?" I tease.

"That was one time, and I haven't heard the end from you girls."

I get to work helping to straighten out the mats. "Well, what can you expect? If you're going to date teenyboppers, then you have to expect to cop shit from your work mates." I laugh at him.

"What about dinner? I'm sure Penny or your other friend would look after Harmony for you."

"So persistent today, I must look extra hot," I tease to distract from the weird tension he's creating.

His face turns serious. "You know you're hot, Ivy. Come on, any night you can?" He's totally for real, I don't get it. Why on earth would he want to go out with me? Has the world gone mad? Two guys after me in the same week. Maybe the universe is playing some joke on me. Whatever it is, I don't like it. The men of this town can go back to ignoring me so I can live my quiet, lonely, but safe existence.

"It's a bad idea, Jam, we work together."

He looks a little wounded. I don't think he's used to rejection. He's a little older than me, but he's a good-looking man and has no trouble getting a date. "Total heartbreaker."

Other students filter in, and Jameson heads out the back. It's not the first time he has tried to ask me out over the last few years, but he was definitely more persistent today.

His class was just what I needed. I feel so much better already and now have the energy to take my beginners class. My mind is calm, and I can think straight again. Jameson didn't stay for my class, though it's probably for the best. There is no way I will ever date him. He's a nice enough guy, but he's my boss. It would just be too weird. We need to keep this relationship professional. Might need to avoid him for a bit.

CHAPTER FIVE

IVY

It's Saturday night and I'm sitting in Jenna's lounge room having my hair styled by Penny—who apparently knows what she's doing, but from the pain in my head as she braids, I'm not so sure. She tells me I will be totally boho-chic when it's done. To be honest, I couldn't care less about how chic I am or what kind. It's not like I'm trying to impress anyone, it's just our normal dinner, a few drinks, then home to bed at a reasonable hour. I'm more interested in the food. Not having to cook tonight is a big motivator in getting me out of the house. For some reason, Penny is taking me in as her project for the night. Lucky me!

Harmony is at our neighbour Fay's for a sleepover. It's something we do one Saturday a month and have for a couple of years now. I used to feel guilty about leaving her for the night, but Fay insists that it's special time they have together and that someone my age should go out and have some fun once in a while before I'm too old! Thanks, Fay, like I need the reminder of how old I'm getting. But man, do I appreciate how kind she is to us.

Penny's finally done with the torture on my poor head

and brings in a mirror to show me her creation. "See? You look divine, totally boho-chic," she says.

I take a look in the mirror, and I have to admit she's done a nice job. Two long braids are running loosely through my long hair. "Nice, Pen, thanks."

She is so excited with herself she's bouncing around as if she is her own cheerleader. "It totally works with your outfit. I've outdone myself this time," she says.

I'm wearing long, knee-high tan boots with little tassels on the sides, a super-short, navy-blue floral dress, and lots of silver bangles up my arms. "Thanks, Pen," I say, trying to pull my dress down a little—it really is very short, and I feel a little more exposed than I would like to.

"Okay, girls, we better go or we're going to be late for our dinner reservation," Jenna pipes up from the bathroom where she's fixing her make-up. She walks into the lounge room and grabs her bag. She looks stunning, like Cleopatra or something with her long dark hair perfectly straight down her back and cat-eye make-up making her hazel eyes look even more beautiful than they normally do. Man, if I were into women, it would be her I'd go for. "You look stunning, Jenna. Where did you get that dress?"

"Oh my God, she does. We make quite the girl gang tonight," Penny says excitedly, still bouncing around.

"It's vintage. I found it at an op shop, nothing special," Jenna says, flattening out the soft chiffon layers of her skirt.

"I don't know what op shops you're looking in to find these amazing outfits. I can never find anything." I'd say at least half her wardrobe would be vintage something. She always has some amazing vintage finds, most of them designer of some sort.

She shrugs. "Just lucky, I guess.

"Go get your heels on, Penny, so we can go," Jenna yells at Penny.

"That will slow her down when she's in them," I say. "She's like an excited Labrador sometimes." I offer Jenna a wink.

"Ready, guys, let's go." Penny comes back in with the tallest stilettos I've ever seen.

"How are you going to walk in those all night?" I ask.

She does a little twirl. "You have to wear them this high. They go with the jumpsuit and make my legs look longer. I'm not tall like you." She's in a red jumpsuit with a super-low front; I don't know how the thing is staying on. "Do I look cute?" she asks as she bats her eyelashes dramatically.

"Very," we both say as we roll our eyes at her. "Now let's go."

OUR DINNER RESERVATION IS AT A FUNKY LITTLE Mexican restaurant near the beach in Byron. It's got the best vibes; it's cosy and super chill with food that's to die for. It doesn't matter what time of day you come here, it's always super popular. We make our way over to our bright red booth, and I get distracted on my way through the restaurant by the eclectic mix of brightly patterned tiles and wall hangings throughout. I've been here a million times before, but somehow you see something new every time.

Seeing all the culture makes me want to travel, and for a split second I let my imagination take me there, hand in hand with the man I love, little Harmony skipping up ahead as we explore the streets of some exotic country. I've never been overseas before, and it's something I've dreamed about, but the reality seems almost impossible. Maybe one day.

"Earth to Ivy." Jenna is waving her hand in front of me. I look up and the waiter is at our table taking our drink order.

"What will you have to drink?" he asks, looking a little irritated with me.

"Sorry, I was a million miles away. Margarita, please." I don't have to look at the menu, that's what we get every time we're here. The girls could have ordered for me, they know what I like.

They're both looking at me with that grin again. "What is it with you two? Stop looking at me like that."

Jenna bumps my arm. "You've been on another planet all week, Ivy. I was just wondering what's going on?"

"Bet you're still thinking about that god from Sunday. Did you call him yet?" asks Penny. She's at it again, hasn't given up all week.

"I thought we decided calling would be a bad idea!" I say, giving her a look.

They look at each other. "That's what *you* decided. *We* think you should live a little."

Smug bitches. It's easy for them, they just have to worry about themselves. I know I should let my hair down a bit, it's been long enough, but how do I ever trust someone again, even if it's just hanging out having fun? I've seen the dark side, and how do I know it won't happen again, that I won't pick the wrong type of guy? I can't afford for that to happen, not now when I have Harmony to protect as well.

I look over the menu—not that I need to, I know this thing off by heart. "Have you girls decided what you want to eat?" I say, changing the subject. "I'm starving."

"I'll call the waiter over. He's cute, right?" Penny motions the waiter over with a come-here gesture and a sexy smile like she's about to ask for more than food—because she probably is. She's so confident, doesn't care what anyone around her thinks. She just goes for what she wants and gets it. None of us can decide what to get, everything is so good, so we just order a mix of different tacos to share.

An hour later, Jenna and I sit picking at what's left of our dinner. It's so good you can't waste a single bite, and I've made a total mess of mine when it all fell apart in my hands. Penny is off flirting with the cute waiter; she disappeared a while ago. She couldn't keep her eyes off him, and he was the same with her.

Jenna has hardly said a word all night, now that I think of it. She has been moody for weeks. I wonder what's going on with her. "Is everything alright, Jen? You seem a bit off lately." She looks up from her taco, coleslaw falling out everywhere. They're the best-tasting tacos around, but they're so messy. It probably wasn't the best idea before a night out.

"I'm alright, I think I'm just kinda bored lately. Work's the same every day, and well, my social life comprises of you, Penny, and Harmony."

"Hey," I say, hitting her across the arm, "we're not boring."

"'That's not what I meant, and you know it!" she says, giving me a look. "I guess it's just that I'm about to turn 28. I thought I would have my life together by now or something. You know, the job I love, the perfect man, the wedding and plans for a family."

"Oh, you mean you want to be a Barbie doll and live in Barbie's perfect dream house." I roll my eyes. She knows I don't believe in any of that shit. "You know life's not like that, babe. Besides, look at us tonight. We're out on the town, two total babes, and we're going to have some fun!" I take her hand in mine and squeeze it. "I'm sure if you really want that life, hon, it'll happen when the timing is right. You just have to be patient. And maybe get yourself out there a little more, like Penny. You will not find your dream guy at home reading every night."

"Yeah, I know you're right. It's just hard to put myself out there. I have trust issues, you know."

"Oh, honey, tell me about it! Look at me, I'm a total mess. A single mum at 30, with no chance of it changing, because just like you, I'm too scared to let anyone else in. Life goals, right?" I grab my drink and scull it and grab her hand. "Come on, let's forget about our shitty lives, get smashed, and dance."

Jen and I walk up the street arm in arm to the bar, with Penny hobbling behind us in her extra-high stilettos.

She shuffles along. "Wait up, guys."

We stop and wait for her so she doesn't face plant trying to keep up. "Thought we'd lost you for the night," I call back to her.

She links her arm with mine. "Nah, found out he's got a girlfriend, so I'm not going there."

"You certainly know how to pick them." We walk through the door of the bar arms still linked, giggling away at ourselves. The vibe is good, music loud, people buzzing about, drinks in hand, and the dance floor is already kinda packed. I think we're a little drunk already.

Tonight's going to be a good night. I can feel it.

Theo

. . .

It's Saturday night. Jasper and I spent the day at the beach with Cooper and Fraser while Elly was setting up a house for an open house. We're lucky the boys are so close in age and they get on so well. I've just dropped both of them over to Mum's for a sleepover. Elly and Fraser are having a kid-free date night, and I'm meeting up with Drew and some of the lads from work, Talon and Sean.

I need to let loose tonight. I have been feeling way too tense lately, and I need a night of fun to feel like myself again. I'm wearing my favourite black jeans and a pale-green T-shirt, standard for going out in Byron. No one gets too dressed up. This is pretty much our usual Saturday night when I get the chance to go out: dinner, drinks, find a chick for the night, have mindless sex, leave before she wakes the next morning. I'm sure this evening will be no different, and by tomorrow, I will have hit the reset button and will feel like life is back to normal again.

It's my release, a bit of fun after I spent my entire week trying to solve cases as a part of the narcotics unit. It's not the most pleasant job, but I get satisfaction knowing I'm giving answers to the families of these victims. It helps me get through this life to know I'm making a difference somehow.

We're playing pool at the back of the beachside locale. This place is big, pool tables down the back, bar in the centre of the room with a dance floor to the side. There's a restaurant with tables, then out the front on the patio area are more tables with umbrellas. The scene is casual and chill, just the way I like it.

"It's your shot, man," says Drew. I get down low, eye level with the pool table, lining up the cue for the perfect shot to end the game. I take my shot, and out of the corner of my eye, see her, standing in the line to the front door. Fuck, she's hot. I miss the shot, which causes Drew to kill himself laughing at my fuck-up. He takes his shot to win the game, celebrating like he's just won the world cup or something. I'm no longer interested in the game, anyway. *She's* here, and I now have another game I want to play instead.

"I need another drink. Loser to shout," he calls out to me over the music.

I watch her as she walks through the door laughing with her friends. There's a pretty brunette who looks vaguely familiar and the blonde with curls I remember from the other day. They were the ones ogling me from the safety of the front lawn.

I'm positive every other red-blooded male is thinking the same thing as me. Ivy's gorgeous, and you can't miss her in that short blue dress and tan boots that run up her legs, stopping at the knee. God, she has legs that go on for days. She and her two friends hit the dance floor. I continue to watch her as she sways to the music, her short dress riding up as she does. What I wouldn't give to touch that arse of hers—fucking perfect, I bet. Drew bumps into me, looking in the direction I am, and I hit him on the arm. "That's her, man, the hottie over there in the boots," I say, pointing to the dance floor.

"Who are you talking about?" he says, rubbing his arm.

"You know, the chick with the cat from last weekend. The one I told you about on Sunday."

He raises his eyebrow at me. "Oh yeah, she's way out of your league, bro, give up now. I can see why she didn't call you."

"She is not. Come and get a drink, man, then I'm going over there." He follows me through the crowd to the bar. My body is on high alert knowing she's around. I've gone to bed getting off at the thought of her every night this week, and I can hardly believe she's just walked into the same bar as me, both of us kid-free. It's got to be a sign or something—not that I believe in that shit, but it's got to at least be another opportunity to chat with her and get her to come home with me.

I take a seat at the bar where I can see them and order a beer. She hasn't noticed me yet, so I'm taking this opportunity to watch her before she does. The friend with the blonde curls looks our way, and I spin my head back to Drew. "Shit, her friend is coming over."

"What did you expect when you've been staring at her for five minutes? She's probably coming over to warn you to stop creeping on her friend."

"Evening, boys, I'm Penny," she says flirtatiously. She's pretty, with a broad smile full of perfectly straight teeth.

I return her smile, trying not to give off a creepy vibe. I didn't mean to stare at Ivy, but I couldn't help myself. "Hi, Penny. I'm Theo, and this is my brother, Drew."

Drew gives her a nod, but he's distracted now, still looking back over toward the girls.

"Who's your other friend, the brunette?" he asks Penny. I look back over, squinting to see better, inspecting the brunette he seems to be fixated on, and I see what he's seeing: it's Jenna. I haven't seen her since the night Fi died. It's a little unnerving to see her again. They must be friends.

"Oh, that's Jen. Come and introduce yourself. She's cute and just as single as Ivy." She touches me on the arm as she says Ivy's name, and it brings my attention back to the present.

"Jen as in Jenna?" Drew says, his eyes going to me. I give him the same look back, not knowing quite how I feel about them being friends. Jenna was the girl we were trying to save that day. She was trapped in the car's boot when her ex-boyfriend hit Fi's car.

"Did Ivy send you over?" I scan Penny's expression, trying to read the situation. Is Ivy keen and she's too shy to come talk to me herself, or is her friend just a massive flirt?

"No way, she wouldn't do that. I was just thinking instead of staring at us from afar, buy us some drinks, you know, to break the ice. Come and join us. You probably owe Ivy a drink anyway, after nearly running over her cat."

"Is that right, hey. So, what's your friend's story anyway, how is she possibly single?"

She laughs at me, placing a hand over her chest, flirtatiously. "Oh, you have no idea, honey. I've known Ivy for five years, and I don't think she's even been on one date. But my girl's got a crush on you, big time. She has been calling you *the god* all week." She laughs again.

Drew pretends to choke. "What did you do to this girl?"

I laugh. "Oh, really? That's good to know." I turn to Drew. "I haven't done anything yet, we just talked. I guess I'm just that good!"

Penny nods with a cheeky smile. "She hasn't stopped all week, really she hasn't."

Interesting. I wonder why? She's stunning, she could get any guy she wants. Well, tonight I'm making it my mission to investigate. "What are you ladies drinking then?"

Penny gives me a look like she won, then leans over the bar to get the bartender's attention. It works because he comes straight over to her. "Pen, what can I get you tonight?"

"We'll have three margaritas," she tells the guy behind the bar.

"No worries, Pen," he says, then leans in to whisper something in her ear.

She giggles. "Maybe later, see how the night plays out,"

she says in reply, probably louder than she should have, she's so openly flirty.

The bartender places the drinks on the bar, and I hand over my card to pay.

"You boys should come and join us. If you're waiting for Ivy to give you a written invitation, it's never going to happen," she says as she bounces away with the drinks I just paid for.

The other two girls take their drinks with surprise. Penny says something to them, and they both turn to look at us. Ivy gives a little wave and mouths, "Thank you."

Fuck, her mouth looks hot. She has more make-up on than the other day. Her lips are red, and they look so fucking good. I can see them around my cock, my hands in her hair, watching her pretty blue eyes bulge as I fuck her mouth. Yeah, that's how tonight's going to go.

I turn to Drew. "You okay if I head over there? You know, with Jenna being there, will it be weird?" He hasn't talked about her at all since the accident five years ago. We've all been wondering what happened between them. But until now, he has just pretended it never happened. And what do I know? Maybe there wasn't something between them back then at all.

He smirks. "Yeah, I'm good with it if you are. I have some unfinished business with her, and I wouldn't mind talking to her about it. I've been wondering how long it would take to run into her once I got home."

The girls make their way over to sit at a table. "We'll have two extra drys," I say to the guy behind the bar as the other boys join us after finishing up their game. I watch the table of girls, all giggling again, as they look back over to us. Maybe they didn't need that extra drink. I can tell they're talking about us. They keep looking over, laughing their heads off. What's so funny, I wonder.

"Boys, we're heading over to that table." I point to the table of giggling girls, and Drew and I grab our drinks and wander over.

Placing my drink down and leaning on the table, I plaster on my most charming smile. "Evening, ladies, mind if we join you?"

Ivy smirks, her eyes roaming up my body, resting on my face. "Well, it's our girls' night, so normally no boys allowed, but I guess since you bought us a cocktail." She pauses, her teeth sinking into her bottom lip. "We could make an exception just this once." She giggles, clinking her drink with Penny's. She's quite the smart-arse when she's drunk.

Jenna's eyes bounce between Drew and me, then widen. Yeah, she's worked out who we are, and she looks a little unsure. I'm not surprised to see that expression from her. It's been a while since she has laid eyes on us, and everything that went down back then wasn't good for any of us.

I motion to the other boys. "This is Sean, Talon, and my brother Drew." They say their hellos, and Penny slides from the bench seat so the boys can shuffle in. Drew's eyes are firmly locked on Jenna, and he moves around the table to sit with her, sliding in close and whispering in her ear. Whatever he says, she seems to relax a little.

Penny points to her friends. "Jenna, Ivy, and I'm Penny," she says, taking her seat back down next to Talon who looks like he has won the lottery judging by the grin on his face.

I move to the other end of the table and purposely slide in next to Ivy. I'm so intrigued by this woman. I want to know more, and she looks like a fun version of herself tonight. This is not like me at all, but there's just something about her, and I'm dying to know what it is. I lean into the crook of Ivy's neck. It's loud in here with all the people and the music blaring, and I want her to be able to hear me. I also want to see if I affect her like she does me. "So, your friend tells me you have a crush on me."

She blinks a few times, her long lashes fluttering as she does. "My friend has a big mouth and likes to make up stories!" she scoffs.

I lightly skate my hand up her bare leg and watch the goosebumps scatter. "Oh, so you haven't been calling me *the god* since I saved your runaway cat last week?"

She drops her head into her hands. "Bloody Penny and her big mouth." Her fingers part, and she looks up to me.

"Don't be embarrassed, it's cute that you have a crush on me."

"Oh, no, you didn't just say I was cute, did you?"

"I think you're very cute, Ivy."

She shakes her head. "I'm not cute. Anyway, you mean you were hardly the saviour, you nearly killed our adorable little kitten!"

I lean into her a little closer. She smells delicious, like lavender or something totally edible. I whisper into her ear, "So, Ivy, how's that little kitty of yours, anyway?"

She looks at me with a cheeky grin, like did I just ask her that? And yes, I did. I know where I want this conversation to go, and I will keep steering it back there all night until she agrees to take me home. I'm not here to get to know her favourite colour and her hopes for the future; I'm here to have a little fun, and hopefully she is as well.

"She's a very naughty little girl," she purrs, the bangles stacked up her arm jingling as she laughs at herself. She leans into me slightly. "She's going to get herself into some trouble tonight." She's just as wound up as I am. That's what I was aiming for. I like this naughty side of Ivy, she's fun.

I run my hand higher up her leg. "Is she now? What kind of trouble is she looking for, Ivy?" I whisper into her ear, placing a small kiss on her neck, biting a little as I pull back. This time I can see a scatter of goosebumps down her neck, and I know I'm affecting her.

"Oh, I don't know, kitty's been cooped up at home for too long. Tonight she's a little tipsy and wants to have some fun." Her words are breathy, like she could come from just my words and kisses on her neck, and if her friend is right, and it has really been as long as she says since Ivy has been with a man, I can only imagine how receptive she will be to what I have to offer her. Her eyes flutter up to me again, and she looks at me through her long, dark lashes, getting braver as she slides her hand along my leg and playing with the rip in my jeans. It sends a message straight to my dick, which is now hard as a rock.

"Oh, really. Well, I'm sure that can be arranged. I'm always up for some fun, especially if it involves your kitty." I continue to place small kisses just below her ear, then down her neck farther.

Her eyes close as she lets out a small moan, then flicker open, and she turns to me. "What are you doing to me, Theo? Why have I thought about nothing but you all week?"

"The same thing you're doing to me, Ivy. I haven't been able to sleep this week from thinking of you."

She licks her bottom lip, and all I can think of is how much I want to taste her. "I bet you say that to all the girls." Her stare is intense, and I meet it with my own. This is some sort of sparring match but one I don't know the rules for.

"I don't, because it wouldn't be true." Her eyes flicker to my lips, and I move my head closer to hers.

The song changes to *Blinding Lights*, and suddenly our moment is broken. She's pulled from the trance and is ready to jump up and dance. "I love this song," she says. "Come on, let's dance."

I'm not much one to dance, but if it means I'm getting close to her, I guess it's worth it. She grabs my hand, and we take off. When we arrive on the dance floor, she's all over the place. I hold her with one hand to keep her up. Not that I'm complaining, but I didn't realise she was this drunk. Her friend Jenna and Drew join us on the dance floor. Looks like they're getting on too, good for him. A few songs in, Ivy stops moving. She looks up at me, slightly swaying on her feet, her face suddenly pale. She doesn't look so good.

She fans her face madly. "Are you hot? It's boiling in here, I think I need to get some air."

I lean into Drew. "Drew, I'm taking Ivy out the front for some fresh air. You guys alright?"

"All good, mate, see you later." I guide a messy Ivy by the hand through the now-crowded bar till we arrive at the front of the building that opens up onto the beach. The fresh sea breeze hits us as soon as we walk out of the pub and into the night. Her colour is slowly returning.

I pull her hand into mine as we cross over the street. "You okay? You had me worried for a sec."

"Yeah, sorry, I don't normally drink like this. I'm a lightweight, my body's not used to it, and with all the dancing..." She shakes it off.

For the first time tonight, I see that girl I met last week, her shyness returning. "Let's go sit on the beach for a bit till you feel better."

"Okay," she smiles sweetly, "that's a good idea."

We wander down the pathway until we hit the sand, and she pulls from my grip on her hand, sitting clumsily down on the sand. She unzips her boots, tugging them off and squishing her toes in the cold sand. I follow suit, taking off my shoes. It's a pleasant night, and there are people mucking about on the sand in small groups, as well as couples walking along the adjoining pathways. Most nights of the week it's busy like this here with all the tourists we get now.

"Help me up." She reaches up to me, and I pull her up with both hands, picking up both sets of shoes. We walk farther up the beach to where it's a bit more deserted, and she plonks down on the sand as I sit next to her. The spray from the ocean mists our faces. It's nice, refreshing after the warmth of the dance floor. The full moon's out, glowing in front of us, illuminating the water. It's picturesque.

Ivy stretches back to lying down, her long hair sprawled out, sand catching in the braids she has woven through it. She's mumbling about the moon and stars and how romantic it would be if there was a perfect life, not this life, some other life that was perfect. I'm not sure what she's going on about, but she looks almost peaceful, like she's going to fall asleep right here on the beach.

I lie down beside her and gaze at the moon. I haven't done anything like this since I was a kid. I just lie there and stare at the night sky. "It's really something, isn't it? The dark night sky with the twinkling of stars and a full moon."

She tilts her head to glance in my direction and smiles sleepily. "It really is. I love the night sky, it's so relaxing." I reach for her hand, lacing my hands with hers as we lie here in complete silence. My thumb skates back and forth over her palm, the connection between us so small, but it feels like it means so much.

Out of nowhere she breaks our connection and stands up. "What are you doing?" I ask, sitting up, confused by her sudden movement.

Her dress is over her head and on the sand before she answers me. She smirks at me, mocking me in just her lace panties and bra. "I'm going for a swim. You coming?"

God, how could I refuse? This woman is fucking hot, from her perfectly toned body to her perky tits just waiting for me to play with. I hop up, stripping down to my briefs in record time so I can follow her in. She gazes at me, her eyes roaming up my body, not hiding the fact at all that she's checking me out.

She tilts her head to the side, her pink tongue slipping from her mouth and wetting her lower lip. I take a deep breath, trying to stop myself from pouncing on her right here and now.

"Are you a god or something?" she asks, looking utterly confused and pleased at the same time.

"I'll be whatever you want me to be, angel."

She gives a little nod, then takes off for the water, running straight through the small wave that hugs the shoreline. I follow her, splashing through the water till I hit waist deep. It's cold, but it's kind of refreshing after being in the hot bar.

"I love living so close to the beach. How good is this, a swim at this time of night?" she says. She seems to be sobering up a bit. "We could never have a night swim back home." She splashes me playfully, and I retaliate by splashing her back.

"I wouldn't know, I've lived here my entire life. Where are you from?"

"Just somewhere more inland. It was over an hour to the beach, so it wasn't a usual occurrence when I was growing up. It was more of a special treat that would take most of the day. You're so lucky, I've only been here five years, but I love it here. It felt like home as soon as I arrived." She splashes me again, and this time I catch her, drawing her into my chest hugging her tight so she can't escape, and we crash into the water together. We both come up laughing.

"It's so cold, refreshing but cold. I'll have to get you back for that." She giggles.

I wrap my arms around her and, holding her close, push her wet hair over her shoulder. "Don't worry, angel, I'll keep you warm," I whisper.

My arms move down farther to her arse, and I pick her up as she wraps her legs around my waist. Her bright blue eyes stare straight into mine, the reflection from the moon making them twinkle. When she looks at me like this, it's like she sees into my soul, questioning me. She appears almost scared. I get this weird feeling come over me like I need to protect her. Maybe it's nothing, but I have this overwhelming urge to know everything about her so I can take care of her.

"Everything okay?" I question.

She tilts her head to the side, taking me in. "Just wondering if I can trust you or not," she says flippantly like it's a flyaway comment that means nothing, but after all my years as a detective, I know it's something.

"Of course you can, angel. I'm here to take care of your every desire. You wanted to have some fun. I'm here to give you everything you need."

Satisfied with my answer, her hands go to the back of my head, running her fingers through my hair. She closes her eyes, and I draw her lips to mine. Her lips are soft and plump, and with that red lipstick, she's driving me crazy.

My tongue swipes through her open mouth as I kiss her

deeper. This is what I've been missing, I don't even know this girl, but this feels right. There is a strange connection between us, a familiar comfortable feeling I get when our lips are locked. Any restraint I had is gone. I'm going to devour her.

Our kiss intensifies to desperate, hurried and rough, like we can't get enough of each other. I'm sure my stubble is scratching up her soft skin, but right now I don't care. This is what I have been imagining all week. I bite down on her lip a little as I pull away from her—not hard, just enough to let her know I don't play fair in the bedroom. She whimpers but keeps her body pressed firmly to mine.

"Theo, that was—oh, no one has ever kissed me like that before. I feel like I can't catch my breath."

I feel it too. That kiss was something else. Another wave crashes into my back, sending salty sea-spray droplets over our faces. "Do you need to get out, are you still cold?" I ask. I'm not done with her, but I don't want her to be uncomfortable.

"No, I'm warm now with your arms around me."

I pull her back to me, smashing my mouth with hers again. Swiping my tongue through her open mouth, she tastes salty from the ocean spray. She moans into my mouth, slowly rocking on my hardened length. It's only a slight movement, but it feels so good with only a thin layer of lace between us.

I dig my fingers into her arse harder, pulling her to me. She clings to me as I kiss down her neck, biting and sucking as I go. Her head is tilted back slightly, her body melting into mine. I suck again, harder this time, hard enough I'm sure there will be a mark tomorrow, but I don't care. I want my mark on her. I want her to look in the mirror tomorrow morning and remember what it felt like to let loose and have a little fun.

My hand roams up her body, feeling her toned abs, then moving higher, running my thumb over her hardened nipple through the sheer lace of her bra

"Your body is scorching hot, Ivy," I groan into her neck. My greedy hands can't get enough. They run over her skin everywhere. Her body feels so fucking good under them, her soft skin, her lean, athletic muscles. Her figure is slim but toned; you can tell she takes care of herself.

I want all of her now, I don't care that we're at the beach. Now that I've started, there is no going back. I slide my hands back down her back and under her arse, pushing her panties to one side, so I can feel her there, at her core. My fingers dance across her sensitive folds, exploring as she lets out a small moan into my chest where her head is resting.

"Feels so good," I growl as my finger slides through her slickness to the bundles of nerves I'm looking for. I circle over her clit as she continues to let out little moans, her head still buried close to me. She raises her lips back to mine, kissing me hard and heated as I continue to play with her, letting one finger tease her entrance, then a second, pushing in harder this time as she grinds down onto my fingers. "You're so tight."

"Like I said, kitty's been cooped up at home for too long. It's been a while." She giggles.

I push in another, filling her up as my lips are back on hers, and she kisses me desperately, her body moving to meet the thrusts of my fingers as they pump her. I move my hand faster as I feel her body tense then spasm around my fingers. She moans, her arms clinging to me.

"Fuck, Theo, what was that?"

"What I have imagined doing to you every night this week, you coming apart as I work my magic with my hands."

She rests her head on my shoulder. "It was fucking amazing. I have never... felt that before."

Still, with her eyes closed, I pick her up and carry her back to shore. She's shivering. "Come on, I need to get you home, you're freezing."

"Maybe, or maybe that was just the first non-battery-operated orgasm I've ever had and my body doesn't know how to react. I think I'm in shock," she says. Her eyes flutter open shyly, a pink blush coating her cheeks.

I laugh at her. Is she serious? I know her friend Penny said she hadn't dated in five years, but I wasn't expecting she had done nothing. And she has a kid, so she's had sex before. "Really? We need to fix this. Let's get you home so you can have a shower to warm up, and I can show you what you've been missing."

We pull our clothes over our wet underwear and grab our shoes. Taking her hand, we wander back to my car. Luckily, I parked close and haven't had much to drink, cause I want to get her home now, with a long list of all the things I want to do with her running through my head. I fumble for my keys, letting us both into my car, and I crank up the heat to warm her up.

She's gone quiet. She sits with her legs crossed, staring out the window. "Are you warming up?" I ask.

She turns her head to look at me. "Much warmer, thanks. Probably wasn't the best idea to go swimming, I was just feeling impulsive."

"That's a good thing. Sometimes you have to just do what you feel like, fuck the consequences. Soon you'll be all warm in your shower."

"Yeah, I guess. I'm not really a spur-of-the-moment kind

of girl. Normally I like things well-thought-out and planned. I think you're a dangerous influence on me, Theo."

I like the way she says my name; it sounds so good rolling off her lips. "Maybe that's what you need, someone to break down your inhibitions and help you relax a little, have a bit of fun."

"Yeah, maybe." She shrugs, not looking so convinced.

I need to keep her talking when it goes quiet. I can see her overthinking and worry creeping in. "So, I know where you live and that you have a five-year-old daughter and a naughty ginger kitten, but that's it. What else makes up Ivy?"

"Do one-night stands need to know anything about each other?" she asks with her eyebrows raised.

"Not normally, but maybe I'm just intrigued by you a little. And who says this is a one-time thing?"

She shrugs. "You implied it. I don't know why you would want to know about me, I'm not very interesting."

"Why don't you let me be the judge of that. What do you do?"

"Besides being a single parent, I teach a beginners yoga class most days of the week. That's about it. Told you, not that exciting."

"Is the class here in Byron?"

She nods. "At the Lotus Studio. Have you heard of it? That's where my friend Penny—you met her tonight—she teaches as well."

"Yeah, I know the place. Explains your fucking hot body!" I look over to her. She looks offended by my comment. She should take it as a compliment. "Must be a nice job to have, feel like you're helping people and keeping fit at the same time."

She's still looking over to me when I glance back at her,

waiting for her response. Her brow is raised. "My body's not fucking hot."

"Ah, yeah, it is."

She rolls her eyes, looking back out the window in front. "I guess it's excellent exercise, but mostly it's good stress relief. Being a single parent can be hard. But I guess you know about that as well. It's all on me, and yoga is my chill-out. What do you do? Actually, wait, let me guess."

I turn into the town of Broken Point, nearly at her place. "Okay, what do you think I do?" I smirk. This should be interesting.

She taps a finger to her mouth. "Let's see... well, all I know about you so far is you like asking lots of questions. You're good at saving small helpless animals, and you're kind of charming, I guess. Oh, and your body is insane. My guess is you're some kind of superhero, like Thor, and this is your human disguise."

I crack up. "Not at all what I was expecting you to say. You're going to be bitterly disappointed when I tell you what I actually do."

"Oh, well, maybe you shouldn't tell me and ruin the illusion. I like the idea that you're some kind of superhero." She smiles. "What do you do, really?"

"I'm a detective."

She nods as if it all makes sense.

"I work in narcotics, nothing as interesting as teaching people yoga or saving the world from supervillains," I say cheekily to change the subject. The last thing I want to do is talk about my work.

"You kind of save the world, though, one drug case at a time I imagine. I wasn't far off."

I shrug as we pull up at the curb of her place. "My

brother-in-law's company built these townhouses. My sister Elly was the one who styled them for sale."

"Really? That's kind of cool. It's a small world round here, everyone knows everyone."

"Even smaller when you grew up here and have worked in the town your entire life. That's why I live out of town a little. But yeah, these places were built with safety in mind. The security system is top-notch, probably good for a single mum, I guess."

"Yeah, that's one reason we picked this place. You can never be too careful. Especially when you have a little one to look after."

"You're not on the run or something, are you?" I chuckle.

She looks at me strangely, her face now concerned. "No... not on the run, that's funny." She fakes a laugh back. Okay, that was a bit strange. Is she on the run?

I go round to her side to help her out of the car, but her mood has shifted, and she no longer makes eye contact with me. "Ivy, is everything okay?"

She looks to the ground, pushing some dirt around with her foot. "I'm sorry, Theo. I just don't think I can do this... " She raises her eyes to look at me, her teeth nibbling on her lip nervously. "I wanted to... I wanted a reckless night of fun just so I could feel, you know, something, anything, like a woman again, not just someone's mum. I wanted to just feel like me again. I'm sorry, I just can't, though. I'm not the kind of girl that sleeps around, and what we did down the beach, I can't even believe I let it go that far." She buries her head in her hands again. I don't know what she's so embarrassed about, her body's fucking amazing.

"You didn't want me to do that?" I take her in, trying to read her. I'm confused, I was sure she was into this as much as I was.

"Yes, I did, I wanted it, wanted you. I still do, I just can't. I'm so sorry."

I take her hands and pull her out of the car and up to me. "It's okay, Ivy, we don't have to do anything. We've had a fun night, haven't we?" I bring her chin up with my fingers so she's looking me in the eye.

"Yes," she breathes. She still wants me, I can feel the desire swirling in the air, and it's not just mine. She wants me, but she's denying herself.

"Then let's just leave it at that, a fun night between two friends. No one has to know, and you don't need to be embarrassed about anything. Your body is perfection, and the memory of your soft little moans when I pleasured you, that will stay with me for a long time."

"Theo, stop, I can't." She pleads with her eyes for me to stop, and I will for now. I don't want to push her to do anything she's not comfortable with, that's the last thing I want.

"Okay, but you have to understand, tonight was the best night I have had in a really long time, and that was because I got to spend it with you."

"It was the best night I've had in forever as well."

"Then feel good about what we shared."

"Okay," she says sadly.

I kiss her on the lips slowly, savouring her in case I never get to do it again and hoping she will change her mind, but when I pull back to look at her, I can see that's not going to happen. "Bye, Ivy."

I walk her over to her gate as she punches the number in.

"Thanks, Theo. If things in my world were different, this would be—"

I cut her off. "It's okay, I understand."

She nods and offers me a small smile.

I watch as she walks over to the gate, opens it, and goes inside her complex without another word. I continue to watch her walk through her front door to make sure she's safe. She turns once she's in and offers a small wave. I jump in my car, satisfied that she is home safe, but with my head spinning from what just happened.

The entire night was so unexpected, and even more, the way I feel right now. I'm not even bothered that she turned me down—well, maybe a little, but there is so much more to Ivy than she's saying, and I want to know it all.

Best of all, the pains I have been getting whenever I hook up with anyone... there was no sign of them. I get the impression that with her it will take time for her to trust me and open up. And for the first time since the accident, I want more. I want so much more with her. I'm prepared to wait for it too, if that's what it takes to earn her trust. So, tonight, I will take my blue balls home to my cold, empty bed and work out my next move.

CHAPTER SIX

THEO

It's Monday morning. I have just dropped Jasper off to Elly and Fraser's so Elly can take him to school when it's time. My work hours mean I only get to take him to school one day a month, and I'm very lucky that Elly and Fraser's son attends the same school as Jasper, so Elly very kindly offered to do the school run for me.

I tap on the table in front of me as I wait for my coffee to be ready. I'm sitting at a coffee shop across the road from the station. It's a funky little shop, dark navy walls with vines creeping up them, the counter a rustic timber, and the smells wafting through are incredible, fresh coffee mixed with home-baked muffins.

"Theo," calls Hannah with a sexy smile, leaning over the counter, resting on her elbows so I can see her huge tits popping out of her low-cut top. She's been flirting with me for years, since that one night we nearly hooked up. I think I dodged a bullet that night. She is a stage-five clinger with a touch of crazy, and turning her down the next time I saw her would have meant having to find a new coffee shop for my morning fix, and I like this place.

I take my coffee. "Thanks, Hannah, have a nice day." I smile politely.

"You too, see you tomorrow, Theo," she purrs, nearly knocking over a coffee, too busy eyeballing me.

When I arrive in our conference room for our normal Monday-morning debrief, most of the team have already gathered and are chatting amongst themselves. I look for Talon; he's sitting towards the back, head down studying something on his phone. I pull up a seat beside him, looking over his shoulder to see what's so interesting. He's scrolling Facebook. He catches me looking and locks his phone, sliding it into his pocket. But not before I saw what he was looking at—or should I say who. "I wouldn't go there, mate, that girl looks like trouble."

"Not going anywhere, and has anyone ever told you to mind your own business?" He gives me a look that tells me he isn't going to do a thing I say no matter how much sense it makes.

"All the time." I laugh.

He shakes his head, about to say something else, when Boss's thunderous voice booms through the conference room, and we all stop what we're doing to listen. Boss—or Detective Sergeant Evans—is a man that commands the attention of all. You can see how he rose to the top of this station at such a young age. He's in his mid-40s with slightly thinning, almost-black hair. He's a solid guy, the type you could see playing rugby just because of the size of him. He has worked in this station for at least as long as me. He's smart, efficient, and doesn't take any shit from anyone. Most of the younger guys here are scared shitless of him, but I've been round long enough to know there is a heart under that tough exterior of his.

"This case is taking a lot longer to solve than we

expected, but the closer we get, the more confusing it is." Boss is in his normal cranky mood, slamming down his coffee as he takes his seat. "We need to wrap this shit up, get it under control before another shipment of drugs slips through right under our noses and we all look like complete fuck-ups to the rest of the state. There is already talk of a turncoat working here with us, and I have assured them there is no way any of my team could be involved, but take this as a warning to all of you... I'm watching closely, and any fuck-ups will be seen."

Sean looks over to us, and I shrug. It's the first I've heard of it, but I fucking hope one of us isn't working for the other side. That would be well and truly fucked up.

"We've had word that the next drop will be here in the next few weeks, so let's look into every potential avenue we can." He points in my direction. "Theo, I want you and Talon looking into the prison system. We think there's someone on the inside orchestrating the entire operation."

Talon and I give a nod to acknowledge.

He points toward Sean. "Sean, I want you down at the docks. There is a boat set up for surveillance, you can make that your office for the week. We think the next drop-off will end up there, so start looking for anything suspicious."

He continues to divide up our team, barking out orders till he's red in the face, then dismisses us to get on with it.

I make my way back upstairs to my office, placing my coffee down in front of me. Talon is close behind, his desk on the other side of the room, as we share our office. I need to get my head straight this morning so I can get this sorted, but I'm stuck back on Saturday night, going over my conversation with Ivy in the car on repeat.

How did I screw it all up so quickly? Was it that stupid comment I made about her being on the run? I have no idea, but somewhere between small talk about our jobs and her getting out of the car, she retreated. I run my hands through my hair. I can't think about that now, I have work to do.

I bring up my emails and scroll through—nothing of importance, so I pull out the file I took home over the weekend. Why can't we figure this out? If this guy is in the prison system, we should be able to trace him.

Two hours later, I'm still drinking my coffee from this morning, but it's stone-cold now. My phone has been blowing up all morning with new statements to add to the file. There is so much evidence, but something's just not adding up, and I keep getting distracted.

My mind keeps going back to Saturday night, running into Ivy, our midnight swim in the ocean and how fucking amazing her body felt under my skin, her soft moans as I brought her to her climax. I'm getting hard now just thinking about it. Let's just say the cold shower when I got home Saturday night did nothing for my aching cock. It was a brilliant start to the night, then on our drive back to her place, she completely disappeared on me. Normally I wouldn't care to get involved with chicks with as much baggage as her, but that's so hypocritical. She's in the same situation as me, and there's just something about her. Yes, she's nice to look at, but it's more than that, something when she looks into my eyes, like she can see me. Not just the fun facade everyone else sees. The real me.

That's exactly the reason you should stay away from her, Theo, I tell myself. She's going to be a whole heap of trouble, trouble I don't need when my life is complicated enough already.

My mind drifts back to Fiona. She was the last girl I let in and look what happened to her. I couldn't go through that again, I just couldn't. Fiona was beautiful, independent, and strong. We connected instantly, but she was my partner, so we tried to keep it professional, just friends. We worked together for two years before I was brave enough to make a move, but once I did, that was it. She was the one for me. We were engaged within 12 months. Shortly after, she was pregnant. The timing wasn't ideal, we would have liked to be married first, but we were happy, blissfully happy. I thought my life was perfect. We bought a house and started planning our wedding.

As soon as I found out she was pregnant, I wanted Fiona to stop working, but she was strong-willed and refused to give up her career, and she assured me that she would never put herself in any danger. And she didn't. She finished up work at six months pregnant, and the anxiety I had about keeping her safe eased off a bit. But life has a way of fucking you over when you least expect.

She was on her way to the shops, just a normal everyday activity. It was the middle of the afternoon. No one could have seen this coming. And if this situation couldn't have been any more fucked up, at the time this happened, I was doing my job, trying to help someone else. But sometimes you don't see it coming in our job.

This guy that ran into her had been on our radar for a while, we were just having trouble tracking him down. This day, we finally had him. We were tailing their car, after him for kidnapping, amongst other things. It shouldn't have ended the way it did. The boys following him were careful. But he was reckless and underestimated the speed he was travelling in the pouring rain—not to mention the driver was high.

Fiona was just in the wrong place at the wrong time. The pain of losing someone, the grief I felt when Fiona died, leaving me to parent Jasper alone... I never want to experience anything like that again. That's why I have been protecting myself by not getting close to anyone. That was my plan forever, but I'm thrown now. Ivy is someone I want to get to know better. The pull I have to her is stronger than the fear of being hurt.

"You finished that report yet?" Talon calls out from his desk, breaking me from my thoughts.

"Nearly, mate, I'll bring it down in a sec," I say, trying to regain my composure and shake off the thoughts of the past. I try not to think of them, but lately, they have been creeping in more and more.

"What's wrong with you today? You have been sitting there staring at your blank screen for ages."

I look at my screen, and he's right. My computer must be running some sort of update and has turned itself off and is now restarting. I hadn't even noticed. "It's just doing a restart."

"You're on another planet today. You daydreaming about that girl from Saturday night?"

"No, haven't given her another thought," I lie.

"What happened to you Saturday night, anyway? You disappeared on us. Looked like you had your hands full too." Talon has no life of his own so wants the info on mine.

"Nothing much. It was too hot in there, so we went for a walk up the beach."

"Likely story, man. Well, you missed out on a good night. Sean got into a fight with the bouncer and got us kicked out, so we headed up to the pub. Didn't get home until five. That friend of hers, Penny, is a little firecracker."

"Yeah, I can imagine. Did you hook up? Is that why you were stalking her Facebook page earlier?"

"I wasn't stalking her. We just hung out. Played pool, had a few drinks, you know how it goes."

"Yeah, I know how it goes with you, and that's why I'm checking. If you hooked up with her friend, I have something I need to apologise for."

"I wish, man. She's fucking hot and a yoga instructor. Imagine what that flexible little body could do. I definitely want to find out."

I shake my head at him, but I know exactly what he's talking about. Knowing that little piece of info about Ivy has me imagining all sorts of positions we could get into.

I decide to do a little online stalking myself. Can't hurt too much, can it? I like to know all the facts, and she hasn't given me much to go on at the moment. I log back into my computer and start the search. She works at the Lotus Studio, so I'll start there. I need a last name if I'm going to look up anything more. The Lotus Studio's page comes up, and there is a picture of her smiling face along with Penny and a few other instructors. But no last name, just her first. So, I decide to go onto Facebook and look up the Lotus Studio. There's nothing linked to her, so I check Facebook and Instagram, looking just for her first name, but nothing relevant comes up. She might be more concerned about safety than I first thought. Who doesn't have a Facebook page these days?

I know who would know some more details—Fraser and Blake. They sold her the townhouse she lives in, but I don't want to ask them just yet. I might just have to work out how to run into her again and do this the old-fashioned way and ask her some more questions.

Ivy

. . .

I cover my mouth, yawning again, for the fiftieth time since I got here this afternoon. It's so nice and warm in my car with the afternoon sun shining in through the windscreen. It's making me want to fall asleep—or it could be the fact I just haven't caught up on my sleep since Saturday night. I wasn't home ridiculously late for a night out, really. But when I went to bed, I just lay there completely wired from that kiss, that moment we had together on the beach, and the mind-blowing orgasm that I still haven't recovered from. Every time I think about it, I get a tingle through my entire body. I shake off the feeling, trying not to get swept up in the desire to have it again. It was a one-off, Ivy. And that's the way it has to stay.

I'm waiting in my car for Harmony's dance class to finish, so I can run in and grab her quickly, trying to avoid the judging gaze of the crazy dance mums. My little Corolla is a safer option than sitting inside trying to make polite conversation. I know it's anti-social, and I should try to make more effort for Harmony's sake, but if I go in there, I'll get stuck talking about costumes or dance competitions, and I'll have to hear how wonderful their superstar kids are.

The moment you walk in is constant chatter about how amazing their kid is. I've learned that the hard way. They're five, for heaven's sakes, let them have fun, not have to compete over everything already. No wonder so many of our kids have anxiety problems with parents like these.

My hands go to my mouth again. I can't stop yawning this afternoon. I need a distraction before I fall asleep waiting for her. I glance down at my hands. The burgundy nail polish that looked so nice on Saturday is now a chipped mess. I make it my mission to have it all chipped off before her class finishes. I don't know how women wear this stuff all the time. It's awful; it only lasts a day looking good, then it chips, and once it does, I keep picking until it's all gone. The only reason I put it on this time was that Penny made me. She's so bossy when she wants something her way, and I give in every time.

I was never really a girly girl growing up. We lived on a big piece of land when I was a kid, so I spent my days outside exploring, climbing trees, and riding my bike. Most of my mates were boys, they were just less hassle to deal with than the girls. They just wanted to play, not do themselves up and bitch about every other girl at school. I think I'm going to have my work cut out for me with Harmony. She's already wanting to paint her nails and try make-up. I blame Penny, she's a dangerous influence. Harmony's probably lucky she's got Penny around, since I've got no idea with any of this stuff.

I hold my hand up to look at my handiwork, one hand done. When I lower it, I see him. It's *him*—Theo —walking across the street with another guy, maybe one of the guys from Saturday night.

At first, I think it must be my tired eyes playing tricks on me. Why would he be walking right past me? It's not likely. I watch them walking down the street towards me, then they go to cross the road. Oh my God, that's definitely him. I duck down, hoping he hasn't seen me. I don't want to see him—or I do, but I'm still so embarrassed about how Saturday night unfolded. Who gets so drunk that she lets a guy she hardly knows finger-fuck her down at her local beach, then freaks out on him? With any luck he'll see me and go the other way.

There's a tap at my window and I know that's not the case. He must have seen me. Dammit. I slowly bring my head up, pretending like I was looking for something. My eyes rise to meet his. This is not happening. Is this guy stalking me or something? As much as I don't want to, I open my door and step out to say hi. I slowly climb out, closing the door behind me with a click. I lean up against it, chewing my lip, uncertain what to say to him.

"You stalking me, Ivy, a little stakeout in your car? You know you don't have to do that, you can just ring the number I gave you last week." He winks. Oh my God, he's so cocky. Why would I be stalking him? I'm mortified, I don't want to see him again after last week.

"I, um, I think it's you stalking me, or is this just a strange coincidence?" I say, putting my hands on my hips, trying to fake more confidence than I have. "I was just sitting in my car waiting for Harmy's dance class to finish." I can feel my cheeks heat under his intense stare. He has this crazy effect over me, I can't think straight around him.

"You remember Talon from the other night."

I give him a brief wave. He smiles at me cheekily, and I wonder how much Theo has told him about the events of Saturday night. "Hi, Talon. Yes, I remember, you spent the night with my friend Penny. Had quite the night from what I'm told."

He lifts a brow, his smile a full-on grin now. "Your friend Penny is crazy." He chuckles.

"She is, I know. What are you boys doing walking the streets, if you're not here to stalk me?"

As he goes to respond, Talon's phone rings, and he excuses himself then walks away to take the call.

"I didn't say I wasn't stalking you. I've been wanting to track you down since Saturday. I had hoped you might call me, but you must have lost my number," he says, taking a step closer to me.

What do I say now? Oh no, I'm just too chickenshit to call you after I flaked out on you? "Oh, yeah, I'm sorry about that, I don't know what happened. Sorry, I must have lost it."

"Of course, I thought that must have been the case. We had so much fun, I couldn't imagine why you wouldn't want to see me again."

I offer a small smile and lower my eyes down to my feet. I see my joggers and remember how much of a dag I am today. I'm still in my yoga pants from this morning with a faded old T-shirt I chucked over my sports tank, my hair in a messy bun, no make-up at all, and let's not forget the chipped nail polish adorning my fingernails. I sigh at how perfect this is—*not*. I suddenly feel even more self-conscious. What is he even doing talking to me? I flick my eyes back to him. He's watching me like he's waiting for me to say something, but I'm not sure what else to say. Should I tell him I'm mortified by how I acted like a total drunk skank or that he's just too good for me?

"I thought I wouldn't have seen you again after I flaked out on you Saturday. I'm sure you normally have a lot more fun with the girls you take home."

He shifts his stance, straightening up, a glint of hurt in his eyes, obviously uncomfortable by what I just said. But I'm sure it's true, isn't it?

"Maybe that's why I'm here, Ivy. I want someone different. Why did you cut our night short suddenly? Did I do something wrong?"

"No, it wasn't you. I was upset with myself for drinking too much and acting like a... well, you know—slut," I say with a flick of my hand.

"Did I make you feel like that?" He looks upset now.

"No, you were perfect. I just don't normally do that..." I can't even say the words, I'm such a child.

"What, Ivy, what don't you normally do?" he says all innocently. He wants me to say it, but I can't.

"You know, hook up in a public place," I say quietly, hoping to God none of the nosy mums are around to overhear this conversation. I'm hot and flushed just thinking about what we did at the beach. He lifts my chin with his finger so I'm forced to look at him. Damn those eyes. He has the most gorgeous blue eyes that light up when he's up to no good. Like right now, when they look straight through me into my soul.

He takes a step closer to me, closing the gap between us. Placing one arm on the car, he's so close I can smell his aftershave, and he smells divine. "You weren't so worried at the time. In fact, I distinctly remember you saying that you were feeling naughty, that your pussy had been cooped up for too long and was looking for some fun," he says, his voice low and raspy. It goes straight to my lady parts, and they beg for his attention.

"Oh God, did I say that?" He nods his head, his lips curving at the ends into a cheeky grin. I think he's enjoying watching me squirm over this. "I'm never drinking again, how embarrassing."

He brushes a strand of hair behind my ear, his hand then falling to my waist as we continue to eye each other off. "Nothing embarrassing about it. We had fun. It doesn't make you a slut, and I think we should do it again," he says, raising his eyebrow in question. Do it again, is he nuts? Standing this close to him, feeling his skin on mine, makes me want to do it again too, but I know I shouldn't.

Talon clears his throat. He's back from his call and is eying us in question. We jump back from one another. I didn't see him come back from his call, we were too wrapped up in each other to notice.

"We've got to go, man, we're needed back at the station. Nice to see you again, Ivy. Tell Penny I said hi," says Talon.

"Sorry, better go. Where's your phone?" Theo asks me.

I pull it out of my pocket, pressing my thumbprint in order to unlock it. He takes it from me and taps in his number, saving it to my phone.

"Now you have no excuses not to call me."

"Okay," is all I can come up with.

"Talk soon then, Ivy," he says with a smug grin. He knows I can't resist his charms.

I watch as they cross back over the street and head around the corner, out of sight. Now I don't know what to do. Was running into him some sort of a sign? I want to call him and see what would happen. Everything he promises sounds like all sorts of wonderful, and my body is craving his touch like crazy since I came apart in his hands at the beach. But—and that's a big but—my head is telling me it's a bad idea. A guy like him, while hot as hell to look at, is only going to be trouble.

I sigh loudly and pull my phone from my pocket to check the time. 4:12, nearly time to pick Harmony up. Guess I'd better head into the dance studio.

CHAPTER SEVEN

IVY

I HAVE JUST ARRIVED AT THE STUDIO FOR MY BEGINNERS class. The room is hot and steamy, and students mingle around chatting amongst themselves. Penny has just finished her hot yoga class, and she's sitting on the counter openly flirting with a good-looking male student. Just her luck. She sees me coming her way. She jumps off the counter, squeals and runs to me, throwing her sweaty arms around me in a hug.

"Thanks for the shower, Pen."

She laughs at me, brushing the beads of sweat from my arm. Nice.

"How did you pull up after Saturday night, Ivy? You disappeared on me. One minute you were dancing with Theo," —she drags out his name to emphasise who I was with—"the next you were both gone."

I continue toward my locker, open it, and pack away my bag. Penny leans up against the lockers, giving me her full attention like she's waiting for me to say something exciting. "I'm sure you missed me, Pen."

She plays with her ponytail, tucking the escaped curls back in. "I missed you, but mostly I just want to know what happened. You look different today, like you finally got laid after five years, and with a guy like the one you left with. I'm sure he would have really blown your mind. Am I right?"

"Whatever you say, Pen." She's not too far wrong, but I don't want to discuss this with her here. I need to get in the right mind space to take my class and thinking back to the weekend and Theo is not going to help me do that.

She hits me across the arm playfully. "I can tell by the look on your face, I'm spot on."

I cover my face so she can't see me, peering through my fingers at her. "How can you tell?"

"Oh, honey, you're practically radiating that just-fucked look. You might as well have a sign pinned to your forehead: freshly fucked."

"Oh my God, stop it," I say, hitting her back. "I don't look like that because we didn't... we just kind of made out a little and..."

"And what? You fucked him, I knew it," she interrupts me with another slap to my arm, harder this time, in her excitement.

I rub my arm. "Ouch. No, we didn't, you're wrong."

Her eyes are wide with curiosity, and I know she will not give up on this. I need to change the subject because I can already feel my skin starting to heat. "Oh, but you did something."

"Maybe. Anyway, enough about me. You look like you were pretty preoccupied with the other boys. Oh, and I bumped into Talon. He says hi," I say, batting my lashes at her. "Looks like you made quite the impression on him."

"I always do." She smirks. "Nice to know he's still

thinking about me. You missed out on such a fun night, Ivy. I didn't get home till five am. After getting kicked out of the first place, we headed to the pub, then once they closed, we spent the rest of the night at the beach. Those boys were cool."

"I'm sure. Well, I enjoyed my good night's sleep knowing I had a five-year-old to get up to in the morning."

"She was having a sleepover with Fay. Next time you're staying out, I've decided we should definitely go out with that crew again."

"Have you now," I say, rolling my eyes at her. Must be so easy to be in your mid-20s with no responsibilities.

She's smiling goofily at someone, twirling her hair, and I turn to see who? Those familiar piercing blue eyes are staring back in my direction. Oh no, it's him, the god himself. "What's he doing here?" I say out loud but almost to myself.

"Looks like he's here for your amazing beginners class."

He's now setting up his yoga mat like he knows what he's doing and him turning up to my Thursday-night class is a normal occurrence. I could almost place a bet he's never done yoga before. I know he's not here for the class. That slight blush from before is now a beetroot red. My face is hot, I can feel it.

"And by the look on your face, things just got a lot more interesting around here, I'd say," teases Penny, throwing me a wink.

He doesn't come to say anything, just gives us a wave and that charming smile of his, the one where his dimples show, then continues to set himself up and stretch. He's in a loose-fitting black singlet and a pair of gym shorts, and the muscles up his arms... Holy fuck, I can practically feel myself drooling. "Why is he so fricken hot?"

"So hot." Penny fans her face dramatically. "You're so screwed, Ivy."

We both watch him. How am I going to teach my class now? I turn back to her so he can't see me. "You've got to take this class for me, Pen." I grab her arms, pleading with her. "I can't teach it now, I'm begging you."

She laughs me off and kisses me on the cheek. "Good night, babe. He's here to see you; he would be very disappointed if I took the class."

"I can't believe you're going to leave me to deal with this. Some friend you are!" I cry, almost stomping my feet like a toddler.

"You'll be fine, Ivy, just breathe. Isn't that what you always say to the rest of us?" She laughs at my discomfort, making her way over to Theo. She starts up a conversation, hitting him on the chest playfully. If I didn't know better, I would think she was flirting with him, but I do, and she's like that with everyone.

I wish I had her confidence. Then I wouldn't just be standing there with my mouth open every time he talks to me. I'd be all witty with something cool to say. They both laugh at whatever she just said and look in my direction. I throw her an evil glare. She sticks out her tongue and rushes out the front door of the studio. She knows she's in big trouble when I see her next.

It's almost impossible to lead this class now with him in the front row watching my every move. I run my palms down my face in frustration and try to breathe so I can calm myself down, and concentrate on what I'm here to do. My class come here to relax, and they expect me to be their calm guide through their practice, not some frazzled mess, which is what I feel like right now. I take my place on my mat, spreading my toes. Grounding myself. Ivy, you've got this, just breathe.

"Welcome, everyone, thanks for coming tonight. We're going to start with our Sun Salutation A sequence, that we were working on last week, but we'll be adding on. If everyone can stand on your mats and let's take a deep breath to arrive at class." I can feel him watching my every move—probably because he has no idea what he's doing! I can tell he's never done yoga before. I bend forward to get into the downward dog, and through my legs he gives me a cheeky wink for my troubles. Oh, save me now, I will not make it through this class.

An hour later, I have somehow made it through, keeping my composure as best I could. My students are in Shavasana, and I'm trying to meditate to calm myself down. Breathe, Ivy, just breathe. Maybe he'll just leave and I won't have to talk to him. Yeah, that's what will happen. He's not here to see me, it's just a coincidence. He's just here for the class so it will be fine.

"Okay, everyone, slowly start to wiggle your fingers and toes, then open your eyes to come to sit on your mat." We all sit up with our legs crossed. I almost laugh watching him try to cross his legs. He looks so awkward. It must be hard with all those big muscles.

Control yourself, Ivy. I close my eyes so I can concentrate. "To the eyes for clear and honest thought, to the lips for truthful speech, and to the heart's centre remembering to always shine, Namaste!" I bow with my hands in prayer pose and take another breath. "Thanks for a great class, everyone. I hope to see you on the mat again next week."

I did it, I made it through! I'm actually quite proud of myself, I didn't fall over or do anything embarrassing. Someone must be watching over me tonight.

I clean up the room, packing away the mats, blocks, and straps we used, and Theo follows my lead, helping me. So I guess I'm not getting away with this as easily as I would have liked. Looks like he is here to talk.

Once the last mat is packed away and all the other students have said their goodbyes, he wanders over to where I stand near the front counter. I feel my face heat again under his stare. At least I can blame it on the class this time. He's looking straight into my eyes as he walks towards me. He stops just in front of me, closer than I would have liked since I've just finished a class—I know how sweaty I am, and I'm sure I stink. He's tall, really tall. I'm pretty tall for a girl so I don't normally have to look up to anyone, but I have to strain my neck to look up at him. He towers over me, still staring straight into my eyes, and again I'm rendered speechless around him.

"Ivy."

"Theo." Words, where are my words? Come on, Ivy, put a sentence together. "Did you enjoy my class?" I almost purr. Who am I even when I'm around him?

"I did." His eyes run up my body, and it should piss me off the way he's looking at me like I'm a tasty treat, but I'm loving it, his eyes eating me up, promising many naughty things I know I can't have. "You're quite the teacher, Ivy. I can see why your class is so full of students, more than half of them men."

I run my eyes over him, really taking my time to appreciate him. He's pure male perfection. That chiselled jaw peppered with stubble, those fucking dimples, and hair I want to run my hands through. Is it bad I want to lick the sweat right off his chest? Fuck, that is sick, I'm messed up. "W-what are you doing here, Theo?"

"Yoga." He pauses. "Okay, I'm here to see you. You haven't called yet."

"I only got your number two days ago."

"I don't care. I wasn't waiting any longer. I'm not a patient man, Ivy. I wanted to see you so here I am. I want to get to know you. You're playing on my mind, and I hardly know anything about you. I don't even know your last name. How am I supposed to scratch your initials into my desk at work?"

I giggle at the thought and cover my mouth to stop it. What is he talking about? "You want to know my last name so you can carve my initials into your desk at work like some lovesick schoolboy? Not what I expected you to say at all."

"Ah, yeah, with a heart around them." He smiles smugly as he traces with his finger in the air what he would write.

I can't help but laugh this time. The image of him like a teenager with a crush is just too much. "If you just have to know, it's Anderson. What's yours? You know, just in case I need it to write on my pencil case or something."

"Walker. So I blew your mind on Saturday night, did I?" he says with that same mischievous grin I remember from that night.

"Is Penny making up stories again?" I say with a smirk, like it's not true. Bloody Penny and her big mouth.

"I don't know, but I hear you're still calling me *the god* so I must have done something right," he says, a bushy eyebrow raised.

I cross my arms over my chest and rise up a little taller, trying to stand my ground against his intensity. "You're so sure of yourself, aren't you, Theo. I bet you get whatever you want. All the girls running after you, throwing themselves in your direction," I say as I take a step back, till I hit the front counter behind me. I need to avoid being in such proximity, with him standing so close. His masculine scent invades my nostrils. Man, he smells so good. It's a total aphrodisiac even after that class, and it's making me forget why I need to stay away from him.

"Why wouldn't I be? And it's more like God's gift, Ivy," he laughs. "Apparently that's what my name means." He laughs again. "But you can call me whatever you like, and if you're a lucky girl, you'll find out why." I have never met someone like him, so confident and full of himself. He's going to be no good for me, I just know it.

He takes another step forward, his eyes back on mine, deep and intense, stalking me like he's a lion and I'm his prey. My skin is back to beetroot red, I can feel it. I'm not used to attention from someone so good-looking—or anyone, really, for that matter. What on earth could he want with plain old me?

I go to take another step back but there's nowhere to go. I'm already right up against the counter. "You're a catch, Theo. Good-looking, a decent job, you seem to have your shit together. Why are you wasting your time on me? I bet most of the mums at school would be all over you knowing you're a single dad."

He brushes some stray hairs behind my ear. "Angel, you don't give yourself enough credit! The moment I saw you, I knew you're not like anyone else. There's something about you. I haven't been able to stop thinking about you since the day I met you."

I drop my head, feeling suddenly very shy by the way his eyes are boring into me. "I came here tonight because you still haven't called, and I couldn't wait any longer to get to know you."

"Theo... I... you don't want me, I'm too damaged," I say in a whisper, barely able to get the words out. I want him, I want him so badly. I want to reach out and touch his chest, run my hands through his hair, wrap my legs around his waist as he kisses me.

"I want you, that's why I'm here. Let go of the fear from your past and trust me to take care of you for tonight." He closes the gap between us completely, leaning down and taking my face in his hands, bringing it up to his and kissing me softly, sweetly. Having his lips on mine is heavenly, every bit as good as I remember from Saturday night, but so different. His lips are soft, but his five-o'clock shadow makes it rough, scratching my face. He slowly circles my tongue with his.

This kiss is nothing like the wild, passionate kiss from Saturday night. He pulls back and looks at me as if he's waiting for me to make the next move. "You're the most beautiful woman I've ever seen, Ivy, standing here in your cute yoga outfit, all sweaty from class, and all I can think of is how much I want to peel you out of it, so I can show you how good life can be if you live a little. Let me take care of you. You spend your life looking after your little girl. Let go for tonight, and I'll take care of you."

I've lost all my practical reasoning for why I'm not supposed to be kissing this sexy man standing in front of me. Enough being little miss goody-two shoes, Ivy. He's fucking gorgeous, and he wants you to just go for it!

The naughty sex kitten inside me is taking over, and she is so much more powerful than me. I can't control myself any longer. My hands go to the back of his neck, I can't help it. I look into his eyes, lean up, and kiss him. All my fears are gone as soon as our mouths meet again. At this moment, I want him more than my fear of whether I can trust him or not. It's just like it was on Saturday night, in his arms with our lips locked. The fear is gone, and all I want is for him to make me feel alive again.

His lips stay connected with mine as he skates his hands down my body to under my arse, scooping me up in one quick move like I'm light as a feather. My legs instinctively wrap around his middle, and he places me on the front counter behind me. I can feel the heat from his body radiating off him and overwhelming me. Our kiss intensifies to desperate hunger. I can't get enough of him. I've never felt such deep desire for a man. He brings something out in me I never even knew was there.

I have to pull back from our kiss to regain my breath. Gasping for air, I stare back at him. The heat in his eyes should scare me, but it doesn't.

"There's something about you, Theo. You make me want to do naughty things with you, things I shouldn't. I lose all control when I'm with you," I whisper, biting my lip trying to control myself and the now-constant throb of desire between my legs.

His lips turn up at the sides. "Let's explore these naughty things, Ivy. Are there showers here?"

I nod. "A shower is a good idea."

He takes my hands and pulls me from the counter. Taking his hand in mine, I lead him down the back to our studio bathroom. I can't even process what I'm about to do. My body has taken over my brain and is leading me now. Whatever this sexy man says, I'm going to do without hesitation.

We enter the bathroom, and I flick on the light. Luckily our studio has amazing facilities with a massive bathroom filled with tropical plants and a waterfall-style shower running the length of the wall. I make my way straight for the shower, turning it on. The water leaves the showerhead in a rush, and I hold my hand under the flow to check the temperature—perfect.

Theo has wasted no time, his singlet, shorts, and underwear already discarded on the floor. He leans against the tile wall watching me, completely naked, male perfection, every last inch of him. So flawless he could be chiselled from stone. My inner sex goddess has to pick her jaw back up off the floor and stop drooling. In all her life she never thought she would be blessed enough to see someone so... I have no words for how much he is.

I swallow the lump in my throat. Things just got real, fast. No turning back now. He's fucking gorgeous with rock-hard abs and a light dusting of hair that comes down into a perfect V shape leading my eyes down to his massive cock that stands to attention, just waiting for me to touch him.

He grabs his cock and strokes himself. "Like what you see? Told you that you wouldn't be disappointed."

I compose myself. Be cool, Ivy, try to act all confident like I'm with men like him all the time. "You're okay, I guess," I say with a smirk. The steam from the shower fills the air, and I remember what we're supposed to be doing, taking a shower to get clean. Or dirty?

He pursues me, his hungry eyes scanning my body as he closes the gap between us. "You have too many clothes on for a shower, angel. Let me help you fix that." He lifts my top over my head, discarding it to the floor, then unzips my sports bra, tossing it over his shoulder while I stand like a rag doll, unable to move, letting him undress me. His hands run up my stomach then over my breasts, his large hands cupping them and toying with my nipples that have hardened just for him. He lets out a low groan, and it's the sexiest thing I have ever heard. He is just as turned on by my body as I am his.

He runs kisses down my neck to my chest, taking one of my nipples in his mouth and sucking hard. I can't help but moan out loud. I'm completely losing control from the slightest touch.

His hand slides down between my legs and he grabs me through my yoga pants. "Your body gives you away." And he's right, I'm soaking wet. My naughty side is betraying me tonight; it's been way too long. She got a small taste of what Theo can do, and boy, does she want more!

He hooks his thumbs into the waistband of my pants and panties, dragging them down my legs, then tosses them to the side. I should feel uncomfortable standing here in front of him nude, but the way he looks at me like I'm a prized possession makes me feel like the sexiest woman on the planet, even though I know I'm not.

"So, being a yoga teacher, I'm assuming you're pretty flexible," he says with a cheeky grin.

"No more talking," I demand, pushing him into the shower with me. He wraps his arms around me, as the warm water runs over my sensitive skin. I'm tingling all over with the anticipation of feeling his skin against me. His lips are on mine again as water trickles around our faces. I can feel his hard length pressed into my front, and I pull back from his kiss. I want to touch him.

I run my hand down his chest, feeling each muscle as I go, until I settle on his hard length, palming it. Fuck, he's so hard, it feels so good. I pump my hand up and down his length a few times, but I want to taste him. I want this big hard cock in my mouth so I can watch him come apart.

As I stroke him, he leans back against the tiled wall. I take the opportunity to lower to my knees. I lick the precum that's dripping from the tip, exploring his massive cock. Rolling my tongue around the tip then taking him deep into my mouth, I continue this process, licking then sucking him in deep. His hands go to the back of my head, first brushing the now-soaked hair from my face then lacing through my hair as he picks up the pace.

"Fuck, Ivy, that's so good," he hisses. I continue the back and forth, loving how much he's enjoying what I'm doing to him. I want him to come in my mouth, but he has other ideas. Tugging on my hair, he brings me back up to him before I can finish.

I slowly make my way back up his chest, kissing him, running my hands up his hard chest as I go. The look in his eyes is pure sin, and right now, I don't care if this is just for fun and games. At this moment, he can do what he wants in the name of fun. I'm all his.

His hands are on my shoulders, and he spins me around quickly. I brace my arms on the wall for support, feeling a little dizzy from the heat in the shower and standing too quickly. He pulls my hair to one side, then places soft kisses down my neck, then harder as he sucks and nips his way down to my shoulder. I'm sure he is trying to leave his mark, and right now, I don't care. It'll be a little reminder tomorrow just for me when all this is over.

His hands explore my body, my stomach, my breasts, my arse. He pulls my hips back a little so my arse is tilted towards him, then he moves down lower, his fingers slipping through my wet folds, exploring. He runs a finger over my sensitive nub almost like he is tracing a pattern, and man, it feels fucking amazing. He is skilled with his hands. He swipes his finger down my centre, and I feel a shiver run through me. Every little sensation has me on edge, my body tingling with need for him. He dips the finger in, teasing my entrances just a little, then he adds a second, pushing in harder this time, circling, stretching me.

"So fucking tight. You feel so good."

I groan in reply, loving the rhythm he's moving in as he continues to work me with his thick fingers. His lips kiss my neck again, and I'm vaguely aware of his erection pressed hard into my arse. He's ready to go, but he's giving me time to be prepared for him, and probably a good thing too—I have no idea how he's going to fit.

His other hand comes to my breast, playing with my nipple as he continues to pump me with his fingers. "God, Theo, I'm going to..." As I say it, he bites down on my neck—not hard but hard enough—and my body convulses around his fingers as I ride the wave of pleasure rippling through me.

I drop my head, trying to regain my breath. He turns me back around, pulling me into his body, wiping the wet hair away from my eyes and kissing me with such intensity it's almost too much, too real. But I want it all just the same.

"Are you okay? Do you want more, angel?"

It's clear that the man is dying to fuck, and he stops to check in with me and make sure I'm alright to continue. Who is this guy? I nod. "Condom first."

I watch him go grab one from his shorts, dripping water all over the floor, but who cares right now.

"Wow, you came prepared, that was presumptive," I tease.

"Of course! I knew what I wanted when I came here tonight, I won't deny that." He's so bloody cocky, and I caved so easily. Right now, I don't care, I just want him inside me.

I watch as he rolls on the condom and comes back to join me in the shower, running his hands up my body to massage my breasts as he kisses down my neck and bites my ear. He then lifts me in one swift move and pushes inside me, knocking the air right out of me.

"Are you okay, Ivy? I won't go any further till I know you're okay."

Fuck, he's big. I can't get my words out. "Yes, just give me a sec," is all I can manage. His lips are back on mine, and he moves slowly as I try to adjust—it's been a long time.

The tiled wall behind me is cold, but the water is hot. He gradually moves to increase the pace. My head spins with every thrust. My eyes close, my mumbled cries of pleasure echoing through the bathroom as I grip onto him.

I'm ready for him now, and I want more. "Theo! Fuck me!" And as if that were the permission he was waiting for, he picks up the pace. Our bodies slap together as the warm water runs over us, and I dig my nails into his back, trying to hold on as he fucks me hard and fast, giving me all he has.

This is heaven. Why have I denied myself for so long? I'm no longer with it. I'm off in la-la land, just feeling the pleasure he's giving me. His fingers dig into my hips, they bite at my skin, and I know there will be bruises there tomorrow, but I don't care.

"Fuck, Ivy, I'm almost there."

I shake as the second orgasm takes over my body. He pumps me twice more, growling loudly as he releases his climax. I still cling to him, my body now trembling. That was too much and not enough.

He pulls out of me, helping me slide down to standing on shaky feet, then hugs me close to his chest, kissing my hair. His forehead rests on mine as we both struggle to catch our breath. The slight gesture of our heads pressed together as we come down from our high feels strangely more intimate than what we just did. This man, I can't even.

As I catch my breath and my heart rate settles, my sex-kitten side is now sated, and my moral conscience takes back over.

Oh God, what have I done? That wasn't supposed to happen. We were just talking.

CHAPTER EIGHT

THEO

Ivy is in my arms, warm water washing over us. Her body feels like silk against my skin. I inhale her scent, and she smells like something relaxing, I think it's lavender. I kiss her on the head, and she looks up into my eyes, but now that scared look is back, and I can feel she's pulling away from me again.

I have no idea why, but I need to keep this connection with her.

"Let me wash you." I'm not ready to let her go yet.

"Okay," she says softly, not completely shutting me out.

I squirt some liquid soap into my hands and massage it over her beautiful body. I can hardly believe that just happened. I thought for sure it would go down much like the other night, but tonight she gave me a small glimpse of her. She let me in just for a little while.

And she is fucking perfection.

This need I have for her will not be a quick fix. I'm not going to be able to fuck her once then have her out of my system. This is the start of an addiction. She is a goddess that I'm going to crave constantly until I can have her again.

She pushes back from me. "Theo, I've got to go. I've left Harmony with Jenna. I should have been home ages ago. They're going to be wondering where on earth I am." She rinses off, squeezing out her hair. "I'm sorry, Theo." She grabs for a towel, leaving me alone in the shower, and rushes around the bathroom drying herself as she tries to jump into her clothes that are scattered around the room.

I rinse off and turn off the shower. She hands me a towel with a sympathetic smile, and I dry off.

Her hair is a mess of wet tangles that she towel-dries then rolls into a messy bun on top of her head, still dripping wet all down her back.

She rushes out to the studio, and I chuck my clothes on quickly so I can go after her. This wasn't quite how I imaged tonight going. I came here to find out more about her, work out why she moved here five years ago. At least I have her last name now. Might give me some answers. But I didn't expect for us to do that, then for her to freak out on me again. She's packing up the studio like a madwoman.

Normally I'd be happy about this scenario, wild sex with a gorgeous girl who wants nothing more. We both move on with our lives, never to see each other again. So why do I get a sinking feeling every time she pulls away? Why is she pulling away, anyway? Surely she can feel what I can when we're together. What's she so scared of?

When I walk back into the studio, I find her on the phone. "So sorry, Jen, I just lost track of time after class. I'll be home in ten." She hangs up and turns to look at me. "I'm so sorry, Theo, I've got to go. My daughter will wonder why I'm not there to tuck her in. My life is just too complicated for whatever this is." She gestures between us, waving her hands around. "I have responsibilities. I can't just lose track of time, fucking in my yoga studio like some horny teenager."

She turns towards her locker, grabbing her bag and slinging it over her shoulder. "What was I thinking?" she mutters to herself as she rushes back into the bathroom. I follow her, still unsure of what to actually say. The pace changed so fast I can't keep up with her.

She throws the towels we used into the hamper and cleans up quickly. Then stalks right past me, back out to the studio, and waits by the door for me to catch up to her. I grab my gym bag and follow her out like a lost puppy, dragging my tail and ego between my legs.

"Ivy, what's going on? I know you're in a rush to get back to your daughter, but I'm sure five minutes more to talk to me won't hurt."

"I'm sorry, I just feel terrible. I haven't done anything like this before. Jenna needs to get home, and Harmy won't go to sleep unless I'm there to tuck her in."

"I'm sure they would have coped without you for a little bit. It's okay to have time for yourself. You're allowed to have a life outside of your responsibilities. Have a bit of fun once in a while." She gives me a look like this isn't up for discussion.

I put my hands on her shoulders to stop her panicking over this. "Look at me." She takes a deep breath and looks up at me. "I know you need to rush off, but can we talk about this over coffee sometime?"

"You got what you wanted, didn't you, Theo?" she says with sad eyes. "You don't have to pretend like this is something it's not." Ouch, that hurt. She's now turned into a complete ice queen on me.

I take a step back, a little offended by her words,

because that might normally be true, but I have never treated her like that. Far from it. "It doesn't have to be one or the other, Ivy. We can have some fun together, nothing serious. I understand your life is complicated. I get it, trust me. We have children who are our first priorities, so I'm not asking for anything serious here, I'm not up for that either, but this doesn't have to be over now. I was never looking for just a quick fuck with you. If I have given you that impression, I'm sorry."

She glances down at the keys in her hand and slowly back up at me. "I don't know, Theo, I just don't do this." She gestures between us. "I've kept myself safe in a little bubble of just me and Harmony for so long, I wouldn't even know where to start. Even if it is just fun. There's just so much you don't know about me, and it's all too complicated. Letting you in even like this tonight is too much for me."

"Okay, you're right. I know little about your situation, so I don't understand, but if you decide you want to talk to me about it, see if we can work something out, you have my number. I'll leave it up to you."

She pulls out of my hands. "I'm sorry. You're a great guy, Theo. Any girl would be lucky to have you, and playing with you is so much fun, but it's just not practical in my life. I shouldn't have let it go this far. I've got to go. Maybe I'll see you around." She locks the door, then turns and heads for her car. I'm left wondering what the hell just happened again. At least I have her full name now, and I can find out a bit more about her.

I UNLOCK THE DOOR TO MY HOUSE AMONGST THE TREES, and Jasper sleepily dawdles in. He had dinner and a bath with Elly, and I have just picked him up, but it's late. I need to get him into bed.

"Go brush your teeth and get into your pyjamas. I'll be there in a sec."

He makes his way up the stairs. This place normally brings me calm and peace from my hectic life, but tonight, I don't feel either of those things. Ivy finally opened up to me and let me in just a little, for her to then reject me moments later. She is the most complicated woman I have ever met. Normally, charming women comes easily for me, but she's so guarded, it's hard to break through to her.

I don't know why I'm so bothered. I should just be happy with what I got, like she said. A quick fuck with the hot yoga instructor. No strings attached or need to see her again. She made that perfectly clear. So why do I feel so empty, so unsatisfied? Like I need more. I have to have more of her. It's because she's not the girl you have a quick fuck with, she's different. I want to spend time with her, to know everything about her. I'm a little annoyed at myself for even feeling this way. It feels like I'm betraying Fiona, even though she's been gone for five years.

I feel lost back in the past, still trapped in that day when she was taken from us. I know everyone says my heart is frozen. It's not. It just shattered that day, and I never thought I would have any hope of rebuilding with someone else. I put everything I had into Jasper. I didn't even want to think about the possibility until now.

I know I should just walk away and be satisfied, but I'm not. I want more.

"Dad?" Jasper is looking at me like he said something, but I didn't hear it. I'm miles away.

"Did you brush your teeth, bud?"

"All done. Can you get me a glass of water?"

"You hop into bed and I'll get you one."

I finish getting him sorted for bed then collapse onto the lounge, phone in hand. I have her last name now. I could look into her more, find out what I want to know, but I can't decide if I should or not. Getting involved with someone, especially someone in her situation with a kid to think about, is a bad idea and the last thing I need.

I promised myself after Fiona was killed, I would never get involved with anyone else again. You only end up destroyed when it ends badly, and for me, it was the worst thing imaginable that happened. I couldn't protect her.

I'm smart enough to know that's just the way it is. One day you can be blissfully happy, then the next, your life is shattered into pieces. So for the last five years, I have protected myself as best I could and not let another soul in. My friends and family are there, and I appreciate their support, and Jasper is my world, but I stopped opening up to other people, and life became a shitload easier. Until now...

This woman that I hardly know has me by the balls. She's a total mystery, and it's one I want to solve. She's fragile, scared, and so beautiful. It's all too much, and for whatever reason, I want to make her feel safe, protect her from whatever it is she's hiding from. I can't do that if I don't know what it is.

I open up my phone and click on the Facebook app, typing her full name into the search engine to see what it brings up. Ivy Anderson. Nothing. I check Instagram and get the same. So I do a Google search. All I can find is what I found before—her connection to the yoga studio. She has no online presence. It's so strange for someone our age. Maybe she is on the run or something, hiding out under a false name, or maybe she is just very private and not into technology. Yeah, that's more likely. I know I could put her name through the system at the station, but I don't want to betray her trust like that. I'm just going to be patient and wait for her to call me, find out more about her the old-fashioned way. But I'm not a patient man. I won't wait forever.

CHAPTER NINE

IVY

I rush in the door, almost out of breath. Jenna looks up over her book. She's curled up on the lounge with a blanket over her lap. "Is she still awake?" I call to her.

"I'd say so, honey. She only came out for a drink about five minutes ago. I told her you got held up at work and wouldn't be too long." She smiles smugly.

"Okay, I'll go tuck her in. You can go if you want. Sorry to keep you so long."

"It's fine, Ivy, not like I have anything else to do with my time. I've got my book, and that's what I would be doing at my place as well. Go tuck her in. I'll make you a tea, yeah?"

"Thanks, Jen." I wander up the stairs. I'm suddenly exhausted. My muscles ache as I step up each stair. I just want to curl up in bed and forget the way Theo made me feel tonight. The way my body reacted to his every touch, the way it felt when his lips met with mine. I touch them, and it's almost as if I can still feel his lips there, the scratch of his stubble brushing up against my chin.

I'm sure tomorrow I will know this for what it is. Too much pent-up sexual frustration from denying myself any action for so long. Now that I have it out of my system, I can move forward with my life. What we did tonight should tie me over for another five years at least, right?

I make it to Harmony's room to find her curled up under her soft pink blanket, her bedside light on an open picture book. By the light highlighting her angelic face as she turns the pages, I can see it's one of her favourites, *Hush Little Possum*.

She must hear me because she peers over her book. "Mummy, you're home." She smiles sweetly.

I drag my tired body over to her bed and lie down beside her. She cuddles into me sleepily. "Sorry I was home so late. I got held up at work with one of my new beginners." Not entirely a lie.

"That's okay. Jenna had time to read me two whole chapters of *The Wind in the Willows*, not just one, so you can stay late every week if you have to. So you can teach that new person all the poses they need to learn. I will be okay."

Oh God, if only she knew. "Oh, thank you, honey," I say, kissing her on the forehead. "I don't think they will be back. Yoga might not be for them."

She tilts her head to look at me, her eyes narrowed in confusion. "Oh, why is that? Didn't they like your class?"

"No, it's not that. I think they just learned all they needed to tonight. They probably don't need to come back for more classes."

"Wow, that person must be the fastest learner ever."

I take the book from her and place it on the dresser next to her bed. "Yeah, something like that. Now it's time for bed. It's already way past your bedtime, and it's a school night." I roll out of her bed and up to standing. As much as I would like to just fall asleep right now, I know I can't. I have to face the music downstairs. Jenna is going to have a long list of questions, I could tell that by the look I got from her. "Night, my beautiful princess. Love you." I bend down and kiss her on the cheek.

"Night, Mummy. Love you too." She rolls over and snuggles in, and I make my way for the door. "Oh, Mummy, I need Mr Sprinkles or I won't get to sleep. Do you know where he is?"

I scan the room, looking for her soft unicorn toy, but he's nowhere to be seen. Damn, I'm too tired for a game of finding the favourite toy tonight. But I know if I don't, there is no way she will go to sleep. "Where is the last place you saw him?" I ask with a sigh.

"In my bed last night." Of course it was. What did I expect the five-year-old to say?

"Okay, let's start there." I go back over to her bed and have a feel around, then pull the sheets back, and sure enough, Mr Sprinkles has been pushed to the bottom of her bed. "Oh, here he is." I pick up the soft toy and place him under her arms, how she likes him to be.

She smiles up at me sweetly. "Night, Mummy, thank you."

I pull up her sheet and tuck her in tight. "Night, sweetie. See you in the morning." I watch her from the door as she snuggles in and closes her eyes. She's so beautiful, and she is my world. She is all I need, isn't she?

I make my way back downstairs to Jenna who is back to reading her book. Two teas sit on the coffee table in front of her. I take one, relaxing into the lounge and taking a sip. It's chamomile with lavender, and it's going to have me asleep in no time.

"You look tired. Big night, hey." She places her book down, giving me a look, eyebrow raised.

"Yeah, the class took it out of me." I take another sip of my tea and settle farther into the lounge.

"Cut the crap, Ivy, and spill. You never leave class late. Something distracted you, and my bet is on a certain sexy cop named Theo?"

I look at her, my eyes widening. "How did you—Penny." I huff. Penny has a big mouth. I shouldn't have been surprised that she would rat me out to Jenna as soon as she could.

"Did you really think she wouldn't text me as soon as she left the studio tonight?"

I shake my head. "I should have known."

She looks over at me, all wide-eyed and excited. The truth is, between the two of us, our lives are very uneventful. Neither of us dates or does anything much other than work and the once-a-month night out, so this probably is exciting to her. "So what happened? By how late you got home and, well, the dishevelled look of you, the wet hair, I'd say you broke the five-year drought. Am I right?"

"Might be," I say, biting my lip, unable to hide the smile forming. Maybe talking to her is a good idea. I'm so confused, maybe she can help me.

"You naughty girl, and in your yoga studio." She bumps my arm, and I nearly spill my tea.

"I know, I'm so embarrassed. I have no idea how it even happened. We were talking, then the next thing, he was asking if we have showers in the building. It all happened so fast."

"Fast, hey. A bit of a letdown then."

"Not fast like that, and no, definitely not a letdown. The man is a god in more ways than just his looks. I have never experienced anything like it." My body tingles with the thought of what we did.

"You've probably just forgotten. It's been a long time, babe."

"No, I don't think I would have ever forgotten if I experienced something like that before. It will stay with me for a long time. And it's going to need to. I told him I'm never doing it again. And I'm sure he got what he wanted anyway. He's probably thrilled with that."

Her brow creases in concern. "Is that what he said when you told him it wouldn't happen again?"

I play with the tea bag, trying to avoid the way she's looking at me. "Well, no, he said I have his number, and if I want to see him again, I should call. But I'm sure he just said that to make me feel better about what we did, you know. Like, call me. But he wouldn't really want me to call him."

"I don't know, Iv. I'm just as out of practice with men as you. But he turned up at your class just to see you. He stayed after class to talk to you. Maybe he is more interested than you think."

Is she right? I really have no idea if he is actually interested in me and not just in what we did. Even if he is, what do I do with that? "Do you think? It doesn't matter, anyway. I can't go there again. I have Harmony to think of, and he has his son, and tonight proves it's not a good idea. They go to school together. The logistics are just too complicated."

"Iv, Harmony was happy with me tonight. Sorry to burst your bubble, but she didn't notice you were late. She was more excited that she got extra story read to her. It's time for you to have a life of your own."

I think over her words for a bit, and I know she's right. Harmony was fine; she told me so herself. She would be fine with me staying late at class every week if I had to. Maybe it's me I'm trying to protect. I'm the one who can't afford to fall for someone. If it didn't work out, I'm not strong enough to cope. And how do I even trust someone enough to let them in, anyway? I know he works on the police force, but that doesn't mean he's a good guy. I have been fooled before when I thought I could trust someone, and I can't risk being hurt like that again.

She gives me a look. "Stop overthinking it. Just call him like he said, go out and have a bit of fun. I'm sure you won't regret it."

"How can you be so sure? I don't even know this guy. He could be anyone. Being a cop doesn't mean I can trust him."

"Yeah, I get it. Hun, I know you have trust issues but hear me out for a sec."

She glances at me, chewing on her lip, like she is thinking something over. Then she picks up her tea, taking a big sip.

"Okay, what?"

"I don't want you to ask me questions about what I'm about to tell you, because it's not something I can talk about, but I kind of know the Walker family a bit."

I look over at her, confused. She knows them? I remember the way she and Drew looked at each other on Saturday night. There was a familiarity between them. They said little to each other while I was there, but their looks gave them away. "I knew there was something between you and Drew." I glare at her, waiting for more information. But she gives me nothing. She sits cross-legged, sipping on her tea. "Okay, I know we have an unwritten rule that we don't talk about what happened in the past, before we moved here, but what do you know about them?"

She places her tea down and turns her whole body to me. She sighs. "Okay, Theo comes from a beautiful family, one that would go out of their way to help anyone. He has a story to tell, one that you should hear from him, so I won't tell it, but I would trust him with my life. He's one of the good guys, Iv. If there is something between you, you should call him."

I cock my head to the side, studying her. What does she know about them and their family that she can't say—or won't? "That tells me very little, Jen. What's the go with you and Drew?"

She shifts in her seat, obviously uncomfortable by the question. "He's just a friend from the past," she mutters into her tea, now avoiding my eye contact completely.

"Okay, whatever you say." I yawn. I'm too tired for this conversation tonight. I definitely want to know more, but it's going to have to wait till my brain is operational again.

She checks her watch, pushing from the lounge, and takes her empty cup to the sink in the kitchen. "It's late, I better get going. See you on Sunday for our beach day."

I follow her out. "Thanks for tonight."

"Any time, hon. You know I'm happy to watch Harmy."

"I'll keep that in mind."

I watch her go into her townhouse and then close the door and make sure it's locked. I put my empty teacup in the dishwasher and turn it on, then make my way up the stairs, checking on Harmony as I walk to my room. She is sleeping like an angel, perfect and peaceful.

I change into my pyjamas then climb into bed. I'm so tired I should go to sleep easily tonight. But my brain is still going a million miles a minute, with thoughts of what we did running through my head—his lips on mine, his powerful body holding me up. It felt so good to be close to him. I felt protected in his arms, and that's something I haven't felt in a very long time. I let my mind wander and imagine what it would be like to have someone like him in my life. I'm sure it would be amazing if this were anyone else's life, but it's not. This is me, and I must have done something bad in a past life and now I'm being punished.

I won't get the happily ever after, I'm smart enough to know that already.

CHAPTER TEN

IVY

"Pass me the sunscreen, Jen." She throws it at my head, and I catch it before it connects.

It's a stunning autumn day. The sun's out, and there is no breeze at all. Penny has twisted our arms with the promise of a picnic lunch and got us out for the day to her favourite place along the beach. I'm sure it's because of the lack of clothing she can get away with wearing as she parades around in her skimpy bikini, but I'm not complaining. This is just what I need.

Since moving here, I try to come as often as I can, let the sun warm my skin and the sound of the waves take my busy mind away to somewhere more peaceful. Harmony is sitting in front of us on the sand, playing with her dolls. I'm feeling good today, trying not to think of my irresponsible behaviour the other night and of him, Theo. As long as I don't close my eyes, because when I do, all I can see is him. And fuck, it's a good sight—water running over that broad chest of his...

STOP, Ivy! I'm not thinking about him. I'm soaking up the sun in my cutest white crochet one-piece and a massive wide-brimmed hat. Penny is fussing over the food platter she has brought, trying to make it look perfect. I'm not sure why since we're just going to eat it. Jenna is sitting up in a stylish sundress almost too good for wearing to the beach. She looks totally out of place, reading glasses on and a book in her lap. She never seems relaxed; she always has to be doing something and looking stylish while she does.

"So, Ivy, what's going on with Theo? Bet it got steamy after I left the other night." And there it is, Penny's real reason for a beach day. She loves the gossip.

This gets Jenna's attention, and she looks up from her book. "And she was over an hour late coming home," Jenna teases, raising her eyebrow at me.

"Thanks, Jen, throw me under the bus, why don't you." I peg one of the sun-dried tomatoes from the platter at her, just missing her head. She gives me an evil glare and throws one back, hitting me in the eye. Luckily, I'm wearing my sunglasses.

"Bitch," I say, laughing at her as she smiles smugly back.

"So," they both say, giving me their full attention. Jenna already knows the story but is playing along.

"I'll give you the G-rated version, as there are little ears around." I gesture over to Harmony, who is busy playing with her dolls in the sand.

"Let's just say we had a chat, we took a shower, and it was a hot one—*too* hot—so like every other time I've seen him, I ruined it by freaking out and running away." I get a sympathetic smile from both of them. They know my past wasn't good, just like I know theirs wasn't, but it's like an unwritten rule between us that we don't talk about it. What happened in our lives before we moved here doesn't exist.

"Gross, I use those showers on the regular," says Penny.

I shrug. "Yeah, and I can only imagine who with." She's

one to talk. I know for a fact that she has been caught in those showers with a guy or two more than once.

"You know nothing, you're just making assumptions." Jenna and I both look over at her in question. It's a known fact that she has been caught doing many things. The girl's a nymphomaniac. "What?" she says, glancing between the two of us. "Okay, fine, I might have been caught, but it was only once, there were just two guys there."

"What, are you serious, Penny?" Jenna says, giving me a look like she can't believe it. I nod, cause I know it's true. Our boss walked in on them. She's lucky he didn't fire her, but I'm pretty sure the only problem he had with it was that he wasn't invited to join in.

She waves her hand in Jenna's direction. "Tell me you wouldn't do the same if you had the opportunity presented to you?"

"I'm positive I wouldn't," says Jenna, throwing her a disgusted look.

"Whatever. Anyway, we're here to talk about Ivy, not me, so spill, missy." They forget their tiff and turn their attention back to me.

"He's so hot, guys, totally too good for me. Besides, no one wants to get involved with a single mum. There's just too much baggage here," I say, looking over at my beautiful baby girl. She's not the baggage, it's my past relationship issues. I wish I could get my shit together to give her a better life with a male role model in it. But there's too much damage from the past. My scars run deep and aren't just emotional. I have actual physical scars on my face from the injuries I suffered that night. Luckily, they are well-hidden with the foundation I use. But every morning when I look at myself in the mirror, they are a constant reminder that I can only trust myself. People aren't always who you think they are.

"Well, his brother seems to think you made a big impression. Apparently he didn't stop talking about you all week," Jenna says.

Somehow, I doubt that. And what is she talking about, his brother? I thought she said he was just a friend from the past. Are they in contact?

"Likely story. Speaking of his brother, what about you? You've been talking to Drew through the week? And you never told me what happened with the two of you on Saturday night. You looked pretty familiar when I left."

She looks down into her book to avoid my questioning gaze. "You didn't miss much. A bit of dancing, drinking, pool, then Drew drove me home. That was that, nothing to write home about." By the look on her face, I can tell there's more to that. She's blushing.

"I know you better than that. Missy, you're hiding something." She just smiles into her book, giving me nothing else to go on.

Penny chucks her unruly curls up into a high ponytail. "Well, if you two won't give up the gossip, this is just boring. I'm going for a swim." She grabs her towel, strolling in the direction of the water. I watch her as she goes. Man, the girl has such sass, I wish I were more like her. Imagine fucking two guys in the showers at work! I would never have the guts. I could barely handle one.

She stops to chat to a couple of guys that have just come out of the water, surfboards slung under their arms. She laughs at something one of them says then they laugh back, and I realise who she's talking to: it's Theo's brother, Drew. They look so alike I have to do a double take, but Drew's hair is longer and has a curl to it.

"Hey, Jen, I think that's Drew coming out of the water," I say, looking over to the shoreline where I've spotted him.

Her eyes widen, and she ducks behind me. "Where is he? Are you joking?" She spies over my shoulder to see if it's him.

"Over there." I motion with my head not to be too obvious. "Talking to Penny."

She peers out from under her hat. "Shit, it is him," she cries, pulling her hat over her face to hide.

"Nothing happened last weekend, my arse!" She wouldn't be hiding behind me if nothing happened. "Too late, babe, I think he's seen us." I laugh at the awkward situation occurring for her. For once the spotlight is off me. I wave him over to say hi. She's going to kill me, but I don't care. It's just too good not to stir up a bit of trouble, and I'm nosy. I want to know what's going on between them.

Drew walks up the beach to us. His wetsuit is unzipped to his waist, his abs on full display. Clearly the Walkers are a genetically blessed family. He's leaner than Theo, but still just as hunky.

"Ladies," he says with a cheeky grin, water dripping down his chest from his wet hair. Jenna is forced from the safety of hiding under her hat.

Harmony, who has been silent until now, runs over to check out his board. "Wow, how cool is this, Mum. Can I learn to surf?" she says, running her hand over his board.

"I could teach you a thing or two, little lady, if it's okay with your mum? I'm giving both my nephews lessons, and they must be around your age."

Oh God, I'm not ready for anything like that. I know I'm a bit of a helicopter parent, but she can try things like that when she's older. "Maybe when you're older, baby. You need to be good at swimming to surf."

"You never let me do anything fun," she says, looking disappointed, as she sulks back to playing with her dolls. I'm sure I haven't heard the end of that; it will be the new thing she wants to do now.

Drew and Jenna both seem to be lost for words. He looks her over, and she tries her best not to seem too interested. But I know her, and she so is. It's getting kinda awkward, so I stand up and brush the sand off my towel, ready to make myself scarce, so they can talk or just stare at each other awkwardly.

"So, I'm just going to go over here for a bit to watch Harmy," I say to relieve the awkward tension filling the air.

Drew tilts his head to the side, his attention back to me. "I hear you're giving my brother a run for his money, Ivy."

I fold the towel in front of me, trying to avoid this conversation. I don't want to talk about this now, especially not with his brother.

"I don't know what you're talking about, Drew. I'm sure Theo got what he was interested in and is onto the next cute thing already," I say, kind of pouting even though I don't want to care. I do like him and saying it out loud it hurts to think he could have moved on to someone else already.

He smiles a knowing smile, and it's just like Theo's with the dimples. "I know he puts on a player act, Ivy, but there is more to him than you think. He's not had the easiest past, and most of what you see is him trying to protect himself. But I know he likes you. You should give him a chance."

"I don't know. I'll think about it, I guess." I shrug. I'm out of here, I don't want to talk about this anymore. He's had a hard past? What, did some girl cheat on him or something? Break his heart once, so now he sleeps with anything that moves and calls it fun? Sounds like he's more trouble than he's worth, if you ask me. And I still wonder what happened to his son's mother. Maybe it was her who did the dirty on him, broke his heart?

"Think I'll go check on what Harmony's doing, leave you two to whatever this is," I say, gesturing between them. Jenna gives me a look, pleading for me to stay and save her. There's no way I'm doing that. This guy is into her, and she needs a bit of fun in her life. I'm sure she will thank me later.

I plop myself down next to Harmony and watch her play. She's lying on her belly, surrounded by mounds of little sand hills she has been building, her long blonde curls dragging along the sand all tangled, wet, and full of sand. That's going to be fun to brush out later.

I could sit and watch her play her little games all day. She is so sweet and innocent. She has the most beautiful soul, and when she plays, you can see her imagination come to life. Sometimes it's hard to believe she's half of me, half the monster in prison. I try not to think of him, but sometimes when I watch her, it's hard not to. She's half him.

Now that she's started school, she's asking more questions too, like, "Why don't I have a dad around like the other kids? Where is he?" I have no idea what to tell her, so for now, I just say he's away for work overseas. I know I'll have to explain it all to her one day, but I'm not ruining her while she's so little. She deserves to think life is all rainbows and butterflies, at least for a little while longer.

I glance back over to Jen, trying not to be too obvious, watching her and Drew chat. She is different with him, shy, fidgety, a little on edge. I wonder what it is between them. It's so obvious he's into her, but there is more to it. Maybe it's time the two of us opened up with each other about our pasts. Might help us both move on with our lives.

Drew finally gives up. He waves to me then makes his way back up the beach, leaving Jen to her book.

"Hey, Jen, I think I'm almost ready to go. I've had enough of the sun for one day, and I should get Harmy home."

"Yeah, me too. I'll go find Pen," she offers as she places her book on her towel, then makes her way down the beach in search of Penny, who could be talking to anyone by now.

I glance back over to Harmony. I don't know what this game is, but she's burying her favourite Barbie in the sand mounds she has created. I listen to her game. Her sweet little voice talks as if she is narrating a story.

"The evil sand monster has taken the beautiful princess and has buried her so the prince can't find her, but the prince is smart because he is Prince Charming, and he will come to rescue the beautiful princess from the evil sand monster. When he does, they will live happily ever after."

Oh, baby girl, if only it were that simple.

"Come on, poss, time to go."

Theo

I pull into the driveway of the place that has always been my family home. I love this house. It's where I spent my childhood, and there are so many happy memories within these walls. My parents have lived here for over 40 years.

The house has changed so much over the years. When we were little, it was an older-style Queenslander, built in the 50s. I'll never forget the colour; it was pale blue-green.

All the kids in the street used to come to our place in the afternoon after school because our yard was massive, and we were the only ones with a trampoline and a mango tree out the back, which we used to climb.

Over the years, Mum and Dad have done a lot of work on it. First, with the help of my sister Elena, who is an interior stylist, they renovated the house inside and out, restoring what they could and adding a modern twist. It now looks more like a modern Palm Springs-style home, all in white, with a bright yellow front door and palm trees and tropical plants all along the front white picket fence. Then once Dad decided it was time to retire from the force, they built three beach bungalows and an entertaining area with a pool, which they now lease out as boutique accommodation. They're able to charge a premium because holiday accommodation here is so popular, and they both like to talk, so it works out nicely for them, having new people to stay all the time.

Every Sunday since the week I moved out, when I was 22, has been the same: a family dinner at my parents' house. Nothing beats a home-cooked meal, especially when your mum can cook like mine. Being a single dad, my dinners are normally pretty boring, whatever I can chuck together as quickly as possible. We rush through the door at night, so I can get Jasper fed, through the shower, and ready for bed before 7:30, so it's nice to have someone fuss over me once a week.

I walk through the front door. Jasper has already taken off through the house looking for his cousin Cooper, and I'm greeted with the most delicious smell. "What's for dinner, Mum?" I ask, kissing her on the cheek.

"That would be right. I don't even get a *Hello, how was*

your day, beautiful mother, before you thought about your stomach!"

"Sorry, Mum. It just smells so good, and I'm starving."

She continues chopping a salad. "Of course you are. When are you not hungry?"

I steal some cucumber from the chopping board. "Where's Dad?" I throw the cucumber in my mouth.

"He's in the study with Fraser. They're looking over some alternative plans. Dad's thinking of extending to make a fourth bungalow."

"Oh really? Do you have enough room to fit another in?"

"That's what they're looking at, trying to make it work."

"I thought Dad was supposed to be retired and taking it easy."

"When have you ever known your dad to take it easy? What's happening with you, Theo?"

"Nothing new. Just working, wrangling Jasper, that's all."

I look out the backyard to see my sister Elena and her son Copper playing a board game as I walk through the large foldout French doors to join them. "Hey, sissy, how are things with you?" I say, kissing her on the cheek. Jasper has taken a seat and watches on as they play. I walk around the table behind Cooper. "Hey, buddy, you want me to make sure Mummy's not cheating?" I mess his spiky hair, earning me a filthy look from him.

"She must be cheating. She's won every game so far!" he says with a little scowl on his face directed at her.

She laughs. "I'm not cheating, I'm just an expert at this game." They're playing four-in-a-row so it hardly takes a genius to win, but he's five, she could let him get one. But it's not the Walker way. We're a little competitive! Come-first-at-all-costs kind of attitude, so the poor kid's got no chance.

"That's okay, buddy, I'm here to watch her. Now we'll beat her this time." I show him where to put the next red chip, and he places it in, all excited. He will not lose with me on his side.

"If you're helping Coop, I get Jas helping me." She pats her lap, and Jasper makes his way around the table to sit with her. He adores her. It's not the same as having a mother, but my sister has doted over him since he was born, and they have a special relationship. Cooper finally gets in a win, and the boys take over to play a game of their own.

There's a loud chuckle from inside, and we all look toward the door as Drew walks through, a goofy smile on his face, as always.

"Uncle Drew's here!" Both boys jump up from their game and run towards him, all excited. He holds out his hands, giving them both a high-five.

"I never get a reaction like that," I complain to Elly.

"That's because you're the boring cop uncle," Drew says smugly, "not the one that just re-qualified for the world surf league."

"What, you're back in?" I jump up, excited for him, bringing him in for a hug. "Fantastic news, we need to celebrate."

"Very exciting news, Drew," says Elly, hugging him. "I didn't even know you were back competing."

"Yeah, I didn't want to jinx it, wasn't sure how I would go after my injury. Sorry I didn't tell you guys. There was a local comp at Avoca Beach. I just had to place in the top three to be back in, and I got second."

"Nice, well done, little bro. Where are you headed first?"

"Looks like Hawaii, probably Maui, then Oahu."

Mum, Dad, and Fraser join us out the back with drinks to celebrate Drew's good news.

"Cheers to Drew," we all say as we clink our beer bottles.

"I'm going to miss you, man, even if you are a pain in the arse." This has been the longest he's been home since we were kids, and I've got to say, it's been nice having him around.

"Theo, you won't believe who I ran into down the beach today," he says, loud enough for everyone to hear.

"Who?" I say, raising my eyebrow, letting him know he better be careful of what he says in front of everyone.

"Just Ivy and her friends." He's such a shit stirrer. He knows what he's doing, mentioning her in front of Mum and Elena.

Mum's head flicks quickly back in my direction. "Who's Ivy, Theo?" Of course Mum has heard every word, she has some sort of radar for this stuff.

"Just a girl Theo has been chasing, but she's a smart one. She rejected him." Drew laughs.

"She didn't reject me, it's just complicated. She's got a kid." I can see the look of hope in Mum's eyes already. She is marrying us off as a perfectly little readymade family of four. She has told me frequently that life's too short. I should find someone special and move on from the past. If only it were that simple.

"A single parent just like you, oh, that's nice. How old is her child?"

"It's not important because it's nothing, Mum. Don't get your hopes up," I say, giving her a look.

She looks disappointed. "I was just hoping one of my boys would finally be ready to settle down now you're in your mid-30s and all. It would be so nice for Jasper to have a feminine influence, don't you think?"

"I think he's got enough of that with you two mothering him," I say, pointing to Mum and Elly. "I think he's fine."

"Well, we could do with some more grandkids around here," she says, her eyes almost pleading with me.

"Elly needs to work on that, she's the married one," I say, trying to deflect the situation onto anyone else but me. I could kill Drew for saying anything in front of Mum.

She shoots me a look that tells me she's not happy. "Thanks, as if I don't hear, '*He's five now. When are you having another baby?*' enough from every busybody around. I don't need it from Mum as well."

"Sorry, sis." I'll leave her with Mum for that conversation.

Fraser takes her hand, pulling her into him. "You don't have to answer those questions to anyone, Elly."

Mum gives her a look and drops it. Not something I had noticed before, but maybe I have hit a nerve. I guess I've been too wrapped up in my own life to wonder why they never tried to have any more kids. Maybe they have been trying and it's not happening. I hope not, for her sake; she's such a wonderful mother.

"I'm going for another beer. Anyone else need one?" Drew follows me inside to help with the drinks.

"That was a dick move, now you've upset Mum," I say to him, opening the fridge.

"Well, if she's focusing on your love life, she'll be off my back for a while," he says with that cheeky grin he always has when he's up to no good—which is all the time.

"So, what did she say, anyway?" I shouldn't ask, but I can't help myself. I'm trying to give her space to come to her senses and call me, but it's so bloody hard. I'm not a patient man when I want something.

He takes the drink from me. "Not a lot. She thinks you're a player, that you got what you wanted from her and now you're done. Don't worry, I set her straight," he says with his hands up in defence, like he fears what I'm about to do to him.

"What. Did. You. Say, Drew?" I say, glaring at him. He'd better not have said too much and screwed this up for me.

"Nothing, just that you like her, and she should give you a chance." Relief washes over me. There are many things he could have said about my lifestyle until now, and they would have been true, but she makes me want to be someone different, and I don't want her to think of me like that.

"Why don't you just call her, man, if you're so hung up on her?"

"I don't have her number. I've left it up to her. I'm not chasing her anymore. If she's interested, she'll call." Except that I can't stop thinking about her, and it's driving me nuts not being in control. I should have just got her number.

"Fair enough. I guess you know what you're doing. If it were me, I'd find a way of getting her number, though, just saying, she seems shy. Or maybe she has you worked out and is right to stay away." That earns him a punch in the arm. He's such a smart arse.

"What about you? If she was at the beach with friends, I bet Jenna was there."

He smiles. "Yeah, she was, but that story is the same as it has always been. We're just friends."

We head back out to the rest of the family where Mum is serving dinner, an assortment of Italian dishes: pizza, spaghetti, garlic bread, and salads. It looks and smells amazing.

CHAPTER ELEVEN

IVY

I PICK UP YET ANOTHER LOST SINGLE SHOE FROM UNDER the dining table. That must be the tenth one now. How is it possible for one little girl to have so many shoes? And all over the house too! We have a place for them just as you walk in the door, but at least once a week they need to be rounded up from all the random places she leaves them and packed away.

I don't know what to do with myself. I have just got Harmony into bed for the night and I'm racing around cleaning, trying to busy myself so I don't cave and message Theo. The hot shower scene from last Thursday plays repeatedly in my head, dirty images of what we did. I haven't stopped thinking about him. Then running into Drew yesterday has made it worse.

Maybe I have judged Theo too quickly, and it sounds like there's more to him. I wonder what happened in his past. I mean, you don't end up still dating at our age and not have some skeletons in your closet, but I wonder what stopped him from settling down.

I still feel horrible for the way I treated him, just

running off like that straight after. He must think I'm a total mess—and he would be right to think that way, cause I am. Every time I close my eyes to sleep, I see him in that shower, water running over his muscular body. I don't know how anyone's supposed to sleep with an image like that in their head. His sexy smile tempting me to lose all self-control, and those eyes—one look from him and I'm gone.

I look at his number on my phone for the hundredth time this week. He put it in under, "The god," of course. I laugh. He's so full of himself. Wish I were more like that. Then I would be out having fun with him right now, not cleaning the house.

I scan around the living room. All the shoes and toys are packed away. What next? I guess I could start on the massive pile of laundry. Man, I hate housework. Sometimes I fantasise about being rich and having someone to do all the jobs I hate for me. Oh, that life sounds wonderful. But it's not real, so I'd better get started on the laundry. No one else is going to do it for me. Least I can watch some trash on TV while getting it done.

Using housework as a distraction is not helping me at all. I keep going over all of our conversations since I met him. What he said is right. I know I deserve a life outside of my responsibilities, but I'm so scared. How do I trust someone again after what happened last time? How do I trust myself to know I'm choosing the right person and I won't end up hurt again—*or nearly dead, Ivy, not just a little hurt?* I remind myself.

I feel the scar on my cheek, my constant reminder to be careful. And I will be this time. I have learned from my past mistakes. I won't make them again.

Jenna says I can trust him, and I believe her. I reach for my phone on the coffee table and look at his number again.

He said let's just have some fun. Maybe that's what I need. It doesn't have to go anywhere or be anything. I'm overcomplicating it by thinking it does. *Just have some fun for once in your life, Ivy.* Okay, good pep talk. Now, how do I do this text thing? I don't know what to write.

Me: Hi. It's Ivy from the yoga studio. I ran into your brother yesterday, and he said I should give you a chance. If you're still interested?

I bury my head in my hands. Oh man, I sound pathetic. *Ivy from the yoga studio.* There is no way he is going to message back. But I send it anyway, because I don't know what else to say. He's probably busy anyway and won't write back. Maybe I should have called? Nah, I would be way too awkward! I would probably be lost for words, and on the phone that would be even worse than face to face. I chuck my phone on the lounge like it just bit me. I don't want to look at it again. I'm too nervous he won't write back or that he will. Ahh. I need to find something else to do, keep me busy. To my surprise, a response pings almost immediately. That was quick. Now my heart is beating fast, I can feel it in my chest. I don't know why I'm so worried, it's stupid.

Theo: I was just thinking about you, wondering how long it would take you to come to your senses. Is this your way of asking me out?

What do I say? What do I say? Why is this so hard? Think, Ivy, come on.

Me: Maybe, if you're interested.

Theo: I gave you my number so you could call when you were ready to come out and play with me. So, what are we doing?

Okay, this is good, he is still interested.

Me: I have no idea. I don't know how to do all of this. It's been so long, and I can't do nights because of Harmony. Can we just start with a coffee? While the kids are at school?

Theo: Well, luckily for you, I have my rostered day off tomorrow if you want to do something then? It's just a bit of fun, Ivy, don't overthink it. I'll pick you up at 10:30. Bring your bikini xx.

Tomorrow, that is sooner than I was expecting. But I guess it won't give me time to back out.

Me: Sounds good. Swimmers to a café?? See you then xx

I wait for the little circles to pop up to show he's typing, but nothing. Okay, I'm left to guess why I would need swimmers for a coffee date.

I have no idea what I'm doing. I need help. I need Penny, that girl will be all over this.

Me: Help! We need to go shopping tomorrow after I drop Harmony at school.

Penny: Miss Ivy's asking me for help? You must be desperate!

Me: Ha ha, can you help?

Penny: Meet you at 915 x

Me: Lifesaver xx

You can do this, Ivy, it's easy. Just get to know him better, see where it goes.

Theo

. . .

I laugh at myself. I'm not writing back, I'll keep her guessing on that one.

Getting to know your date, hey? Well, it's not my usual style, but the cop side of me is curious to know what she's all about and why she just appeared five years ago. The rest of me—mainly my cock—just wants a way to get her naked again. An afternoon swim in my pool will be a good start, I'd say. I'll take her for a coffee, a swim, then... we'll see what happens. We both have school pick-up, so unfortunately, we don't have all day, but that's life as a single parent, and at least she will understand.

I double-check the locks around the house like I do every night before I head up to bed. Jasper has been asleep for a couple of hours. He has been exhausted since starting school this year and crashes out early most nights. Tonight is no exception since we have been at my parents' for our Sunday dinner where he and Cooper ran around until I dragged him out of there because I knew how tired he was. He fought it all the way then fell asleep five minutes before we got home, so I carried him up to bed and tucked him in.

I peep in his room. He's sleeping soundly so I turn off the hall light and head into my room. I sit on the end of the bed, and the photo of Fiona on my dressing table catches my eye. If things work out the way I want them to, Ivy is hopefully coming back here tomorrow. What do I do? What's the right thing to do here? Fiona will always be Jasper's mum, and she will always have a place in my heart, but something about Ivy is different, and I want to be open to moving forward with my life, not living in the past.

Tomorrow, I will put her photo in Jasper's room. He loves that photo of his mum. He loves to sit holding it, asking me questions about her. It breaks my heart that he wasn't able to meet her. She would have been such a wonderful mother. She was the one that knew all about kids, not me. I had no idea, and when she was gone, and I held his little body against my chest, I didn't know how I was going to do it. I was all he had, and I had to work it out. I don't always get it right, and I'm sure that's only going to get worse as he gets older, but I love him with everything I have and make sure he knows it too.

Until now, Jasper was all I needed. I didn't even think of the possibility of anyone else actually being a part of my life. Until Ivy. I don't even know what has come over me when it comes to her. I'm like a horny teenager, constantly thinking about her, and when I do, I'm hard as a rock. That body of hers is out of this world, toned muscles with curves in all the right paces, long hair I want to wrap around my fist as I fuck her. I'm hard again just thinking about it.

I'm wanking off twice a day in the shower and still no relief. It's more than just the sexual attraction, though. That's kinda all I want it to be, it would be safer that way, but I know this is more, and I hardly even know her. She is a complete mystery. We have had four conversations tops, and really, I know next to nothing about her life and past. She is so guarded.

I have never really met anyone like her. Most girls I can't get to shut up about their past. They want to tell you every little detail of every relationship they have ever had and why they fell apart. Maybe tomorrow will be different and Ivy will open up to me. Maybe she will see that she can trust me.

Ivy

. . .

I can see Penny waiting for me at our usual meeting place, our favourite coffee shop down near the beach. She's preoccupied, chatting away to one of the baristas. Thank God she's on time today because we only have an hour, and I have a feeling I'm going to need every second of it.

Her eyes meet mine. "I've ordered for you," she calls to me, holding up a coffee in a takeaway cup.

"Thanks," I say, taking the steaming hot coffee from her hand. I take a sip. Ouch, too hot! I do that every time. I have no idea why I haven't learnt to wait so I don't burn my lip. That's going to be a good look for my date, turn up with a fat lip from a coffee burn. I have to drag Penny away by the arm from the young barista she's flirting with so we can get going, then start to walk up the street.

She waves goodbye, then turns to me with a filthy look. "Why are you in such a rush? I was doing my thing."

"I could see that. Sorry, but Theo is picking me up at 10:30, and I really need your help."

"We better get going then. Wait... what? You're going on a date with Theo?" She walks in front of me, stopping me in my tracks.

"Well, kind of. I don't know what it is. He's picking me up for coffee and he said to bring my swimmers, so I'm guessing we'll go for a swim somewhere. That's where you come in. I want something a bit, you know, hotter than my boring mumsy one-piece that hides the stretch marks."

She grins at me. "Nice, okay, I know just the place. I'm so excited for you, babe." She hugs me. She's bouncing down the street now, dragging me by the hand, energised by the task I have set her.

"I knew you'd be able to help." We stop when we get to a surf shop. The window displays are all posters of models with their bums barely covered by their swimmers, so I guess this is the right place.

We walk in, and Penny loads my arms up with bikini sets to try. "What? Why do you look so scared?"

"I just don't know if I can pull these off," I say, holding up the tiny bikini in front of me.

"Stop being silly. You have a hot body from all the exercise you do. Show it off! What's the point in all the yoga you do if no one sees it? Now hurry and try these or you're going to be late." She pushes me into a fitting room. "Start trying, and I'll be back in a minute with some more."

The first few I try are awful. There's no way I'm going out in public with them on. Then I get to one that's a pretty pale blue. I love the colour so maybe it will be okay. Just as I get it on, Penny opens the curtain and comes in with some more.

"You're lucky I'm dressed!" I say, mortified, covering my belly. She has no boundaries.

"What are you worried about? It's not like I haven't seen you naked before."

She's right, she has. We were both drunk and jumped the fence of the local swimming pool to go skinny-dipping. Jenna refused to join us and kept watch on the other side of the fence instead. We thought it was hilarious at the time, after having a few too many cocktails. We were lucky we didn't get caught and thrown in jail for indecent exposure in a public place. Penny's such a bad influence.

"Not sober, you haven't!"

"You should definitely get that one, it's totally hot on you!"

"Thanks. What about my stretch marks? They look awful, don't they?" I feel over the faded lines on my tummy.

"Ivy, I can barely see them. Your body is perfect. Theo will not notice some tiny stretch marks."

"They're not tiny, but thanks."

"He's not even going to be looking at them, trust me. I know guys. He'll be looking at your arse and your tits."

"Oh God, these are too small, aren't they? They show too much." I cover my arse. "And I'll be lucky if my boobs don't pop out of this top!" I say, adjusting the top to try and cover myself better, but it's no use.

"You wanted something sexy, Ivy. Now stop your whining and own it. Brazilian cut is all the fashion at the moment, everyone is wearing them." I roll my eyes at her and push her out of the dressing room. "Try these, then we better go," she says, handing me the last few pairs she has found.

I find one other I like and decide to take them both. You never know, today might go well and I'll need it. I pay for the swimmers, and we make our way out of the shop to walk back down the street towards our cars.

"So, what else do you need help with?"

"I don't know, everything? It's been a lifetime since I have been on a date. What should I wear?"

"What you're wearing is fine. Just relax, babe. He obviously already likes you or he wouldn't be seeing you again, so just be yourself and you'll be fine. Maybe just don't end it by running this time. Poor bloke is going to get a complex."

"Ha, you're so funny, Pen. I won't run this time." I feel a hot nervous sweat roll over my body when I think of the last few times I have seen him and ran. What if I run again? He's going to think I'm a total nut job. And I can't help it! I have so many triggers that make me want to run these days.

This never used to be me. Until everything that happened with Dominic, I was trusting and easy-going, a normally functioning human. But when the man that's supposed to love you turns your home into a battlefield and beats you to within an inch of your life, you learn to protect yourself—and that's what I have been doing. I don't know that I can trust Theo, and until he proves otherwise, I'm always going to be on edge with him. I just don't trust men now. I don't know if that will ever change.

I turn to my friend, grabbing her by the arms. "I don't think I can do this, Pen. I haven't been on a date since I was a teenager when I met my husband." Shit, did I just say that out loud? See? This is a mistake. It brings up all the old memories I've been so successful at suppressing until now.

"Of course you can, I was only joking. Has it really been that long? Wait... what do you mean husband?"

Why did I have to slip up on this with her? She won't give up now until I tell her more. "Oh, I just meant the last long-term boyfriend," I lie to hopefully stop the line of questioning coming my way.

"Harmony's dad, was it him you were married to? I've always wondered what happened there."

"Nothing happed there!" I say, annoyed with myself for the slip-up. "I don't want to talk about this, Pen, not today." I know she loves the gossip, but hopefully, she can see by the look on my face this isn't shit you want to talk about.

"Yeah, of course. You know you can talk to me if you ever need to, though, right? I love the scandal, but with the serious stuff, I wouldn't say anything to anyone. I've got your back, babe."

"Thank you, I know, I just can't talk about it. It's too hard."

"I understand." She takes me by the arms. "Forget I brought it up. We need to get you ready for this date. And you can do this. It's just coffee and a swim, easy stuff."

"Easy for you."

"Live a little, Iv. What's the worst that can happen? You'll have a bad time and never do it again."

I offer her a little shrug. If only that was the worst that could happen. I try not to think of the worst-case scenario, because as soon as I do, my mind runs away on me and I'm back in the nightmare, running, scared for my life.

Shake it off, Ivy, don't go back there, this is not Dominic.

"You okay, hun? You disappeared on me."

I shake my head and plaster on a fake smile. "Yeah, sorry, I'm fine. I'd better get going so I'm not late. Thank you for your help." I give her a quick hug, then head for my car.

"Call me after. I want all the juicy details, woman."

I throw her a look that tells her *no way*, and she blows me a kiss before turning and heading back up the street.

You can do this, Ivy. And man, do I want to, I really do. I'm just scared.

CHAPTER TWELVE

IVY

I check my reflection in the hallway mirror for the fiftieth time this morning. Nice, natural make-up with a bit of mascara. I'm wearing Mum's sapphire earrings for good luck. I don't wear her special jewellery very often, but today, I feel like I need her with me for an extra boost of confidence. I apply my favourite cherry lip gloss and take one last look. That will have to do. I'm not into the overly made-up look even though Penny left some make-up here for me. She's trying to micromanage me for this date as best she can, and I love her for it.

I'm wearing a simple knee-length cotton dress with an intricate flowery pattern all over it and tan sandals. It's supposed to be a beautiful sunny day, so this should be perfect. Who am I kidding? I have no idea what's perfect to wear for a date. I'm so nervous. It's been years since I've done anything like this, I have no idea what I'm doing. What if we have nothing to talk about? I should just cancel, save myself the trouble.

The buzzer for the security gate sounds, and I jump, my nerves a little on edge. Looks like it's too late to back out—he's here. I grab my denim jacket, bag, and phone from the dining room table, checking my reflection one last time as I go past the mirror and make my way out the door.

Theo is leaning against the passenger side of his white Jeep. His gaze is focused on me, and I feel so self-conscious making my way from my house to his car. Just don't fall down the driveway now, Ivy, and we're off to a good start. He holds the door open for me with that same charming smile I remember from the other night at the yoga studio. He appears relaxed and carefree; I guess you would be when you do this kinda thing all the time. I'm making assumptions, maybe he doesn't do this all the time, but he certainly seems like the type that would. Overconfident, cocky, and sexy as hell.

"Good morning, Ivy. You look beautiful today."

"Morning, Theo. Such the gentleman, holding the door for me," I say with a shy smile as I climb into his massive car. My hands are a little shaky, making it hard to do up my seat belt. It eventually clicks in, then I tuck my hands under my legs to stop the shaking.

I do not know why I'm so nervous around him. I mean, we've already slept together. He's seen me naked, for God's sake. I should be able to sit in his car and go for a coffee. Somehow the talking seems so much harder than a quick fuck in the studio bathroom.

He hops into the driver's seat and gives me a brief smile. He smells divine. Some expensive aftershave designed to entice women, I'm sure, and it's working. I want him already. No sex for five years until Theo, then one smell of this man's aftershave and I practically want to beg him to take me home for another go. But I need to show some control if I want to actually get to know him. And I'm not doing anything else with him until I know at least something about him.

He turns the car around and drives away from Broken Point towards the mountains. I wonder where he's taking me for coffee. I was assuming we would go to some place in town, but we're driving in the opposite direction. I wait for him to say something, having no idea what to say myself. But nothing—this is awkward. "Where are you taking me?"

"A café just a bit out of town."

"Oh, okay, that sounds nice." I look out the windscreen again. What now? "The weather channel says it's supposed to be a nice day today," I say, trying to make conversation. Man, I'm talking about the weather? This is bad. He looks over at me, snapping out of his thoughts, and gives me that cheeky smile I'm growing to like.

"I was planning on that. Did you bring your bikini?" he says, raising his eyebrow.

"Yes. Why do I need my bikini for a coffee date?" I say, feeling kind of silly for having to ask. I'm so new to this dating thing. Maybe you always go for a swim after coffee.

He laughs. "Well, if all goes well and you can still stand the sight of me, I was thinking of a swim at my place might be nice? I live near the café."

His place? I'm a little surprised he has thought that far ahead, but I have nothing on for the day and a swim sounds nice. "Oh, okay, that would be nice. I have to be back at three for school pick-up, but I guess you do as well."

"Yeah, I only get to pick Jasper up from school one day a month when I have my RDO, so we try to make the most of it—get ice cream or go for a swim at the beach or a walk if the weather is nice."

"That sounds lovely. What do you do with him the rest of the time?"

"He goes home with my sister Elly and her son Cooper."

"You're lucky you have family so close by to help."

"I know. I would be lost without her. She helps a lot. Her son is the same age, so they have fun together."

"That's nice then." I wonder what happened to his wife or Jasper's mum. He said he has been raising him by himself since he was born. Maybe she did a runner, couldn't handle being a parent or something.

We have been driving for about 15 minutes, and I don't recognise this road at all. "Where are we going? I haven't been this way before." All I see out the window is tropical-looking trees; looks like we're heading into the rainforest.

"Just a hidden-gem coffee shop. It's not as busy as the ones in town, and it's on the way to my place, so I thought it would be a perfect place to get to know you better," he says, pulling into the parking lot of the coffee shop.

It's cute, one of those country-looking, bakery-type coffee shops with big open windows at the front and people sitting on bar stools looking out at the view of the tropical rainforest all around.

I go to hop out of the car, but he's at my door already, helping me out. It's so unexpected, but it's kind of nice to have someone fuss over you. He holds out his hand, and I take it and jump out of the car. He doesn't let go once I'm out, holding my hand on the walk to the café. I smile to myself. This is cute and not what I was expecting from Mr Let's-just-have-fun.

The elderly lady behind the counter sees us and shuffles straight over to welcome us.

"Theo, it's lovely to see you today. And you brought a friend! How nice for you, dear."

"Yes, Wendy, I would like you to meet Ivy."

She wears a kind smile. "So wonderful to meet you, Ivy.

Follow me to the best seat in the house." We follow her through the café to a booth with dark brown vinyl coverings and rustic timber tables. I'd say the original furnishings from when this place was built, in probably the 80s. It's charming, but it's a little worn around the edges. She sets down two cardboard menus that she pulls from her frilly white apron.

"I'll be back in a minute to take your order, dears," she practically sings as she wanders back to the kitchen.

The smell of fresh oven-baked goods wafts through the air, and my tummy rumbles right on cue. I wonder if I'd look greedy ordering pie and cake so early in the day.

Theo places his menu on the table and turns his attention back to me. "What do you feel like?"

"I know it's only early in the day, but the smell of the pies is just too good to resist, so I'll get a chunky steak pie and maybe some carrot cake." I give him a cheeky grin. "Does that make me a total pig?"

He laughs. "No, I was thinking the same thing. They make the best pies, and it's nearly 11 o'clock, that's lunchtime, right?"

"Yeah, close enough."

He calls Wendy over, and she takes our orders then shuffles back off to the kitchen, returning moments later with our pies and cake plated up. "I'll bring out your coffees when they're ready, dears."

I offer her a smile, and she makes her way back to the kitchen.

It looks as good as it smells. I dig into my carrot cake first. I can't help myself, the cream-cheese frosting is calling my name. Theo is giving me a questioning look. "What?" I say.

"Dessert first, hey?"

"Yeah, it's the best bit, why would I wait? And there are no kids here to see me do it." I laugh as I take a big scoop of cake. "Yum, this is so good. Do you want to try some?"

He's already smashed most of his pie. "Told you this place is worth the drive out of town. This is where I take Jasper when we want a treat. It's our special place."

"And you brought me here."

"Of course, you're very special." He smiles a little seductively. This dude knows what to say to get a lady swooning over him. Not a player, my arse, but I can't say I don't like it.

"I have to admit I was a little worried you were driving me out here so you could kill me and dispose of my body with no one around." I laugh nervously as a look of shock washes over him.

"Why on earth would that be the first thing you thought of? Do I look like the type of guy that would kill pretty girls for fun?"

I shrug and pull a face that says I don't know.

He shakes his head. "I'm glad I'm getting some sort of insight into your morbid mind."

Guess it's best he knows up front how fucked up my head is. "I'm not morbid, I just don't know you. I know very little about who you really are. Just because you're nice to look at doesn't mean you're a good person."

"You know a little about me, and I don't think I have given you any reason to worry as yet, have I?"

"No, but I know from experience people are good at hiding what they don't want the world to see."

He looks offended by my comment. "Well, I can assure you I'm an open book, and you have nothing to worry about when you're with me. And I hope after today we can get to know each other a little better so you can see that and stop worrying."

I look down at my pie, picking up a fork to dig in, trying to take a break from his intense expression. He is full-on when he gets himself worked up over something. I can picture what it would be like to get interrogated by him, those piercing eyes staring me down.

"Sorry, I wasn't trying to offend you. It's just, since becoming a parent, I'm always on the lookout for the worst-case scenario. It's like a protection thing, you know." I shrug, trying to brush it off as nothing so I don't look like a completely paranoid psycho and so I don't have to explain my actual reasons for being so mistrusting of him.

He jabs his fork into his cake forcefully. "Yeah, well, just so you know, I'm one of the good guys. You will never have to worry about when you're with me. I will protect you with my life. So just relax and stop worrying." He shovels the cake into his mouth, his focus still on me. I feel like a five-year-old who was just told off by her dad, but also kind of pleased that he was so willing to tell me he would protect me and that I have nothing to worry about. I feel like it's true with him, but I'm not stupid enough to let my guard down with him yet. He's going to need to do a lot more than just tell me he will keep me safe before I trust him completely. I have nothing to say back to him, so I just play with my pie, breaking a bit of pastry off and nibbling on it.

He rests his fork on the side of his plate. "Tell me about yourself, Ivy."

Oh great, the moment I have been dreading. The date interview. I take a deep breath, brushing a long strand of hair away from my face. "There's not much to tell. I'm a single mum, with a five-year-old daughter, who teaches yoga. That's as exciting as I get," I say a little more sarcastically than I intended to.

"What about your family, do your parents live around here?" he asks, scarfing down the last of his cake.

"My parents lived back in Dorrigo, where I grew up. They died in a car accident one night when I was 17, and I'm an only child. So, there is no other family. It's just me and Harmony now." I talk fast without taking a breath, just like ripping off a band-aid. I hate it when people ask about my family. I instantly get that pain in my stomach where it feels like someone is squeezing my insides.

He pities me, I see it in his eyes. I knew he would. That's why I hate telling people and didn't really want to have this conversation with him.

"That's awful, you lost both your parents on the same night. I can't even imagine how hard that must have been as a teenager. Your entire family just... gone." His expression has completely changed from the cheeky guy I first sat down with. He looks completely shattered by what I've just said.

"Theo, I'm okay. It was awful when it happened. I was devastated, and I miss them both every day and wish they were here, but it was a long time ago, and I'm lucky I have lots of wonderful people in my life now. Jenna and Penny, who you already met, and one of our neighbours, Fay, have become my family now. You do the best you can with what life throws at you, right?" I say with a small smile.

I need to get this talk off me because I know what comes next—more questions. Like why am I a single mum? What happened to Harmony's dad? Do you share custody? And the list goes on, and I don't want to have that chat right now. "Tell me about your family, Theo. I already know you have a cheeky brother that's just like you." He looks up at me, differently this time, his smile returning.

"I'm super close to my family. My mum and dad live

here in Byron, still in the same house I grew up in. I have my annoying little brother—who is nothing like me, by the way—and I have a little sister, Elena. They're twins. She lives here as well with her husband Fraser, kind of near you in Broken Point. She's the one that looks after Jasper for me. I'm sure you two would get on really well. She's got a little boy, Cooper, who's the same age as Jasper and Harmony."

You can see how much he loves his family by the way his face lights up when he talks about them. It must be nice to have such a close-knit family.

"That's lovely you all live close by each other. Your brother Drew, he's like a professional surfer, right?"

"Yeah, spends most of his time away on tour, but he's home at the moment with an injury."

"Jenna told me a little about him. How do they know each other?"

A crease forms across his forehead. I can see this is something he doesn't want to talk about. "It might be best if she tells you that story of how they know each other."

"Oh, okay. Sorry, it's just she said she knows your family but said little else, so I was just curious," I reply quietly. That was a strange mood change. Now I really want to know what happened with them, because it obviously hit a nerve with Theo as much as it did with Jen. And if there is something I need to worry about here, I want to know before I get more invested.

"It's okay. It's just her story to tell, and it's complicated. I was a little surprised to see her again that night I ran into you at the bar. It had been quite a few years since Drew and I had seen her last. Are you two close?"

"Yeah, she's like family to me. We met five years ago when I moved into the townhouse next to her. She has been there for me ever since. Looks after Harmy while I teach yoga classes or if I need to duck out to the store. It's hard raising a child on your own, and she's a total sweetheart. I would be lost without her."

"It's nice you have her to help you. I know exactly what you mean, I would be lost without my mum and Elly. There is no way I could raise Jasper on my own without their help."

"Your sister sounds like an angel."

"She is. I think I need to introduce you two. You're very similar, and with kids the same age, I reckon you will get on well."

"I think you're getting ahead of yourself, don't you? Introducing me to your family? I haven't even decided if I'm coming back to your house for a swim yet." I laugh.

"I have. I'm not finished with you yet." The look he gives me, the desire in his eyes. We've had a weird conversation where his mood flip-flopped like crazy. But then he gives me that look, and I melt. I don't know if we are compatible in any other way, but the fucking chemistry is off-the-charts sizzling.

Wendy appears at our table to collect our plates. "How did you kids go?" She stacks the plates and cups in her arms like she has done it a thousand times before.

"It was delicious, thank you. I'll be back again." Quickly sipping the last of my coffee, I hand her my mug.

Theo smiles at her warmly. There is such familiarity between them; he really must come here a lot. "Thank you, Wendy, delicious as always."

He turns to me, patting me on the leg. "Right, we better get going if we're going to fit in a swim before picking up the kids." He reaches over for my hand, and I let him take it as we walk to the counter to settle the bill and thank Wendy again. The way he looks at me on the way to the car has my heart beating a little faster and butterflies dancing in my stomach. I'm nervous all over again.

Theo

My place is just a short drive from the café. Ivy has gone quiet. Every now and then she glances at me, but not for too long before she drops her head to look back out the window.

I can't stop thinking about what she said happened to her family. How sad to have been a teenager and left all alone in this world? I don't know what I would do without my family. And I know I have only just touched the surface of what has happened in her life. I'm still wondering how on earth she ended up a single mum. That was one of the many questions I had prepared for today's getting-to-know-you date. I can't see any guy in his right mind leaving her with a baby, and there's no sign of him in Harmony's life now from what I can see, so they're not co-parenting. I wonder what happened to him.

I pull into my driveway and she gasps. "This place is amazing, Theo. I've seen nothing like it."

"It's pretty special, hey. I had it designed by Elly and Fraser, exactly the way I imagined it."

"We have something in common then."

"I'm sure you will find we have lots of things in common once you get to know me."

She is still looking over my place in awe when I open her car door. "You getting out or just going to admire my place from the car? I can assure you it's better when you get inside."

She takes my hand tentatively, and I help her out. I can see she's a little uneasy about being somewhere new. Her eyes are big, and she has that deer-in-the-headlights kind of look going on. She's definitely a little on edge.

My place is quite amazing, if I say so myself. It's all-timer work with 360-degree views of stunning tropical rainforest and large glass windows all around, bringing the outside in. You almost feel like you're camping out at night. Sometimes we do, in the massive hammock that's out the back.

We make our way up the pebble walkway to the double timber front doors. I open the door, and she stops in the middle of the room, looking around.

"Stop it! Theo, this place is... I have no words... I can see why you wanted to bring me here. It's like a treehouse for adults. I'm sure it gets you laid every time." She drops her handbag on the lounge and rushes excitedly to the back doors, opening them to the large deck, taking in the view in front of her. Nothing but beautiful tropical rainforest. "Whoa."

I follow her out the back, standing behind her, wrapping my arms around her front to whisper in her ear, "What about the pool? It looks pretty good. Are you ready for that swim?" I can feel the goosebumps run up her arms, and I hope that's a good thing.

She turns slowly around in my arms, facing me. I'm lost again. She is perfection. Tanned skin with a scattering of pale freckles across her nose. She has pale blue eyes, and her waist-length dark blonde hair frames her face with strands of gold highlighted by the sun.

I reach down, cupping her face and drawing her closer

to me so our lips meet. She wraps her arms around me, kissing me with such intensity I know she wants this just as much as I do. It's what I need to know. She feels the same—this insane chemistry isn't just in my head. She pulls back, wriggling out of my grip, her warmth gone as she heads back inside towards her bag. And so, the dance continues. She lets me get close for just a second, then she is gone again.

She rummages through her bag and grabs her bikini, holding it up. "Where should I change?"

I show her through to my bedroom. "You can change in here or in the bathroom if you like." Without another word, she walks into the bathroom and closes the door, flicking the lock. As soon as I feel like I'm getting somewhere with her, walls go up and she locks me out again. Literally. She is going to change in the bathroom when we both know I have seen her naked before.

I change into my boardies and go to the hallway cupboard to grab some towels. When I turn to walk back into the room, she's standing shyly in the doorway. Fuck me, her body is insane in a tiny floral bikini, her toned, curvy body on full display. I have no idea why she is so shy about it.

"Wow, you look incredible." I have to adjust myself to hide the raging boner I'm sporting at the sight of her, but luckily, I'm holding our towels. "You could give a boy a heart attack wearing a bikini like that!"

She giggles. "I was going for hard-on, but if you need me to change, I can. Don't want to be taking you to the ER today."

Miss Shy and Innocent knows exactly what she's doing. "You're a tease, you know."

"Am I? You said to bring my swimmers. I was just

following your instructions." She smirks, her teeth biting into her bottom lip. "Come on, let's get wet."

She saunters towards the open deck doors, her hips swaying as she goes. I don't know if she's doing it on purpose or not, but she is driving me fucking crazy. The fabric on those swimmer bottoms barley covers anything. That arse, those long, tanned legs... Fuck. She's lucky I don't drag her back to my room and do exactly what I want to her right now.

I have to remind myself that's not what today is about. I like this girl and actually want to get to know her, not just play with her—as much fun as it would be to have her in an array of positions, screaming my name.

She looks back at me and catches me checking her out. My eyes snap back up to hers. "You alright back there, Theo?"

"Yep, I'm good, just enjoying the view." I drop the towels on one of the sun lounges next to the pool and dive straight in the water. It's refreshing, just what I need to calm my raging hard-on. Fuck, this woman drives me nuts. She eases down the steps of the pool one foot at a time, checking the temperature tentatively.

"It's nice and warm once you're in," I say, trying to entice her to jump in as I swim over to the stairs. I grab her hand, pretending to be nice and caring, then I pull her in on top of me. The water splashes around us, and she screams for me to stop.

"It's too cold!" She laughs and, wriggling free of me, splashes me in the face.

"Don't worry, baby, I'll keep you warm." I pull her up into my arms, bringing my hands under her arse. She stiffens, her body on high alert again.

"Is everything alright?"

"Yes, it's just... I'm not used to all of this."

"You can trust me, angel, I'm not going to do anything to hurt you." I kiss her neck and pull her into me closer, and she relaxes a little, wrapping her legs around my waist and her arms around my neck, her hands playing with my hair. I draw her in for a kiss, but before I have time to kiss her again, she pushes off me and launches herself into the water. She comes up laughing.

I pull her back into me, this time not letting her get away, blocking her in between the side of the pool and my body. We're hip to hip, her warm body pressing into mine, her long hair messy and tangled, draping down her shoulders. Her eyes look into mine, and I'm gone. With her, I'm under some sort of spell. She's intoxicating, and I have to have her. I wrap my hand around the back of her neck and draw her to me, our lips about to meet.

"Theo, I..." she tries to protest, but I don't let her finish.

My lips eat up her words as I kiss her, swiping my tongue through her open mouth. She lets out a little sigh as I feel her body melt into mine, her hands roaming over my back as our kiss intensifies. It's passionate and desperate, so different from what I'm used to. I could do this all day, just hold her, our bodies close, our lips locked. I feel alive, not the numbness I have been feeling for so long.

I want to give in to this feeling. Maybe my existence can be more than just getting by. I can have true pleasure in my life again, but it's also scary as fuck when I know all good things don't last forever, and this girl is already on edge. Every time she flinches or stiffens when I touch her, I know she's not just some normal girl. There is so much more to her situation, and before I get more invested, I want to know what it is.

I pull back from her, and she looks lost, her eyes almost teary. "Are you okay?"

"I don't know. I'm too damaged for this, Theo." Her sad eyes hold mine, and I wish I knew what she was talking about. Why is she damaged?

"You're not the only one," I offer, and it's the truth. I'm definitely too damaged for this, and that's why I have avoided getting close to anyone else... until now.

"What are we doing here? This isn't just fun, is it?"

"It could be."

"But it's not. I may not have a lot of relationship experience, but this is so much more than fun, and if you're as damaged as me, we have no hope." She drops her head.

I lift her chin so she is looking back at me. I don't want her hiding from me. I need to see what she is feeling. "Maybe we can work it out together, heal each other." I don't even know what I'm suggesting, but I'm not ready to stop whatever this is, so I'm grasping at straws to keep her here in my arms where it feels so natural for her to be.

"Maybe, or we could also mess each other up more, and I can't afford to do that," she says sadly.

"Always the pessimist, aren't you, Ivy?"

Her eyes snap to me. "No, just realistic. I have to be. Life isn't all rainbows and butterflies, Theo. No matter how much we want it to be, and both of us have little people we have to think about."

"I'm a cop, Ivy, I know that more than most, but it doesn't mean you should be so scared of the bad that you can't try to have the good. What's the point in living if you don't get to do anything fun because you live in fear?"

"Yeah. I know you're right, I'm trying." She drops her chin, breaking eye contact, then takes a deep breath and lets it out before glancing back at me. "Sorry to be such a downer," she adds with a cute little smile on her face.

I kiss her again. I need to comfort her; I can see she is trying today. My hands run along her arms, and I can feel the goosebumps. "Come on, you're cold. Let's get out."

We make our way out of the water, and I hand her a towel, wrapping it around her and rubbing her arms to warm her up. Come upstairs to the hammock. It's in the sun this time of day, that'll warm you up." I know I have to take her home soon. We have kids to pick up, but I don't want her to go. Today has gone too fast.

Sitting in the hammock, I wrap my arms around her to keep her warm. "Maybe we should take a shower, warm you up," I suggest.

"Nice try, we both know how that ended last time, and I can't be late to pick up Harmy, and it's nearly time to go."

That was the idea, but she's right. We better get going. It's the hardest part of being a single parent; there is always someone you have to put before yourself. Most girls wouldn't get that, but because Ivy is in the same situation, she knows how it is.

"Come on then. Let's get dressed and go before I can't help myself and make us both late for school pick-up."

She smiles then surprises me by pulling me in for a kiss, her body falling on top of mine as I lie back and pull her down into the hammock on top of me. Cocooned by the hammock, we kiss slowly, passionately. She feels whatever this is too, I can tell. And she wants it just as much as me. Our tongues meet, our kiss escalating quickly to hot and heavy as I move my hands down to her arse. She runs her hands through my hair as she slowly grinds against me, her movements slow but controlled. She knows exactly what she's doing, going back and forth, driving me nuts.

She pulls back from our fierce kiss, gasping for breath. "Time to go," she whispers.

"You are a tease today. What am I supposed to do about this?" I say, rubbing my massive erection against her pussy.

She lets out a small groan, just as disappointed this is ending. "You're just as much of a tease. Come on, the school bell won't wait." She places a small kiss on my lips then pushes out of the hammock, heading towards my bedroom, arse swaying as she goes. She is killing me, and she knows it.

The drive back into town goes quickly as our time together is running out. She's opening up to me now and telling me about her crazy friends and some funny things Harmony does. She looks so happy when she talks about the women she's so close to.

I know I probably shouldn't ask, but I can't help myself. This question has been on the tip of my tongue since the day I met her, and I can't let her go today without knowing the answer. "Where's Harmony's dad? Does she get to spend time with him as well?"

She has gone quiet. I look over to her, and she's playing with the rings on her hands. I can see her shut down, and immediately I regret asking.

"Argh, he's... she doesn't see him, she never has." She sighs. "He's in prison and has been her entire life, but I haven't told her. She thinks he's just away somewhere overseas for work." She doesn't look up to see my reaction.

Prison—I knew there was more to her story. This makes more sense to her behaviour. What did that fucker do to end up in prison? "Oh, I'm so sorry, Ivy. I'm sorry if I upset you by asking."

She raises her head to look out at the road. "It's okay, it's not your fault, it is what it is."

"What happened, if you don't mind me asking?"

"I... I can't, I don't want to talk about it. He's not a good person, and he deserves to be in prison, so don't be sorry. We're better off without him in our lives. I hope she never has to meet him."

There is rage in her voice as she says the words. She's not just scared, she's angry. Whoever Harmony's dad is, she hates him. We pull up at her place, and she grabs her bag, pulling it onto her lap, ready to run again, I'm sure. But she doesn't. She turns to me, grabbing my face and kissing me lightly on the lips.

"I had fun today, Theo. If you want to do it again sometime, and I'm not too fucked-up emotionally for you, let me know." She turns to leave, and I grab her wrist to stop her, immediately regretting it when she flinches again, pulling her arm back.

"Sorry, I was just going to say, what about Saturday? Can you get someone to look after Harmony? Jasper is having a sleepover with Cooper, so I would be free if you can."

"I'll see what I can do," she says as she kisses me once more, then she slips out of the car and walks up to her house. And I'm left wondering what that fuckwit did to end up in prison and how a sweet girl like Ivy got involved with him in the first place.

CHAPTER THIRTEEN

IVY

A fter my date with Theo yesterday, I came home and bawled like a baby until it was time to pick up Harmony. I don't want to be this damaged shell of a person anymore. I want to be strong, be able to have a normal relationship, the chance to have a happy future, but I'm just so scared of everything. I'm scared of how fast I want to take things with Theo. When I'm with him, it all feels so right. I get carried away with the idea of how good we could be together, but how could I possibly be falling for him already? That's just crazy. It must just be hormones or something because I'm horny as hell for him. I need to get some control before I'm blinded by lust.

And he had to ask about her dad. Of course he did. Why wouldn't he be wondering where he was? I want to open up to him and let him into my life, I really do. If there was anyone I would want to let in, it would definitely be him. He's so kind and caring. Without even knowing what's wrong with me, he's there to comfort me every time I need it, but I just don't know how to open up to him yet. I guess over time that might change.

I don't have time to think about him now. We have the girls coming over, and I need to get this place straightened up. Every flat surface is covered with Harmony's paintings laid out flat so they can dry. Fay spent the afternoon here with Harmony, trying to teach her a new painting technique she learnt. She has ducked home for a bit to get changed out of her now-paint-stained clothing for our weekly dinner.

"We need to clean up this mess before the girls arrive for dinner."

"It's not mess, Mummy, it's art." She stands there with her hands on her hips, all sassy at my insult.

"Sorry, baby. Can you please find a new home for all your beautiful art?" I pile them up for her because we're running out of time.

The girls will be here soon for our Tuesday-night dinner. It's our weekly catch-up. We normally have tacos because it's something we all love and Harmony will eat. She's not a fussy eater, but there's a long list of foods she won't eat, and it changes weekly so, for now, we cater to keep her happy.

The buzzer goes, and I run over to the door to grab it, still with a pile of art in my arms. She's early, bloody Penny. I'm not ready for them yet. I swing open the door to a sad-looking Penny holding a bottle of wine.

"What's wrong, babe?"

"It's nothing." Her words are wobbly, then the tears start.

"It must be something, you never cry." I try to put my arm around her and usher her in as best as possible with the pile of art in my hands.

"I'm just having a bad day. I need wine." She takes her bottle straight to the kitchen and grabs two glasses. She fills the two glasses then cries again, tears trickling down her face.

"What's wrong? It must be bad. Tell me, maybe I can help."

She goes to her bag and pulls out a white stick. I know what that stick means—shit, she's pregnant.

"My period is over a week late, and it's never late! I've been really careful, I don't know how this could even be happening," she says, crying harder.

"So, the test is positive?"

"I don't know, I haven't taken it yet. I'm too scared to see the answer!" she wails.

"You might be worried about nothing. Come, let's go take it before the others get here." I take her hand and drag her to the bathroom, pushing her through the door and closing it.

"I can't do it. If I am, I don't want to know," her muffled voice comes through the closed door.

"I'm not letting you out until you do, so you better hurry."

"You're such a bitch," she snaps.

"Hurry up." I stand at the door waiting for the results, silently praying to whoever will listen to me. *Please don't let her be pregnant, she's not ready for this!*

Three minutes feels like forever when you're expecting bad news. It takes me back to the day I found out I was pregnant with Harmony. I thought my life was over. There was no way Dominic and I were ready for a baby. I had been trying to work out how I could leave him for so long, and I had almost saved up enough money in a separate bank account he didn't know about too. I knew running away from him was going to mean losing my parents' house, but I couldn't stay. He wasn't a good man.

So, I had my plan. I would run, start a life somewhere else. But fate had other ideas, and before the month was out, I was holding a white stick with two blue lines. I was on the pill, and I shouldn't have gotten pregnant. We hardly even had sex, but there was a night when he had come home drunk, and instead of fight, I gave in. I had been sick earlier that week with a tummy bug and apparently that can cause the pill not to work, so there it was.

I was so close to my escape but so far. There was no way I could do it when I found out. When Dominic promised to change, assured me he would take care of us, I believed him. So stupidly, I trusted him.

The door slowly opens. "I'm too scared to look." She cries, handing me the white stick.

I glance down at it, still praying for her. "Babe, it's negative! Stop stressing."

She grabs the test out of my hands and stares at it, the smile returning to her face and tears instantly drying up. "Thank God, it's negative! This is the happiest day of my life." She throws her arms around me. "I need that wine now to celebrate."

And that's Penny. She's fun, but she brings the drama with her wherever she goes. This is not the first pregnancy scare she's had since I have known her, and I'm sure it won't be the last.

We grab our overfilled glasses of wine and sit on the lounge. Tiger pounces onto my lap, curling up in a ball to sleep. She is settling in nicely now. She has learnt the house rules. I play with her soft fur as I listen to the next drama in Penny's life. Who needs to watch TV soaps when you can watch it play out in real life?

Harmony comes out of her room to join us. She must have been busy playing and missed all the drama. She picks Tiger up and puts her in her dolly stroller. I don't think Tiger likes it much, but she lets her do it. They wander off down the hall, and I try to concentrate on Penny.

"The worst part would have been that I wouldn't have known who the father was. I slept with three different guys in the last month."

"This might be one of those learning lessons, you know? The universe trying to tell you something, like slow down with the random guys." I roll my eyes at her.

"You know, I actually think you might be right. I'm going to take a break from men. No more one-night stands. From now on, if I meet a nice man, I will make him wait till it's serious before we hook up."

"Yeah, okay, Pen, if that's what you say."

She taps me on the leg. "No, really, this time I'm serious. I'm getting older now. I need to be more responsible. I'm not an excellent judge of these things. From now on, I'm waiting for your approval before I go any further with a guy."

I laugh, probably a little too sarcastically. "I wouldn't go off my opinion. I might be older, but I have no idea what I'm doing."

"Oh yeah, how did the date go yesterday?" She bumps shoulders with me, nearly spilling my wine.

"It was okay, I guess?"

The doorbell rings. It must be the others. I place my glass on the coffee table and go to answer the door, Penny by my side.

"Evening, ladies."

"We're just about to hear about Ivy's date yesterday," Penny says, just as Harmony walks back into the room.

"Pen," I warn with my best shut-the-fuck-up face.

She gives me a look of apology. "Sorry. I mean, we're

just about to hear all about how much Ivy likes coffee and swimming."

I shake my head at her and make my way into the kitchen. Jenna grips my arm, and Fay follows close behind.

"So, missy, you have kept this one quiet," she whispers.

"I wasn't hiding it. I would have told you myself tonight, I just didn't see you yesterday," I say quietly back. I'm not ready to talk about any of this with Harmony within earshot. I don't want her to get her little heart set on him and it all turning to shit. "I want to know more about how you know him."

"Maybe later when it's just the two of us."

Dinner was the usual tacos, and most of the talk centred around Penny, as per usual and just the way the rest of us like it. Fay has taken herself off to bed, and Penny headed home for a quiet night after all the drama, so it's just Jenna and me. I have had too much wine, and I think Jenna is the same. We're a little giggly.

"So, now's the time. Spill what you know about Theo. I want to know what I'm getting myself into."

"He's a good guy, Ivy. Stop your worrying, just enjoy yourself for a change."

"Yes, but you know him. What happened? How do you know him and Drew?"

"It's a long story."

"I have all night, hun, and so do you."

She gives me a long look then rolls her eyes. I'm not going to back down tonight. "Fine. But like I said, it's a really long story. About six years ago, I was in with a bad crowd and found myself on the streets. I got the only job I could... it attracted a less-than-ideal type of companion."

I smack her on the arm. "Stop talking cryptic."

"I was working at a strip club, if you have to know." She rolls her eyes at me again.

I give her a look of surprise because I just can't see it. My quiet friend, the librarian, dancing on a stripper pole. "Oh, okay, go on."

"You have to understand, I was in a really shitty place. I mean, I had the clothes on my back and that was it. I either did that job or live on the streets. I ended up as the girlfriend of one of the heavies from the club. Vinnie was a bit older, but he was nice enough. He showered me with gifts and offered me a place to stay, and well, beggars can't be choosers, so I did what I had to do to get by."

"Okay, you're painting a very different picture to the one I see here today. You're so put together with your perfectly matched outfits and so sensible. You're the one around here that has her head screwed on. I had no idea you went through any of this, Jen."

She gives a small smile at my compliment. "That's all because of Drew and the whole Walker family. Not long before I met Drew, I walked in on Vinnie torturing some poor guy who looked little older than I was in one of the back rooms at the club. I was so shocked and scared, so I took off, catching different trains and buses, until I ended up here. I thought I was far enough away from him. I thought I was nothing to him anyway, and he would forget about me. But guys like that... they don't forget. He saw me as a possession, one that had seen too much, and when I took off, he took it personally and came after me."

I can't believe what she's telling me. It sounds like a movie or something. How was this her life before we met? "What happened, did he find you?"

"I met Drew when I was dancing at the club here. He

was on a buck's night with a few friends. It just happened to be the same night that Vinnie turned up to find me, and Drew got me out of there. He took me back to his parents' place. They were all so lovely, like the nicest people you could ever meet. His mum helped me get the job at the library, and Drew, he was my friend. For a long time, he and Blake, another guy that also helped to get me out of that life, were my only friends. They helped me get this place and start a new life, one I could be proud of. I owe them everything."

I place my hand on hers and give it a squeeze. "I'm so shocked, I had no idea what you've been through."

"Don't look at me differently, that's why I haven't told you until now. I didn't want you to see me like that. I just wanted you to know they are good people, and if there is something between you and Theo, explore what it is. He's one of the good guys."

"I don't look at you differently. I know who you are. You have been my friend for long enough now that I know you're a strong, kind-hearted woman. I know you must have been in a terrible place when they found you. I think you're amazing, Jen. You're so much stronger than me. I'm just surprised because you're kind of prudish. I can't see you as a stripper on a pole."

"Have you thought maybe that's why I am the way I am now? You might not think less of me, but I sure as hell do. I wish I wasn't that person. That's why I don't talk about it. I don't want to remember that pathetic girl."

"You shouldn't feel like that, because she's the one who made you the strong woman I see before me today. You're you because of everything you went through, and so am I. I want to tell you why I'm finding it so hard to move forward with Theo, but I don't think I can get the words out. I haven't told anyone about what happened to me, except a psychiatrist I saw a few times. It's so hard to talk about."

She squeezes my hand. "You don't have to tell me, Iv, it's okay. But if you ever want to talk, you know where I am." She hops up, taking her wineglass over to the sink and rinsing it.

I want to tell her, though. I need to talk to someone about it. Trying to move on with my life is bringing up so much anxiety about the past, and I know I can't move forward unless I deal with at least some of these feelings before the dark cloud of apprehension completely fogs my judgement and I stop trying because the fear of the unknown is stronger than the desire to live again.

"It was Harmony's dad," I blurt out. I pause, trying to work out the words to say. She turns to look at me, then makes her way back over to where I sit. "He was a horrible, violent man who gambled away all our money and had an issue with drinking—and possibly worse as well."

She sits beside me. "What did he do to you, Ivy?" she whispers.

"He ruined me. I'm broken because of him. I can't be a normal person, I live in too much fear." Tears blur my eyes, and I try to blink them away. I want to get the words out, but they're stuck.

"Hey, hey, honey, it's okay. Whatever he did, he's not here now, is he. So you're safe. We can work this out, you're not too broken."

A sob escapes my throat, and I force the words out. "The night he nearly killed me, when I was seven months pregnant with Harmony... that was the end. I found enough strength to save her, and I ran away from him." My hands are shaking, and just saying the words, I'm right back there at my parents' old house, blood running down my face, broken ribs, my chest heaving for breath while I hid behind the big gum tree in the open paddock, praying he wouldn't find me.

"Ivy, I'm here." She wraps her arms around me, pulling me into her shoulder as I break down, my tears leaking onto her shirt, unable to finish what I started saying. When I say the words out loud, it's too much, I can't deal with it. "Shh, it's okay, baby, don't cry. Whatever happened to you back then, you're safe now, I've got you."

She holds me, and I try to get myself under control. I sit up, rubbing my hands over my face and taking a breath, counting to four, trying to calm myself down like I was shown by my psychiatrist.

"I'm sorry, Jen, I didn't mean to start crying. I just... I want to open up to you like you could with me. I feel like after all this time, it would be good to have someone who understands me and what happened. But I can't say it. The words get stuck."

"It's okay, honey, you can talk to me when you're ready. Just remember you're safe now, though, okay?"

"I'm safe for now. He's in prison. But he will get out one day, sometime in the next six months I think, and then what?"

Her eyes widen in fear. "Is that a possibility?"

"I hope not. We changed our names when we came here, but what if he works it out? He will not let this go. He's the kind of man that will look for me, and I'm sure he hates me and will want revenge. I was the one that got him locked up."

"It sounds like you covered yourself, changing your name. And these places are super safe, Drew's brother-in-law made sure of that, with all the tech they used on them.

He won't be able to get to you. I'm sure you're safe. And for now, he's still in prison, right?"

I nod. "Yeah, for now. They will notify me when he's released."

"So you're okay to continue on with your life, honey. Don't let the shit from your past ruin your future. You say I'm strong, but look at you, raising Harmy on your own. You're super strong."

"I'm not on my own. I have you and Fay and Pen. But the problem is I'm scared. How do you trust anyone after you have been through something like that? He wasn't always evil. When we first started dating, he was a nice guy, but he changed over time. How do I know that won't happen again?"

"I guess you can never be sure of someone, but you know Theo is a different person, and you can't judge him on someone else's actions. He's been through a lot himself. Talk to him, tell him why you keep running from him. I'm sure if anyone would understand, it would be him."

She's right, I know she is, but how do I get past the fear so I can let him in? I wonder what happened to him. "What about you?"

She tilts her head, looking back over to me. "What about me?"

"You said you can't let what happened in the past ruin your future. Why are you holding back from Drew?"

"That's different."

"I don't see how, and it's blatantly obvious the two of you like each other. You're more than just friends, aren't you?"

She smiles sadly. "I think I missed my opportunity there. I know Drew did like me, but that was years ago, and I wasn't ready for anything after what happened, so it went nowhere. It's too late now. I missed my chance with him, and that's okay. I'll just have to stick to my book boyfriends for my happily ever after. Did I tell you I'm writing a book?"

"No, what kind of book?"

"It's kind of a hot romance." She blushes.

"I think I have learnt more about you tonight than the whole five years I've known you. Who would have thought shy, bookworm Jenna had a sex kitten hiding inside of her?"

"I don't have a sex kitten hiding inside of me. And it's not what I normally write. All the other manuscripts I've drafted have been urban fantasy books. I don't even know where this one has come from. I just have such a boring life I need to live through my books." She giggles. "Anyway, speaking of book boyfriends, I need to get back to my latest one. You can borrow him when I'm done if you want."

"Might need to if I can't get my act together before Theo grows tired of trying with me."

"He's into you. You just need to give him a chance." She throws her arms around me in a quick embrace. "Night, hun."

"See you tomorrow." I check the front door after she leaves, then head up to bed.

Theo

I know I shouldn't be snooping around behind Ivy's back, but I got to talking to Elly this morning when I dropped Jasper off before school, and she thinks Fraser would probably have the documents filed somewhere from when the townhouses were sold. If I can have a look at them and see what name is on Ivy's, I might be one step closer to working her out. So, I have taken a brief detour on my way back to the office on my lunch break to see what I can find out.

Claudia, the receptionist at The Green Door, Fraser and Blake's company, is at her desk and smiles gently when I walk through the impressive foyer, all polished timber, leather, and marble. "Morning, Claudia, is Fraser in his office?"

"Hi, Theo, yes. I'll let him know you're here." She calls his office and waits. "You're right to go straight in, Theo."

"Thanks," I say with a wave.

I enter his office, and Fraser is sitting behind his desk focusing on his computer monitor. "Hey, man, what brings you in here?"

"Just in the neighbourhood, thought I would drop in and say hi."

He raises a questioning brow. "Is that right? How nice of you. Nothing to do with wanting info on a certain hot chick you're trying to stalk, would it?" He smirks.

I take a seat across from him. "I'm not stalking anyone. Who told you...? My sister has a big mouth."

"What do you expect? You know your sister tells me everything. She's excited you're seeing someone. She texted me not long after you left this morning."

"Of course she did. I'm not seeing someone, we just had one date. Elly needs to calm down."

"Yeah, you know that won't happen. She and your mum will be planning your wedding before we know it."

I run a hand through my hair. "God, I hope not."

"So I took the liberty to look up who bought number two from us, but you know I shouldn't be giving you this information, right?"

"Yeah, I know. I just want to know if the name on the

paperwork is of an Ivy Anderson. You don't have to show me anything."

"Sure is. How can I help if you already know her name?"

"I think she changed her name about five years ago, the same time she moved here to this area. I'm trying to work out who she was before."

"Don't you think you should wait for her to tell you that info, not go snooping? You're going to end up shooting yourself in the foot, man. If I know chicks, this seems like a terrible idea."

"Yeah, I know all that. But before five years ago, she didn't exist, and curiosity has the better of me. I can't just go out and ask her, because I shouldn't even know that much. I only started looking into her because she's so skittish, she has some sort of trauma or something. I just want to understand her better, and she said Harmony's dad's in prison. I want to know what I'm up against."

"I'd go talk to her about it, man. Take it from me, if you like her, you don't want to fuck it up before it's begun."

And I know he's right, but I have been a snoop my whole life. I like to have all the information I can, that's why I make a good detective. Get the facts, then you know what you're dealing with. I'm also not very good at stopping once I start investigating something, and I have a feeling that Ivy's not going to just tell me what happened for her to change her identity. If she's in witness protection or something, she wouldn't even be allowed to.

The biggest problem is I already know how invested I am in her, and a part of that is knowing I can protect her. I won't go through losing someone again like I did Fi. I need to know the facts so I know I can keep her safe.

On my way out, I pop my head around the corner of

Blake's office to see if he's in. "Hey, man, you got time for a quick chat?"

"Theo, yeah, come in, take a seat."

I take a seat across from him as he finishes up what he was doing. "I won't stay long, I know you're busy, and I have to get back to the office. Just thought you might help me with something."

"Anything for you," he says sarcastically, but he actually would. What we went through trying to save Jenna from Vinnie and to keep Indie safe all those years ago gave us a bond that means we look out for each other. Even if he was brought up on the other side of the law, I know he's one of the good guys and is trying to do what's right for everyone.

"You haven't heard any whispers about a huge drop-off happening up this way in the next couple of months, have you?"

"Never just a friendly chat with you, is it, Theo? Always work."

"Well, I could ask you about all the kids, make small talk, but I'm not a chick, so yeah, straight to business. Just thought it was worth asking in case you know something I don't—a name, drop location."

He frowns. "Not asking for much then, are you. You know I'm not involved in any of that shit anymore."

"Yeah, I also know I got you out of trouble not that long ago when you were supposed to be out of all that. There is another thing that's been playing on my mind as well."

"What's that?" He rubs the back of his neck.

"Back when we were working the Vinnie case, we always had a feeling there was someone with inside information who was working with the Barrett brothers."

"There was definitely someone working with them, one of you." He gives me a pointed look.

"Not one of us if they're helping drug smugglers, but yes, someone on the force. I know one of the brothers is dead now, and the other's in prison, but we've been working this drug case for three years now, and every time we get close, things disappear."

He crosses his arms over his chest and sits back in his chair, giving me his full attention. "What kind of things?"

"Evidence, witnesses. One of the guys from our team. Things that lead me to believe there's a dodgy cop working within my team. And if that is the case, we need to work it out and fast."

"Okay, let me see what I can do, but if we couldn't find who it was back then, I don't see how we will now."

"Just see what you can find out and I'll do the same. Don't mention what you're looking for to anyone, though. I don't want whoever it is to know we're onto them. They are one step ahead of me every time, and it needs to end now. That's the only reason I'm asking you."

He gives one nod. "Understood."

"That's all I'm asking, buddy. Anything you can come up with would be much appreciated. So how are those crazy kids of yours?"

His face softens. "Crazier than ever. There will be four of them before we know it, and I don't know how we'll manage that."

I shake my head. It's hard to imagine how crazy it would be, when I just have the one. "You guys need a nanny or something for four kids, when you're both running businesses. It's just insane."

"Yeah, I think you're right."

CHAPTER FOURTEEN

IVY

Now that Theo has my number, he has been putting it to good use, and we have been messaging back and forth all week ever since our date, sometimes very late into the night. It's nice and really the only way for two single parents to get to know each other. He's very persistent in seeing me again. I'm trying not to give in because I know the further I take this, it's only going to end one way, and that's in heartache.

He's so hard to resist, though. If he would just leave me be, I would be fine. I could just go on with my life like I never met him. All of these damn butterflies in my tummy would go away.

Who am I kidding? Even if he wasn't texting me, I couldn't just forget him. There's something about him, something I've never felt before—like I'm safe with him. All my fears just melt away. He feels like home, which is weird since I haven't had that feeling since my parents were alive. It's not like I don't have a wonderful home and life with Harmony, but there's just that niggling feeling that something is missing, and when I'm with him, the feeling's gone.

It is fun to play around with the idea, though. I haven't smiled this much in a long time, seeing his flirty messages at random times of the day. He tries hard, I'll give him that. Apparently, I've left him with blue balls all week. I suggested a way he could fix that by himself, but he wasn't impressed with my suggestion. But that's what he gets for telling me his problems.

Yesterday, once I knew both the kids were in bed, I got close to calling him and just testing out phone sex, but I chickened out. I'm too insecure about my lack of experience. I'm sure he gets involved in scenarios like that all the time, but I have never done anything like that, and it just didn't feel right.

It's Thursday now, and I think he's worn me down. Every day it's harder to say no. *Have some self-control, Ivy!* But I don't. It's not that I don't want to see him again. Who wouldn't? He's so freaking hot! I can feel my girly parts throbbing with need just at the thought of him. But the logistics are kind of tricky with our work hours and kids. There's also the minor matter of how the hell do I trust another man after what I've been through? Especially if he's just in it for a bit of fun. Even if it's just fun, it's still hard to let anyone else in. He seems like a decent guy. His line of work should imply that, but I've been fooled before, and it's hard to come back from that kind of life lesson.

I have just put Harmony to bed after my yoga class and head into my room to get ready for bed myself. Checking my phone that was lying on my bed, I see a text from 'The god' himself.

Theo: I have just put Jasper to bed and was thinking I had given you about enough time to organise yourself for Saturday. Are you ready for our next play date? x

Play date, he's such a smart-arse. I know I probably

shouldn't, but I can't help myself. I want to see him again, experience the way he makes me feel. So alive. And if I don't get back out there now, it may never happen. I will be too old, and no one will want me.

Me: Yeah, the kids would love that. We should go to the park.

I laugh to myself as I press send for being a smart-arse back.

Theo: Not what I meant and you know it! I want you all to myself this time.

Theo: But another time we should get the kids together for a play, when we're all ready.

Me: Lol So my neighbour Fay can have Harmony from 10, if that works for you?

Theo: Good girl, you won't be disappointed. I've organised something fun for the day. I'll pick you up from your place, and bring your bikini x

Me: What is it with you and the bikini? Didn't you get a good enough look last time? Don't you know how to date with your clothes on? lol

Theo: I grew up in the water, it's all I know. Plus, you can't blame a guy for trying. You've got a beautiful body, baby. I want to see it.

I wait a minute, not quite knowing what to say when he compliments me like that, and then another text pings in.

Theo: How was your day?

Me: Long. I'm tired from someone who has been keeping me up at night, and my muscles are sore from a new class I took yesterday. I'm sitting on the end of my bed, too tired to make my way to the shower.

Theo: I'm in bed already. Someone has been keeping

me up as well. Probably going to happen again tonight. Can I call you?

Me: Yeah, Harmony is asleep.

My phone rings straight away, and I hit the green call button to stop the noise, so it doesn't wake her up.

"Hello," I whisper into the phone.

"Hi, beautiful, sorry to call, but I wanted to hear your voice."

His voice is husky and sounds so sexy it sends a flutter through my body. "That's okay. It's nice to hear yours as well," I say, grinning stupidly. How he does this to me I have no idea.

"What class did you take yesterday? Some fancy new yoga class?"

I giggle. "No, I wanted to try something new. It's a self-defence class." And that's all I'm going to tell him about it. He doesn't need to know why I feel the need to take these classes.

"You don't need to go to some class for that. If you want to learn self-defence, I can teach you." His tone is a little annoyed. He doesn't like that I didn't ask him for classes.

"Thanks, but that's okay. It was good to go to a class. I met some really nice people and learnt a lot. I think I'll keep going."

"Okay, if that's working for you, but just remember, the offer stands. If you want my help, I'm an excellent teacher." Even through the phone, I feel his cocky confidence, and I'm sure he would be more than capable of teaching me, but this class is something I need to help me move forward in my life, to try and loosen the grip my past has on me, so it's something I need to do on my own.

"I'm sure you are, but I don't know how much I would

learn. I would be too distracted by all the muscles." I bite my lip, waiting for his comeback to that.

"Speaking of muscles, you said yours are sore. I was thinking you should go take a bath."

Not what I was expecting him to say. "But I'm talking to you."

"Yeah, that's why I called. I think you should run a bath and I can talk to you while you're in there," he says cheekily. I knew there was an ulterior motive to this call.

He wants to talk to me while I'm in the bath? How do I do this?

"Stop overthinking, angel, go run the bath."

How does he know I'm overthinking this? "Okay?" I creep down the hall to the bathroom, closing the door behind me, and turn on the tap. Water rushes into the big freestanding tub. The bathrooms in this townhouse are stunning and one thing I liked most about this place when I bought it, with large cement-looking tiles on the floor and white subway tiles in a herringbone pattern on the walls. The bath is the feature of the room with a large woven bamboo pendant light hanging above it.

"So, I can hear the bath running. Put me on speaker so you can get undressed."

"You're very bossy tonight, Theo."

"You might have to get used to that, I'm always pretty bossy. But tonight, I'm just trying to help you because you're tired."

"Is that right? And what are you going to do while I have a bath to relax?"

"Talk to you, listen while you make yourself come."

Oh, that escalated quickly. "I'm not going to make myself come just because you say so."

"Yes, you are. Tonight, you're tired, so I'm going to take

control for you so you can just relax and enjoy yourself. Get out of your head, Ivy, just listen to me." His voice holds so much authority. It's sexy as fuck.

"Okay," I say in a small voice.

"Put the phone on speaker," he demands.

I put it on speaker and place it on the stone countertop. "It's on."

"Take off your clothes and tell me what you're doing." I can hear ruffling around on his end, and I assume he's getting undressed as well.

"I'm removing my tank top and unzipping my sports bra." As I say it, I throw them one by one in the hamper.

"Watch yourself in the mirror as you do it. I bet you look amazing."

Is he kidding? I don't want to watch myself. "Theo," I say, removing my yoga tights and panties.

"Your body is absolute perfection, Ivy."

I look at myself, but I don't see perfection. Can't he see what I see? The stretch marks over my stomach from my pregnancy, the incision mark from my C-section, the cellulite on my legs because I eat too much sugar, the dark circles from lack of sleep, and the worst off all, the scar on my cheek from that night. The water is heating the room, and the mirror is clouding over with the steam.

"See? Perfection, long toned muscles, gorgeous face with sparkling baby-blue eyes, perfect tits, and that long hair. Fuck, you drive me crazy. I'm hard just imagining what you're seeing."

"You're always hard," I tease as I turn off the bath and check the water temperature. It's just right.

"Only around you I am. What are you doing now?"

"Putting Epson salts and lavender oil in the bath. What are you doing, Theo?"

"Touching myself thinking about how unbelievably hot you are."

"Are you really?"

"Yes. I'm so fucking hard thinking about you. Get in the bath, Ivy."

"Yes, sir," I say with a hint of sarcasm, but also, I want to do everything he says. My body is throbbing with the need for his next instruction.

"Good girl. I can't wait much longer. I'm not coming before you, and I'm already on the edge."

I leave my phone on the bathroom counter. The bath is full, and the water splashes a bit as I hop in and slide down into a comfortable position. My muscles are thanking me. "This is just what my body needed."

"You should listen to me more often. I know what's good for you, Ivy."

"Do you? What do I require now then?" I'm surprised by how breathy my voice is. He's not even in the room and he has the same effect on me, just knowing he is turned on by me.

"To relax and play with that naughty pussy of yours."

Oh God, can I even do this? I knew that was what he was going to say, and I pushed for it. *Stop thinking, Ivy, just do.*

"Slide your hand down your body to your pussy." His voice is deep and commanding, so without another thought, I follow his instructions. "Spread your legs."

My hand goes between my legs over the small patch of hair and over my clit. My breathing is ragged from nerves, from excitement, from just hearing his heavy breathing on the other end of the phone. "Theo, I don't think I can do this."

"Yes, you can. Circle your clit, rub your hand over it,"

he orders, and I do. I'm so sensitive, and it's just from his words. Hearing him tell me what he wants me to do has my lady parts buzzing with excitement. It won't take me long.

"Tell me what you're doing."

"I'm holding my thick cock in one hand, stroking back and forth, imagining what your wet pussy would feel like in that warm bath, my fingers stroking over your most sensitive spots. I bet you feel so fucking good."

"Yes, I'm so wet for you, Theo. I wish you were here."

"Push a finger into that tight pussy of yours."

I moan out loud as I do.

"Another," he groans.

I push in another. "Fuck, Theo, this is so hot."

"Rub your clit with your other hand," his husky voice demands.

I pick up the pace, finger-fucking myself just how he wants me to, as my other hand rubs over my sensitive bundle of nerves, water splashing over the sides of the bath. But right now, I don't care. I'm somewhere else in a better place where there is only pleasure. My body tenses, and I can feel how close I am.

"You need to come now!"

I let go. My body tightens around my fingers, my clit pulsing as my orgasm ripples over my body. "Fuck, Theo, oh my God."

"Ivy," he groans into the phone, and I know he's had his release as well.

I take a minute to regain my composure, quickly getting out of the bath and grabbing a towel. I sit on the side of the bath, picking up my phone.

"Fuck, Ivy, you have no idea how hot that was."

"Yeah, I think I do." I run a hand over my face. I'm overheating, and sweat beads run down my forehead. "I'm going to need a shower just to cool off."

"I wish I was there to hold you right now."

"Me too," I whisper. It's hard for me to say the words out loud, but I want him here now, with me, his strong arms wrapped around me, holding me like last time.

"Saturday."

"Yeah, I'll see you then."

"Sleep well, angel."

"You too."

I hang up and miss him immediately. Fuck, I'm screwed. This isn't just some sexy attraction. I mean, that was just phone sex, but this is so much more, I can feel it.

Theo

She is perfection in every way.

Hearing her soft moans as she got herself off at my command was fucking hot. I never thought she would agree to do that, and it wasn't even where I was expecting tonight to go, but once I start something with her, I can't stop myself. And she has agreed to see me on Saturday. I'm going to pull out all the stops to get her to notice me and keep seeing me.

Man, I don't even know who I've become—a sappy lovesick fool practically begging a chick to date me. This isn't me at all. But there is something about her I want, something I have to have in my life. The fact that she has a kid should be enough to scare me away, but it doesn't. We have been through almost the same situation at almost the same time, like we're the missing part of each other's puzzle, and it has me picturing the four of us going on picnics and having family movie nights.

It scares the shit out of me after everything I have already lost, but it's not a deterrent. I want her more than I have wanted anything in my life, and if she comes with a ready-made family, even better. That smile, those eyes... she's fucking sent from the heavens to bring me back to life.

But there is someone I need to see before I can really let myself explore what this is between us.

I'VE WALKED THE PATH THROUGH THE CEMETERY MANY times before. I come here often, sometimes with Jasper so he can talk to his mum, sometimes alone so I can talk to her about him, ask for her advice. I know she can't answer, but she was the one who was good with kids. She wanted a baby, she knew what to do with them, so when we found out she was pregnant, I was happy because I knew it was what she wanted. I knew she would be an amazing mum, and I could support the two of them.

Instead, I had to do it all alone, and most of the time I have no fucking idea what I'm doing. I just pray that I'm not fucking him up too badly.

Today, walking through the tombstones feels different, like the air is thick and it's hard for me to breathe. I'll still come here with Jasper so he can visit his mum, but today I need to say goodbye so I can move on.

The pain in my chest is back, the heavy feeling weighing me down, stopping me from moving forward and being happy again. I used to be fun and energetic; I didn't take anything too seriously. Now I feel like all I have is seriousness, the heavy feeling of dread because I was missing that spark in my life. I have Jasper, and I'm eternally grateful for that, but I've been feeling like there is a missing piece in my life. That is, until I met Ivy. I've only known her for such a short time, but she has my thoughts looking to the future, to something better than what I have now, and I know it's time.

I sit by Fi's gravestone and place pale-pink roses in the little vase. "You should see how well Jasper is doing at school. You would be so proud of him. He loves reading and is excited to go to school every day," I tell her, but to give her an update on Jasper isn't really why I'm here today. It's just hard to say what I want to.

"Fi, I know when we buried you, I swore to you I would never move on. That you would be my one and only, and until now, you have been. I wish things had been different and we could have had the life we dreamed of together. But you're gone... and you're never coming back. I can't live this lonely existence anymore, just living to solve cases and put criminals behind bars and take care of Jasper. I need *more*. I need to truly live again. So... I need to stop coming here.

"I've met someone. Her name's Ivy. She has a little girl the same age as Jasper, they go to school together. She's beautiful and kind, and I want to see where this is going to go. I just—I needed to see you first, before I can let myself explore whatever it is.

"I need you to know I will never forget about you and the amazing person you were. No matter what happens, you will always be my first love and hold a special place in my heart. I love you, Fiona. I will always love you." I kiss my hand and touch her gravestone. I sit there for a little longer, not ready to leave yet.

Eventually I stand and brush the grass off my pants. I walk away, my heart still heavy. I'm having second thoughts about moving forward. In some sick way, it was easier to live in the pain of the past; it can't hurt me any more than it already has. But I don't want pain anymore. I want to heal. I want to love again. Everything in me tells me Ivy is the one I can do that with, so I have to try.

CHAPTER FIFTEEN

IVY

It's Saturday morning and Theo picked me up ten minutes ago. We're walking up the street towards the beach, I think. He has been quiet ever since he got to my place. I glance at him, white shirt and boardies ready for a day at the beach. His blond hair has that messy look like he just got out of bed, and he looks like he hasn't shaved in a few days. I've noticed he doesn't shave often; he's got that hot surfy vibe going on. I'm really not sure why he is interested in me at all. Maybe that's what he is thinking about right now, that's why he is so quiet. This might be a mistake. Maybe he's not that keen after all.

"Is everything okay? You seem different today?"

His eyes roam over me, taking me in, and I feel even more insecure than normal around him. "I'm fine, just got lots on my mind."

"Oh, a case at work?" I forget how heavy his job must be at times.

"Amongst other things."

He's giving me nothing, and I'm starting to feel a bit

uncomfortable. "We can do this another time if that would be better."

He turns to me, taking my hand. "This is exactly what I want to be doing today." His lips form a small smile for the first time since he picked me up.

I tilt my head to the side, trying to gauge his expression; he looks kind of sad or down. What's going on with him? "Okay, but if you—"

He cuts me off, placing his hand under my chin, making me raise my eyes to meet his. "I have been thinking about you all week, and we're finally getting to spend some time together. I'm going to make the most of it."

He takes my hand, and we continue down a narrow pathway to an opening onto the beach. The view is stunning! "This is beautiful. I haven't been here before."

"That's because it's a local secret," he says, wrapping his arms around me. We both just stand and enjoy the view in silence. "Come on, I have had a spot set up for us." He takes my hand and leads me along to a blanket that's been set up with a picnic basket. Looks like he might have had a bit of help with this. There are also two surfboards and wetsuits.

"Um, who are they for?" I say, pointing to the surfboards waiting on the sand.

He raises his brow. "Who do you think? I'm taking you for a surfing lesson."

I shake my head. Growing up in Dorrigo, we didn't have a beach anywhere near us. I'm not that great in the water, and I'm sure I'm going to embarrass myself in front of him. This seems like a bad idea. "Oh, I've never been surfing before. I'm kind of scared of going out that far in the water."

He wraps his arms around me protectively. It feels good to have him so close. "That's what you've got me here for, to keep you safe from the big bad sharks."

I hit him on the chest playfully. "I wasn't even thinking about sharks until now, thanks for that. Maybe I'll just watch you."

"No way, you're not getting out of it that easily. I promised you a fun day, and this is one of my favourite things to do. You'll love it! Come on, strip off and let's get in."

I don't know who he thinks I am, but this is not my thing. And now all I can think about is sharks!

"Come on, Ivy, live a little."

I roll my eyes at him and earn myself a playful slap on the arse with his towel.

"Okay, I'll give it a go," I say, knowing I will not win this battle. He's got his bossy boots on and looks very determined to get me in there. I pull my dress over my head and drop it on the sand so I can wiggle into the wetsuit he brought for me, and somehow, it's a perfect size. He does the same, then he passes me a board and we walk down the beach towards the small waves rolling into the shore. I silently pray to whoever is listening. *Please don't let there be any sharks today*.

THE WATER IS PERFECT, AND AFTER AN HOUR'S SURF lesson from Theo—one of the best surfers around, according to him—I honestly can't believe how much I enjoyed it. Theo's mood has improved as well, and he seems back to his usual self, playful and cheeky.

I'm definitely not great at surfing, but I will try it again, and maybe I'll let Harmy get the surfing lessons she wanted, as soon as she can swim better. Being in the ocean was like meditating, listening to the sounds of the waves as I lay on the board. I can see why Theo likes it so much. We make our way back up the beach to the little picnic area he has set up with a blanket and basket of food.

I lay my towel on the sand and strip out of my wetsuit. I can feel his eyes on me as I lie down on my front on the sand in just my bikini. I love this bikini; it's a pretty pale blue colour that shows off my tan, with Brazilian-style bottoms that barely cover my arse. It's tiny, not something I would normally wear on a family day at the beach, but I picked it with Theo in mind. He's kind of fun to tease, and by his expression, I can see I'm getting the desired effect.

"I'm glad this is almost a private beach. There's not much to your bikini!" he says, having to adjust himself in his board shorts.

"I thought you would like it. You didn't seem to mind the other day," I say, trying to play it cool, relaxing my head down onto my towel, enjoying the warm sun heating my back.

"I do like it, but I don't want anyone else to see what's mine!" he says, flattening his towel out beside me and throwing his T-shirt over my arse in an attempt to cover me up.

"What's yours, hey? I thought this was just some fun, Theo." I roll over onto my side to face him, raising my brow in question.

"I think we both know this is more than just fun, Ivy," he says, his eyes intense. I hold his gaze, not sure what to say next. He's gorgeous like this, his hair wet and messy from the saltwater, his chest on full display, muscles still glistening with beads of water dripping over them. All I can think about is how much I want to lick his chest. What is wrong with me? I've turned into a sex-starved animal ready for her next meal—and what a fine meal he is.

As if he can read my mind, his lips turn up at the side as

he reaches out for me, wrapping his enormous arms around me and pulling me into him. I can feel how hard he is through his thin board shorts. It's nice to know I have the same effect on him as he does me.

His hands slide down to my arse. "Mine," he growls into my mouth as our lips meet and he kisses me with desperate need. "I want you to be mine, Ivy." Him getting all possessive was the last thing I was expecting. Suddenly I feel like I can't breathe. I pull back to look at him.

"I'm not in need of someone to take ownership of me, Theo." I wasn't prepared for this, to let someone else in. I don't know if I can.

"That's not what I meant. I want to be yours as well."

"You hardly know me, and I have a lot of issues. You don't even know what you're saying. You should be out there looking for some young fun thing with no baggage. Not a 30-something with suitcases full."

He rolls me over onto my back, locking me in place with his legs so I can't move. Normally being locked in a position like this would freak me out. The lack of control I have over the situation and his dominance, it should scare me—but it doesn't. I trust him. His big, blue eyes are warm and kind, and I know I'm safe with him.

"I know enough to know you're someone special, and I don't want to waste time playing around. When I decide I want something, I make it happen, and I want you in my life, beautiful."

"You know I'm a package deal, though, right? If we try this, you're not just getting me. It's not all going to be rainbows and butterflies with me. I have Harmy, who is my entire world."

"I know, and I'm good with that. The same goes for me and Jasper, but I want us to work out a way to do this, the four of us, somehow. Can you trust me to be a part of your world, Ivy?"

I blink up at him. My mind is racing a million miles a minute, with all the scenarios of how hard this is going to be and all the things that could go wrong. "I think so... It's just hard for me to trust anyone. I've been hurt before."

"I can see you've been hurt in the past, but I promise you I won't do anything to hurt you. You *can* trust me."

His eyes are beautiful and so kind; I could get lost in them, and it's so easy to believe what he's saying right now. This close to him, I can feel his honesty, and I hope to God the words he's saying are true. I want them to be. I want him and everything he's promising me. I don't want to live my life alone anymore. I want someone to share it with, someone to talk to at the end of the night when Harmony is in bed, someone to share all the little moments with.

"Stop overthinking it and let me in, angel." He leans down, placing a kiss on my lips, soft and slow.

And I let him in. I want all of this with him.

His tongue sweeps through my open mouth, claiming me so I can't think anymore, and I cave, my body melting into his. This is too good to stop. All thoughts are gone, and my horny inner goddess is taking over. She just can't get enough of this sexy man in front of her.

Our kiss intensifies as my hips rise to meet his hard length pressing into me, my hands running over his back. We're practically dry humping on the beach in the middle of the day. And I don't even care, I want him so badly.

His hand drops to my pussy, pushing my swimmer bottoms aside, slightly brushing over my sensitive spot. "You're so wet for me." He teases my entrance, dipping a finger in then back out, tracing over my slick folds. Fuck, this feels so naughty. We're on a public beach, but it feels so good, I don't want it to stop.

He pushes another finger in, deeper this time, and I groan into his mouth. "Oh, feels so good." He continues his pace, his lips never once leaving mine, as he pumps his fingers into me, and I arch my back with a desperate need for him and how good he's making me feel.

I'm about to go over the edge into bliss when I hear someone else, and we both freeze. Theo quickly pulls his fingers out.

"Hey, man," comes from a familiar voice from a bit farther down the beach. I can't put my finger on who it is.

Oh my God, who is it? I cover my face in horror of being caught. I'm just praying he was far enough away that he didn't see anything.

"Hey, Drew, what are you doing here? You don't normally surf this spot." Shit, it's his brother. I sit up, wrapping my towel around me as I do. How awkward! I bet he can read all over our faces what we were up to. I can feel the heat radiating off my cheeks; they would have to be bright beetroot red by now.

I smile politely. I have no words. I'm a grown-arse woman with a child and I shouldn't be getting caught on a public beach being fingered.

"Hey, guys, yeah, just trying something different. This spot's great because no one's around, but I guess you guys already knew that," he says with a cheeky laugh.

Oh God, I need to crawl into a hole and die, this is so embarrassing.

"I was just giving Ivy her first surfing lesson. We came here since it wasn't as busy."

"Nice. Well, I'll leave you two love birds to it. See you

tomorrow at Sunday dinner, Theo. Say hi to Jenna for me, Ivy."

"See you tomorrow."

Still too mortified to speak, I just nod. As soon as he turns towards the beach, I bury my head in my hands. "Oh my God, Theo, do you think he saw?"

"Don't stress, he wouldn't have seen much. He was too far away."

"We need to be more careful. All I need is one of the bitchy dance mums seeing me and the entire town will gossip about me. I won't just be the poor single mum—I'll be the *slutty* single mum."

"You overthink things way too much. No one else is around to see you, and if anyone says anything about you, they will have to deal with me. I'll protect you from the bitchy mums. You're safe with me, baby."

Nice of him to say, but he doesn't know how badly other women judge each other, especially when you're a single mum.

Theo

Well, that was a little awkward, being caught knuckle-deep in Ivy's pussy. Luckily, he didn't find us a few minutes later or I would have been balls deep—not so easy to hide. This is what Ivy does to me; I lose my mind when I'm with her. My cock takes over, acting on impulse. I have never in my 35 years been caught doing anything, but with her, I forget where I am. Poor Ivy is head down in her hands, obviously embarrassed.

"I'm sorry, angel, I got carried away."

"We both did," she says, looking up shyly at me. "Let's just have something to eat. If I keep your mouth busy, it might keep us out of trouble for a bit."

"I still have my hands."

She gives me a look. "Well, put some food in them. We're not doing that again."

"I don't know what's in the basket, but I'm sure it's good. Elly packed it for us, and she's got a knack for this type of thing." I flick open the basket and it's full of food, all on little wooden platters. Cheeses, veggie sticks, fancy bread, chocolate-covered strawberries—there's even wine and two glasses.

"I knew this was too good for you to have come up with all on your own," she says finally, with a little smile on her face again.

"Yeah, when you're not good with something—outsource. You can't be good at everything," I say, shrugging.

We sit quietly, devouring the fancy lunch my sister has put together. Ivy is deep in thought, and I hope it's not still because we got caught. I hope it won't scare her off, we were just getting somewhere. "You want something to drink? She packed wine."

"Yes, *please*." She exaggerates the please. I fill a glass for her and hand it to her. She takes a big gulp, then reaches for a strawberry, biting into it. "Your sister certainly knows how to pack a lunch."

"She does."

Her cheeks are flushed with colour, and she looks relaxed and happy for the first time since I've known her. It could be the alcohol, but I hope she finally trusts me. "So, tell me, Ivy, I still feel like I know little about you. What are your dreams for the future?"

She raises a brow. "Are all your dates like a job interview? Or is it a police interrogation?"

"Ha, yeah, sorry. I really don't date that much. I haven't in a long time, anyway, so if we're not making out, I'm kind of at a loss as to what to say to you."

"Least you're honest." She shrugs. "I don't know. I love teaching my beginners yoga, but I have this idea to start kids' classes at some local schools, where I can help kids suffering with anxiety to manage their feelings through yoga and meditation. I think if I can help people early on when they're kids, it could be a real life-changer for so many, and you don't know what some kids are going through. This might be something they really need, but their parents don't have the money for classes."

There's definitely more to her past if that's something that's on her mind. I wish she would open up and tell me what happened with Harmony's dad, but today we're having a good time, and I don't want to ruin it by pressing her for more information about her past, so I let it go.

"That's what you use yoga for?"

"Yeah, to start with, it was. Now it's just become a part of my life."

"I think that sounds like a nice idea. I'm sure lots of kids could benefit from it."

"I hope so. I'm just not sure where to start. Harmony is so funny; she knows it's something I want to do, and she said last week she gave a yoga class as her show-and-tell and got all the kids to do some stretches she knows. She said I should definitely go to her school first because the kids didn't have any idea what they were doing, and they need my help."

I laugh at the thought of her trying to teach the other kids and getting frustrated because they wouldn't listen.

"She sounds very confident. You're going to have your hands full with her when she's a teenager."

She shakes her head. "You have no idea. I have my hands full with her already with the sassiness. She's a beautiful kid, but she is strong-willed and so self-assured. I wish I had just a little of her confidence."

"What do you have not to be confident about?"

"I don't know. I've just never felt that good about myself. I have never been very popular or outgoing. When I was at school, I had just a handful of friends. I'm not the type of person to stand out. I can see that's not something you have an issue with."

"Yeah, not really, but Jasper's more like you. He is shy and hasn't really made many friends at school yet. His teacher is worried about him. She said he's really smart and is doing really well with all his work, but he's not really making friends. He has Cooper, his cousin, but he's in the other class so he only has him in the playground."

She bites into a strawberry, thinking about what I said. "That's no good. What did his teacher recommend? She must have some ideas on how to help."

"She wants me to organise some play dates with some other kids in his class. I've made a couple of attempts, but that's easier said than done when you're a single dad. Some of these mums are crazy, and it never seems to be the dad who wants to be involved."

"That's what I was telling you about before! They're nuts! What happened on the play dates?"

"I've only tried two. The first one, the mum spent the entire time talking about how much she hated her husband, then tried to hit on me in their house, so I got out of there as quickly as I could. Jasper wasn't worried because he and the kid weren't really gelling anyway. The other mum spent the whole time telling me about how outstanding her kid was and comparing him to Jasper in every way. They're only in kindy; it's a bit early for any of that, don't you think?"

She rolls her eyes, and I can see she has had just as much trouble with some of the other parents as I have. "Totally! Can't they just be kids and have fun before we have to push them to be something amazing? That's why I avoid other parents as much as possible. I can't deal with all the bullshit. It's only early days. I'm sure he will find his group of friends."

"Hope so, it's hard not to worry." I run my hand over the small sunflower tattoo on the back of her arm. "Why the sunflower?"

She puts her hand to the back of her arm, feeling it almost like she forgot it was there. "Why not? Sunflowers make me happy." She looks off into the distance as if contemplating what she's about to say. "They were my mother's favourite. She used to plant them in our front garden every year. She loved them because they make people happy. They're so big and bright.

"We would plant the seeds together, and it would take weeks for them to grow. At first, they look like nothing but tall green stalks in the ground. They were the giant type, and some of them would get taller than me. Then one morning, you wake up to bright yellow sunflowers dancing across the front of your house. So pretty and happy. When I moved up this way, I drove past that big farm with all the sunflowers, and it reminded me of a better time when my parents were still alive and I didn't know the harsh truths of life." She shrugs. "So that's why I got it, a little reminder of better times since everything else was gone."

She's still sitting with her hand on her arm. I reach out

to her, pulling her back down onto the sand on top of me. "That's beautiful, angel," I say into her lips as I kiss her.

I didn't mean to bring up old memories, but it's nice she's finally opening up to me and showing me parts of who she is. I'm dying to know everything, but I'm trying not to push, which is very hard for me. I'm not patient in the slightest, and in my job, I'm used to getting information out of people. It's what we do, interrogate until they tell us what we want to know.

After lunch, we wandered down to the local markets in town. They run along the beachside every Saturday until the sun goes down. The atmosphere is great with live music and street performers. We walk through the crowd hand in hand, and she looks happy, carefree, and relaxed. I finally feel like I'm seeing the real Ivy.

Every few stalls, we stop to look at what they have on display. She seems to like this one stall with long hippie-style dresses, and I can't help but admire how beautiful she is. She stands looking at herself in the mirror with the long red dress held up to her front. As I watch her, my cock jumps to attention in my pants, and I have to adjust myself so it's not obvious. She's been driving me crazy all day, testing me. I don't think he can take much more. I've got to get her home before I take her right here at the market in front of everyone.

I come up behind her, kissing her neck. "You should get this one, it would look stunning on you," I whisper in her ear. "Then we need to get you home to finish what we started at the beach, before we have kids to pick up," I say as I press my hard cock into her arse. I can see her face blush in the mirror in front of us at the thought of what we were caught doing. I take the dress from her and take it to the counter to pay for it.

"No, you don't have to get it for me," she protests, a look of unease on her face.

"I know I don't, but I want to. You can pay me back later." I give her my cheeky smile, so she knows I'm just playing, but honestly, if I want to buy her something, I'm going to. I finish paying, and I'm rewarded with a kiss.

"Okay, take me home, Theo. I think I have kept you waiting long enough." She playfully bites her lip and takes my hand. This time she won't run.

We turn to walk out, and I hear my name being called through the crowded walkway of the market stalls. I can't see her yet, but I know who it is. Shit, I'm not ready for this. She'll be all over Ivy, asking a million questions. Ivy will run after this interrogation for sure!

"Mother!"

She throws her arms around me like she hasn't seen me in ages, when really, it's been a week.

"What are you doing here, Theo?" She stands back from me, her eyes running over Ivy with a knowing smile. She's loving this.

"Just shopping with my girlfriend, Ivy. This is my mum, Anne." Shit, did I just say girlfriend? Ivy's eyes go wide in surprise then she gives mum a shy wave to say hi.

"Oh... well, this is a surprise, Theo, how lovely. Nice to meet you, Ivy," she says, giving Ivy a hug and kissing her cheek. My mother is very affectionate. It doesn't matter if you have just met her for the first time, you're getting the full greeting. She stands holding Ivy's hands as she talks to her. "Now, Ivy, every Sunday night we have a family dinner —you must come tomorrow. I'm sure the entire family would love to meet you."

Oh no, she didn't just invite her to family dinner. She's going to run for sure! Ivy looks to me then back to Mum. I can tell she's a little uncomfortable.

"Mum, I'm sure Ivy doesn't want to join our boring family dinner. This is new between us, and I don't want to scare her off with you lot," I say, trying to get her off the hook. Mum looks a little wounded, but she's full-on.

Ivy smiles sweetly at my mum. "That's okay, Anne, dinner sounds nice. I haven't had a family dinner since I was a teenager. As long as you're alright with it, Theo?" she says, looking at me with her big, blue eyes blinking. She looks a little overtaken by emotion, like she's about to cry.

"Of course, I would love you to come. And Harmony as well, she could play with Jasper and my nephew Cooper." I turn to Mum. "Ivy has a daughter. Harmony, she's five, just like Jas and Coop."

She squeezes Ivy's hands, that she has yet to let go of. "Oh, how wonderful! Well okay, it's settled then. We will see you all at dinner tomorrow at four."

I place my hand on Ivy's back in an attempt to get her out of this conversation. "Okay, Mum, we have to go now, see you then." I wrap my arms around Ivy's shoulders and lead her away from Mum. She smiles and waves bye.

"See you both tomorrow," Mum calls through the crowd.

"Are you okay?" I whisper into Ivy's ear as we walk away. "We can cancel if you're not ready for my family. It's pretty full-on."

"Yes, I'm okay with it, as long as you are. I was just a little surprised you called me your girlfriend."

"I told you at the beach, I want you to be mine. That means you're my girl, right?" We stop walking now so I can look her straight in the eyes. I need to know she feels the same way.

"It's just... I thought you didn't do the whole girlfriend thing, and I'm not just a girlfriend. I come with a child too. I know we went over this at the beach but are you sure you've thought this through?" She has her eyes down, looking at the ground. I lift her chin so she has to look at me.

"Angel, I haven't stopped thinking about this since the first day I met you. I thought I couldn't do this again, but now that I've met you, I don't want to be without you either. We both have a child, and it's going to complicate things, but it's going to make it more fun too. I want to try this if you do."

"What do you mean by again? Do you mean like with Jasper's mum?"

"Let's go back to your place so we can talk properly."

We sit in almost silence as we drive, both deep in our own thoughts. It's pretty clear we have both had a lot of shit to deal with in our past, and we both carry scars that are hard to live with, but I want this to work. For the first time since the accident, I can see a life with someone else, and I hope if I open up to her, she might do the same with me.

CHAPTER SIXTEEN

IVY

We arrive out the front of the complex, and I tap in the code to open the gates. I'm still not sure how I feel about him coming to my place—it's my safe place, and it's scary letting someone else in—but I feel like he's been so open with me. Maybe I need to give him a chance. When I'm with him I feel safe. Plus, he's a cop, so he's got to be safe, right?

I open the front door, and he follows me in. He's unusually quiet, and it makes me wonder if he's changed his mind.

"Would you like a drink or something? I don't have a lot, but I have coffee or tea," I offer, walking towards the kitchen.

"Coffee would be great, thanks." He follows me, pulling out a stool at the breakfast bar, taking a seat while I make our drinks. "When do you have to pick up Harmony?"

"In about an hour, but she's just next door so Fay won't mind if we're a bit late." I place the coffee down in front of him as he glances at me. He appears sad. He's definitely changed his mind. I knew it was all too good to be true. "Is everything okay? You're quiet again, like this morning."

He pats the seat next to him, and I sit. "Ivy, I know you've had some stuff in your past that wasn't ideal, and you'll tell me about it when you're ready, but if we're going to move forward how I would like to, I need you to know where I'm coming from."

"Okay, you can tell me anything." Now I'm scared. What's he going to say? He can tell me anything, but it doesn't mean I'll be able to handle it.

"I've only really had one long-term relationship. It was a few years back. I thought she was the one." He pauses, taking a breath like this is hard for him to say. I reach out, placing my hand on his leg, trying to comfort him, even though I have no idea what's going on with him.

"She was my partner at work, and we were engaged to be married." He stares into his drink, not making eye contact with me at all. "I thought I had my life all planned out. A few months after our engagement, we found out she was pregnant. It was earlier than we planned, but we had talked about having a family, so why not start early. I felt like the luckiest man in the world, everything in my life was perfect." He pauses to have some of his drink, looking like maybe he can't get the next part out.

I don't like where this story is going. It can only have a bad ending because he's now a single dad, no wife. "This is your damage, isn't it? That day at your house you said you're damaged too. This is why?"

"This is why. It's difficult for me to talk about, and until now, I really haven't, but I want you to know where I'm coming from when I say I really want to try this with you. I never thought I could even think about a future with anyone else, but since the moment I nearly ran over your cat, it's all I've thought about. You're on my mind constantly. The day I lost her, it was the hardest day of my life. In a split second, she was gone. Jasper was born, and I was a single dad with no idea what I was doing."

His story is so tragically sad, but he doesn't cry. The pain is etched on his face, the fear in his eyes like he is reliving everything he witnessed that day as he's telling me. I reach for his hand, lacing my fingers with his, hoping the contact will help him tell his story.

He takes a deep breath. "The cops were chasing a wanted man. He was high on drugs and smashed into her car. Fiona, my fiancée, was driving, on her way to the shops, a normal everyday activity. Just in the wrong place at the wrong time. She was rushed to hospital, but they couldn't save her. I'm thankful every day that they somehow saved Jasper. I don't know what I would have done without him. He gave me hope and a reason to go on."

I'm in shock. He lost the love of his life in a tragic accident and became a father the same day. Here I was thinking he was just a player who'd had a bad relationship and ended up with a kid out of it. My face is wet with tears, and I sniffle to hold back the sobs that want to escape. It's just so sad. I get him now; he makes so much more sense to me.

I wrap my arms around him and just hold him. "I'm so sorry, Theo. I can't even imagine what you went through." The tears continue to roll down my face as I attempt to comfort him. I can't believe that's what he needed to tell me. Of course he didn't want to go through that again.

"That's when I decided not to get close to anyone again. Then I couldn't lose them, you know? I just wanted to be a good dad." His hands are gripping my face as though his life depends on it. "But I couldn't stay away from you. I kept telling myself it was just fun and that I could walk away at any time, but now it's too late. I can't walk away from you. I'm in love with you, Ivy."

He's in love with me! I'm so surprised to hear him say those words. I don't know what to say back so I cuddle him a little tighter.

"I want to try. I want to push past the fear of loss and live again with purpose towards a future. I want a second chance to be truly happy with you, Harmony, and Jasper—if you'll have me."

I run my fingers through his hair and close the space between us, meeting his lips with mine, slowly kissing him. I can't take away what happened, but I can be there for him now. We stay like this for ages, neither of us wanting to let go.

"I want you, Theo, and I feel the same. I can't let go of you. I'm yours just as much as you are mine." I finally pull back, taking his hand and leading him up the stairs to my bedroom. I'm not fighting it anymore. He says he's in love with me. I might not say it back just yet, but I know I feel it too, and I'm going to sure as hell show him.

We make it to my room and stand at the end of the bed. He takes in my perfectly made room then turns back to me. I cup his face in my hands and draw his stubbly face to mine, kissing him slowly, tasting him as his tongue swipes through my mouth. He pulls me into him. I can feel how much he needs me close to him, and it makes me want him even more.

He runs his hands down my back until they stop on my arse, and he scoops me up. My legs wrap around his waist as our kiss intensifies. I feel so close to him right now, not just physically, but on every level. This is so much more than I have ever experienced.

He lowers me onto my bed, our bodies entangled, still lost in our kiss, unable to let go even for a second. Instead, we start to clumsily peel the layers of clothing from each other, not breaking contact. My dress is reefed over my head as I tug his shirt over his and reach for his shorts, yanking them down his legs while he unties my bikini top.

His hands are everywhere, and as the layers come off, the touch of his skin on mine is heaven. My bare chest presses into his hard pecs as I roll on top of him, and he drags my bikini bottoms over my arse and down my legs. Our kiss is hungry, and his stubble scratches my chin in our desperate need to satisfy our desire for each other and the necessity to be as close as possible.

My hips rock into him, and I can feel his hard erection pressed into my pubic bone. I'm desperate for him. "I need you now," I whisper.

And in one more roll of my hips, I slide up a little higher, so the tip of his cock is at my entrance, then I lower down. He fills me with his massive cock, and the stretch burns, but I don't care. This is what I need.

"Fuck, Ivy." He reaches his hand through my hair, pulling me back down to him. My lips are swollen and sore from our aggressive kissing, but still, I want more of his mouth on mine. I rock back and forth on him, riding his cock. My hips seem to take over on their own, taking what I need from him, as he does the same, thrusting into me. His hands skate down my back to rest on my hips, and he digs his fingers in, picking up the pace.

It all becomes too much. It's as if my mind completely blacks out. I don't even know what I'm doing anymore. It all feels too good, too much, but I don't want it to stop. "Theo, I'm... Fuck, oh God." My orgasm rips through me so intensely that it feels like I'm having on out-of-body experience.

He thrusts into me harder, twice more, and I feel his release as he lets out an animalistic groan.

I collapse onto his chest, a sweaty mess. I focus on the sound of his heart frantically beating in his chest.

He strokes my hair, and as I slowly come back to earth, I roll off him and he pulls me into his side. "That was off the charts."

"It was, angel." He pauses, looking at me, worried. "Please tell me you're on the pill, because in the moment, I completely forgot about protection."

I sit up quickly. "Fuck, that was stupid. I wasn't thinking either. I'm on the pill, we're covered." How could I have forgotten about that, though? That was really dumb.

"Okay, that's good. I didn't mean to ruin the moment we were having. I just suddenly thought about it, and an unplanned pregnancy is probably the last thing either of us need right now."

"Definitely the last thing I need."

He pulls me back down to his side, hugging me into him. We lay in each other's arms for as long as we can before I know I really need to get Harmony.

Theo

Last night was definitely a turning point for us. I opened my heart to her, and she didn't run or shut down. She took me to her bed and showed me how she felt about me. It was so intimate, both of us kissing, tasting, teasing to climax. This was so much more than just lust-filled sex. It was us knocking down our walls and letting each other in, and it felt unbelievable. I didn't think I could do this again—

imagine a life with someone else—but with her, that's what I want.

This morning I have some time with Jasper, and I'm hoping to have a little chat with him about Ivy. So, I have driven us in to Byron so we can go for a walk up to the lighthouse. It's a long, steep walk for a little dude, but I have driven up closer to the top.

I take his little hand and we start the walk. "Are you excited to see if there are any whales today?"

"Do you really think there might be?"

"Some guys from work said they've seen them this week, so we might get lucky."

He beams with excitement and walks a little faster. He is such an animal lover, and he's going to go nuts if we actually get to see some. We haven't been lucky enough to see them any other time we've been here.

The walk is really picturesque, and although we're on a timber boardwalk-style pathway, it's still surrounded by trees, with the sound of the waves crashing to the shore on the beach below and tropical rainforest birds calling from the trees.

By the time we get to the top, we're both a little puffed from the steep incline, and the humidity in the air today isn't helping. I pull a water bottle from my backpack for Jasper.

He has a big drink, hands me the bottle, and bolts for it. "Beat you to the lighthouse."

I throw the bottle back in my bag and take off after him. Such a Walker kid, always looking for the next competition. He's fast for his age, but he's got nothing on his old man, and I catch up with him quickly, running just behind him so he can win. "Yeah, I win! You're getting slower, Dad."

"You're getting faster, mate. It's hard to keep up with you now."

"I'll never be as fast as Uncle Drew," he says with a grimace.

"You will be one day," I say, messing up his short hair.

He looks to me with a cute little smile. "Do you think I will be as good at surfing as him?"

I'm surprised by his question. I knew he was enjoying their lessons together but not that much. "Do you want to be?"

"Maybe. I like surfing," he says with a nod of his head like he's deciding this is a good idea.

"You need to get really good at swimming then, and I'm sure Uncle Drew will teach you to be just as good at surfing as him, if not better."

We walk down the stairs to the lookout platform and take a seat. For a Sunday it's surprisingly quiet. Normally this place is crawling with tourists on the weekend. We must have picked the right day to come for once.

"There is something I wanted to chat to you about today, buddy." I pull an apple out of the backpack and hand it to him.

"What is it?" His little face has a look of concern, wrinkles forming across his freckled nose.

"Do you remember that day when we were going for a surf lesson and I nearly ran over that cute little ginger cat on the way?"

"Yeah, I remember. That was Harmony's cat." He bites into his apple.

"You know her?"

He nods, swallowing his mouthful. "She's in the other class, but her friend Quinn and her like to play tip with Cooper sometimes, so I know her a bit."

"Okay, well, that's good then. Her mum and I have become friends, and Nana invited them over for Sunday dinner tonight. Do you think that would be okay if they come with us?"

"I guess, but they're not family. Sunday dinner is for family."

"Yeah, you're right, but Harmony's mum, Ivy, is a very good friend of mine and she doesn't have any family of her own, so Nana thought it might be nice if they share ours and join in with our dinner."

He thinks for a bit then nods. "That's okay then. Harmony won't take Cooper away from me, though, will she?"

"Is that what happens at school? Do you feel left out when he plays with the other kids?"

"No, not really. They ask me to play too, but it takes me a long time to finish my lunch, and by the time I'm finished, I can't find them."

"Oh, really? Okay, maybe we need to give you less in your lunch box then, so you have time to play."

"That would be good because the teacher said we have to eat everything in our lunchbox before we can play. I don't think Cooper does, but I don't want to get in trouble."

He's such a rule follower, and now what his teacher was saying about him not really making friends and sitting alone makes more sense. It's not that he can't make friends. He's just trying to follow the rules and eat his lunch, so he's missing out. Least this one is easy to fix. "Well, from now on, I'll put less in your lunchbox so you can go play when Cooper does. And tonight, you might get to know Harmony, so you have another friend at school. How does that sound?"

"That sounds good."

"Look, Jas, over there, I see something in the water."

He jumps up, running to the side of the fence where I'm pointing, and sure enough, today must be our lucky day. There is a burst of water from the ocean below, and moments later, another one.

"Whales, Dad! We finally get to see them!" He's so thrilled, and this is why Sundays are my favourite day of the week, seeing him experience all the new and exciting things life has to offer.

CHAPTER SEVENTEEN

IVY

I slip into my shoes. "Come on, baby. Theo and Jasper will be here in ten minutes to pick us up."

"Where are we going again, Mummy?" We already had a chat about this over pancakes this morning, but she was preoccupied with her unicorns and wasn't listening.

"Just for a BBQ with my friend Theo at his parents' place. There will be kids for you to play with as well. Theo's son Jasper and his nephew Cooper, they both go to your school.

She looks up from where she's playing with her unicorns with a questioning look. "Someone to play with? I'll just pack a bag." She rushes off into her bedroom, returning with her handbag full of unicorns and wearing her red sparkly heels. "I'm ready," she announces.

She has refused to let me dress her since she was three, so she's in an interesting combination of striped tights under a glittery tutu, with a bunny T-shirt. Now with the addition of the red sparkly shoes, she is uncoordinated perfection. I have gone for simple white shorts with cute buttons down the front and a loose floral blouse with tan slip-on sandals.

With some things, we couldn't be more opposite. She loves the bling with all the frills that will draw as much attention as possible, and I prefer a more understated look that will definitely not get me noticed.

I'm so nervous my hands are sweating, and I feel kind of sick to the stomach. I'm even more nervous than our first date, and I was bad enough for that. I know I have technically met his mum already, and she seemed nice enough, and I know Drew a little, but officially meeting his whole family seems a little too real for me. There are going to be so many of them, and I'm not used to the big family gatherings.

And I'm a little apprehensive for Harmony to meet them all as well. I'm worried we might be rushing things, letting the kids meet each other already. After yesterday, I should feel good about it all—and I do—but I still want to protect her.

I wish I'd had the guts to tell Theo about my past. It would have been the perfect opportunity to open up to him, but every time I try to, I can't. I'm so embarrassed to admit what I let happen to me for years, and I know as soon as I tell him, he's going to see me differently. I'll be poor, weak Ivy. I don't want his pity, and I don't want him to see me like that.

I hear Theo's car pull up out the front. "Come on, baby girl, let's go."

We walk tentatively hand in hand down the driveway towards his SUV. He smiles kindly as he hops out of his side and opens the door for us. His son Jasper is in the back in his car seat, and he looks us over as if assessing us. I wonder what he thinks about all of this and what Theo has told him about me.

Theo's in his standard T-shirt and jeans. I have no idea how he makes it look so good. He's just so hot, I don't think it would matter what he's wearing. He gives me a simple kiss on the cheek and takes Harmony's car seat from me so he can put it in his car.

"There you go, little miss. This is my son Jasper, but I think the two of you know each other from school already."

I can see Harmony's little smirk as she hops into the back. She may only be five, but she's smart and she can see what's going on—which makes me more nervous! Theo says he's in this for the long haul, but he doesn't really know what he's getting himself into, and if he did, I'm sure he would run for it.

"Thank you. Hi, Jas, I know you from school. You're Cooper's friend."

Jasper smiles at her.

"Jasper, this is my friend Ivy," Theo introduces me to his son. He's a sweet-looking kid with strawberry-blond hair and freckles across his nose. He smiles shyly. "You girls both look beautiful. Harmony, I can see how much effort you put into your outfit. My sister Elly will be very impressed."

She grins, flattening out her skirt. "Oh, I hope so. I'm so excited to meet your family. I have a bag full of toys for us to play with."

"That was very thoughtful of you. There is also a trampoline in the yard, so you kids will have lots to do."

"Oh, really? I have wanted a trampoline for forever, but Mum says our backyard isn't big enough." She smiles excitedly over to Jasper, who is very quiet, just assessing us.

I hop in the car and look out the window, trying to distract myself, but my bouncing knee is giving away my nerves.

"Are you okay?" Theo says, resting his hand on my leg to stop the bouncing. It works; I can feel myself calm down just knowing he's there.

"Just a bit nervous. Family gatherings aren't my thing. What if your family doesn't like me?"

He throws his head back and laughs at me like I've said something ridiculous. "They're going to love you, both of you," he says, looking in the back at Harmony. "I've already received multiple texts today from Mum trying to make sure everything is perfect. I think she's a bit excited. As you know, I haven't brought someone home in a very long time."

He hasn't brought someone home in a long time. I wonder if he's only bringing me because we ran into her yesterday and he didn't have a chance to say no. Stop being so pessimistic, Ivy. Just enjoy yourself for once and stop looking for the negative all the time.

The rest of the drive goes by quickly as he chats to Harmony about fairies, unicorns, and her dance lessons. I'm surprised how much he has remembered from what I have told him about her. Jasper is quiet, but I can see he is taking it all in. He's more of a silent observer like me.

We pull up to a beautiful, traditional-style Queenslander home, with a front deck that wraps around the house, a white picket fence, and perfect tropical front gardens. Theo's mum is outside to greet us before we even have a chance to leave the car, and his dad follows closely behind.

"Mum, Dad, this is Ivy and Harmony. Ivy, you remember my mum Anne, and this is my dad, Jim."

Anne reaches out and gives the warmest welcome hug I think I've ever received, and Jim shakes my hand, while Harmony clings to my leg, her head buried. She has lost the confidence she had in the car.

Anne takes Harmony's hand. "Come on, Harmony, why don't you and Jasper come out the back with me. Cooper has been waiting for you two to get here." They both happily go off with her.

"So nice to meet you, Ivy. Anne is a bit excited. Theo, she has been carrying on all day about meeting you yesterday," Jim says.

"Nice to meet you too, Jim. You didn't have to go to any fuss for me."

"You don't know my mother," Theo says, eyebrows raised, and it scares me a little. She seems really nice, and I remember what Jen said about how she helped her start her new life, so I'm sure she must be okay. Maybe just a bit full-on if you're her kid.

Jim walks in front of us through the house to the yard. I can hear the happy squeals of the kids on the trampoline already.

My nerves are calming. I can do this. Theo steals a quick kiss, then takes my hand, and we walk out the back to meet the rest of the family.

"You okay?" he asks.

"Yes, Jasper is very quiet, though."

"I think he is as nervous about meeting new people as you."

"Is that what it is?" I ask, concerned for the poor kid. I'm not quite sure how to connect with him yet.

"Yeah, he'll warm up."

We walk around the corner and are greeted with lots of smiles. "Wow, your family are all so good-looking!" I whisper to him. They really are. I don't think I've seen so many good-looking people in one backyard. I feel so out of place.

"Good genetics, I guess. They all take after me."

"Yes, that must be it." I laugh. As we arrive in the backyard, I see Harmony has already made herself at home on the trampoline with the boys. They look like they're having fun.

She sees me and calls out, "Hey, Mum, this is my friend Cooper."

"Friends already?"

"No, he's my friend from school. We're in the same class."

I look over to Theo. "There you go, they're already friends. It couldn't get any easier. I knew the two of you would fit in easily."

A beautiful blonde who would have to be around my age comes to stand with us, handing me a glass of wine. "This is for you, thought you might need it. I'm Elly."

"Thank you, Elly, that's very thoughtful and very appreciated. I'm Ivy, as I'm sure you have heard." I take a sip.

"Where's my drink, sis?" complains Theo.

"Sorry, Theo. You're a big boy, you'll have to go find your own." She winks at me, and I start to relax. These people are nice.

"Typical. I'll be back in a sec." He kisses me on the cheek and walks toward the house.

I turn to Elly. "Thank you for helping Theo with the beautiful picnic you packed yesterday."

"My pleasure. It's just nice to see him happy again. Looks like our kids are friends already. We'll have to organise a play date for them."

"That would be nice. Harmony doesn't have that many friends yet, so I'm sure she would love to."

"Theo said you bought one of the townhouses my husband built in Broken Point. It's funny, they were the first place I styled when I started my business, and I always wondered who would move into them."

"Oh, really? Yeah, I guess that is kind of funny."

"Theo really likes you, hey. He would kill me for saying, but he doesn't ever go to the effort he did for you yesterday."

"Yeah, he said he doesn't really date. I was surprised until he told me about what happened. It's nice to know I'm someone he's able to open up to. I really like him as well."

"He deserves happiness after everything he's been through. And selfishly, I hope you can make it work. I need another girl around here—too much testosterone."

We're not there for long when Anne brings out the salad, placing it down the centre of the table. Jim is on the BBQ, and it smells amazing. Now that I'm finally relaxing, I'm starving.

Theo was right. His sister Elly is lovely, and we have hit it off straight away, chatting while we watch over the kids playing on the trampoline. Having kids the same age helps. Elly is also keen to come and try out one of my beginners yoga classes she said Theo told her about. I really hope he didn't tell her all the details, just that I'm a good teacher.

I can see Theo and Drew in deep conversation about something. As I'm watching them, he looks up to check on me and I'm caught. He rewards me with that cheeky wink of his.

I could get used to this, being a part of a family. It's so lovely. The warmth and affection they share for each other is something I have missed so much since my parents passed.

Theo

I sit here in my parents' backyard, beer in hand, with Drew talking my ear off. He plans to re-join the surfing tour, and the line-up of countries he will be competing in sounds amazing. He wants me to bring Jasper to visit him along the way somewhere so he can watch him compete. It's not something we have attempted before, but he's old enough to travel with now, and he has taken an interest in surfing, so it might be a nice idea. I wonder if Ivy and Harmony would want to come with us?

I glance over to where Ivy is standing with my sister. She's so beautiful in the afternoon sunlight. The two of them have been chatting away since we got here. I just knew my family would love her, and somehow, this all feels right. She fits into our family so nicely. I can't help but imagine what a future would be like with her and our kids. Some sort of a normal family, a second chance. I'm just so scared that it could all be ripped away in an instant. I wish I knew how to get a grip on the fear.

Mum announces dinner, and we all make our way to the table. Mum's super health conscious after the heart attack Dad had a few years back. All the food she makes is healthy, so there are always loads of fresh salads to go along with the BBQ, and today is no different. The table is full of platters of food.

The kids have their own little plastic table down the end. Harmony, Cooper, and Jasper are laughing hysterically at each other's jokes. They seem to be having a good time. Ivy and I sit across from my mum and dad—Mum's way of making sure she gets all the gossip she can.

"So, Ivy, Theo tells me you're a yoga and meditation teacher and you would like to introduce a program into the local schools to help kids deal with their anxiety."

Ivy looks over at me, a little surprised that I've told my mum. "Yes, it's something close to my heart. I have seen from personal experience how much yoga and meditation can help with the stresses of society today, and I think if we teach our kids when they're little, we can give them tools for life."

"Sounds like it would be an amazing program. Did Theo tell you I'm the principal at Byron Primary? We would love to work with you on creating this program if that's something you're interested in."

"Really? That would be amazing!" She looks at me like she can't believe it. I knew my mum would love her. I can't believe I'm saying this, but she's perfect, and her dream sounds like such a good idea. I didn't tell her Mum was a principal because I didn't want her to be more nervous about coming here, but I'm sure together they'll make a great team to bring this dream to life.

"I'll get Theo to give me your number, and you can come by one day next week so we can get started. If that works for you."

"Okay, thank you, that would be amazing."

Mum's cooking is delicious, the table is noisy with chatter, and for a while I forget about the past.

After dinner, Mum gives the kids paddle pops and they sit on the grass, the chocolaty mess dripping all down their hands and messing up their faces.

Ivy and I stand just by the yard, watching them. Tonight has been a little hard. I just want to hold her, wrap my arms around her, kiss her when I feel like it, but we're both on our best behaviour because of the kids. She bumps arms with me. "We better get them home so they can get into bed at a reasonable hour. It's a school night."

"I'd like to get you home and into bed."

"I'm sure you would. But we have responsibilities tonight."

"Jasper and I could come for a sleepover. I'm sure the kids would love that, they're getting on so well."

She gives me a look. "The kids have school in the morning. Why don't we try to do it next weekend? That way if they don't get much sleep, they can sleep in on Sunday morning. I'll even cook my special Sunday pancakes for you both in the morning."

"That's nearly an entire week away. Are you saying I have to wait that long to be with you again?"

"Theo, you knew this was going to be tricky—don't make it harder. I want to spend the night with you just as much, but they,"—she points toward the kids—"have to come first, and we need to manoeuvre this carefully."

"I know, you're right. Next Saturday night sounds perfect for a sleepover with the kids. But don't think that means you're off the hook. You need to work out a time I can see you this week, cause I'm not waiting that long."

"I'll see what I can do, bossy pants." She pokes out her tongue as she walks away from me, heading in the direction of the kids.

Ivy

My heels click on the vinyl-tile floor as I walk down the long school hall on my way to Anne's office with my proposal clutched in my shaky hands. I don't normally go for heels, but today I felt like I needed to be professional for this meeting, so a fitted floral dress, a touch of make-up, and the only heels I own were as good as it was going to get.

I still can't believe she wants to hear my ideas on how we can implement this program into our schools. I check my watch again. Two pm, I'm right on time. There's only an hour before I have to pick up Harmony from school, so hopefully this is quick, but this was the only time she could do this week when I wasn't already teaching a class, and she wants to get the ball rolling. She's excited to start the program trial in the second term of school, so I had to take this appointment time.

After Sunday night's family dinner, I have Elly's number in case of emergencies, so if I need to, I could probably call her and get her to grab Harmony if I'm not going to make it in time. Now that I know who she is, we have been running into each other at school pick-ups all week. It's so nice to have a friend with a child the same age. I've never had that before.

"Ivy, so lovely to see you." Anne's warm face greets me, and she gets up from her desk to hug me. "Take a seat, dear." She's a really beautiful woman, dressed immaculately in a sage-green fitted dress and cropped jacket. Her skin is nearly flawless, and she radiates a beautiful, warm glow. I hope I look that good when I'm in my 60s.

I sit across from her, clutching the folder. "Here's a copy of the proposal I was telling you about," I say, passing it to her over her desk.

She takes the folder, opening it and flicking through.

"This program is really important to me. I have seen firsthand how much yoga and meditation can help when you're dealing with a lot of stress or if you naturally have awful anxiety—or even just to build confidence. Kids these days also have way too much stimulation with screens. They don't get the chance to have downtime and relax their little minds, and meditation is so good for that.

"I'm hoping that if we can start with kids when they're in kindy like Harmony, Jasper, and Cooper, by the time they reach high school and the stresses of school life increase, they will already have the tools to deal with whatever life throws at them."

I'm rambling and probably talking way too fast because I'm excited, but I can't help it. I have been working on this idea for years. I know I can't change the world and the fucked-up things that take place in it, but if I can help some of our younger generation to cope a little better, I can leave here feeling like I've done something positive for humankind.

"It's a wonderful idea, Ivy, and I can see how passionate you are about helping these kids. Have you thought about how you will run the program by yourself?" She lowers her glasses down her nose to look over at me.

"The studio where I teach has four instructors. This is something we have been talking about for a while, so to start with, it would be me and my friend Penny, but eventually, if all goes well, my whole studio will be on board, so we should be able to run the program through all the schools in the district." I can feel my nervous knee bouncing underneath the table, but luckily Anne can't see that.

"Sounds perfect. You have thought this through. If you can let me know both of your availability for term two, I will get a timetable drawn up for you to work with the junior school here, then we can start talks with some other schools in the district, see if we can roll out the program to them by the start of next year."

I beam with excitement. I can hardly believe she is so supportive of my idea. "Really? That sounds amazing. Thank you so much, Anne. I think the kids will really enjoy the program we have planned, and hopefully it will help with all areas of their well-being."

"I'm sure they will be very excited to try something new.

You will both need your working-with-children checks up to date as well before you're allowed to start."

"No problem, we will organise it straight away."

She grins. "I'm looking forward to working with you on this, Ivy." She stands, and I can hardly believe it was that easy. I push back my chair, standing as well as she comes round her desk to shake my hand.

"Thank you again, Anne. You have no idea what this means to me."

"Not a problem... and Ivy, whatever you're doing to Theo, keep it up. I haven't seen my boy this happy in a very long time. You're good for him."

I feel my face heat. "He's making me just as happy. I'm lucky to have found him." I give her a brief wave. "See you soon."

"You and Harmony are welcome anytime for Sunday dinner. We loved having you this week."

"Thank you, it was a lovely night. We will definitely try to come again."

I walk to the car quickly, checking my watch. I've just got time to make it to school pick-up. I think I'll pick up Harmony and take her for ice cream to celebrate this win.

CHAPTER EIGHTEEN

THEO

I pull up out the front of the florist. I don't even know what I'm doing here, flowers are not my thing. In fact, I don't think I've ever bought flowers before. But I feel like I need to get Ivy something special tonight. Jasper and I are going for dinner and officially meeting her friends.

I walk into the florist. It's rustic-looking with hanging plants all around. I scan the room, not seeing any bunches made up. This is a bad idea. I've got no idea what I'm doing. I turn to walk out when a young girl with bright pink hair and tats running up her arms pipes up from behind the sales counter.

"Done something wrong, have you?" That's very presumptuous of her.

"Not that I know of, just trying to do something nice to get my girl to smile." I feel self-conscious that I look like *that guy*, the one that has cheated or at least fucked up bad enough to need a get-out-of-the-doghouse present.

"Or get laid? That's the only two reasons guys come in here: they've either fucked up or they want to fuck!" For someone so young, she seems very dark, or maybe she has seen it all before and that's the only reason men buy flowers. I laugh at her forwardness.

"Okay, can't a normal guy just do something nice for his girlfriend? I didn't realise we were all jerks."

She looks slightly taken aback. Her scowl changes to a small half-smile. "Sorry, it's just been one of those days. What are you looking for?"

"Just a nice bunch, something happy and bright—maybe some sunflowers if you've got them." I know for a fact they're a flower Ivy loves.

"Sure, no worries, give me a couple of minutes." She grabs flowers from the vases on the shelves behind her, and within no time at all, she's pulling them into a bunch and wrapping them up in front of me.

"Wow, that was fast," I say, handing her my credit card.

"That's my job. You want a card on there?"

"No need, I'm giving them to her in person." She finishes up tying the bow, then hands me the enormous bunch of flowers.

"They're beautiful, thank you. Hope your day improves." She gives me a small smile, then turns, grabbing her broom, and sweeps up the mess she made creating the arrangement.

I head back to my car, placing the flowers on the seat next to me. I hope she likes them and doesn't think I'm a dick for buying flowers.

I'm actually a little nervous to be a part of her weekly dinner with her friends. They're all so close, and I will be the only guy. Not that I normally have any trouble with a room full of women, but tonight seems important. I need them to like me.

I stop to pick up Jasper from Elly and Fraser's on the

way. Elly answers the door. "He's just getting together his school stuff."

"Thanks, Elly. How has he been this afternoon?"

"Perfect as always." She sighs. She looks like she has had a big day, and it makes me feel worse than I already do that she has to help me out so much. She always says she doesn't mind, that it's better this way because they keep each other occupied, but I'm sure it's still difficult. "He's the easy one, Theo, you know that. You sure you don't want to trade for a bit?"

"I think I'm good, but if you want me to have Cooper over on the weekend, just let me know. What trouble has Coop got himself into now?"

She steps to the side, and I can see the hole in the window in their lounge room. I cover my mouth to stop the laugh when she is clearly unimpressed. "Oh shit, how did he do that?"

"Soccer practice."

"Well, he must have a good boot on him then. You should be proud."

She rolls her eyes. "That's exactly what Fraser said."

"Sorry, Elly. The offer stands, I can have him for you, give you a break."

"It's okay, Theo. I'm sure you have better things to do... like see your new friend," she teases in a singsong voice.

Jasper appears in the doorway, dragging his over-sized school bag behind him. "I'm actually on my way over there tonight for dinner. I'm meeting her friends."

"Well, have a lovely dinner then, you two. I'll see you in the morning for all the gossip."

"Thanks, sis, see you in the morning."

Jasper and I head off towards the car. "How was school today, bud?"

He beams with excitement. "It was so good! I finished all my lunch the same time as Cooper, then we ran down to the playground and found Harmony and her friend and played tip the whole time. It was the best!"

I give him a high-five. "That's fantastic news. I'm glad the two of you are getting on because we're on our way over there now for dinner."

"Yes!" He pumps the air with his fist.

Things are going better than I could have hoped for. With the two of them getting on so well, this might just be easy after all.

Ivy

THE GATE BUZZER RINGS, AND I GO TO CHECK IT. There better be someone this time. I swear it rang half an hour ago, but there was no one there, so maybe I'm just losing my mind.

Ever since I met Theo, things like that keep happening. It's so strange. The other day I was driving Harmony home from school, and I swear this black SUV with dark tinted windows was following me the entire way. Then when I pulled into the driveway, he slowly drove past and parked just up the street. I couldn't see the driver properly because the windows were too dark. It totally could have just been a coincidence, but it freaked me out just the same.

Harmony is at the door, ready for it to open. She is so excited that her new friend Jasper is coming for dinner, but this time, it's Fay and Jenna. They're here for Taco Tuesday.

Tonight I've made nachos, so not technically tacos, but it's close enough. I get sick of the same thing every week.

Theo has been invited to our dinner for the first time. The girls want to get to know him, and honestly, I want their opinions, so I know it's not just me in a loved-up bubble. These women mean everything to me, and I know they will tell me the truth. He won't be here until a bit later because he has to stop off at Elly's after work and collect Jasper.

As I go to close the door, the buzzer goes off. That must be Penny. I buzz her in. We all make our way to the lounge room.

Harmony hugs Fay and Jenna then jumps into Penny's arms as soon as she walks in the door.

"Come play with me, Auntie Pen."

"Maybe after dinner, baby girl." She puts her down, playing with her curls that are in cute pigtails.

Jenna takes Harmony's hand. "Come, I'll put on your favourite movie. What is it this week? Barbie and the Secret Door or Mermaidia?" They sit on the floor in the lounge room setting up the DVD player.

"Oh, I don't know. I want to watch something Jasper would like. What movies do boys like?"

"Hmm, I'm not really sure. What about a classic like *Matilda?*"

"Yes, I love that one."

I head into the kitchen in search of wine. Opening the fridge, I pull out the bottle of sangria I bought earlier, knowing I would need something to take the edge off my nerves tonight. I unscrew the top and pull down four glasses from the top shelf.

"Anyone want wine?" I say, holding up the bottle. I'm not normally a big drinker, but Theo has me all over the place. I feel frazzled when he's around, and I need something to calm my nerves tonight with my friends meeting him, and my usual go-to of lavender oil's just not cutting it.

I really hope they like him. These women are so important to me, and I trust their opinions, so if they don't, I would say we're screwed before we have really begun.

"It's a Tuesday, Ivy!" Jenna scolds me.

I shrug. "Thanks for pointing that out, Captain Obvious! I need it tonight; my nerves are on end with you guys meeting Theo properly. So, I take it you don't want one?"

She comes to stand with me, wrapping her arm around me. "If you are, I guess I will. I could use it tonight as well."

"I'll help." While I pour the wine, Penny comes to help, never one to say no to a drink.

"Is everything alright, honey? You don't seem yourself," Penny says, topping up her glass. She's already sculled the first one.

"I don't know. It's all going well, but it's moving so quickly, and I wasn't ready for this, you know. I just didn't see myself settling down with anyone after Harmony's dad."

"I totally know what you mean. Why settle down with one man when you can try something new every night?" she says with an over-the-top smile.

"Not what I meant, but you do you, honey."

"Oh, I get bored easily. Life's short, you know. Got to enjoy it while you can. Maybe that's what's wrong with you, you're just bored with him already."

"I am not bored with him already. Have you seen him?"

"Yeah, I have! You're right. What is it then?"

"She's self-destructive," Jenna says, nudging me on the arm. "It's all too perfect, so she's trying to find faults so she won't be happy."

"That's not what it is," I say, swatting her away. "I'm just scared, that's all."

Fay tuts, pouring herself a glass of wine, having given up on me getting her one. "Ivy, it's okay to be scared, but don't push away a good man because you fear your past. Theo's not that man. You keep pushing him away, he'll eventually get the message and you'll end up like me. In your 60s, going home by yourself because you wasted too much time running from your past."

"You've got us," I told her. "Man, we're a sad bunch. Lucky we have each other."

The gate buzzer goes off, and a tingle of excitement runs through me knowing I'm going to see him again. I have a quick scull of my wine and head for the door to greet him. Opening the door, I'm surprised by him holding the hugest bunch of flowers I have ever seen. They're bright and colourful, a mix of sunflowers and pale pink roses with some other pretty flower I don't know the name of. I'm in shock. Harmony is at the door, pushing past me to get to her new buddy Jasper.

"Theo, these are beautiful. No one's ever given me flowers before." He pulls me in for a quick peck and the nervousness melts away. I'm consumed by his scent and his warmth.

Harmony has Jasper's hand and is dragging the poor boy inside with her. "Come on, we have a movie to watch," she says, pulling him with her.

"Hey, kiddo," says Theo, stopping her before she can get too far. "I have something for you as well." He pulls out a single pale pink rose.

Her eyes widen, and she hugs him. "Thank you, this is so special." She runs off in the kitchen's direction, calling out to Jenna for a vase.

"Hi, Jasper honey, go inside with Harmony. She has the bean bags set up and a movie for you guys to watch."

He looks to me a bit warily, then over to his dad.

"Go on, bud, I'll be inside in a second."

"You didn't have to do that," I whisper once Jasper has disappeared into the house.

"Yes, I did. You two are my girls, and I have to look after you."

"Thank you, I feel very special." I smile, wrapping my arm around his waist and burying my head into his chest. "You ready for Taco Tuesday?"

"I'm not sure, but I don't think I have a choice, do I?"

"Come on. They're not that scary. We won't gang up on you, I promise."

"I just need one thing first." He pulls me into him for a proper kiss, this time without the kid audience. This is all right, I know it is. When I'm with him, all the uncertainty disappears. He is my man, and I have to stop fighting it. We pull back from each other, my eyes still on his, lost in him, my heart hammering in my chest after just one small kiss. The effect he has on me is insane.

I keep my arm wrapped around him and usher him through to the lounge room where the others are. They are chatting away, but all eyes are on us as we enter the room. "Ladies, this is Theo. Theo, this is Fay, and you met Penny and Jenna already. I'm just going to find a vase for these."

"Ladies, I hope you don't mind me crashing your dinner."

"Not at all. It's so lovely to meet you after hearing so much about you," says Fay kindly.

I take it as my chance to leave and go into the kitchen to find something to put my flowers in. Since I have never been given flowers before, I have nothing to put them in. I look under the sink in my collection of recycled food jars, and there's a big coffee jar that will be perfect. I rinse it out and place the flowers on the breakfast bar. I can't help but smile to myself. He is something special. What am I so worried about? I just need to give him a chance and stop stressing before I screw up the whole thing.

Theo gets on with the girls like he has known them for years. Everyone—including the kids—like the nachos, and the rest of the night goes well, everyone chatting and getting to know each other.

Harmony has really taken to Theo and has been grilling him with questions, sitting on his lap since we finished dinner. It's so nice to see how well they get along. I don't think I ever realised how good it would be for her to have a male around.

Jasper is a quiet but lovely boy. He is so much like me, and after dinner I asked him to come and help me get dessert ready. He was excited to be involved and beamed as he handed out the desserts to everyone. He looks so much like Theo it's crazy. He even has the little dimple happening when he smiles.

I can see Fay really likes Theo, and what she said to me earlier has gotten to me. As much as I love her to bits, I don't want to end up like her—alone. I've got Harmony, but one day she will have a life of her own and won't need me anymore. Then what?

It's time, Ivy, time to get your life back.

CHAPTER NINETEEN

THEO

It's finally Saturday. After a long week of missing Ivy and really only getting to chat over the phone—except for our Taco Tuesday dinner with her friends—it has made for an extra-long week, and I can't wait to get my hands on her. Even if I might have to wait until the kids are asleep tonight until I can do what I really want to do with her.

We have a big day planned with the kids.

"Are you excited about having a sleepover at Harmony's house tonight?"

"Yes, I can't wait. She said we're going to watch a movie tonight and I can pick whatever one I want."

"That's exciting."

We pull up at Ivy's place, and Harmony is already standing out the front, the door wide open. She beams with excitement when she realises it's us, then runs back inside, I assume to get her mum. They come out shortly after and make their way down the driveway hand in hand. Ivy looks stunning as always in a short, burgundy-coloured floral dress and knee-high boots, her long hair braided to one side.

Harmony is wearing a dress as well, but hers is covered in unicorns and rainbows, and on her feet are glittery pink gum boots. Very cute.

"Morning, my lovely girls, you both look beautiful today."

Harmony throws her arms around my legs in a hug. "Morning, Theo! It has been so long since I saw you last, and I have so many stories to tell you."

"Okay, Harmy, you have all day," Ivy says. "Why don't you get into your seat so we can get going, and you can tell Theo all about your week once we're in the car."

I help Harmony into her car seat, and she immediately starts up a conversation with Jasper about something her cat did this morning. I close the door and turn to Ivy, pulling her into a kiss. Just a little one in front of our kids, but I wasn't waiting for that until tonight.

She hugs in close to my chest. "I've missed you this week," she whispers.

I brush a stray hair behind her ear and breathe her in—lavender, so calming. "I've missed you too, angel."

There's a little tap at the window, and we turn to see both kids peering out at us. "Guess we better get going."

"Unless you want to be in big trouble with Harmy, then yeah, we better." She hops in the car, and I make my way round to my side.

"Okay, gang, let's go have a fun day out."

"Where are you taking us?" asks Harmony.

"Just to a special place I'm sure both you and your mother will love."

It's just a short drive, and as we pull up to the farm, Harmony's excitement erupts in a squeal. Jasper feeds off her and squeals as well. Ivy smiles over to me; I know she loves this place. She told me how much she loves the sunflower fields here on one of our earlier dates, and I just knew this would be the ideal place to bring the kids. There is a park and plenty of space for them to run around while we walk the paddocks looking at the animals.

We all hop out of the car, and the kids take off straight for the park. I slip my hand into Ivy's as we walk over to catch up with them. "Thank you, this was the perfect idea for today," she says.

"The sunflowers are out as well. We can have a walk over that way if you like, then maybe get some lunch here. Their menu is insanely good."

"That sounds wonderful." She smiles back at me.

We watch the kids play in the park for a while, then we take a tour of the farm. The weather is perfect for an autumn day, warm, with the sun shining. The deciduous trees are losing their leaves, and the kids jump around, playing in them along the way as they run from paddock to paddock, checking out the animals.

There are piglets that Harmony begs her mother to take home with them, chickens, and Scottish highlander cows that are so friendly they come over to the fence. They're Jasper's favourite, and he thought he might try his luck and ask for us to take one of them home like Harmony had with the piglets. But the best part was Ivy's face when she saw the field of massive sunflowers. Her eyes were glossy, but she smiled the most beautiful smile.

We then had lunch, and the kids played in the park again, not wanting to leave at all. When it was time, we headed home to Ivy's to get dinner ready for the kids—homemade pizzas so everyone could choose their toppings.

The kids watch a movie while Ivy and I chop ingredients and smear tomato paste over pizza bases. I can't help but wonder if this is what it would be like every night if we're to one day merge our lives and live together. It's so much nicer to have someone to share all the mundane things with, like cooking.

When the pizzas are done, we make our way into the living room to check on the kids and discover they have made a blanket fort with sheets and pillows and are snuggled together in the middle of the cubby watching their movie.

"Time for dinner, guys," calls Ivy.

"Oh, can't we just stay here? It's all cosy," begs Harmony.

"Nope, not for dinner. You can come and eat at the table with us, then go back to your fort."

Harmony pauses the DVD and they both make their way to the table.

Everyone is quiet for a bit while we start eating our homemade pizzas.

After her first piece, Harmony looks my way, a little smirk on her face. "Theo, are you and my mum friends like me and Jasper, or are you boyfriend and girlfriend?"

"Um." I look over to Ivy then to Jasper, trying to work out what I'm supposed to say right now. Ivy just grins at me, waiting for my response. "We're boyfriend and girlfriend, Harmony, why do you ask?"

"I was just thinking about it. I thought you might be, because I saw you kiss my mum today. And I thought that would be good if you are, because I like Jasper and I want him to stay over all the time."

"Yeah," Jasper agrees.

"Well, we're glad that you like each other, but at the moment the sleepover will just be occasionally," I say, trying to defuse the situation before it gets out of hand, with their little imaginations running wild.

"Like every weekend?" she asks, her brow furrowed.

"Like some weekends," Ivy says, giving Harmony a look.

"Oh, okay." She bites into her second piece of pizza. She looks between us, then over to Jasper. Her head tilts to the side as she takes me in. She thinks hard about something, her lips pursed together. "Does it mean that you will get married and then we can all be together all the time? And what about when Dad comes back?"

Ivy coughs, nearly choking on a mouthful of pizza.

She said Harmony can be hard work with her questions and her inquisitive mind, but I had no idea she would be so clued up about relationships. I wasn't ready for these questions tonight, and by the look on her face, Ivy certainly wasn't either. She looks like she might hyperventilate at any time.

I glance over to Jasper. He looks happy enough, eagerly waiting for my reply. I feel like I should have talked to him about all of this before tonight. He seems okay with it all, but I think after all of this has been brought up, I need to make sure later tonight that he really is.

"That's enough questions, Harmy. How about you and Jasper work out what movie you're going to watch next, while the adults finish their dinner."

The kids jump up and run back to the lounge room. "You okay?" I ask. "You look a little rattled by her question."

"Aren't you?" she says, her eyes wide.

"A bit, but it's not a big deal. She's smart and curious. They were going to ask questions eventually."

"Well, I don't know about you, but I'm definitely not ready to answer any of her little questions."

She seems really irritated by it. I was thinking it was a little funny but now I'm worried. Why is she so averse to the thought of marrying me? "Because you don't see yourself getting married to me or because it's too early to discuss?"

"Ahh..." She looks lost for words. "Because it's too early for us to even contemplate and because I don't want to tell them anything that will get their hopes up when we don't even know where this is going. They already have it harder than other kids because they only have one parent. I don't want them to be excited about this, then for it to be taken away if things don't work out between us."

"I understand that. But if things kept going the way they are, you would want to get married one day, wouldn't you?" I know it's too early to discuss this with her, but now the question has been raised, I need to know how she feels.

"I don't know." She collects some plates from around the table and heads into the kitchen. I follow her, wanting to know what is going through her head. Is the thought of marrying me so bad that she is freaking at the prospect?

"Is that what you want, Theo? To marry me someday?" she says, staring into the kitchen sink.

I turn her around so we're facing one another. It's not something I had really thought about until now, but I know the answer. "Yes. I know we've only been dating a little while, but I know what I want, and that's to marry you someday."

Her face is serious, and I feel her pulling away from me. "Give me time to catch up with you, Theo. I'm really enjoying where everything is going, and I hope we can have a long future together, but I still have a lot to process before I can even think about marriage—even if it is with someone as wonderful and handsome as you."

Okay, she's not pushing me away, she just needs time. That's alright, I can deal with that. "I'm pretty wonderful."

"And handsome." She smiles.

I take her hands in mine. "Okay, let's just put this conversation on the backburner for a while. I wasn't even thinking about any of this until Harmony mentioned it, so let's just go back to having fun together."

"Sounds good to me." She reaches up, kissing me. For now, I'm just happy that she didn't freak out completely and ask me to leave.

After we cleaned up the kitchen together, we all sat in the cubby the kids had built and watched a movie together with buttery popcorn. It was what I always imagined having a family would be like. Jas and I have had movie nights before many times, but this was different, and it felt like this was what I had been missing out on while doing the whole parenting thing alone—having someone to share the little moments with.

This day with these three special people made me feel whole again.

Ivy

I yawn sleepily, and my eyes flutter open to see Theo propped up on his side watching me. It was so nice to have him in my bed last night. We're lucky the kids are so young and haven't questioned us having a sleepover, they just think it's all a bit of fun for them. "How long have you been staring at me?"

"Not very long. I was just thinking about how beautiful you are."

"I'm sure I look a total mess right now." I laugh, sitting up so I can wrangle my out-of-control hair into a messy bun on top of my head. It's so long now, down to my waist, and by the morning, it's always a knotty mess.

Luckily, after our almost fight over marriage last night, we recovered pretty easily and had an enjoyable night. It's not that I hate the idea of marrying Theo one day. It's just that I'm still technically married, and I really don't see how I'm going to get out of that easily. There is no way Dominic will ever agree to a divorce. He is possessive and jealous, and he would never let me out of our marriage. That is one of the reasons I haven't tried to ask for one. It would also make it easier for him to find me, so it's not worth the risk. And since I haven't told Theo about the minor matter of me still being married—or that I was *ever* married, actually—that conversation would never go down well.

"You look perfect." He reaches out for me, pulling me back down to him.

I squirm free. "I better go check on the kids. I can't believe they haven't been in to wake us up yet. Harmy is always up by now."

He lets me go reluctantly. "Well, when you're done, come back to bed then and cuddle me."

I jump up to check on the kids in Harmony's room. I push open the door just slightly to make sure I don't wake them if they are asleep still. Harmony is on the mattress on the floor, and Jasper is in her bed—they must have swapped—but they are both still fast asleep and so cute.

I make my way back into the room quietly. Theo is lying in the middle of the bed, hands behind his neck, chiselled abs on full display. I can't get over how ridiculous his body is. I'm sure my goofy smile gives away the effect he has on me.

"So, have we got a little more time together before they wake up?" he asks, eyebrow raised.

"I'm in shock, they're both still asleep. We must have worn them out last night with the late movie," I whisper, not wanting to wake them.

He pulls me back down to the bed. I know what he wants because I want it too. I would never take my hands off his body if I didn't have to. He rolls on top of me, pinning me below him and taking over my mouth with his kiss. Then travelling down my body, he places small kisses on my neck, lowering my pyjama camisole strap as he goes, exposing my breasts. My nipples harden instantly in the cool morning air. He takes each one in his mouth, sucking slowly, teasing me. My body responds instantly to him, hips rising off the bed, greedy for more of him, wanting him inside of me again. My hands wrap around his neck, pulling him down to me as he sucks harder. "Feels so good."

He continues farther down my body, hooking his thumbs in the silky bottoms of my pyjamas. Then we hear her.

"Mummy," Harmony cries out from her room.

I giggle, I can't help it. Her timing is terrible, but this is how it's going to be with both of us having kids.

"Right on cue. Our family is determined to cock-block me," he grumbles.

"Better luck next time, big boy," I say, slapping him on the chest and getting up to go collect Harmony.

"I guess I'm going to have to get used to this," he calls after me.

"Yes, you are. It's not too late to back out now if you want to."

"It most certainly is! I'm all in. There is no backing out now, and if that means I have to be patient, I will learn."

"If you're a good boy, I will reward you for your patience with special Sunday pancakes." I smile at him cheekily. It's just as hard for me, but this is being a parent. They will always come first.

I push open the door to Harmony's room to find the kids in bed together, Harmony showing Jasper one of her most loved storybooks. It's the cutest thing I have seen since they built the cubby together last night. I can't believe how well they are getting on with each other. I know it probably won't always be like this, but it's nice while it is.

"Who wants pancakes for breakfast?" I ask.

Their little faces rise to me and beam with excitement.

"I do!" Harmony calls out.

"Me too," says Jasper.

"Well, why don't you two get yourselves dressed for the day, and I will get started on the pancakes."

I head downstairs, filled with excitement for today. It's so nice to have the boys here with us, a brief glimpse into what it would be like to have a normal family—except we're not normal.

But I'm not going to dwell on that today. I'm going to make the most of our time all here together. I get to work making the breakfast, mixing the ingredients together, then pouring the batter in a frying pan. While the first batch cooks, I get started chopping up the berries and making a fruit salad to go on top along with the maple syrup. It's the way we have it every Sunday.

I hear the kids running down the hall and turn to see Theo in the doorway, freshly showered, hair still wet, just faded blue jeans with a rip in the knee on, his shirt in his hand. My thoughts are way too inappropriate for a family breakfast. By the look in his eyes, so are his.

"You going to put that thing on? Cause it's very distracting having you in my kitchen all wet and sexy from your shower."

"That's the idea," he says, closing the gap between us, kissing me slowly, tugging on my bottom lip with his teeth as he pulls away.

I groan, my hands resting on his six-pack. He's just too good. I want him to do so many bad things to me right here, right now—but no. "Shirt on now or I'm going to ruin your breakfast."

"I don't care about breakfast. I want to go back to bed with you."

"Well, they care," I say, pointing to the two little people who have just entered the room. "And since you don't care, they can have the first batch," I say, sticking out my tongue.

"Yeah," they cheer together as they take their seats at the breakfast bar.

I serve the first two pancakes to them with the berries and maple syrup.

Jasper's eyes look like they're going to pop out of his head. "My dad doesn't know how to make pancakes like this."

"Hey, I make you pancakes," Theo protests.

"Yeah, but you use that instant mix stuff and there are no berries and syrup," he says, licking his lips.

"He's got me there. These do look extra special."

"And you know what the best part is?" asks Harmony.

"What?" both Jasper and Theo say.

"The secret ingredient." She beams.

"What's the secret ingredient?" asks Jasper, leaning into Harmony.

Harmony puts her hand up to his ear to whisper but says it loud enough for us all to hear. "It's love, just a sprinkle."

Jasper smiles, and he gets the little dimples in his cheeks just like his dad. Looks like he likes the sound of that.

Theo worms his arms around me as I cook. "I knew I was missing something in mine. Now that I know, I will have to add it in. How much do you add, Ivy?"

"Just a pinch should be enough," I say, flipping the next batch and playing along. Kids at this age are the best, still naïve enough to believe in the power of magic.

I finish cooking our breakfast, and we sit next to each other at the breakfast bar to eat. "We're having a party for Drew next Saturday night. I want you to come. Maybe you could see if Jenna and Penny what to come as well?" asks Theo.

"That sounds nice. I'm sure Penny will be more than happy to accept the invitation, and Jenna too, if I tell her it's for Drew."

"You can find a sitter for Harmony?"

"I'll talk to Fay, I'm sure I can work something out."

"That's good. I would really like you to be there."

Around lunch time we picked up Cooper to take with us to the park, hoping to give Elly a break from the craziness, but she came along. I really like her. She's just lovely and keeps Theo grounded with her smart-arse comments when he gets a big head. The banter between the two of them is funny to watch. We then joined the rest of the family for Sunday-night dinner.

It's been a wonderful weekend, one of the best I can remember, and I'm feeling very lucky and blessed to have found Theo and to have been welcomed into such a warm, loving family.

CHAPTER TWENTY

THEO

I RUN MY TOWEL THROUGH MY DRIPPING HAIR, THEN dry off my body. I'm just about to hang the towel back up when the doorbell rings. *Who's that?* It's ages before I told them all to arrive.

I couldn't drop off Jasper to his Nannie's—Fiona's mum's place—until midday, and she lives an hour away, so I have been running behind since. Now and then she likes to have him for the night. She is a lovely woman and Jasper adores her, so any chance she gets to have him she jumps at.

We're having a bit of a party to celebrate Drew being back in the World Surfing League. He leaves for his first competition in Maui, Hawaii next week. It's probably Mum and Dad at the door, they always arrive early. I grab my towel and wrap it around my waist, and head downstairs to the front door.

Holding my towel to stop it from falling, I open the door, my frustration fading as soon as I see her.

"Sorry, I came early to help you set up. Hope that's okay?" Ivy's standing there gripping on to her overnight bag, looking a little anxious. Fay has agreed to have Harmony for the night so Ivy can stay, but I'm not sure she is totally comfortable staying here. So, I'm just going to make sure she is by the end of the night, because for once, we're both kid-free, and I intend to make the most of it. Starting right now.

"I'm already all set up, but I have something you can help me with." She looks sexy as fuck wearing a red strappy wraparound dress that runs to the ground, with an oversized belt at her waist showing off her curves and a slit up the front, going almost all the way up her leg. It's the one I bought her at the markets a few weeks back, and she wears it well. I'm hard already. I won't make it through this party with her in that.

"Do you need me to lay your clothes out for you so you can get dressed? Cause that towel just won't do. You're going to scare all your guests off." She laughs, walking through the front door.

"You're going to pay for that little comment, missy." I pull her in for a kiss. "I like this," I say, sliding my hand through the slit in her dress and grabbing her arse, bringing her closer into my body so she can feel me. "See what you do to me?" I say, pressing my hard cock into her as we kiss.

I push the door closed, our lips still locked, and smack her on the arse. "Upstairs, now."

"What, don't we have to do stuff for the party?"

"No, it's all done, but I've got something I need taken care of upstairs." I smack her on the arse again. "Now get going quick or we'll run out of time, and I won't last the party like this."

I chase her up the stairs, and she squeals as I pick her up and throw her on the bed. I stand back, dropping my towel to the floor, trying to decide where I want to start. She looks fucking edible, so why not start there? My hands crawl slowly up her legs to where her panties are, and she lifts her hips, allowing me to hook my thumbs in the sides of her panties, dragging them down her legs. I push the excess fabric of her dress up around her waist and lift her legs over my shoulders, giving me easy access to her pussy. Lowering my head towards her, I inhale her scent, and she smells divine. I lick through her wet folds, tasting her. "You taste so fucking good, I could eat your pussy all day."

She rises on to her elbows. "We don't have all day, people will be here soon."

"I don't care about them, they can wait. I have been imagining how good you'll taste all week, and now I have you here like this, I intend to enjoy myself."

I place the palm of my hand on her tummy, pushing her back down to the bed. Burying my head back in her pussy, I lick circles around her clit then suck hard. She squirms underneath me, but I hold her in place with my other hand, still pressing her into the mattress, holding her firm so she can't move too much. Her hands tug at my hair.

I push in one finger, then two, as she moves her hips off the bed, rocking gently into the thrusts of my fingers. I continue to devour her, enjoying the sound of her soft moans as her climax builds, and I fuck her harder with my fingers, tipping her over the edge. Her body contracts around my fingers as she cries out. Her body trembles as she comes down from her orgasm, and I climb up the bed next to her, pulling her into me so I can hold her.

Her breathing is ragged. "Theo, that was..."

"Earth-shattering," I joke.

She giggles at me. "Something like that."

"I haven't finished with you yet."

I roll over on top of her, reaching her hands over her head to hold her in place with one hand. I immediately feel the shift in her body language as she stiffens under me. "What's wrong, did I hurt you?"

"No, I need my hands free." Her voice is panicked. I release my grip on her wrists at once.

I feel like an absolute arsehole. "I'm so sorry. Are you okay? We can stop."

She relaxes again, letting out a breath. "No, I'm good, just don't like being restrained. It makes me panic. Don't stop." She moves her hips again, rolling them under me.

"Are you sure?"

"Yes, come on, fuck me."

With that plea, I wrap my hands around her waist and flip her on top of me, so she's sitting, legs straddling me. Giving her all the power. I don't ever want to see that look of panic in her face again. This way she can feel comfortable to do what she wants.

She reaches down and kisses my lips, and I pull her into me, wrapping my hands through her hair as she crawls on top of me. I feel so close to her like this, not just physically but emotionally too.

Her body close to mine, I can feel the brush of her hardened nipples on my chest while she moves, and I continue to kiss her, our tongues fighting in our hurried desperation to get enough of each other. Her hips rock back and forth, moving a little quicker. I slide my hands from her hair down her back to settle on her arse, pulling her into me faster, not able to get enough. I can feel the need to orgasm building. I don't want this to be over, but what she is doing with that roll of her hips, it's just too good.

"Fuck, Theo, I'm going to..." I can feel her body pulsate around my cock as I lose control of myself, filling her with my seed.

She collapses on my chest, our sweaty bodies still

connected. I can feel her heart hammering in her chest. This is where I always want to be, with her this close to me. I never want to let her go. I run my hand through her long hair. "That was..."

"Something else," she finishes my sentence.

"Yes."

The doorbell rings, and we both jump up in panic. I check my clock on the nightstand, and whoever it is has arrived early. I throw on my underwear and pull up my pants, grabbing my shirt as I run for the door. "I'll go let whoever it is in. Don't rush, come down when you're ready." I throw my shirt on as I head for the stairs.

I get to the bottom of the stairs, and sure enough, I can see my mum looking through the glass door. I open it. "You're early," I snap.

"Lovely to see you too, Son." She kisses me on the cheek. Dad's hands are full, so I push the door open wider to let him through. "We came to help. I have a car full of food. You can help us unpack."

"Where do you want these?" asks Dad.

"Anywhere in the kitchen is fine, Dad. Sorry, Mum, thank you for coming early to help."

"That's better. Is that Ivy's car in the driveway? Is she here already?"

"Yes, she'll be down in a minute, Mum."

I help them unload the food trays from the car.

"I hope you're treating her well. She's a keeper, Son. Such a warm heart and radiant personality. Have the two of you talked about the future?"

Oh God, not this already. I know what my mum is like, but I was expecting her to at least give us a few months before there was talk of settling down. "Not really, Mum, it's only early days. I don't want to scare her with thoughts of having to spend her future with me." Truth is, I have been thinking about the future with her. Since the day I met her, it's all I can think about. But I don't need to talk to my parents about it, and I really don't want Mum bringing it up with Ivy.

"I was just thinking how lovely it would be if you got married and the two of you could move in here with Harmony. You would make such a lovely father to that little girl, and I'm sure Ivy would be just the perfect mother to Jasper. What a family you would be."

"Mum," I warn.

"What?" She smiles, her eyes bright with excitement. You can see the cogs of her brain ticking, she is planning the bloody wedding already.

"Don't go getting ahead of yourself. Let's just see how things pan out, and don't go saying anything to Ivy either." That's the last thing we need when things are finally going so well.

"It's just that you're getting older, Theo, and after what happened, it's nice to see you so happy with someone. But if you want to have a family of your own, you need to settle down before you're too old to do it. You don't want to miss out like Uncle Mitch. That's what happened to him. Too much of a ladies' man when he was young, then ended up all alone, missing the opportunity for a family."

"I have a family of my own already. And I'm pretty sure that's the way Uncle Mitch likes it, Mum. He's still a ladies' man. That dude would never settle down, and I don't think he feels like he missed out on anything. Besides, the point is, I want to settle down with her. I just don't quite know what she wants or what her situation is."

"What do you mean by that?" She gives me the side-eye,

and I know I need to stop talking, and fast, before she starts asking more questions.

"Nothing. We just don't know each other that well yet. That's all." We walk back into the kitchen with the last load from the car, and Ivy is already in there talking to my dad. She's still flushed from what we just did, her skin glowing. She's so beautiful; not just on the outside but the inside too. She has a gentle soul that wants to help wherever she goes. Of course I want this woman in my future, I would be stupid not to, but I'm just not sure where she stands on all of that, and I don't want to scare her.

But now I feel like I have Mum's voice in my head. Great.

After Ivy helps Dad organise the trays of food in the fridge, we all grab a drink and head out onto the back deck. The rest of the guests filter in. Drew is here with a couple of his school friends, as well as Fraser, Elly, Blake, and Indie. They've hired a sitter for the night so they can enjoy themselves without the kids. Ivy's friends Penny and Jenna are here as well, as are the two guys from work I'm closest to, Sean and Talon.

The once-quiet house is abuzz with excitement. Delicious finger food being served on trays, cocktails from the makeshift bar Dad set up on the deck, and everyone seems to be having fun.

Ivy stays by my side for most of the night. We can't keep our hands off each other. I actually just wish everyone else would go home so I could have her to myself.

She seems relaxed tonight. It could be the number of strong cocktails she has consumed throughout the evening, but I would like to think it's because of me. She's finally more comfortable around me and my family. We stand on the balcony, looking out over the pool below. Her arm is wrapped around my waist and mine around her, pulling her into me tightly as we look out over the party below.

"Have you seen Jenna?" she asks.

"No. I haven't seen Drew for a while either. You don't think they might be together?"

"I'm positive they are." She smirks. "She keeps saying nothing is going on with them, but I can see right through her. Just friends, my arse." She giggles.

There's a loud commotion over near the pool, and we both go to the other end of the balcony to see what it's all about. Penny has fallen or jumped into the pool fully clothed and is splashing about.

"Oh my God, I'm not going in there after her," laughs Ivy.

"Don't think you'll have to. Looks like Talon's going to be the one to help her." He has stripped off his shirt and jeans and dived in after her. The two of them continue to swim about. I don't think poor Talon has any idea what he's getting into with that one.

"I'm just going to the bathroom, back in a sec." She takes off toward the bathroom, and I watch her. I can't help but feel like the luckiest man here.

I top up my drink and take a seat in the hammock.

A few minutes later, Ivy comes back from the bathroom looking strange, a little pale and kind of pissed off. She was only gone five minutes max. What could have possibly happened in that time?

"Is everything okay?"

"How well do you know Sean?" she snaps. "I mean, I know the two of you are friends from work, but how close are you?"

"Why?" What has the stupid fucker done. He's not the

smartest, and I swear if he hit on Ivy there will be hell to pay.

"He stopped me in the hall just now and was asking some weird questions about my past. Did you put him up to it?"

I don't know what she's talking about. Why would Sean be asking about her past? I've barely said two words to him about her.

"If I want to know something about you, I'll ask myself. I wouldn't get a mate from work to do it. What kind of questions was he asking?"

"He wanted to know where I was from, like where I grew up. He was asking about Harmony's dad and where he was. Why would he be asking if not fishing for information for you? Why would he care about my past?" Her eyes are glassy, she's really upset. I don't know what that was all about.

I take her hand and try to comfort her. "I don't know, but I promise you it wasn't for me. I'll have a chat with him on Monday, but he's drunk, he was probably just trying to get to know you. The dude has no personality and wouldn't know how to talk with a chick at all. I'm sure that's all this is. Trust me, you have nothing to worry about with him. I have worked with him for years. He just has no idea how to communicate."

She softens, believing me, and I'm glad because I really have no idea what that was all about. I wrap my arm around her and lead her over to the hammock, pulling her in tightly and kissing her forehead. I want her to know how safe she is with me. I will deal with Sean on Monday. He is such a drunk idiot tonight. I'm sure that's all it was, but still, I'm going to make it clear he needs to stay away from her. She snuggles into me, relaxing again, and that's where we stay for the rest of the party, cuddled up with each other.

Ivy

Sunday morning, we lie tangled in his lush cotton sheets, our bodies still wrapped around each other. By the looks of how much daylight is filtering in, we must have slept in. It would have to be after ten, but I'm too comfy to look.

Theo is still asleep. He's even more handsome when he's asleep, if that's even possible. I want to run my hand over his stubbly jaw, but I won't. I don't want to wake him, as we had such a late night. I still can't believe someone like him wants to share a bed with me. It blows my mind. I have no idea what he must see in me.

My thoughts keep going back to last night and the weird conversation I had with Theo's work friend, Sean. I didn't tell Theo the entire story because I didn't know what to say, but he was definitely threatening me with his line of questioning.

I could feel his eyes on me for most of the night, then he waited until I was alone in the hallway on my way back from the bathroom. He stood too close and wouldn't let me pass. He had the hairs on the back of my neck standing up. It wasn't a comfortable conversation. My entire body knew something wasn't right with him.

He asked me why I was mucking around with Theo if I was already married. How did he even know that? I haven't even told Theo that yet. I denied it. It's none of Sean's business anyway. That made him mad, and his words are still ringing in my ears: *"You're a liar as well as an adulterer."*

He wouldn't tell me what he knows, but he knows more about me than anyone else around here. I guess he could have looked into my past through the police system or something, and he was just looking out for his mate? Seems like a really odd way to do it, though.

Theo thinks he's harmless, he was just drunk—and Sean had definitely been drinking. His words were a little slurred, but I got the impression there was more to it than just a drunk mate looking out for his friend. His eyes bored into me like he could read my mind. The memory of the way he looked at me still turns my stomach this morning. I'm sure I'm probably overreacting—I had been drinking myself, so maybe I'm remembering it differently to how it happened because I'm a bit paranoid. I'm sure that's all it is.

Theo stirs, his lips curling into a smile when he opens his eyes to see me staring at him. Dimples showing, his hair is messy, but he is hot as sin. How can he look this good first thing in the morning after a party? I'm positive I look a total fright.

He pulls me towards him, so he is cuddling my back. "Well, I think that was a successful night. Drew had a good time."

"It was. Are you going to miss him?"

He runs his hands down my body, kissing my neck as we talk. "Of course, but he has been going away like this since he finished school, so I'm used to it. That's why we make the most of it when he is home."

"I think someone else is going to miss him too. Did you notice the two of them disappeared for a sizeable chunk of the night?"

"I was too busy focusing on you to notice what anyone

else was doing. But I think you're right, there is more going on there than either of them will admit."

I roll around in his arms so I'm facing him. "I'm going to have questions for that girl when I see her later this week."

He places a kiss on my lips. "It's nice having you here in my home, I like you in my bed." He kisses me again, and I soften into him.

"It's been a nice weekend," I whisper into his lips.

He moves back a little so he's looking at me, his face serious. "I want you here all the time, you and Harmony with me and Jasper." He pauses, searching my eyes for a reaction. Is he asking what I think he is? I half expect him to laugh and say just joking but he is deadly serious. "I have given this a lot of thought, and I think the two of you should move in with us."

My heart kicks up a beat. Oh no, no, no, he has no idea what he's saying. We have been dating for such a short amount of time. I pull out of his grip. "Are you serious?" I splutter.

"Yes, why not?"

I sit up, pulling my legs up to my chest. "Because we hardly know each other. Besides, I like my place, I'm comfortable there, and I don't want to uproot Harmy before I really know what's going on with us." And what I can't say out loud is that sometime in the next six months, Dom will be released, and then I need to know I have the security of my home, with all its high-tech security systems, just in case he works out where we are. My heart is pounding now, and I'm starting to freak out. I can feel the beginning of a panic attack, and I try to concentrate on my breathing to calm myself down.

He rolls away, sitting on the opposite side of the bed to me, his back turned. "You're just making excuses. You know we know each other well enough. I'm crazy about you, Ivy. I want to be with you every day, not just try to catch you when we have a free moment from our kids. I want to come home to you, have you here in my bed every night. This feels right to me."

I want to cry, because this is all too much for me. "Theo, I'm crazy about you too, but... but I'm not ready for this type of commitment. I need to go slow with this till I get my bearings."

"I just don't get it. I know you feel the same way as me, I can see it, but you continue to keep me at arm's length. I want to give you everything. I want you to be a part of my world and me yours. What are you waiting for? Neither one of us are getting any younger. I know what I want, and it's my girls at my house with me."

"Don't go getting all possessive of me, Theo. You don't even know what you're talking about. I want to have a life with you. I want everything you want, but I just need more time to get used to all this. Plus, I know my house is safe. I feel protected there with all the security."

He turns back to look at me. He is hurt, and I feel terrible, but he has to see this from my perspective. "You would have me here, I can be your security. What more do you need?"

I don't know how to explain it to him without telling him everything, and I'm just not ready for that. "You can't be here all the time, Theo, and I need to be able to look after myself."

"You act like you're constantly under threat. What could you possibly need protecting from that warrants the type of security you have in that house?" His tone is filled with anger.

I turn away from him. "You wouldn't understand," I

whisper, trying not to cry. I don't want him to be annoyed with me, we were having a nice time. Why can't we just keep it at that?

He comes around the bed and reaches for my hands. "Try me. Talk to me, I want to understand."

"I didn't have a very good past. There are things you don't know."

He cups my face in his hands, tilting my chin up so I have to make eye contact with him. He's so wonderful and it makes me feel even worse. "Well, tell me, beautiful. I want to be able to understand your demons so I can help you. I'm here for you, but I can't help you if you don't open up and talk to me about it."

I want to open up and tell him all of it. I want to open my entire world up to him like he has me, but I can't. I don't want him to see me as some helpless victim. The pity in his eyes would kill me. I can't do it. "I... I'm sorry, Theo, I can't talk about it. It's in the past and I don't want to talk about it with you."

He drops my hands and takes a step back. He's annoyed, and he has every right to be, I get it. "But it's not in the past if it's affecting your future with me. You're still struggling with it now. Don't think I don't notice you looking over your shoulder when we're out around town and how jumpy you are when I touch you. I know it's not me because you warm up to me, but something has you shit-scared, and it's time you tell me what it is."

He watches me, waiting for me to say something, but I can't. I'm only going to disappoint him. I can't tell him any of it. "I can't help you if you don't talk to me. Let me help you with whatever scares you so much. Is it to do with Harmony's dad?"

I look back at him. Blinking quickly, I can feel the tears

welling in my eyes. This is too much, I need to leave, I need to go home. I roll from the bed, pulling the loose, tangled sheet with me to cover up my body; I don't want to be naked around him right now, I feel too exposed.

He follows me, grasping me by the shoulder. "Where are you going?"

"I need to get home to Harmony. Fay will wonder where I am."

"No, she won't, she knew you wouldn't be home till midday. You're running from me again. Stop running, Ivy." His tone is serious, and it scares me that I might push him too far and he'll just give up on me. My heart is racing, and I don't know what to do. The flight or fight is kicking in, and I want to run but I don't want to lose him.

"I'm not. I just can't have this conversation with you, and you keep pushing me. I can't open up to you, Theo, you won't like what you see if I do."

He looks away from me. I can see how tense his body is, and I know it must be frustrating for him. I know how messed up I am. He lets out an audible sigh and his gaze comes back to me, his face softening. "I'm sorry for pushing you, angel. I won't push anymore. Just come back to bed and we can forget about the whole thing. I know I'm moving too fast, I just really care about you. I'm excited to move forward with our lives—but if you're not there, then that's okay. I can wait for you."

He rubs his hands up and down my arms, and I don't know what to say to him. Tears roll down my face. This man is pure perfection, offering me everything I would want in a perfect world. But this isn't a perfect world—this is a fucked-up world, and I'm damaged goods too broken for him. I have no idea why he even bothers with me.

"Come on, just come back to bed with me." He takes my

hand and leads me back to his bed. We lie down, and he wraps his arms around me, pulling me into his chest, and I sob. I can't even tell him why, but he holds me all the same as my tears fall on his bare chest.

We lie like this for a long time, neither of us wanting to move or deal with what just happened between us. I don't even know how to deal with it. I'm embarrassed that I broke down in front of him, sad I couldn't open up to him and give him what he wanted, but I'm just not there yet. Honestly, I don't know if I ever will be.

CHAPTER TWENTY-ONE

IVY

When I finally got home, it was nearly midday. Fay had Harmony sitting at the kitchen bench with a sandwich and chocolate milk in front of her. They both seemed to be happy. The room was yet again littered with art they had made together.

Harmony came running over immediately and threw her little arms around me, hugging me as if her life depended on it. I clung to her just the same. It had only been one night, but I missed her. I was still clinging on when she squirmed out of my hold, running off up the hallway after Tiger. It's nice to know I'm missed by her, even if the feeling is only fleeting.

Fay filled me in on their fun night together, with pizzas, a movie, and popcorn. I felt bad I had little in me to chat with her after she had done me a favour and sat Harmony for me for nearly 24 hours. But I was exhausted, and I think she could tell, wrapping up our conversation quickly and heading home.

Not long after she left, I got out the fluffy blanket, and Harmony and I have spent the rest of the afternoon vegging on the couch. I let her pick whatever movie she wanted, so it's been a lot of *Barbie and the Dream House*, but I don't mind. I'm too lost in my own thoughts to care what we watch.

I feel so confused about everything. I know it's getting to the point where I need to tell Theo about my past. He wants to move forward, and I have a lot of things stopping me from doing that. I'm still married, for one. How do I tell him that? *Oh, you know how you keep asking about Harmony's dad? Well, actually, I'm still married to him,* and *yeah, he's in prison where I put him after he beat me up when I was pregnant.* Just watch how fast Theo runs for the door then!

The beautiful man I have come to have actual feelings for would be gone in a flash. I'm sure I would never hear from him again. And the generous offer for us to move in with him would be a distant memory of a bullet he dodged with someone way too damaged to be loved by him. He's got his own issues from his past; the last thing he needs is me and mine.

I can't see how this all ends well, it's just not possible. The longer I wait to tell him, the more he will resent me for keeping it from him, but it gives me time to enjoy being with him and dream about how differently things could have been in a different lifetime with different circumstances—and as selfish as it is, I'm going to hang onto that for as long as I can.

Theo

. . .

I know I shouldn't be doing this, but I want to know what I'm dealing with. I have this sinking feeling that all my happiness will be ripped away at any moment. Her reaction to me asking her to move in with us was anything but what I expected. She is haunted by something in her past, and it's more than just having some guy break her heart. She's damaged. I can see the pain in her eyes. The fear.

Talon has been my partner for five years and my best mate. He's smart and reliable, and he's always got my back, which in this job is what you need. I probably shouldn't ask him since it's technically not police business, but if you want to track someone down that doesn't want to be found, Talon's your man. He's got the knack for it.

We work two feet apart sharing an office, so he knows this shit is driving me crazy, and I'm sure he'll help me.

"Hey, man, can you give me a hand with something?"

He looks up from his desk with a worried look. "Yeah, what's up?"

"Well, it's not a police matter, but you know Ivy, the girl I'm seeing?"

"Yeah... this already sounds like a bad idea, man."

"It probably is, but I have to know more about her. Her past is a mystery, and she won't talk about it. What I suspect so far is she changed her identity five years ago when she moved here, about the same time her daughter was born and her husband went to prison."

I go to his desk, standing over him as he starts to open new tabs. "Did you look at social media?" When I give him a look, he corrects himself. "Okay, of course you've checked social media."

"She has no online presence at all. From what I can see, her name didn't exist until five years ago. Come on, man, I know you're good at this stuff. Can you track down her past?"

"Do you know where she grew up?"

"She said she grew up on her parents' property in Dorrigo. Oh, and her parents were killed in a car accident one night when she was 17."

"Both of them, that's awful."

"Yeah, she's an only child as well, so she doesn't have any other family around."

"Okay, so let's start with police reports on car accidents in Dorrigo for that year." He jumps on my computer and starts typing, searching for around that time and place. He scans through article after article, not finding anything. I stand over his shoulder, watching him run searches, knowing this is a bad idea but unable to stop myself either.

Then when we are about to give up and look elsewhere, he spots it, bringing up an article.

"Bingo. Read this, man, it's got to be them." He points to the screen and a newspaper article he's found.

A man in his late 40s is assisting police after the semi-trailer he was driving killed two in the early hours of the morning.

Emergency crews were called to Whisky Creek Road in Dorrigo after a head-on collision just after one am.

Police were told the black SUV was hit head-on by a semi-trailer.

Both occupants of the vehicle were killed on impact, and a crime scene has been established at the location.

He points to another article farther down the page. "There's another one here the following week. This must be them."

> Dorrigo community pays tribute to local entrepreneur Ray Green and his wife Brittany after their tragic head-on collision with a semi-trailer in the early hours of Sunday morning. Ray and Brittany were upstanding citizens in our community and will be sadly missed. They leave behind their only daughter, Lauren (17).

The second article is accompanied by a picture of the car accident and a family photo of the three of them, the teenage girl in between her parents. She's so much younger, sweet and innocent, but I know that face.

"That's her." It's definitely her. It's so awful. I still can't believe she had to go through that at such a young age. When she told me about it at the café that day, my heart ached for her loss, but seeing the article and the photo of the three of them, it's devastating.

"Well, we know her name now. Let's look it up on the system." He types Lauren Green into the system, and it brings up a report about the car accident and another report under a Lauren Sanders.

"Why would her name be different...? She's married," I say almost to myself. I can't believe she's married. It explains a lot, though, why she freaked out so much when Harmony brought up us getting married one day. I knew there had to be an ex because of her daughter, but I had originally hoped it was a one-night stand gone wrong or something. I would have hoped if she was married, she would have told me about it by now, but there has been no mention of a husband. I'm shut down every time I try to ask about Harmony's dad. All I knew was he was in prison, and she was happy about it.

"I'd say she was married, not sure if she still is. According to this, she charged her husband, Dominic Sanders, with domestic violence. The police report says he beat the shit out of her while she was pregnant. That's why he's in prison."

I run my hands through my hair. I don't want to believe it. What the actual fuck! What kind of animal does that to his pregnant wife? No wonder she's so frightened. How could you trust someone you haven't known for long, when your husband puts you in hospital with his own fists while you're carrying his child.

This guy is never getting near her or Harmony again. I will make damn sure of that.

"Fuck," I mutter.

"Yeah, fuck! His police profile says he's due to be released next year, but it might be earlier for good behaviour. That's all I can find, man, I'm sorry."

"Thanks, I think I've seen enough." I walk back to my desk and collapse into my chair. I feel sick. These are the lowlifes we deal with every day in this job, but to know what she must have been through breaks my heart. It also explains a lot as to why she acts the way she does. She might have lived with him for years like this before she could press charges.

I have seen so many cases like this. It's very unlikely this was the first time he beat her up. No wonder she's jumpy and constantly worried about her safety. How could you ever feel safe when the threat was living under the same roof as you?

I turn to Talon. "Hey, if you find anything else on the fucker, let me know. I'm going out for a bit. I need to clear my head." He's still looking through reports and nods in recognition of what I've said.

CHAPTER TWENTY-TWO

IVY

I'M SITTING IN MY CAR WAITING TO PICK HARMONY UP from school. I should have walked, we're just around the corner, but I just didn't feel like it today. I'm so tired because I haven't slept properly since Sunday after having that argument with Theo.

I check the time. She should be here soon, I'd better walk up to the school. I jump out of the car and stroll slowly to the front gate. As I'm walking, I get that creepy feeling again, like someone's watching me. I look behind me, but there's no one there. I must be imagining it. A text pings on my phone, and I stop to check it.

Theo: Hope you're having a good day, angel, can't wait to see you tonight x

I send a quick message back and put my phone back in my bag to continue the walk up to school, but I run straight into someone. "I'm so sorry," I say, rubbing my head.

"You should be more careful, Ivy."

It's Sean, who works with Theo, and I get that uneasy feeling again. "Oh, hi. Sorry, Sean, I wasn't looking. Are you okay?"

"I'm fine. I'd be more worried about yourself, sunshine," he says smugly.

"Oh, I'm fine, thanks. Sorry again." I try to brush it off and get going before I have to talk to him anymore. I know Theo says he's harmless, but I don't like him at all.

He stands in my path, blocking me. "Not so fast. I'm talking about you and Theo. I'd be more worried about what's going on there."

This guy is really pissing me off. Who does he think he is? "I'm not sure what you're talking about or how it's any of your business."

"Let's just say I have worked out who you are, *Lauren.*" He raises an eyebrow and glares at me.

The hairs stand on the back of my neck at the mention of my actual name, the one I was born with. No one has called me that for a long time. "I'm sorry, what did you say?"

He smiles down at me. "You heard me, Lauren. I'm just here to give you a message. Stay away from Theo. This thing you have with him will not end well for either of you, and I don't want to see him get hurt again."

My mind is racing a million miles a minute. What the fuck does he know? How could he have connected the dots? I've been so careful, but I guess they have ways to access information if they want to. I know they're mates, but why would he care so much about Theo's feelings?

He raises a brow. "Cat got your tongue? Just listen then. Stay away from him or I'm going to fill him in on your past. Do you really think a top bloke like Theo wants someone else's damaged goods? Cause there is no way he does."

I blink back at him, tears dangerously close to the surface. I'm shocked by his insult, the reality of his words hitting way too close to home. I know that's the truth, I *am* too damaged for him, but that doesn't mean hearing it out loud doesn't sting like a fucking bitch.

"Sorry, love, didn't mean to upset you. I'm just looking out for my mate, and you have that little girl of yours to worry about. Maybe just concentrate on keeping her safe and leave Theo alone."

"I... I have to go." I step around him, and he lets me. I knew this guy gave me the creeps. A tear escapes down my cheek, and I swipe it away. I'm shaking from the strange confrontation. I just want to grab Harmony and get the hell out of here.

I look over my shoulder as he crosses the street, and I see the car he gets into. I recognise it—it's the same black SUV I saw the other day following me. What the fuck is going on? It could just be a coincidence, but my gut tells me it's not. This guy has given me the creeps since the day I met him. And now he is threatening me to stay away from Theo. What the hell?

I get to the gate and Elly is there, waving at me to come over. Great, Theo's sister is the last one I want to see right now. Most afternoons we stand by the gate and chat until the kids come out, but today I just want to hide. I offer a small wave back, and she makes her way over to me.

"Ivy." She takes one look at me. "What's wrong?"

"Oh, nothing, I'm fine, just got something in my eye."

"Yeah, right, how stupid do you think I am? What's my brother done? I knew he would mess this up."

"No, no, he hasn't done anything, really. He's perfect. I'm fine." I wish I could ask her about Sean, see if she knows anything, but I'm too scared to now. I don't want to get someone else involved, and I shouldn't have got involved with Theo in the first place, even though it hurts to hear. What Sean said is true, I'm too damaged, and why would

Theo want me once he knows who I am and what I've been through?

Elly looks at me like she doesn't believe me. "Really, I'm fine," I say. The bell rings, and the kids come running out, chatting loudly, running and screaming towards the group of parents who have gathered. Elly has both of the boys and has to take off up the street after them. "See you tomorrow," she calls.

"See you then." I'm still waiting on Harmony. Where is she? I have no idea why it takes her so much longer than anyone else to get out of school at the end of the day. She makes her way out of the gate, in her own little dream world, as usual. I paint on my best fake smile for her. I don't want her to know how upset I am. She smiles back and runs to me, cuddling in. I take her heavy backpack. "Did you have a good day?" I ask.

"Yes, we had sport, and it was so much fun."

We chat as we walk back to the car. As I get closer, I notice Sean's car is still parked where it was. He's sitting in the driver's seat on the phone with someone. He watches me, the look on his face scaring the shit out of me, his lips turning up to one side into a smug smile. I'm completely freaked out.

I know what I need to do. Even though it's what I have been thinking for a while anyway, now I know for sure. Theo is too good for me, and I will not let him get caught up in my bad decisions from the past.

Theo

. . .

Ivy has been acting strangely all week. When I talk to her, she's distant. I can only assume it's because I asked her to move in with me. I knew it was a mistake as soon as I asked her. But it was too late, the words had already left my mouth. I haven't seen her all week. She has made excuse after excuse why she can't catch up, and today I've had enough. I need to talk to her. She needs to know what she means to me, and I have to tell her I know about her past and it's okay. I'm here to protect her. She doesn't have to be afraid of her arsehole ex anymore, she has me.

I pull up at Elly and Fraser's place to drop Jasper off so Elly can take him to school. As soon as she opens the door, he takes off looking for Cooper. "Have a good day, mate," I call.

"Yeah, Dad, see you later," he calls back, not turning round.

Elly stands in the doorway, and I hand her his school bag.

"What have you done to Ivy?" she says.

"Good morning, Elly, nice to see you too. Why do you assume I've done anything? What are you talking about?"

"She's been quiet with me all week, then yesterday, I could have sworn she was crying at school pick-up. Something's up with her, she's not her normal happy self. Thought you might have known something about it." She gives me an accusatory look. Bet she's been sitting on this all night. She probably would have questioned me last night, except when I picked Jasper up, only Fraser was here.

"It might have been me. I don't really know."

Her eyes narrow. "What did you do, Theo?"

"I asked her to move in with me."

She looks shocked, not unlike Ivy when I asked her.

"Shit, Theo, are you for real? You've only been dating a little while, you probably scared the poor girl off."

I run my hands through my hair, frustrated at my stupidity. "I know it was dumb, but things have been going so well, and Mum was in my ear about how nice it would be to have a lovely normal family. I know I should never listen to her, but I just thought maybe she was right."

She pokes me in the chest. "Never listen to Mum about this stuff, she just wants us all married with a million grandchildren for her to play with."

I throw my hands up. "Too late. Now what do I do?"

"Talk to her, tell her you're a dope and you're sorry for moving too quick."

"There's more to it now, though. See, I kept waiting for her to talk to me about her past, about Harmony's dad, but she kept saying she wasn't ready. Then after she turned me down on Sunday, I kinda looked into her past."

"Theo, what did you do?" She covers her mouth with her hand.

"I just wanted to understand why this was all so hard for her, but what I found wasn't good. It explains why she's so scared to move on, but now I know all her secrets, and she's going to kill me when she finds out I went behind her back."

She pokes me in the chest again. "Yeah, she is, and you're going to deserve it."

"What should I do? I don't want to lose her. I know she's scared because she's been hurt, but there is something real between us."

"All you can do is come clean. Tell her what you told me, let her know how important she is to you, and you know you fucked up. Then you pray she can forgive you."

"What if she doesn't?"

"We work that out if it comes to that. You have to tell

her what you know, it's not fair to keep it from her. Nothing good ever comes from lying, Theo." Man, she sounds like Mum. She even has the same condescending voice as she tells me off.

"Yeah, I know you're right."

"Good luck." She smiles sympathetically.

"Thanks. I'll see you tonight."

I hop back in my car to head to the station and send off a quick text to Ivy before I take off.

Me: We need to talk. No more avoiding me.

Ivy: Yeah, we do.

Me: Will you be home at 1pm?

Ivy: Yes.

Theo: See you then.

As I pull up in front of the station, my phone rings. It's Blake.

"Hey, man, wanted to talk to you before you got to work."

I stop the engine. "I just arrived, but I'm still in the car."

"Okay, well, all I can say is you want to look into Jimmy Barrett for that job we were talking about."

That's interesting. I wonder what he's heard, because last I heard one of the Barrett brothers was dead and the other was in prison, and I don't think he's out yet. "Okay, I thought we dealt with them years ago."

"Nope, Jimmy went to prison, has been there about four years. You want to have a look into that. Alright?"

I tap on the steering wheel, thoughts running through my head faster than I can process. Those fuckers were the ones helping Vinnie, and they're the reason for what happened to Fi. "Got it, thanks, man." I hang up and make my way into the station.

Talon is sitting at his desk already. "You in a better mood than this morning?" he says, raising his eyes from his computer.

What is he talking about? We did our normal gym session this morning; I wasn't in a mood. "There was nothing wrong with me this morning."

"Yeah, you've been a pleasure to be around since we looked into Ivy's past the other day. Having second thoughts about snooping?"

"I'm just tired," I huff, taking a seat at my desk.

"Yeah, okay." He lowers his eyes to continue what he's working on.

"I've got a new lead for you to look into. Jimmy Barrett—he's in prison, but before he ended up in there, he and his brother ran a lucrative drug-smuggling business in Sydney. He might just be our connection on the inside. See what you can find."

"On it."

CHAPTER TWENTY-THREE

THEO

I'M STANDING OUT THE FRONT OF IVY'S HOUSE. IT'S THE middle of the day, the only time we can really have an actual conversation without little ears around to hear. I buzz at her front gate.

Knowing what I now know, all the security makes sense. She knows he's going to be released one day and could potentially try to find her. I'm glad she's smart enough to think of that. What I can't understand is how someone like her got involved with a piece of shit like him in the first place—and she married him! It makes no sense to me at all. I mean, in this job, I see it all the time and wonder how these girls get involved with guys like this, but she is so smart. How did it happen to her?

She opens the door. She's in skinny jeans that hug her long legs and an off-the-shoulder sweater. I'm not quite sure what to do, so I kiss her on the cheek, and she hugs into me. Okay, she has missed me as well. Maybe things aren't as bad as I was thinking.

I smell her hair—lavender, so comforting. As I hold her, regret washes over me. Why did I have to research into her past? I should have just waited. She's going to be mad, I know that for sure. I just hope she can see it from my perspective and forgive me.

I lift her chin so she's looking at me. "I'm sorry about Sunday." I gaze at her beautiful face and I can see the little scar on her left cheek—it matches the one in the police report photos. I have noticed it before but didn't think anything of it. I can feel my temper rise. I'm so mad that he did this to her.

"Come in, Theo, we need to talk. Do you want a drink or something?"

"No, thank you." I follow her as we walk through to the breakfast bar. As she takes a seat, her pretty features give her away, and she hasn't even heard what I need to tell her yet. "What's wrong, Theo?" she says, looking more serious now, with her knee bouncing. I've noticed she does that when she's nervous. I take her hands to try to calm her nerves, running my thumb over the back of her hand.

"Angel, I don't want you to be mad, but I couldn't stand not knowing anymore."

"Not knowing what, Theo?" She's staring me down, already looking pissed.

"I've told you everything about my past, even the shit bits I don't talk about with anyone, and I just wanted to understand you better, know why you're so scared, why you don't open up to me."

"What have you done, Theo?" She pulls her hands from mine and stands up, folding her arms in front of her, holding her body protectively.

"I know, Ivy, I know why your husband went to prison, why you're so scared. It all makes sense now."

Her face changes from fear to anger, her eyes narrowing in on me. "You did what? You looked into my past, so you could *understand* me?" She blinks, and I can see tears in her eyes. "I would have told you when I was ready, I told you that. This isn't simple stuff to talk about."

I can see how much I've hurt her, and it's killing me. The last thing I wanted to do was hurt her more. Her tears break free, running down her face. Why didn't I just wait for her to tell me? I knew this was a bad idea, but I couldn't help myself. I shift uncomfortably, not knowing quite what to say next to make this better.

"I'm sorry, angel, but how long did I have to wait before you told me? How could I keep you safe if I didn't know what was going on?" I try to reach out for her arm, but she pulls away, she's so hurt.

"I have been doing a good job of keeping myself safe for long enough. I don't need you to do that for me. How am I supposed to trust you now? You went behind my back! Did you see the notes from the hospital social worker?"

"I saw it all: the report from the social worker, the photos of what he did to you, and the police report. He's a monster."

"You probably think I'm pathetic for staying with him for so long! But you don't know, you don't know what it was like." Her voice is shaky.

"I don't think that at all. Tell me what happened. I want to know about your life, I want to understand you. It's not healthy to keep stuff like that all bottled up inside."

She takes a deep breath and moves to sit on the lounge, her head down. "I know I should have left him when everything changed, after we got married, but I had no one else. No other family, my parents were gone."

I move over to sit with her. She's finally opening up to me.

"Harmony wasn't a planned pregnancy. You wouldn't

plan to bring someone else into that relationship, but once we found out we were pregnant, I hoped she would change things. I was kidding myself; he was a narcissistic prick who wasn't going to change for anyone.

"He wasn't always that way. In the beginning, our life was good. I met him while I was studying nutrition at uni. The company he worked for was doing some renovations on one of the uni buildings, and we ran into each other there.

"He was the one who picked me up and put me back together after my parents' car accident. A lot of my high school friends didn't know how to handle it, and over time, I grew distant from them, relying more on him. After a couple of years, I asked him to move into my parents' farm with me, as we were inseparable anyway, and 18 months later, we got married." The tears are still rolling down her face as she talks.

"It's okay, Ivy, you don't have to go on if it's too hard."

She just shakes her head. "I have to tell you now. You can't just think it's like the report says, you have to understand. I have to tell you." I nod for her to go on, putting my arm around her as she talks, but she brushes me off.

"Maybe it sounds cliché, but that's when everything changed. He had started work for a new construction company with a new group of guys, and he hung with them on weekends. Then, it was most days after work as well. I didn't mind because I was busy with work. I had just started at the hospital in the nutrition clinic, and there was so much to learn. I was working six days then going home and researching to help my patients as much as I could."

I brush her hair out of her face, so I see her looking down like she's numb when she says the words.

"For the first few months, I didn't notice much of a change. But as time went on, he started coming home drunk a lot. Not just drunk, but irritated and irrational. I'm sure he was high on something. He was always out of money and relying on me to help him out.

"After months of this going on, I confronted him and told him I wasn't giving him any more money for whatever it was he was doing, and that's when he lost it at me for the first time. He threw me across the room and told me my money was his because he owned me now that we were married. He demanded full access to my inheritance, and after that, this was the new normal.

"Our relationship completely broke down. It was a vicious cycle of him going out with his mates, gambling or whatever it was he was doing, losing money and taking it out on me. Then sucking up to me with gifts and being all Mister Nice Guy like he was in the beginning, then taking more of my parents' money and losing it again.

"The night I left, I thought he was going to kill Harmony. I was seven months pregnant and—well, you've seen the report. I didn't know what I was going to do, but I wasn't going back! Harmony was born early. I was so stressed, and my body just couldn't handle being pregnant. I was lucky she survived."

She's not crying anymore, just staring into space. I go to hug her into my chest, and she lets me.

"Theo, I told you I was broken. Why didn't you believe me?"

"Ivy, I'm in love with you, you're my girl. I wanted to make sure I could keep you safe. I'm so sorry this happened to you. I will never let anyone hurt you again." I pull her into me, not taking no for an answer. I love her, and I'm not letting go. She looks up at me with tears in her eyes again and kisses me slowly. Time passes and we cling to each other, not moving. She breaks the contact, pulling away slightly, her hand still in mine. She looks so sad.

"I can't do this, Theo... I really care about you, and it's going to break my heart to do this, but I need you to go. You deserve better than me." She's still looking into my eyes, not letting go.

"Don't do this, Ivy. I can take care of you. You just need a few days to calm down to see my side." I kiss her desperately, hoping it changes her mind. I can't leave her like this. She's a mess, and it's because of me. She kisses me back for a second, then pulls away.

"I'm sorry, Theo, I need you to go," she says, tears running down her face again. Feeling defeated, not wanting to make this any worse than it already is, I walk towards the door then turn to face her. She's looking down now, back to shutting me out.

"You're just looking for an excuse to push me away, Ivy. Let me take care of you," I say, getting frustrated with the situation. She looks up at me, surprised.

"Stop, Theo, just stop. I'm not making excuses. I opened my heart to you, I let you in. I told you I was too broken, and I couldn't tell you all this, and you proved to me what I knew all along. I can't trust anyone but myself. I'm better off alone." She gets up and heads to the front door, opening it.

"I'm so sorry, Ivy." I turn and walk out, completely defeated. I have left my heart with her. This isn't how this was all supposed to happen. I want to be the one there to comfort her, not the one making it worse. She closes the door, and I can hear her sobs get louder.

What have I done?

Ivy

"Lauren, Lauren," he calls from downstairs. I think I'll just pretend I'm asleep. I don't want to fight tonight. "Lauren, I need to talk to you," he slurs. "Where's the money? Where have you stashed that last thousand you took out?" What the fuck is he talking about? He knows it's all gone.

He stumbles through the bedroom door and stops when he gets to me, hovering above me. I can smell the stench of stale beer on his breath. It's almost too much for my pregnant tummy to take.

I reluctantly open my eyes, taking him in. His dark eyes stare straight into mine with a flicker of anger already showing. He looks terrible tonight. He hasn't shaved in weeks, and his once-handsome features have taken a toll from all the drinking and late nights. He was such an attractive man when we first started dating. The classic tall, dark, and handsome. I always thought he was too good for such a plain girl like myself, skinny with mousey dark blonde hair. I'm nothing special, and I wondered what he ever saw in me. But now he's a shadow of the man he once was.

"What's wrong?" I say, slowly sitting up in the bed, propping myself up with a pillow and trying to avoid his stare.

"I'm in the middle of the best hand of my life and I need some more money to win! But I'm all out. I know you have something stashed around here somewhere." He pulls out the bedside drawer, rummaging through.

And I know that's what it was. That's what he saw in me all those years ago... the money. My parents' money. But that's where he's wrong this time!

"It's all gone," I whisper, trying not to piss him off, but it's true, there is nothing left. He stands over me again, one hand *on either side of me. He stares straight at me, his nostrils flaring. His breathing is heavy. He's trying to contain his temper in his drunken state. My heart kicks up a beat. He scares the shit out of me when he's like this, but I try not to show him that.*

"You're lying. I know you've got some stashed," he spits. I flinch and cover my belly as he bangs his hands on the bed in frustration. "You're lying," he growls at me through clenched teeth.

He turns to our dressing table, pulling all the drawers out. He throws them across the room, rummaging through the contents, emptying each one in his desperate need to find some cash. I feel completely helpless to say anything, because I know from experience, he'll turn on me if I do. He's a big man, and I have absolutely no power against him, especially in my current condition.

Finding nothing in the drawers, he turns again, stalking his way over to me with renewed determination, ripping me out of bed by my hair. Tears sting my eyes instantly from the pain radiating through my head.

"What do you mean, it's all gone?" he screams.

"There's nothing left," I say with tears of pain escaping down my face.

He throws me to the ground, and my face connects with the bedside table on my way down. I feel my cheek throb instantly. Oh, the pain. A small trickle of blood runs down my face, over my hand. He smiles at me with a sadistic smile I've never seen before.

"Where's your mum's jewellery then?" He snickers.

"It's... it's in a safe deposit box across town. We can't access it till they open in the morning," I stutter out, barely able to talk through the pain in my head. He lifts his leg, and I instinctively cover my belly as he kicks me in the chest, his

work boot connecting with my sternum. I hit the dresser behind me with the force.

I gasp for breath through the pain. "The baby," I cry out.

"The baby, the fucking baby that we can't even afford! We'd both be better if it dies anyway," he slurs at me.

Oh God, this is so much worse than normal. He's going to kill the baby! I've got to get the fuck out of here!

I turn my head away from him and see the baseball bat he keeps under the bed in case of intruders. I don't have time to think. I grab it, and with one huge swing with all I've got, I smash it into his knee cap. He's so drunk, he goes down like a sack of potatoes, screaming at me in pain. I'm up and out of there as fast as my body will take me. I can hear him trying to get up, screaming at me, but I run and don't look back.

"Lauren, you fucking bitch, you're going to pay for that! How dare you! I fucking own you, bitch, you can't run forever."

I can and I will! Anything to save my baby girl from this monster.

The adrenaline is rushing through me now, and I run as fast as I can down the stairs and out of the house. My head throbs as I run and my breaths are short, but I keep running out the front door and through the paddock, as far as I can get away from him. I feel twigs and rocks breaking the skin of my bare feet as I run, but there was no time to stop and look for shoes. I don't care, I just keep running.

I get to the big gum tree in the back paddock and hide behind it, sliding down to the ground, trying to catch my breath. Praying to any god that will listen that he can't see me. He's calling out for me from the front porch, but he's gone the other way. The door slams again, and he's back inside. I see a torch shining through the paddock I'm in, then I hear him scream out in frustration.

"Lauren!" It echoes all around in the normally quiet night. I hear my racing heartbeat in my ears. The constant thump of it is almost deafening, and I'm sure he'll be able to hear my laboured heavy breathing as I try to catch my breath, through the pain of my injury to my ribs.

I WAKE IN A HOT SWEAT, GASPING FOR BREATH, MY heart speeding in my chest and tears running down my face. Thank God I woke myself up from that. I roll over to look at the time—it's only two am. I haven't had a nightmare like that since before I met Theo. But I'm not surprised it was back tonight.

After Theo left this afternoon, I fell apart. I knew this was all too good to be true, and I knew this day would eventually come. It was only a matter of time before we broke up. It wasn't how I expected it to go down, with him going behind my back. I thought it would be me confessing how sorry I was for keeping it all from him and begging him to stay with me. But now I feel betrayed.

If it was so important to him, why didn't he talk to me about it? You don't use your police connections to stalk your girlfriend's past. That police report would have been horrendous to read. It's so much worse than me explaining my story. He would have seen all the photos of my injuries and read every gory detail of what went on. It gives me an icy shiver at the thought.

I know I'm not being fair. I guess he did try and ask me, but I wasn't ready to talk about this and he should have just respected my wishes. I would never push him on something he wasn't ready to talk about.

I could see the pity in his eyes, the way he looked over my body, imagining my injuries. I knew this is how he would be, that's one reason I put off telling him for so long. Then it had been too long, and I couldn't tell him because I didn't want to lose him—and now I have. I forced him to go behind my back. It's my fault, I know it is, but it hurts just the same. Because now the trust I needed from him is gone.

I grab my pillow and put it over my head. I can't stop the tears, and my head is thumping. He went behind my back and looked up my past. Our conversation keeps playing repeatedly in my head. *Grrr!* I'm so frustrated, I throw the pillow across the room.

I've got to get something for this headache. I tiptoe downstairs to the kitchen so Harmony doesn't hear me. The last thing I want to deal with is trying to settle her back to sleep when I feel like this. I fill a glass of water and take two painkillers. Hopefully, this helps me sleep.

I get back into bed, and all I can smell is him. My sheets smell like him, and it's both overwhelming and comforting at the same time. I wrap them around me. How could I have let myself fall in love with him? He said he loved me too. I don't even know if that's true or if he was just trying to soften the blow of what he was saying.

Tomorrow's a new day, Ivy, everything will feel better in the morning.

I roll some lavender oil on my wrist and rub it to my other wrist. This normally helps when I can't sleep, but it's going to have to be some pretty powerful stuff to work tonight. I inhale the lavender and start another body scan and pray to whoever is listening to let sleep take hold.

But everything didn't feel better in the morning. It was worse. Theo wasn't there for me to wake up next to, and my face was blotchy, my eyes red and sore from all the crying. I looked terrible, and my heart ached. But one thing about being a parent is that life doesn't care if you feel terrible and just want to hide in your bedroom all day, the curtains drawn, the covers pulled up, out of sight from the rest of the world—you can't.

You have to get up and fix breakfast, get a little person ready for school, and you have to get yourself ready for work —and in my case, that means covering up the tired, blotchy face with some thick foundation, finding my cutest pink paisley crop top and tights, plastering on the best fake smile I can muster, and teaching my class. I actually feel sorry for them. With the mood I'm in today, I'm going to kick butt. They won't know what hit them when I walk through the door this morning.

That was the hardest class I have led in the whole four years I have been teaching. I'm in such a foul mood. I really shouldn't take it out on my class, but I had to take it out on someone. I'm still furious Theo went behind my back, using his police connections to get information on my past. I'm probably overreacting, and maybe he's right, maybe I should have told him what happened to me by now, but I wanted to do it in my own time when I was ready.

The problem is, as much as I'm still angry, I can't stop thinking about him, and my heart hurts when I think of living life without him. I miss him already. How could I have fallen for him so quickly? I know I should call him and try to work things out, I'm just not sure where to start.

I slowly drag my broken heart around the studio, packing the mats away.

I hear the door slide open. One of the students must

have forgotten something. I turn to see who it is. "Elly, what are you doing here?"

She stands by the door, looking out of place and a bit unsure. "I'm sorry to turn up at your work, but I didn't want to wait until school pick-up. It's always hard to talk with the kids around, and I needed to talk to you."

I turn away from her and continue to pack away the mats. One guess as to why she's here. "What did you want to talk about?"

She comes to stand by me. "He's a mess, Iv. He knows he fucked up majorly, but he doesn't know what to do."

"So you came for him. Do you know what he did?" I say, probably a bit shorter than I should be with her. She's not the one I'm angry with, but I'm in a terrible mood and I really don't want to discuss this with anyone, let alone his perfect sister.

"Yeah, he told me the entire story. I'm sorry, hun, he can be a dick when he wants to know something. I should know. He has always been super nosy. He used to read my diary when we were kids just so he wasn't missing out on anything."

I turn back to look at her. I need to stop being a bitch. She's so kind, and she's just here trying to help her brother. "He didn't!"

"Yep, he did!" She laughs. "I know it's not the same thing, but I get how annoyed you must be."

"I thought you would be on his side. Didn't you come to plead his case?"

"I came to make sure you were okay. We're friends, aren't we? And you've been through so much. And now you have my brother to deal with. I figured you could use someone to talk to that knows what you're dealing with." She offers a warm smile that I can't refuse.

She's right. I need someone to talk to. And we have become friends over the last few months. She is such a genuinely nice person. Not sure she is going to be able to help much, but it will be good to get it off my chest. And she already knows the story from Theo, so there is that.

I offer a small smile back, about as good as I can get today. "Do you want something to drink?"

"Thanks, a tea would be nice."

I lead her into our kitchenette and start on making two teas. She takes a seat at the small table we have. "Milk?"

"Yes, please."

I place the drink in front of her and take a seat across from her.

She takes a sip. "You guys are going to be okay, I know you will."

"How can you be so sure?"

"He adores you, and I see the way you are when you're with each other. You're meant to be together."

I want to believe her words. When I'm with him, everything feels so amazing, and I love the idea that we're meant to be, but somehow, I just don't know if that's our reality. Is that just something people say? What is *meant to be together* anyway? How can you even tell if you're meant for someone?

"How do I trust him again?" I ask softly.

"I don't know, honey. You're the only one that can answer that. But you have to maybe try to see it from his perspective, so you can understand why he felt like he had to go behind your back. He works as a detective, and he's used to solving puzzles, protecting people. If he can't get the answers he wants, he works out a way to do it. He knew you were scared, and he wanted to protect you, but he didn't know what from. He really felt like there was no other way.

He didn't break your trust to hurt you—he did it to understand you. He loves you."

I'm sure everything she's saying is true. It all makes sense, and some of that I have been telling myself already.

"I'm in love with him as well. I haven't told him that, but I know I am. I do kind of get it from his perspective. I know this was my fault because I wouldn't tell him. Every time he asked me, I told him I wasn't ready to talk about it, because I was too scared to tell him, worried I would lose him—or worse, the pity in his eyes would be too much for me. I don't want him to see me as that pathetic girl. I want him to see me for the strong person I am now."

"That's exactly how he sees you. He thinks you're amazing, Ivy. All of us can see how strong you are."

I shake my head. "Except I'm not strong," I say sadly. "I want to be, but I can't even move on from the past so I can try to have a better future. It's still holding me back. Even one of his mates from work has told me to stay away from him, that he deserves better than me after everything he's been through."

"I guess the desire to move forward has to be stronger than the pain from the past so you can let it go and let yourself be happy. I wouldn't worry about what anyone else thinks. This is between the two of you." She squeezes my hand across the table. "I better get going, I have a client I need to see before I get the boys from school." She places her cup in the sink, and I do the same.

Her words make a lot of sense. "Thanks, Elly, you didn't have to come and help me."

"Yeah, I did. You're family now, and we all look after each other. Talk to him, I'm sure you guys can work this all out."

"Yeah, maybe. I just need a little time to process it all."

She wraps her arms around me in a hug. "Don't wait too long. Theo's a mess."

I nod and offer a small smile. "I'll see you this afternoon at pick-up."

She takes off for her car. And I'm left alone with my thoughts.

Where do I go from here? The conversation I had with Sean last week still plays on my mind as well. I mean, the threat isn't valid anymore. It wouldn't matter if he told Theo about my past because he already knows, but things he said don't add up. Like we would both get hurt if we stayed together? If he was just being a good friend looking out for Theo, he should have just told him everything he knew, let him be the judge of what to do with the information. The fact he has come to me twice now with a threat to stay away from Theo doesn't sit right with me.

There is more to this, I'm sure of it. I just don't have any idea what it could be.

CHAPTER TWENTY-FOUR

THEO

Today has been a really long day. I messaged Ivy to apologise again for what happened yesterday afternoon—but nothing. She's still pissed at me, and I get it. I know going behind her back was a shitty thing to do, but I don't regret it. I needed to know, and now I do. Now, I just need her to forgive me so we can move on together.

I knock on the door at Elly and Fraser's to pick up Jasper. Fraser answers.

"Hey, mate. Elly says you're staying for dinner, she needs to talk to you."

I raise a brow. First I've heard of it, but honestly, the company would be nice. As long as she's not going to have another go at me. "So, that means I have no choice?"

"That's right. You know what she's like. You better just do what she says." He laughs.

"Okay then. I couldn't be bothered fighting with her tonight," I say as we walk through the house. I really don't have the energy to cook anything either. "Where are the boys? The house is silent."

"They're out the back."

"Not with a soccer ball, I hope." I'm trying to crack a joke, even though joking right now is the last thing I want to do.

"No, they're on the swing." He gives me a telling look. "You fucked it up, didn't you?"

"Don't act like you don't know what I did. I'm sure Elly has already told you all the details."

"Yeah, sorry, man. She tells me everything. But I warned you what snooping into her past would get you."

"You sound just like your wife," I joke, but it's true. The more time these two spend together, the more they've started sounding like each other.

Elly is setting the table and offers me a sympathetic smile. "How was your day?"

"Pretty shitty. What about yours, Sis?"

"It was okay." She gives me a guilty look. I can read her so easily, and I know she's done something.

I raise a brow to her. "What, Elly?"

She places the last of the cutlery on the perfectly decorated table. I don't know how she has time to work in her business, look after the boys, and keep a perfect house. It's always clean with fresh flowers in vases and cushions fluffed —it looks like one of her show homes. "Fray, can you take over stirring the dinner? I want to have a quick chat to Theo before the boys get in."

She turns to me with a small but still very guilty smile. "Don't get mad with me, but I went to see Ivy today." She slumps into a seat across from me.

"Why?" I say, my voice a little irritated. I don't need her meddling in my business.

"I just wanted to make sure she was okay and plead your case a little, I'm sorry."

I can't be mad with Elly. She's always just looking out

for me. I would be lost without her and her help. I'm kinda glad she went to see Ivy, since she won't talk to me. I need to know she's alright.

"How was she, is she okay?"

"Not really, Theo, she's as much of a mess as you. The two of you belong together, but you're getting in your own way."

I have so many questions. I just want to know that there's still hope. "What did she tell you, do you think it's over? Did I go too far? She won't return my messages, and it's driving me crazy. I just want to know she's okay."

"It's not over, there is definitely still hope. She's just hurt you went behind her back."

A small twinkle of hope enters my heart. Elly thinks it's not over, this is good. I have time to fix my mistakes. "She was saying more than that yesterday, though. She was annoyed at me, yes, but I got the impression she was going to break it off with me anyway. She was saying I deserved better than her, that she was too broken."

"I think she's just really down on herself, Theo. She said one of your work mates made her feel terrible about herself, said you deserved better after all you had been through, and she should let you go if she didn't want to hurt you."

What the fuck? Who would have been talking to her from my work? "What? It doesn't make any sense. Who was it?"

She shrugs.

"I bet it was Sean. She said he was giving her a hard time at Drew's party. She came back upset from talking with him but wouldn't really tell me why."

"That guy has always been a dickhead, Theo," Fraser adds from the kitchen. "He probably wants her for himself or something."

"Yeah, I don't know, but I know now he can't be trusted. There is no way he is looking out for me, we're not that kind of friends. The only time we hang out is if we go out drinking."

Fraser serves up dinner on the kitchen island and places the bowls on the table. "Boys," he calls to them out the back. "Dinner."

"Hey, Daddy, I didn't know you were here." Jasper runs from the sliding door over to me, hugging my side.

I mess up his hair. "Did you have a good day?"

"Yes." He smiles cheekily, and I hope he and his cousin haven't been up to no good again.

"Okay, well, I want to hear all about it over dinner. Go wash your hands." He runs off to the bathroom.

"Spaghetti bolognaise, yum. Thanks for having us for dinner and for looking out for Ivy. I owe you, Sis."

"It's okay, Theo. We have all been there. It's hard work when you fall in love, but it's worth it. I'm just trying to avoid you having to wait as long as we did to sort your shit out. I can tell she's your person, Theo. I know you two will work this all out."

She seems so confident. "Thanks, Sis."

I really hope she's right. I know Ivy is my person too, and I'm not naïve enough to think that even when you are in love with someone, you won't have your difficulties. I just hope she can trust me again and see I was coming from a place of love and the desire to protect her.

Ivy

. . .

It's Tuesday morning, and I've just dropped Harmony off to school. Jenna and I are going for a walk then having lunch down at the beach café. I feel like I've been a bad friend lately. With all the drama in my life, I've been neglecting our friendship. Ever since Theo left my place last week, I have been a total mess. I'm so emotional. I haven't stopped crying, and it doesn't help that it's that time of the month and I feel like I'm bleeding to death.

"Are we still on for Saturday night?" asks Jen.

I feel so guilty. We're so close normally, in each other's lives so much, and I know she needs me, but I've been caught up in my shit and I hadn't even realised it was this weekend. "Ah, I don't know, I'll probably give it a miss this month."

"What's wrong with you, babe? You've been a moody bitch all week!"

"Thanks, Jen!"

"You know what I mean, you haven't been yourself. *The god* not keeping you satisfied?" she says, laughing and hitting me on the arm.

I glance at her, tears almost about to burst already. "I ended it with him."

A look of shock washes over her. "What? I thought it was all going so well."

"It was, then he went behind my back and looked up things about my past and Harmony's dad. I couldn't handle it, so I kicked him out," I say, shaking my head and burying it in my hands, the tears breaking free. I have been so sad since I kicked him out of my life, I just can't stop.

Jenna rubs my back. "It can't be that bad, can it? I'm sure we can work this out."

I raise my head to look at her, trying to wipe away the

tears, embarrassed I'm so upset in a public place. "I was so pissed at him. I still can't believe how much I overreacted."

"Hey, it's going to be okay, Iv."

"I've told him everything now. Once I started, I couldn't stop, then I asked him to leave because I couldn't deal with it all. Saying everything out loud brought it all back. I know he was just trying to understand me but talking about it was just too much. You know?"

"I totally understand. I would be the same, babe, but he's one of the good ones, and he clearly cares about you, or he wouldn't have even been interested."

"He messaged me yesterday, and I ignored him—I'm such a bitch."

"Yeah, that's what I'm saying, you're a total bitch lately!" She laughs at me, trying to lighten the mood. "Just message him already, put the poor boy out of his misery. You clearly have strong feelings for him, or you wouldn't be so hung up on letting him go."

Tears threaten to break free again, and I sniffle them back. "I'm in love with him, but that's half the problem. I know if I message him and we work things out, I don't want it to end, but what if we can't make it work? Our situation is so tricky, with the kids, with our pasts; we both carry a lot of hurt."

"No one can answer that at any time, babe, you know that. You just have to open your heart and give it a go."

"Yeah, maybe. I don't know."

She hugs me again, handing me a tissue out of her bag. "Come on, let's get you some comfort food before you make any big life decisions." She puts her arm around me and guides me into the café.

I can see Penny already has a table for us, so we make

our way through the line-up for coffee. This place is always so busy, but it's the best so it's worth the wait.

"Hey, Pen, what's going on with you?" I say, trying to gather my strength and pretend I didn't just have a meltdown. She gives me a weird look.

"Everything okay, Ivy?"

"All good." I plaster on my best fake smile to hide the inner turmoil I'm really going through. I've already talked to Elly and now Jenna. I don't want to go through it all over again with Penny. It's now time for me to work this shit out myself.

The look of concern lasts all of two seconds before she demands all of our attention on her, and I'm glad for the distraction. "Okay, well, you're never going to believe it. You boring bitches left me Saturday night to my own devices, so I went out with some girls from one of my classes. You know the ones, Ivy, the ones that talk through the entire class."

I roll my eyes so Jenna can see. "Yeah, that would have been awesome, they're super annoying!"

"Go on, Pen, tell us the story we just won't believe," Jenna says.

Penny gives me a look. "So anyway, we're out and we get chatting to this team of footy players, and we start playing pool and drinking. It was the best night, it totally flew by, and the next thing I know, it's two am and I'm walking home with two of them," she says, raising her eyebrow. I can only guess where this is going.

"And?" Jenna says impatiently.

"And the night didn't end there... It was unbelievable. I mean, of course I've been in a threesome before, but this was with two guys! And they really knew what they were doing, if you know what I mean."

"I think we do, Pen," I say, trying to process what she's

telling me. How on earth does she manage to get herself into these situations?

"Lucky you," is the best I can come up with. Jenna hasn't said a word, she looks shocked.

Penny smacks her hand on the table, causing others around us to look our way. "Damn right, lucky me! It was the best night of my life, and I've had some pretty good ones to compare it to. Are we going to order? I'm starving."

"Yes, let's eat," Jenna pipes up. "I need food, and I think I've had an information overload this morning. I feel like I should write this stuff down and put you two in my next book."

"Lucky for us you write fantasy for young adults," Penny says, not looking fazed by the idea of being an inspiration for a novel.

"You never know. My next series could be a romance..." she says, giving me a cheeky smile.

"Oh really, well, if it is, you can do your own relationship research," I say, making sure she knows my life is not to be included in her stories.

"You can write about me. I'll give you all the juicy details too," says Penny, all excited.

"On second thought, I might just stick to my made-up world of fantasy, sounds safer," Jenna says, looking a little scared.

We order lunch and continue to catch up on our week. I don't know what I would do without these girls. They keep me sane. My mind keeps going back to Theo. I need to fix this, but somehow a message seems like it won't be enough.

"Jenna, do you have anything on Friday night?" I ask.

"You know I don't. What are you thinking?"

"Can you watch Harmony for me? I need to do something."

"Of course, babe, you going to fix it?" She gives me a warm, sympathetic smile.

"I'm going to try anyway." But first I need to go back home. I need to face my demons. Not him—Dominic—but the rest of it. I think mostly I haven't moved forward from the past because I have been clinging onto the fear of everything that happened.

I don't want any of it to have a hold over me anymore. I want to be strong enough to move forward with Theo if that's what he still wants, and if not, I want to be strong enough for myself.

I need to say goodbye to everything holding me back.

CHAPTER TWENTY-FIVE

IVY

Harmony helped me pack up the car nice and early this morning. I have given her a day off school. She is so excited to see where I grew up. I've never taken her there since the day I left for Byron.

I've never come back, not even to visit my parents' graves. Until now, I haven't felt strong enough to, but I think it's one of those things I need to do so I can move forward with my life.

We have been driving for three hours already and stopped three times for toilet breaks—the joys of having a five-year-old along for a road trip. It shouldn't be much longer now, and we'll be there. My palms are sweaty on the steering wheel, and I'm not so sure this is such a good idea anymore. I'd felt like this was just what I needed, and when I talked it over with Jenna, it seemed like a great idea, but now that we're close and the scenery is becoming more clear, I'm hit with the overwhelming feeling of grief. This wasn't just the town I grew up in. It was the town where my parents died and left me all alone to fend for myself.

In my new hometown, I can pretend I don't miss them

so much, but here the feeling engulfs me. A stray tear escapes down my cheek, and I wipe it away. Luckily, Harmony is in her car seat in the back so she can't see me. What if I have a panic attack and it's just me and Harmony?

We drive past the old soccer field where I used to go watch my dad play soccer every Saturday afternoon, then past the primary school I attended for seven years. It all still looks the same. Then we drive out of town a little on the way to my parents' old house.

As we approach the driveway, I pull over to the side of the road so I can take a closer look. I can hardly believe my eyes at how beautiful it is. The new owners must have done a full restoration on the facade, at least. The paintwork is fresh and white, the gardens perfectly manicured in cottage style with white rose bushes lining the driveway, and the garden beds closest to the house have tall stems of large yellow sunflowers growing in them.

I try to swallow over the lump forming in my throat, but I can't. The house is once again picture-perfect, and just the sight of it makes my heart happy. Selling my parents' home was one of the hardest things I have ever had to do, but seeing it like this, I know I made the right choice. Another family lives there now and is making it a happy home.

"Look, Mum, horses," Harmony squeals excitedly from the back seat of the car.

"They're magnificent, aren't they? This is where I grew up, baby, right until you were born and we moved to Broken Point."

Her eyes are wide in disbelief. "You lived here, Mummy? You're so lucky! Why would you ever move away from such a beautiful place?"

"I was too sad here, baby. This was Nanny and Poppy's

house. I missed them too much when I lived here, so it was best we started a new life somewhere else."

This house has had a hold over me for so long, because this is where it all happened. This is where he made me feel small and weak, and I was so scared of him and of life without him at the same time. It's the house I see when I close my eyes and return to the nightmare.

I have also felt bad for so long that I wasn't able to afford to keep all that was left from my parents. But being here and looking at it today, it has lost its trepidation. I'm not that girl anymore. I have grown and changed. I am stronger now, and I would never let him control my life again. Even if he gets out and finds us, I will stick up to him this time and make sure he knows he will never have any power over me again.

I take a breath, feeling stronger and more determined to move forward with my life.

Harmony's small voice comes from the back. "I know I never got to meet them, but I wish I did. I look at the photo you have of them in the lounge room and wonder what they were like."

"They would have loved you, baby, they were such good people. I know it's not the same as meeting them, but we can visit the place where they're buried. It's been a long time since I have been to see them, and I would like to take you there today if you want to go."

"Yes, I would like that." She smiles.

"Okay, let's go there now, then I want to take you to my favourite bakery for lunch. Hopefully it's still there."

"Can I get a sausage roll?"

"You can have whatever you like today."

Today was a good idea after all, it was just what I needed.

CHAPTER TWENTY-SIX

IVY

I pull into Theo's driveway. I hope he's pleased to see me and I haven't left it too long to contact him. But I really needed that time to work out what I wanted and to process how to move on from my past. Now I feel ready to commit to everything with him.

He knows about my past so there are no more secrets between us, and if he'll have me, I want to spend the rest of my life with him, trying to make this all work.

His car is parked out the front, so I know he's here, and I messaged Elly earlier today for a favour. She was more than happy to help by looking after Jasper for us. She was just going to tell Theo the boys wanted to have a movie night and he should take the night off to rest. Or something to that effect. She is on team love and wants us back together. I've been lucky to have found a new friend out of this as well. He didn't message me last night for the first time since we broke up, so maybe he's given up.

I step out of my car, straightening out my short layered skirt, suddenly feeling overwhelmed with nervous butterflies. My hands are clammy, and it feels like all my rings are going to slip off. The words I had so clearly rehearsed are now a jumbled mess in my head.

Oh God, what if he's decided I'm not worth the trouble? He could have, and I wouldn't blame him if he did. From the start, none of this has been easy, and it never really will be with our modern family situation of two single parents. But I really hope more than anything he thinks I'm worth it and still wants to make this work with me.

I slowly walk over the pebble driveway to the front door of his house. I take a deep breath, trying to prepare myself, somehow mustering the strength. As I knock once, the door swings open, and I'm left with my fist still held up. Theo is obviously surprised to see me. He's standing there in his doorway looking like pure male perfection in blue jeans and a white shirt. I can't find my words—no words at all—the sight of him has left me completely speechless.

"Ivy, what are you doing here?" he says, crossing his arms over his chest. He's annoyed with me, and since I have ignored him all week, he has every right to be.

"I... I needed to see you. Can I come in, please?" I say, looking down and fidgeting with my rings. He's so intimidating when he's serious, I can't even look him in the eyes.

"Yeah, I guess." He stands back, giving me space to walk into his house. Then he closes the door behind me. "I'm a little surprised to see you. I thought since you have been ignoring my attempts to contact you all week, maybe you were done with me."

I follow him through the front of the house till we get to the living room, and he sits on the armchair. I take a seat on the sofa across from him. He's staring at me. I take in his face, and it's the first time I notice how tired he looks. I'd say he hasn't slept all week, just like me.

"What did you want to talk to me about, Ivy?" His words

have lost the warmth they usually hold for me, making me feel like I shouldn't be here. I can feel tears threatening to fall already, but I need to hold it together so I can tell him how I really feel.

"I... I'm so sorry, Theo. I'm sorry for what happened last week." I sniffle, holding back the tears that threaten to break free. "I'm sorry. I wasn't expecting to have that conversation with you, I wasn't ready for it. I didn't handle it well, I know. I should have listened to your side more, talking about what happened. It was just too much for me. It brought it all back, forced me to have to deal with it."

His features soften a little. "I know, and I'm sorry, Ivy. That's not what I was trying to do. I just wanted to understand you better, so I could protect you from whatever it was you were so scared of."

"I talked to Elly, and she helped me see things from your perspective, and I'm sorry I didn't tell you sooner. I wasn't trying to hide my past from you, I just couldn't deal with talking about it."

"Why didn't you respond to any of my messages? You must have known how bad I felt for what happened."

"I'm sorry. This week I've had time to reflect, and I took a drive home for the first time since it all took place. Most of what I'm so afraid of isn't even my reality anymore. I'm so much stronger now, and Harmony's dad is in prison. The likelihood of him finding us is so slim. I'm ready to move forward and stop living in the past's fear. This week without you has been awful. I thought I didn't need anyone, that I could do it all alone, but I have realised that even if I can do it all alone, I don't want to. I want you with me... if I'm not too late?"

He gets up from the armchair and comes to sit next to

me on the sofa. "I thought it was over, Ivy," he says, his voice shaky.

"I'm still not sure what this is between us, Theo, but I don't think it could ever be over. I'm completely in love with you," I say, reaching up to touch his face. "This week apart has just proven that to me. I want a life with you, if you'll have someone so broken."

He wraps his arms around me and pulls me close to him. "You're not broken, you've just been through a lot and need time to heal so you can see there are good guys in this world as well." He kisses me slowly, holding me close to him as the tears continue to fall. "I understand where you're coming from because I've been there too. When I lost Fiona, I wanted to shut myself off from the world. I was happy never to have another relationship again, so I didn't have to feel that hurt. It was easier not to feel anything for anyone. Until I met you and everything changed. I knew I couldn't stop the feelings I was having for you, even if I wanted to. I love you, Ivy. I'll never let anything like that happen to you again, that's my promise to you."

"I know you won't. I have felt safe with you since that first night at the beach. I should have trusted my instincts more."

"From now on, no more running or shutting down. We're in this together. You, me, and our two crazy kids."

"I like the sound of that." Our lips meet again, and I feel like I'm home. His scent surrounding me, his warm body pressed against mine. I never want to be apart from him again.

Theo

. . .

She just needed time to process. All week I've thought I had gone too far and destroyed what we had started together. But she was trying to deal with the demons I forced her to look at again. For that I feel terrible, but if it can bring us closer together, then it was all worthwhile.

"So, this is why Elly is holding on to Jasper for longer tonight?"

"Yeah, I kinda asked for a favour. Hope that was okay? This isn't the conversation you can have with kids around."

"It's definitely okay. I'm glad you feel close enough to her you can ask. It also means we have time to make up properly."

"What do you have in mind, Theo?" She smiles with that naughty glint in her eyes, and I know she's thinking the same thing as me.

Instead of answering, I pull her onto my lap, her short skirt fanning out over my legs. I wipe away her tears. She has black mascara tear stains down her cheeks from crying, but she is still so beautiful, so perfect. And I need to show her just what she means to me.

Her arms wrap around my body as I caress her face, pulling her in for a kiss. Soft, slow, gentle, our lips meet over and over again. Her hands roam up my body under my shirt and mine lace through her hair, pulling her closer to me. I'm not able to get enough of her.

My lips travel down her neck, tasting and nibbling my way down. I slide my hands over her jacket, making it drop to the floor so I can get my hands on her bare skin. They roam down her body, tugging at her singlet and pulling it over her head. Her tits look amazing in a pale-pink lace bra, the thin layer of lace leaving nothing to the imagination, her pink nipples hardening under the cool night air. I cup her breasts, running my hands over her nipples as she hauls my shirt off, and our lips meet again.

I pull away from her and continue placing kisses down her chest unit I reach her breasts. I push the thin lace fabric down, pushing her breasts out, and I lower my mouth to suck each hardened nub while I play with the other, twisting her nipple just slightly. She lets out a little whimper, and I move my mouth back to her lips.

Our kiss is more hurried this time, our tongues battling as she rolls her hips over my lap. My jeans feel like they're strangling me, my erection so hard with her slowly grinding on me. I need to get them off. She must have the same idea because her hands go to my top button, undoing it and sliding down the zipper of my fly. I help her push them down far enough that my cock can spring free. She teases me with her hand, sliding back and forth. I push her panties to the side and run my finger through her slick folds.

"God, you feel so good."

"Mmm," she moans into my neck as she continues stroking me.

I push a finger in, then another. She's so wet, so ready for me, and I can't wait another second longer. I pull my fingers out and position myself at her entrance as she lowers down onto me.

She moans again, louder this time. "God, I've missed you."

"I've missed you too, angel." I position my hands on her hips, helping her rock into me. Every time I do, she lets out another little whimper, a plea for me to go harder, faster—so I do, our bodies moving together. The many bangles that she likes to wear on her arm jingle around as she bounces on my cock; it's a sound I could get used to.

"Theo, I'm going to…"

"I can feel it, yes…"

Her body convulses around me then she collapses down onto my shoulder as I pump her once again, letting go myself and filling her. I pull her into me, closely, and I can feel her body trembling.

"Are you okay?"

"Yes, it's just, this thing with you is so intense. When we're together, it's so unbelievably good. I just know this is it for me now." She takes a deep breath then glances back to me, her eyes glassy. "You are the only one for me, I'm completely in love with you."

"I'm so happy to hear you say that because that's exactly how I feel, Ivy. I love you too."

I pull her into me once more, kissing her perfect lips. We collapse down onto the lounge together, and I hold her as tightly as I can. I thought I had lost her this week, and I was devastated. I will never get enough of her. After tonight, she'd better be prepared to make this arrangement permanent, because I'm never letting her go.

CHAPTER TWENTY-SEVEN

THEO

The last month has been one of the happiest of my life. Ivy has let her guard down and has opened up to me. She is relaxed in my home, and she and Harmony are talking about moving in within the next few months. We just need to organise to put her place on the rental market. She wants to keep it as an investment property, and I think that's a great idea.

Because we've all been spending so much time together, the kids are getting on like siblings, perfectly loving to each other one minute and in World War III over a toy or what television show to watch the next. Ivy and I are navigating our way around the tiffs as best we can. Most of them are just plain funny.

Tonight, I'm back at the station with Talon, like I have been every other night this week. We're still stuck on this case, but we know from one of Blake's contacts that the drop will happen this week. Sean is without a partner currently and has been working this case for a while as well, so this week we have joined forces to see if we can all somehow piece it together before the drop lands.

I'm tempted to ask Sean what the hell was going on with him and Ivy, but I won't for now. While we're all trying to work on this case, I don't want to do anything to fuck it up. It feels like we're getting close, and I need to keep my personal life separate from work. But I'm keeping an eye on him now.

Jasper is at Elly's for dinner, and Harmony is with Jenna at Ivy's place until Ivy finishes her class at the yoga studio. Then she'll pick them both up and meet me back at my place. The logistics are a nightmare, but that's the reality of two working parents, and we're lucky we have so much help.

Sean taps on my desk, an annoying habit of his when he wants my attention. "Just ducking out for a bit."

I push back from my chair. "I'll come with you. I need to clear my head."

He looks to the door then back to me. "Oh, it's probably best if you stay here, I won't be long."

"Okay," I say, turning to Talon to give him a look. I haven't noticed it before, because even though we've worked together for a while, Sean and I have never worked all that closely, but his behaviour this week has been strange. It might just be that he's used to working alone since it's been a while since he had a partner, but there is definitely something odd with him disappearing at different times of the day, and he always takes phone calls outside or to the hall so we can't hear.

Sean leaves, and I turn to Talon. "That was weird," he says before I have the chance. He feels it too. Our intuition is telling us something is off with him, but we can't put our finger on what it is.

"Yeah, there's something going on with him. You spend more time with him on the weekend than me. Is there something going on with him? Like with his family or something?"

"Not that I know of, but to be honest, we haven't been spending much time together at all lately, he's always busy. Probably just girlfriend trouble?"

"Does he have a girlfriend?"

"Don't know." He shrugs then drops his head back to his computer and gets back to work.

Might be why Boss has put him in with us as well. Maybe he's noticed something suspicious with him and we're supposed to be keeping an eye on him.

"You want a coffee? If we're going to be here half the night again, I'm going to need another to get through."

"Yeah, mate, thanks."

This week has been tough. I finally have Ivy with me at night, and I'm here at the station for half of it. What I wouldn't give to be going home right now to spend time with her and the kids. All I can hope is that we work this case out soon so my life with her can return to some sort of normal before too long.

CHAPTER TWENTY-EIGHT

IVY

I PUT THE LAST MAT BACK ON THE SHELF. ALL THE students have left, and I'm nearly done for the night. I'd better text Jenna that I'm on my way.

I grab my phone from the front counter and start to text her when I feel a presence behind me. I get a chill down my back like someone has just walked over my grave. One of my students must have left the door open and the cold air is getting in... yeah, that's what it is. I'm just freaking myself out because I'm tired.

"Honey, I'm home," a voice says from behind me. I know that voice instantly, and I feel the blood drain from my face. He's found me.

With shaky hands, I quickly press call to Jenna instead of sending a message and put the phone in the front pocket of my jacket. Years of knowing this moment might come but hoping it never would have prepared me. I'm not going down without a fight. I'm not the same girl he was married to. I'm strong, and I've got my baby girl to fight for.

I slowly turn to see Dominic standing in the doorway to the studio, his arms crossed over his chest and the look of pure evil in his eyes. He looks so different, bigger. His muscles bulge, the arms of his T-shirt stretched tight over the size of them, like he's spent the last five years working out in the prison gym or something. Probably with one thing in mind—to strangle me with his bare hands for putting him in prison. With that thought, I can feel the beads of sweat running down my back.

"Well, well, well, look at you, if it isn't my beautiful wife, hot as fucking ever. I can't say I mind the improvements you've made to your body. Being a yoga teacher suits you." His eyes roam over my body. The way he looks at me and the smile that forms gives me the creeps. "I thought you would have organised a welcome home party for me on such a special day," he spits at me with venom in his tone.

I don't get it, they said they would contact me. I should have had warning that he was out. I did have a missed call this afternoon from an unknown number, but I was in a rush to get to class, I wonder if that was them?

"H-how did you find me?" That is all I can muster as a reply. *Good one, Ivy, way to show him how strong you are now!*

"It was easy, wifey. Just because you're in prison doesn't mean you don't have friends on the outside looking out for you. One of mine is in the business of tracking people down who don't want to be found. Looks like you've made quite the new life for yourself here."

He throws a pile of photos down in front of me. I glance at them, not wanting to move too much closer to him or take my eyes away from him, but I can see what they are of—me with Theo, Jenna, Penny, and Harmony. All in different locations around Broken Point. Ha, I was right all this time, someone has been watching me. I thought I was just being paranoid. But this makes it pretty obvious someone has been watching us all.

God, I hope the call went through to Jenna and she's getting help. He's gone fucking mad.

"Does he know you're married, Lauren? Or should I be calling you Ivy now? Cute how you changed your name. I like it, Ivy suits you. Did you really think moving away and changing your name would stop me from finding you?" He aggressively lunges forward from where he was standing in the doorway. Closing the gap between us in a couple of quick steps, he grips my shoulders, his fingers digging in. "You're my wife, you belong to me," he spits out, holding me by the shoulders and shaking me.

I want to be brave to stick up for myself, but he's so close, towering over me as he breathes down on me, so much anger in his eyes.

"You lost the right to call me your wife when you beat the shit out of me that night. You might have been released, but I want nothing to do with you—which you already know by the restraining order that should have been issued to you on your release."

His nostrils flare as he growls at me. "No fucking piece of paper is going to keep me away from what's mine." He leans in to grab me by the back of my head and pulls me into him by my hair. My eyes prick with tears instantly. He's looking straight into my eyes, furious with rage. "And you are mine."

He leans in to kiss me, pushing his lips into mine violently, his stubble scratching my face, his tongue forcing its way into my mouth. I feel sick to my stomach, but I know I need to try to remember what I learnt in self-defence class. I'm not going down without a fight. Think, Ivy!

I lift my leg and knee him in the balls as hard as I can.

"Ahh!" he screams, letting go of me, bending over and grabbing his crotch in pain. "You fucking bitch."

I grab my bag and keys and run as fast as I can from the studio to my car, opening the door and jumping in with the same motion. As I go to slam the door, I feel his hand grip my arm.

"No!" I scream in frustration. How did he get to me so quickly? He pulls me from the car, dragging me by my arm and my hair. I try to kick at him and push him away but there's no use, he's too strong. He pins me up against my car, my hands trapped in his grip. His other hand closes around my neck as he pulls my head back to his chest.

"Really, wifey, you thought you could outrun me? I'm twice as fast." He talks into my ear, his words slow and calculated, and every one of them sends chills straight through me. "You have no fucking chance. As much of a turn-on as it is to chase you around—you know how much I love the fight—but you should really just give up now and start doing as I say." He laughs, a torturous sound that vibrates through my body.

I try to move but I can't, I'm pinned to the car with his strength. The fear overtakes me because I know he's right. No fucking self-defence class is going to save me from him. But if I go with him and do as he says, I'm going to be lucky if I get out alive. What were those statistics of people abducted by their abusive ex-husbands? I can't remember, but they're not good. I know going with him is not an option.

Maybe I can try to talk to him, buy me some time before someone realises I'm not home yet. Both Elly and Jenna will be waiting for me to pick up the kids, and by now, I would have to be late. They must be wondering where I am.

"Why don't we just go back inside? I won't run again, I know there's no point. We can just talk, work all this out." I try to sound braver than I am, but my voice still wavers with the threat of his hand on my neck.

"How dumb do you think I am? I'm running this little reunion we have going on, not you. I don't need to talk right now. I need you to do as I say so we can get out of here. We can talk somewhere less likely for someone to find you."

Fuck, he's going to take me. I try one last ditch effort to escape him, turning my head as if I'm going to say something, then I bite him as hard as I can. He loses his grip and I try to step out of his hold, but he catches my leg and drops me to the ground, his knee pressing heavily on my back in one move. The gravel bites into my face, and it's hard to breathe with the pressure of his weight on me. I have no options left.

"Nice try. You've gotten so much feistier, I'm impressed, but it still all ends the same for you, I'm afraid."

Tears well in my eyes with the pain in my back and the realisation that he's right—I'm no match for him. Then he covers my mouth with a rag and the overwhelming smell of chemicals fills my nose. I try to fight the need to sleep, but the chloroform is too strong. I can't resist anymore.

Theo

I check my watch. It's nearly 8:00 pm, and I'm still at the station. It's about this time I've been calling Ivy every night this week to check in with the kids before bed. I ring but the phone goes dead straight away. That's weird. I try again and the same thing.

I hear the ping of my phone vibrating in my pocket and look down to see a number I don't recognise. "Hi?"

"Theo, it's Jenna. I hope you don't mind I got your number from your brother. I think Ivy's in trouble. She's at the yoga studio, but her class finished an hour ago. I normally get a text to say she's on her way, but tonight she pocket-dialled me. I couldn't hear much of what was going on, the voices were muffled, but there was someone else there."

My blood runs cold. "Jenna, what do you mean?"

"She was arguing with someone, a man, then her phone dropped out."

Shit, Ivy was right. He must have come after her the first chance he got. We haven't even been told he was released yet. "It's got to be her ex, he must have been released. Is Harmony with you?"

"Yes, she's worried and so am I." I can hear the panic in Jenna's voice. She knows all too well how serious this is.

"Okay, keep her with you, try and distract her. I'll work this out. I'll be in touch as soon as I can."

"Alright. Please bring her back safely," she pleads, her voice scared.

"I won't let anything happen to her." I say it as confidently as I can, but I can't be sure. How can I? I don't even know what we're up against. My worst fears are coming true. This can't be happening again, I can't lose her. I have to work this out and get to her before she comes to any harm.

I look over to Talon. "What's wrong?" he asks.

"He might have found her."

"Who?"

"Ivy's ex. She hasn't arrived home. I'll go check the

studio, that's where she was last. Can you look into his release, see if he's out of prison?"

"On it."

On my drive out to the studio, I call Elly to ask her to have Jasper for the night and get her up to speed with what's happening. Hopefully, they're still at the studio.

Please let her be alright.

From the reports I've seen from five years ago when she was pregnant, this guy is a total monster, and he's had a long time in prison to think about his revenge, I know from experience—you rarely see these cases end well. But please not this time. I can't lose her.

I should have been there tonight to pick her up. I should have been watching her. I knew he was being released soon, I should have been there to keep her safe. My mind is racing quickly with all the possibilities. Please let her be at the studio, safe.

I pull up to the studio, and I know she's not here. The first thing I see is her car with the driver's side door wide open. *Shit.* There is no sign of another car. The studio door is open too, and I walk through with my gun drawn.

"Ivy? Ivy, are you here?" I call out, hoping to God this is all just some sort of misunderstanding. My heart is thumping so loudly I can hear it in my ears.

There's no response as I sprint through the studio, checking all the rooms and out the back as panic and realisation settle in. She's gone. I knew it before I walked in here. But I didn't want to believe it could be true.

When I get back to the front entry, I notice a pile of photos on the floor, all of Ivy with her friends or Harmony and me. The bastard must have hired a private detective to track her. That's how he found her so quickly.

Where the hell has he taken her? My hands are shaking,

but I've got to keep it together so I can find her. I call through to Talon to see what he's found.

"He's found her, Ivy's husband," I yell through the phone, my frustration taking over. "He must have been released early, he's found her. I'm at the studio now, and she's gone."

"Shit. Okay, man, we'll find them."

"Did you find anything on him?"

"Yeah, he was released yesterday. We have all the resources we need. We'll track her down. Is there anything at the studio that could help us find him?"

I look down at the photos I'm still holding. "Some photos of her with friends and me. Send a car to give the place a once-over."

"Are there markings on them, a print date? Anything we can use to identify where they came from?"

"Yeah, actually there is. I'll send you a photo." I take a quick picture with my phone and send it through.

"I'll look into it. Get back to the station so we can get a crew out to look for her."

I'm already driving as fast as I can back to the station. This is a nightmare. How the fuck will we find her now? Every minute we don't know where she is, is time lost.

I pull up at the station and check my phone. While I've been driving, it's been blowing up with messages from Talon. I don't have time to check them, and I'm here now, so he can brief me inside. I go straight to the conference room where the briefing has started without me. Boss sees me enter and gives me a sympathetic nod before going on.

"We'll split into two crews: one to go find where Dominic has Ivy, while the other needs to get to the docks and work out which shipping container has the drugs. Our new intelligence is saying they're supposed to be transported tonight." I have no idea how this all relates, but Boss is fuming mad. "This is to stay between this crew. No one else in the office is to know, understood?" We all nod.

The drug team heads out, leaving Talon and Sean with me to work out how to find Ivy.

"Talon, what's going on? How does any of this relate to Ivy?"

"It seems Ivy's ex-husband has been a busy man while in prison."

My hands form into fists at the word *husband*. If he's touched her, I'm going to fucking kill him.

"He's now got big connections in the drug ring," Talon goes on. "It took us a while to piece it all together, but he's the man on the inside we've been trying to find, and he's going by Dom."

"I'd say your girl is in more trouble than we originally thought," says Sean.

"Walker, in my office now," Boss yells as he's heading for the door. I pursue him.

"What's going on, Boss? I need to be out there trying to find Ivy," I say in frustration, running my hands through my hair. Why aren't we moving? I'm pacing back and forth in his office.

"I know, son, but you need to be careful. This isn't just some ex out for revenge. He's a dangerous man and has lots of help around him. He's working with Jimmy Barrett. There's something more too. I didn't want to say it out there because I don't know who we can trust, but one of us is leaking information to him. Those photos you found at the studio... they're from this station."

"What?! One of us set this up? I don't believe it." I can't. I've been working in this station for 15 years, this crew is like family. No one here would do this.

"I'm not happy about it either, but we've known for some time that someone was helping evidence disappear."

"Yeah, we have. What do we do now?"

"Keep your wits about you, son. Don't trust anyone until we get this sorted and we find your girl."

I walk back into my office, not having any idea where to start. I just want to find her.

I'm fuming mad one of our own has helped a madman kidnap my Ivy.

"Come on, Theo," Sean says, "you're with me. We'll go look for your girl. Talon, you stay and see what you can find here, and let us know if you come up with anything worth looking into."

"On it." Talon types away at his computer. I have no idea what he's even typing in, since we have no real leads as to where Dom could have taken her.

"Where are we even going to start looking?"

"Some abandoned warehouse in the industrial estate. Boss thinks they might have the shipment leaving from there, and he could be holding your girl there as well."

"Okay, what are we waiting for then?"

We take off in the direction of Sean's car. The thing I don't get is why Boss didn't tell me all this when I was just in his office with him? It seems odd to me, but I just want to find her, so guess we should just go with it.

CHAPTER TWENTY-NINE

IVY

OH, THE NOISE... WHY ARE THERE SO MANY SEAGULLS this morning? My hands go to my head. It's thumping, and the screeching of the birds is not helping.

What did I do last night? I can't think, my mind is blank.

I slowly open my eyes, squinting as I try to focus on the surrounding room. I'm not in my room or Theo's... What is this place? It's a small room with just a bed and a small window with sunlight peeking through the blinds, and it looks like a door that leads to a bathroom of some sort. The floor is a rustic, aged timber, and the walls look like they're fibro with paint peeling off. Wherever I am, it's very run down.

I can still hear those bloody seagulls. They're making my head pound. I need some painkillers. I can also hear the slight sound of tumbling waves, and I can smell the salt in the air. I must be near the beach.

I feel a heavy arm on my hip—then the memory washes back over me. He's back! I blacked out at the studio, and he took me!

Beads of perspiration form on my forehead as the realisation hits me. This is bad—very, very bad. Where the fuck am I? Oh God, what happened while I was blacked out? I suddenly feel sick.

I need to run, I need to escape. I try to slowly wriggle out of his grip, but he's quick to wake up, rolling on top of me and pinning me to the mattress. *No!* I cry internally as he looks down at me, a sardonic smile reaching his lips. He didn't spend his time in prison thinking about how he could redeem himself and become a better person. No, this man has been working on reaching some new status as pure evil.

"Morning, my beautiful wife. Where do you think you're going so early?" Think quick, Ivy, and try not to piss him off.

"Just to the bathroom," I say as innocently as I can. I've got to work out how to get away from him. Harmony will be with Jenna, but she'll be worried. I need to get home to her. I just have to pray that Jenna worked out what was going on and called Theo and he's coming to save me.

"Okay." He drops my hands and lets me walk to the bathroom. He walks close behind me, and when I go to close the door, he puts his foot in the way to stop me. "The door stays open. How stupid do you think I am? I'm not allowing you to escape."

Gross, he's such a fucking creep. He's right, though—as soon as he turns his back, I'm out of here. I finish up in the bathroom and splash my face with water, trying to get rid of the pain in my head.

I look at myself in the mirror. I look terrible, minor cuts all over my face that must be from the gravel driveway last night. *Be strong, Ivy, you can do this. You have escaped him once before. You can do it again.*

I make my way back into the bedroom and sit on the end of the bed. He follows me, his eyes never leaving me.

"What do you want, Dominic?"

"I want my life back, the one you destroyed by going to the police." His eyes bore into me.

"What was I supposed to do? You nearly killed our baby! I wasn't letting you do that."

He looks like he's on the edge of losing his shit. He takes a deep breath, and I flinch as he stands, thinking he's about to hurt me.

"You don't need to remind me of that. If you can just be a good girl while I get a few things sorted out here this morning, then we can go back to our old life, before you got pregnant." What is he talking about? He's deluded!

"The baby didn't die. She was born, you know that, right? I can't go back anywhere with you. I have a child to look after and a life here." He's freaking me out. I expected him to be angry, but he's talking like this is a simple mix-up that will be straightened out in no time. At least when he's mad, I know what to expect. I don't know what this is.

"I'm sure your friends back here can take care of her. You, on the other hand, will be coming with me!"

"Like hell! I'm not going anywhere with you. You've lost your mind." He comes up in my face, his nostrils flaring, his breathing heavy, trying to control his anger. He puts both his hands on my shoulders and shakes me, but I'm not scared of him anymore. I just need to stay alive so I can get the fuck away from him and back to my baby.

"Don't make me mad now, wifey. I have spent five years setting up a better life for us. You won't have to worry about a thing. Just do what I say, and I won't need to hurt you, okay? We can be happy in this new life I have sorted."

"What have you done, Dominic?" What is he on about?

He's been in prison that whole time, what could he have possibly done that would set up his future?

"That's not something you need to worry your pretty little head over. Everything is going to be perfect." He kisses me on the forehead, and I cringe. "Now, I don't want to, but I need to go into town and grab a few supplies for our trip home, so I'm going to have to tie you up while I'm gone." He's still looking straight at me, waiting for my reaction.

"You don't have to do that, I won't go anywhere," I whisper in a feeble attempt to avoid being tied up.

He just laughs in my face. "Nice try, but I'm not taking my chances on that." He grips both my wrists, pulling them behind my back, and makes fast work of tying them together, then he pushes me back to the bed and starts on my ankles.

"Now be a good girl and have a little rest while I'm gone. It's going to be a long drive home," he says as he closes the door to the bedroom.

And I'm left alone.

Theo

It's the early hours of the morning now. Our entire crew has been out looking for Ivy since she was taken last night.

I've been trying to piece it all together. This drug case is something we've been working on for three years now, but how does it all relate to Dom and Jimmy Barrett? How could he have been running this operation from prison, and who in this station is helping them?

Talon has traced the photos back to a computer downstairs that is not being used by anyone. He has hacked their user account, and we now have access to their emails. They go back a while, most of it trivial shit, so it's not helping at all.

Ivy's phone hasn't been used since she was taken.

I've been on the road with Sean, checking all the abandoned warehouses in the industrial estate that Boss put us on to, but there was nothing there. It all feels so hopeless, we just don't have enough to go off.

Sean has pulled into the petrol station so we can refill and keep looking. As he hops out of the car, he makes a point of putting his mobile phone in his pocket. Odd, since he'll only be gone a few minutes, but he has been acting strangely all night. He seems on edge, jumpy even. I don't trust him at all. There is something so off with him.

I take the chance to look around his car while he's filling up. I can't see anything that would help me work him out. Once he's filled the car, he heads inside to pay. I hear a text ping, but it's not my phone, and Sean has his on him. Then, another ping. It's definitely a text and sounds like it's coming from the glove box.

I know I shouldn't snoop, but it's weird that he would have a second phone... and the curiosity gets the better of me. I look over at the shop, checking what Sean is doing, and he's at the fridge looking at the drinks, so I click open the glove compartment and pull out a phone. I check what it says. I don't have his password so I can only see what comes up on the home screen, and it's cut off.

Unknown: *Everything is going to plan. The honey's at the old beach shack. Shipment is arriving at 7am, dock 4. Just keep' em away at your end and...*

That's it, that's all I can see. But that's enough for me to know it's him. *He's* the one that has been screwing us over from the inside. So much makes sense now. I check where he is again, and he's paying, so I slip the phone back in the glove box exactly where I found it.

Think, Theo, how do I get him to take me there? He hasn't seen this message yet so he won't know the exact location or time, but he would have to know where the beach shack is, and there is no way he will willingly take me to her.

I quickly call Talon. "Tell Boss it's Sean. A text arrived on his phone while he was getting petrol. I'm going to need backup at the beach, north end I'm guessing by the text. It's an old beach shack there. It's close to the drop-off point."

"Where is the drop-off point?"

"Dock four, seven am. Got to go, he's coming back." I disconnect the call.

Sean climbs into the car.

"That was Talon. Dom has been spotted at the local shops heading north down Shirley Street. We're the closest to him so we need to move."

"Okay, alright, I'm on it." He jumps in the car, slamming the door, obviously irritated we're heading in the right direction, and there's not much he can do about it.

Now to find out what the fuck is actually going on. "Thanks for staying back and driving round all night to help me find her. I know you're probably used to flying solo these days, but I really appreciate it. You're a good friend."

"Yeah, no worries, anything to help you, mate."

I can't believe this guy. But now that I know it's him, I want to know as much as I can that might help. "Did they ever find out what happened to your partner? I haven't heard anything around the station. So strange, he just disappeared?"

"Ha, yeah, it was weird. No, nothing yet. Honestly, I think he was doing the dodgy on his wife and did a runner." He laughs—he actually thinks it's funny. I have a pretty good idea of what happened to him. I'd say he worked out what Sean was up to and that's why he disappeared.

Sean puts on his indicator to go right. "We're heading towards Shirley Street, it's left."

"Oh yeah, sorry." He changes his blinker and turns left to head towards Shirley Street and the beach. He drives up the road a bit, then pulls over to a secluded spot on the side of the road.

Before I work out what he's doing, he pulls his gun. "I'm sorry, man. We've worked together a long time, and you're a good guy, but you're going to fuck up my plans."

Ivy

As soon as I hear his car drive away, the tears tumble down my face. I try to wriggle my arms free, but it's no use. There's no way I'm getting out of these knots. The rope burns my skin as it rubs, but I will not give up, I can't.

I close my eyes and try to imagine what the rope looks like as I feel it will my fingers. I've found the end of one bit. Maybe if I can push it back through, it will loosen a bit.

Just as I think I'm getting somewhere, I lose it. Fuck, this is hopeless. All I can do is pray Theo has worked it out and is coming to help me.

Who are you kidding, Ivy? That's the shit that happens in movies, not in real life. It won't happen.

. . .

It's got to have been over an hour. He's going to be back soon. My wrists are raw from trying to wiggle free, and I'm a sweaty mess, but I have to keep trying. I'm not going anywhere with him. He won't win, he can't.

I push to my feet and hop into the bathroom, trying to find anything that might help me in here, but there is nothing. But I catch sight of myself in the mirror, and if I can see the knot...

I got it! This time it pushes through, and I wiggle my hands again. This time, the knot loosens up. My hands are free! They're bloody and bruised, but I don't have time to worry about that. I quickly untie my ankles and rotate them around to get the blood pumping properly again.

As the pins and needles ease in my hands and feet, I slowly stand up, looking around the room for my shoes. Then I remember I was barefoot when he took me. I don't know how far I'm going to get without shoes, but I have no choice. The familiar feeling washes over me from my past, barefoot and desperate to escape him before it's too late. Shoes aren't important, I just have to run.

I'm ready to make a run for it when I hear a car. I hope it's not him, but when I dart over to the window to check—fuck, it's him! Of course it's him.

I have no time to escape. What am I going to do? *Think, Ivy, think.* I run to the tiny kitchen. There's got to be a knife in here or something I can use as a weapon. I madly pull out all the drawers. He's going to be inside any second. No knives, but I see a saucepan sitting in the bottom cupboard. That will have to do, it's all I've got.

I run behind the front door to hide, saucepan in hand. If I can hit him hard enough, it might just buy me enough time to get away.

He throws open the door. "Honey, I'm home," he calls,

and without another thought, I swing the saucepan as hard as I can toward his face. He catches it in his hand and tackles me to the floor.

No, this can't be happening! I was so close to escaping this time.

He's on top of me, his legs on either side, pinning me to the ground. "You fucking bitch, you thought you could escape me?" He slaps me hard across the face, then his hands are on my neck. "I did this all for you so we can have a fresh start, a better life together, never having to worry about money again. We would have it made, and this is how you repay me?"

His hands are squeezing down hard on my neck now as he yells at me. I gasp for breath, but it's no use. This is how it's going to end.

I try to push him off, but as I struggle, my breaths get shorter.

Theo

THERE IS NO WAY THIS SLIMY FUCKER IS GOING TO GET away with this. "There's back-up on its way now. What are you going to do, shoot everyone?"

His smile leaves a sick feeling on my insides, because I know he has gone too far already, and we both know there is no coming back from this.

"Give me your gun, Theo."

I reluctantly hand it over. All I can think about is if he shoots me, I'm not going to get to Ivy in time. And what about our kids? My chest constricts at the thought. I can't think about them right now—I need to keep a level head and remember my training. I can get out of this.

"Out of the car, and don't try anything stupid, Theo. I will kill you."

I ease out of the car, his eyes on me the whole time, gun drawn. He follows me around to my side of the car, positioning the gun to my back. "Walk until I tell you to stop."

There's a secluded beach path and I walk down it, stumbling over the uneven sandy pathway deeper into the scrub. "Turn here." He's leading me off the track where the scrub is denser. If I'm going to do something and not just accept my fate, I need to do it now before we go any deeper.

I feign tripping on an old log and stumble to the ground, grabbing a broken branch and knocking his legs from under him at the same time. Lucky for me, he didn't see it coming and goes down quickly into the bush. Without hesitation, I grab for his gun, wrestling him.

I hear Talon shout, "Sean, stop where you are or I'm going to shoot!"

The distraction is enough for Sean to get the upper hand and take control of the gun. "Yeah, you don't want to do that or I'm going to shoot your man Theo here."

Talon looks between us, assessing what to do. "There is an entire team on their way here, you have no chance of getting away with any of this. Put down the gun now before you do anything stupid, and we can talk."

"Too late for talking."

I give Talon the nod to shoot. It's the only way we're going to get out of here. He looks at me, worried, but we can read each other well enough that we know what has to happen. He looks once more between us and pulls the trigger. As he does, I dive out of the way.

But it's too late.

Sean's gun has gone off as well, and the pain radiates through my leg where I've been hit. I grip my leg, looking behind me to see Sean on the ground. Talon's bullet has hit him in the chest, and he's clutching the wound, bleeding out.

Talon grabs Sean's gun and comes to help me. "How bad is your leg?"

Boss has finally caught up and comes running through the shrubs. "I heard shooting what happened?

"Go see Sean," Talon yells to him as he drops down to look over the damage to my leg.

I take another look and can see how lucky I actually am. The bullet has grazed my outer thigh. It stings like a bitch, but I'm going to be okay. "Not as bad as it feels. We need to get out of here and try to find Ivy. I'm pretty sure she's at the beach shack down at the end of North Beach."

Talon rips off his shirt and passes it to me. "Here, wrap this around to slow the bleeding." I do as he says, and he helps me up to standing.

"Boss, we're going to find Ivy. You okay here?"

"Yeah, I'll organise an ambulance." He talks into his police radio. "We need an ambulance to the beach path on Shirley Street."

I limp out of there as fast as I can, following Talon. We make it back to his car and jump in.

We arrive and park across the road near the beach, so they won't hear us. The front door is ajar. "You go round the back, and I'll try the front."

"You okay?"

"I'm fine, just get around the back. We have no idea what we're dealing with. There could be a few of them around."

I stagger up to the front door of the beach shack slowly,

gun drawn, my leg throbbing and the blood soaking through the shirt and running down my leg. The first thing I see is Ivy. She's lying on the ground, and it doesn't look good.

I'm too late.

I scan the room, but there's no sign of Dom. I rush over to her, checking for her pulse. She's warm, and I can feel her heartbeat. She's still alive!

"Ivy, it's me, Theo. You're okay, everything is going to be alright. Open your eyes so I know you hear me." She doesn't move. Then I feel the cold steel against the back of my head.

Dom is standing right behind me.

"You came to save her, did you, lover boy? How romantic. It's such a shame you're too late. Drop your fucking gun and stand up." I throw my gun down in front of me, standing up slowly, like he instructed.

"What did you do, Dominic?" My poor angel lies lifeless in front of me. I know she's alive but only barely. She needs urgent medical attention. There are marks on her wrists and ankles—obviously from being tied up—bruises on her neck and face. It looks like he's strangled her.

I've failed. I didn't get here before he could hurt her again.

"She couldn't follow instructions and was going to screw up my plans. She became a problem, and problems need to be eliminated... much like yourself."

"Put the gun down," I hear from outside. Talon must have scoped the place and come back around the front. Thank God.

Dom laughs, the gun still firmly positioned to the back of my head. "As if you pretty boys are going to be shooting me. I have been watching you lot for a while now with a friend of mine, and we've orchestrated quite the operation right under your nose."

I can hear the faint sound of sirens in the distance. Back-up was slow, but it's on the way. My eyes are on Ivy, begging her to wake up.

"That's where you're wrong," I say. "The mate you have been working with, Sean—he is as we speak bleeding out while waiting for an ambulance to arrive, so unless you want to end up like him, put the gun down now."

I see her move slowly, her hands going to her throat as she gasps for breath. Her eyes search the room and find me. She's alive! My eyes plead with her not to say a word, then I flick my gaze down to the ground where my gun is. Dom mustn't be able to see her from where he's standing behind the front door, or he's too preoccupied with Talon, who is now negotiating with him, to notice.

Ivy slowly inches over to where my gun sits, while Talon keeps Dom busy. She grips the gun. Using all the energy she can muster, she lines the gun up with his upper body. I give her a slight nod, and she pulls the trigger, then collapses back to the ground. Dominic flies back, clutching at his chest.

"You fucking bitch," he screams, spitting up blood. His gun drops to the ground. He won't survive that kind of bullet wound. Even with the ambulances on their way, I'd say he has minutes, if that.

Ivy pushes up, crawling over to him with whatever strength she has left. Her breathing is shallow, and I rush to stop her, but she looks to me, pleading like she needs this, so I let her go.

She looks him right in the eyes. "You deserve to rot in hell." She spits at him, her voice hoarse and barely a whisper.

He goes to say something back to her, the look in his

eyes murderous, but he can't get the words out through the spluttering of blood now gurgling from his open mouth.

I rush to her as fast as I can with the wound in my leg. "It's okay, angel, you're going to be okay."

I fall to the floor beside her, exhaustion overwhelming me. I cradle her in my arms, pulling her in as close as I can, whispering to her, "He's dead, he can't hurt you again."

Her tears run freely down her face, and I can feel the sobs escape as I hold her close. I can't even imagine what she's been through tonight. The thoughts that must have run through her head, the fear. But I have her now in my arms where she belongs, and I'm never going to let her go.

CHAPTER THIRTY

IVY

I feel so woozy, but I can hear sirens all around and feel Theo's strong arms holding me, assuring me. I say *I am safe* on repeat in my head. My body trembles uncontrollably, even in his warm arms. I can't seem to make myself stop. He brushes the hair away from my eyes and whispers to me how much he loves me, his bright blue eyes dull. I can see it in them; he thought I was gone.

A lady's voice breaks me from the trance of his eyes, and there's suddenly a lot of movement around me. Someone with a booming voice yells instructions—I think it's Theo's partner, Talon. Then warm hands wrap around me, and I'm being hoisted up and carried to a stretcher.

The kind face of the paramedic comes into view. "So cold," is all I can say.

"It's okay, dear, we're here to look after you, you just need to lie down for a bit. Let us take care of you." She holds my hand. "Do you understand? Squeeze back if you do."

I grip her hand as hard as I can with the trembling. "I'll get you a blanket." She disappears, returning moments later, to cover me in a warm cotton blanket. It doesn't help. I still shake and shiver, my body cold right through to the core.

"It's shock, sweetie, it looks like you have been through a lot. I'll run some checks." She wraps the blood pressure sleeve on my arm.

"I'm fine, I don't need any help," I hear Theo say. "I need to make sure she's okay." I turn my head to the side to see him limping towards me. He takes my hand. "Is she okay?" he asks the paramedic. His worried eyes meet mine, and I feel so terrible to have caused him so much concern.

"She'll be going in for checks and observation. She's in shock. You need to ride with me to get someone to look you over."

"I'm fine."

"Yeah, but you're not." She looks down to his leg.

I'm not sure what she's talking to Theo about, but I close my eyes and try to block it all out, try to calm my beating heart and get control over this persistent shivering.

I'm wheeled inside the ambulance, and I hear the door shut. Theo is by my side. I grip his hand, too frightened to let go. I can hardly believe he's here with me and we're both alive after everything we've been through in the past 24 hours.

"I called Elly and Jenna. The kids are fine, happy to hear they'll be able to see us soon, but they have no idea what happened, and I think it would be best if we keep it that way," he says quietly.

I open my eyes to look at him. This beautiful man hasn't left my side since I came to. I have no idea how I'll explain all of this to Harmony, she must have been so worried. Theo brushes some hair behind my ear and smiles down at me. I look over at him, my saviour. My eyes drop lower and I realise he's hurt as well. That must have been what the paramedic was talking about.

"Your leg, what happened?" My voice trembles, now I'm worried about him. His leg is wrapped in some sort of white fabric and it's covered in blood.

"Sean shot me. It's just a flesh wound, I'm fine." He shakes his head.

"You're not fine, you've been shot. You need to have it looked at," I demand, starting to panic. He was shot by one of the guys he works with?

"Lucky we're on our way to the hospital then." He smiles at me cheekily. Somehow, he hasn't lost his ability to be a smart-arse to me even in this situation, and I know it's all for my benefit, because he would be in a lot of pain.

Everything is all starting to make a lot more sense now. Sean was warning me to stay away from Theo because he was working with Dominic, and he must have been feeding him all the information about me all along. That's why he found me so quickly. I should have trusted my instincts and got Theo to look into him sooner. Maybe then this all wouldn't have happened. "I knew there was something off with Sean. I can't believe he was working with Dom all this time."

"Yeah, you and me both. He had us all fooled. I'm so sorry I didn't work it all out sooner." He squeezes my hand. He looks so defeated but none of this is on him.

"Theo," I say, gripping his hand even tighter, "I thought I was going to die. There was no way out. I tried everything to get away from him." I sniffle to hide the fact I'm about to cry.

He brushes his other hand over my face. "Hey, hey, it's okay, it's all over now. He can't touch you again, angel, you're safe." He leans closer to me, and I feel so safe with him. He did everything he could to get to me, to protect me, just like he promised he would—and he was shot and still kept fighting to get to me. Somehow, we both survived. I owe him and his partner Talon my life.

THEO

WE'VE SPENT MOST OF THE DAY IN THE HOSPITAL. Ivy has just been released, the shock having worn off, and the rest of her injuries will heal up over the next week or so. She is safe and will never have to deal with Dom again.

She sits with me while my leg is stitched up. We have avoided having our statements taken until we have the all-clear from the hospital staff, but I know what's coming, and it's not going to be easy for her to go through. There is no way she will be charged with Dominic's death because she was acting in self-defence while he was threatening her and two officers, but we still have to go through the process, and she will have to relive every detail as they take her statement.

Talon pops his head around the curtain, still dressed in the same clothes from last night; he obviously hasn't been home. "Is he going to live?" he asks the doctor stitching me. "Ivy," he kisses her cheek.

The doctor turns to him. "He'll be fine as long as he doesn't go trying to stop a gun-wielding madman with his body again." She gives me a serious look.

"Yeah, about that. Sean survived. Boss stayed with him until the ambulance arrived." His brow knits together when he says it. He's not happy he survived. A part of me feels the same. He might have been our mate and colleague once, but he was the one all along causing all this trouble, helping Dom and Jimmy Barrett. He is scum just like them.

"What are they doing with him?" Ivy asks nervously.

Talon watches the doctor stitch me back together and winces at the sight. It's not that bad; I've been watching her the whole time.

"I have given a statement, but they're waiting on your statements before we go any further. For now, he's under police guard in ICU. He lost a lot of blood so it will be hit or miss if he makes it through the night or not."

"I just don't understand how this all happened. Sean used to be a decent guy—at least I thought so."

"Yeah, you and me both. You're not going to like this, Theo, but apparently this has been going on since Vinnie was in town."

"What?" I snap. My heart aches all over again. Knowing someone I so close to me could have been responsible for hurting me and my family so much. He was the one who helped Vinnie back then. He was one of the ones responsible for Fi's death. All these years he has acted like a mate, and he was working for the other side the whole time. My fists are clenched. I want to get out of here and deal with him myself.

I feel a tug at my side. "Theo, you need to relax so I can finish stitching you up," says the doctor. I take a breath and try to relax but it's no use, I'm fuming mad. Ivy rubs the back of my hand in slow stokes. She offers me a sympathetic smile, and I soften a little.

"Do you want me to go? We can talk about this later," Talon asks, looking between me and ivy.

"No, it's alright. What else do you know?"

"Sean got involved with Vinnie, who introduced him to the Barrett brothers, and he has been working for them ever since—well, Jimmy anyway. He might have been in prison but the operation he built is still forging ahead. He just found new contacts on the inside to help, so when he's released, it's all still in place for him."

"New contacts like Dominic?" asks Ivy.

Talon nods. "We will have more details about it when we dig a bit deeper."

The doctor finishes up the stitches and places a bandage over the top. "Keep me posted," I say.

"Will do. For now, I'm heading home for some well-deserved sleep." He squeezes Ivy's hand and turns to leave.

"Talon..." says Ivy. "Thank you."

"Just doing my job." He offers her a smile before walking away.

And we're both lucky he's so good at his job. He saved my arse twice today.

CHAPTER THIRTY-ONE

IVY

It's been one month since that day, and things couldn't be better. I no longer have to fear Dominic will come and find me, because, as awful as it sounds, he's dead. Sean spilled every detail and ratted out all of their accomplices to the Boss when he thought he was dying at the beach that day. The rest of Theo's team managed to stop the whole drug shipment from ever leaving the dock area, and they're hoping that everyone involved is now behind bars.

The kids don't know what happened that night. They just think Theo had to stay back at work and had a fall, injuring his leg, and I was in a minor car accident. Harmony never needs to know what kind of evil monster her dad was, and when she's older, I will explain that he's never coming back, and that's all she needs to know.

I have decided to keep my new name. As much as I appreciate the name Lauren as what my parents gave me, it holds bad memories as well. Besides, Ivy was my new start. It's the only name all my friends and now family up here know me as, and I want to stick with it. Lauren was broken, but Ivy is strong.

"Hey, kids, we're here," Theo announces, pulling me from my daze staring out the car window. We've been driving from his place to the cute café he took me on our first date. I told Harmony about it, and she has been begging us to take her so she can have what she is calling a *family date* with us. Hope it lives up to her high expectations.

We get the kids out of their car seats, and as soon as their feet hit the ground, they're running towards the café. They're stopped at the front by Wendy, who kneels down to talk to them at their level. Theo takes my hand, and we catch up to them.

Wendy smiles to us warmly, her hands clutched together in front of her. "This is just too cute. The kids tell me you're on a family date, is that right?"

"They wanted to see what they were missing out on." I laugh.

"Well, I better show you to the best table we have and get you some menus then. Follow me," she says, marching straight towards the table we shared on our first date here. We've been here quite a few times since, but just the two of us while the kids were at school.

Theo has had the last month off work. He needed some time away from his job after everything that happened. The time together just the two of us during the day has been wonderful, then we go to school pick-up together and collect the kids for the day, have dinner together, and work out where we're all staying for the night.

We also took the kids to watch Uncle Drew compete at one of his surfing comps in Rottnest Island in Western Australia. We had the whole week there, even though he was only competing for three days. It was so nice to have a family holiday. Jasper and Harmony are both keen to be pro surfers now. Jasper is really into it and is actually quite good in the water for his age—Harmy not so much, but I will let her take some lessons with Drew when he gets back. It has been one of the most wonderful months of my life; we haven't had a single night apart. Other than me working, we're together.

Wendy stops at our table, and the kids hop up into their seats. She hands them two menus, and they sit looking over them like they can read what they say.

"I already know what I'm having," Harmony says. "A sausage roll. I saw them in the front counter." She licks her lips. "They're my favourite."

"Ooh, I might get one of those too," Jasper says. "Can I have a sausage roll, Dad, please?"

"Of course you can, buddy. Just give me and Ivy a sec to work out what we want, then we can order."

We take our seats, Theo next to Jasper and me next to Harmony. I glance over the menu, but I already know exactly what I want as well. The carrot cake and chunky-steak pie—in that order.

We give Wendy our orders, and she disappears to the kitchen. Theo takes my hand across the table, and Harmony gives Jasper a sassy look.

"We wanted to bring you two here today to have a little chat," says Theo, turning towards the kids.

Their little faces look worried. "Oh, I thought it was for the yummy food," says Harmony, thinking she might be in trouble.

"It's not a bad chat," I say quickly, "it's just something Theo and I have been talking about, and it affects both of you as well, so we wanted to check with you and see your thoughts on it."

Theo takes over from me. "We think that all the going between houses is a bit disruptive for all of us, and it might be nice if..." He pauses, looking at me, and I nod for him to go on. "It might be nice if we all moved into the same house together."

"What would you both think of that?" I ask.

They look between each other, then over to us. "So like, all live in one house all the time, like a family?"

"Well, yeah, kinda like a family. Would you like to do that?"

"Yes, that would be so much fun." Harmony beams, clapping her little hands in front of her.

Jasper is quiet and looks to be thinking it all over. "What about you, Jas, how would you feel about us all living together?" I ask. "We don't have to do this straight away if you're not ready, we can wait." I want to make sure he's comfortable.

Harmony wears her heart on her sleeve. She's dramatic and always quick to voice her opinion, so you always know what she wants. Jasper is quiet, he's more calculated. I've noticed how he likes to think things over before he decides.

And truth be told, we *are* rushing into this. We haven't really been together all that long, but I just know that with Theo, he is the only one I have ever felt like this about, and I want to spend the rest of my life with him. If we need to wait for Jasper to catch up, I'm totally fine with that. We will stick it out until he's ready for this big change.

Theo turns to him. "What are you thinking, mate? We don't have to rush this. We can wait awhile if you like."

Jasper gives a little nod. "I think this is a good idea, but I'm just not sure where everyone will sleep. At Ivy's place there are only three bedrooms, and at our house... well, we do have four, but one is a junk room and there is so much stuff in there, there's no way a bed would fit. There's four of us. Dad, Ivy, Harmony and me."

"Oh yeah, where will I sleep?" huffs Harmony.

Theo chuckles, and I can't help but laugh a little too. We were so worried about how he would go with the changes, and all he's concerned about is the sleeping arrangements.

"We think maybe Ivy and Harmony and Tiger could come and live with us, Jas, and you don't need to worry about the sleeping arrangements. Ivy has agreed to share with me so you can keep your room, and Harmony can have her own room as well. We won't even need to touch the junk room. How does that sound?"

The kids grin with excitement. "Yes, yes, let's do that," they say.

I smile over at Theo. Everything is falling into place.

The kids' eyes widen as our food is placed on the table in front of us. "Can we have dessert first, Mum?" Harmony asks. This kid knows me too well.

"Why not, it's a special day." I laugh, taking a big bite of my cake.

They dig into the chocolate cake they both ordered, and within seconds, they are covered in the sticky, chocolaty mess.

We enjoy our pastries and cake, and when the last crumb is eaten, I stack the plates into a neat little pile on the table and try to brush the crumbs into a serviette to hide the gigantic mess we have made here today.

"Are we going to move all of our things in today, Mummy?"

"Theo and I have other plans for today, baby girl. We will try to move our things over slowly this week and the big things next weekend."

"Oh, okay," she says sadly.

"Don't be disappointed, we have a surprise for you this

afternoon, and I think it's something you're both going to like." Her frown turns into a grin, and she grabs my hands, dragging me from the table.

Theo

Just a short drive through town and we arrive at the location of the surprise. I glance over to Ivy. Her face is relaxed as she leans back in her chair. "Are you ready for this?" I whisper so the kids can't hear.

"I'm ready for anything with you," she says with a definite nod of the head.

She has been so different since the night her ex kidnapped her. She's relaxed and so happy. I would like to think it's because of me, and I'm sure some of it is, but knowing what she went through with him, and her knowing he's gone for good now and she will never have to face him again—she has been able to truly let go of her past and live in the now. She wakes up every day excited and ready for what's coming next, and our relationship has progressed quickly.

I can hardly believe I'm the same person. It wasn't that many months ago that I never wanted commitment again. Nothing scared me more. But with her, I knew the second I laid eyes on her, she was it—my future. And I can't believe how lucky I am.

I park the car, then turn around to see the kids' reactions. Ivy is looking over her shoulder as well, huge smirk on her face. She's so excited about this. I'm waiting for some sort of reaction, but the kids both look confused.

"This is where we got Tiger," says Harmony.

"Are we getting another cat?" asks Jasper excitedly.

I shake my head. "Not a cat. Tiger is enough trouble for all the cats in the world."

Ivy laces her hand with mine. "But we wouldn't have her any other way. That naughty kitty is the reason we found each other."

I kiss her lips, remembering that day. Who would have thought me nearly running over her cat would have brought us together. I don't really believe in fate, but there was a higher power working in our favour that day.

I turn back to the kids. "What have you been asking for, for as long as I can remember, Jas?"

He looks to Harmony. "It's a dog!" He squeals, and she squeals back.

The four of us make our way out of the car and push through the front door to the pet shelter. The kids can barely contain their excitement. Ivy chats to a lady on the front counter who then makes her way out from behind the desk and over to us. Her uniform is a white shirt with shelter's logo on it. Her name badge reads "Crystal." She's young, and you can tell by the swing of her long dark hair when she walks and the gigantic smile plastered on her face that she loves her job.

She bends down to talk to the kids. "I hear you kids are getting a new family member today."

"Yes," they say excitedly together.

"Well, follow me, I'll show you through to where the dogs are so you can pick out your new friend."

We walk quickly behind the lady, trying to keep up with her and the kids. Once inside the room with all the dogs, my heart sinks a little. It will be harder than I thought to pick just one. Looking at them all lined up in their cages just makes me feel sad for them, even though most of them look happy enough, with tails wagging.

Harmony has taken Jasper's hand, something I have noticed she likes to do a lot. She leads him over to a cage right down the end of the room with a medium-sized fluffy white dog who has her face pressed right up against the enclosure, tongue out, tail wagging happily. They crouch down by the cage and talk to her. Ivy takes my hand, and we join them.

Crystal smiles. "You kids have made a good choice. This dog has a beautiful nature and is great with kids." She turns to Ivy and me. "Very gentle. She's a Spoodle—a poodle crossed with a cocker spaniel."

"What do you kids think, is this the dog for us?" asks Ivy, going up to the cage and inspecting it more closely.

"She's the one," says Jasper quietly, looking at the dog lovingly.

"I'll get her out so you can have a pat," says Crystal. Opening the cage, the bundle of white fur comes bounding out straight to the kids, pushing up against them as they run their hands along her soft fur. They giggle as she licks their hands, her tail working overtime as they pat her.

"She is the perfect addition to our blended family," I say.

"I think you're right, she's the one. What are you kids going to name her?" asks Ivy.

"Her name is Daisy." Jasper points to the label on her cage, where there is clearly a name printed.

"She looks like a Daisy, that's the perfect name for her."

And our little blended family is complete. I couldn't be happier. I look at Ivy, and she smiles over at me. I wrap my arm around her and pull her into me, kissing her hair. I feel so lucky to have found her.

EPILOGUE
THEO

It's the peak of summer. The sun is warm and the air smells like fresh-cut grass. I have been putting this off for longer than I would have liked to, waiting for everything to be perfect. Today, it's time.

I pat my pants pocket for the fiftieth time this morning, just to make sure it hasn't fallen out. So many thoughts are going through my head. Is she going to think this is all too soon? We have been together for less than a year. But what a year it has been. Ivy and Harmony moved into the treehouse with me and Jasper. The kids have taken to each other really well and enjoy having someone to play with—when they're not fighting with each other. Tiger is still just as crazy, and our new addition, Daisy, fits in perfectly.

Ivy has no idea what's going on this morning. The rest of my family has known all week, because I needed a little help, but they have been sworn to secrecy. We all arrived at the beautiful farm I brought Ivy and the kids to earlier in the year. This has become a special place for us, and we got here early enough so we could have brunch with everyone.

I lean over to whisper in her ear. "Mum said she'll watch the kids. Come for a walk with me."

She gives me a curious look. "Okay... it's a stunning day, a walk would be nice." I take her hand, pulling her from the table, and we leave the rest of my noisy family behind.

The farther we walk from my boisterous family, the more I can hear. I hear my heart hammering in my chest. *Thump, thump, thump.* I hope I'm doing the right thing. She agreed to move in with me no problems, and life has never been better. But this is something we haven't talked about since that night Harmony brought it up right back at the beginning of our relationship, so I really have no idea where she stands on it. She has been there before, and maybe it's not something she wants to do again.

We walk through the paddocks past the little piggies the kids love so much. She gives me a sideways glance. "You're strangely quiet today, Theo. Is everything okay?"

"Yes, everything's fine, angel. Did I tell you how beautiful you look today?" She smiles, a light blush coming over her cheeks. She has to know just how gorgeous she really is, but still, every time I compliment her, it's the same reaction: a blush of the cheeks, shy smile like she has no idea. She's wearing my favourite pale-yellow sundress today. It highlights her tan and really makes her cobalt-blue eyes stand out. Her hair is in a loose braid over one shoulder, and it really suits her.

"You've said it at least three times already." She giggles.

"Well, you do, I can't believe how lucky I am to call you mine."

"I'm the lucky one." She smiles sweetly.

I stop walking and pull her into me, cupping her face and drawing her close to me with a long, slow kiss to her sweet lips. I pull back. "Come on, there's something I want to show you." I lead her by the hand towards the sunflower field. She gasps when she sees them, just like the first time. It is quite a sight, fields of beautiful sunflowers standing almost as tall as me, raising their big, golden-yellow heads to the sun.

"I love this place. They're just so... wonderful." She smiles, and her whole face lights up.

I search around in my pocket, trying not to be too obvious, and clasp the small velvet box in my hand, lowering to one knee and taking her hand.

Ivy looks at me, her eyes wide, blinking down at me. "Theo?" she starts, but I cut her off.

"Ivy, I know we haven't been together all that long, and I know this isn't something we've really talked about. But I love you, I adore you, and so does Jasper. You have been such a wonderful influence in both of our lives, and I just know that I have to have you forever. I understand if you can't do this, and it won't change anything if you say no, but I had to ask. I've known this is what I wanted since I met you."

I pull the box from my pocket and pop open the lid. There sits a ring with an oval-cut diamond cluster on a rose-gold band. God, I hope she likes it. I had Elly's help to pick it out, and she assures me this is the right one. I don't know how she knows that, but I'm trusting her. "Ivy Anderson, will you marry me?"

She continues to blink back at me, her mouth not moving.

My heart hammers in my chest. *Please say yes, please say yes*, I chant in my head.

Her lips turn up into a smile at the side and she opens her mouth. "How could you ever think I would say anything other than yes?"

She pulls me to my feet, and I pick her up, swirling her around before lowering her to the ground and pulling her in for a kiss. Before we know what's happening, there is loud cheering and whooping from behind us. I told them to wait, but they must have been unable to help themselves.

Jasper and Harmony come running towards us, and we swoop them up together, pulling them in for a family hug.

The End

COMING SOON
FOREVER DREW

JENNA

My heart hammers in my chest, and I feel the familiar uncomfortable churn of my belly. I can't believe I'm back doing this again. This was not my plan. I had hoped I could get a job as a waitress or in one of the cute boho retail shops along the main street. But just my luck, no one was hiring, and I couldn't afford to wait. I needed a job and fast. The life I'm trying to flee was dangerous, and in all honesty, in the end I was scared for my safety. I had seen too much and was afraid I was next. I probably am if my ex-boyfriend manages to track me down. I just pray that I'm far enough away that he won't.

It's been six months since I have needed to work, but the shitty circumstances of the past few weeks have brought me back to the only job I seem to be able to get. One I'm good at —and why wouldn't I be? I have been doing it since I was 15, and the moves come naturally.

This club is different to most I've been in; the room

surrounding me is set up like a circus tent, with a high ceiling of yellow-and-red-striped shiny satin fabric. There's a circular stage in the centre of the room where two girls are hanging from long silk apparatuses attached to the ceiling. I stand and watch in awe from the doorway to the change room.

"Arial acrobatics," says one of the other girls, making her way past me to start her shift, in a sparkly next-to-nothing outfit.

"They're amazing," I murmur in wonderment. I could stand here and watch them all day, their strong bodies twisted in silk as they twirl around. These girls are gorgeous and toned, with flashy sequined costumes that leave little to the imagination. They're more like gymnasts than strippers.

But we're all strippers here, no matter how talented they are with their acrobatic routine.

This is my first night at this club. I have been in training with them all week, learning the dance routines. The manager here has very high standards with her dances, so the routines need to be perfect. I have no idea why; from my experience, men couldn't care less how well we dance. They're here for the booze, tits, and arse. But I need this job, so I have learnt my routine carefully from Ariel, one of the other girls who has been here a few years.

It has been nice to get to know Ariel this week. I don't have any other friends in town yet, and she's been kind, taken me under her wing so to speak. So caring that she heard my sob story and offered me her spare room to stay in until I'm back on my feet. She's stunning, with long strawberry-blonde hair and sparkling green eyes. Her name was picked from her resemblance to the little mermaid.

As I watch, a rowdy group enters the club and heads straight for the roped-off area down the back, where I'm working tonight. I take a deep breath, trying to mentally prepare myself for the night ahead. *You've got this, just like riding a bike*, I joke to myself, trying to get my nerves under control. Ariel grabs my hand and drags me to the bar alongside her. She motions for two shots, and the bartender places them on the bar.

She holds the glass up to me. "Come on, this'll help. I can see how nervous you are." She has been such a lifesaver this week, and she's right, I'm nervous as hell.

I glace at the clear liquid in the shot glass. Tequila. I'm not sure if this is a good idea but I throw it back, and it burns my throat.

She does the same, then motions to the bartender for another two. We tip them back in unison, and she pulls a face. I giggle at her. I like this girl. She is fun and easy-going, everything I'm not. I feel the tingle of warmth radiating through my body already. Much better.

"You good now, girl?" She smiles.

I nod. "Let's do this."

"Good. It's our lucky night; we have a buck's party of young sexy rich guys to dance for in the private room."

I follow her through the back onto the smaller stage and take my place on the pole. As the music starts, we move, and for the most part it comes back to me.

I should feel lucky, because this club is different to any I worked in Sydney. The manager is nice and actually gives a shit about the girls who work here. I pay attention to the music and follow the moves Ariel taught me. I think I'm nailing it. My confidence starts to return, and I'm relaxing. I can do this.

This isn't my chosen profession, but things in life haven't always gone my way. Or ever, really, starting with being dumped on a doctor surgery doorstep when I was six months old, with a note saying that my parents had both died and I needed someone to take care of me. To this day I have no idea if they actually died or if they just didn't want me, but that was the start of the series of unfortunate events that has been the life of Jenna West.

I came to work as a stripper when I was 15 because I had no other options. I couldn't stay at the foster home I had been placed in. Things had gotten out of hand with my foster brother, and it got to the point where the home that was supposed to be my secure place in this world didn't feel so safe anymore, so I ran away. While on the streets, I met a girl who was a little older than me, and she hooked me up with the job. I was too young to be working in a club at the time, but armed with a fake ID, they didn't think twice about giving me the job.

So I was a stripper. The money was decent enough, and I was able to survive on my own just fine. I was doing okay until I met Vinnie. I kinda knew he was going to be trouble right from the beginning. He was one of the heavies for Mr Donovan, the owner of the club where I worked. Mr Donovan was a big name in the city, mostly because he owned half of it. He was the one everyone bowed down to, so Vinnie had a lot of power, and he knew it.

I should have known better than to get involved with him, but he was nice to me and offered me a place to stay. He didn't want me to strip anymore, so he paid for everything and took care of me. It seemed like a sweet deal, and for a while it was—until I walked in on him murdering some poor young guy.

The scene was horrific and still plays over in my head when I close my eyes, even now a few weeks later. I can't unsee it, it was so awful. Tears instantly prick at my eyes, and I blink them away. I can't cry now, I need to focus on what I'm doing. I can't fuck this job up, I really need it.

I always knew Vinnie was one of the heavies for Mr Donovan, but I had no idea he took things that far. It scared the shit out of me. I wasn't hanging around another day, so I grabbed the few important possessions I had—which weren't many, they all fit in a small backpack—and I got the hell out of there. It was like déjà vu, running from my foster home all over again.

So now I'm back where I started all those years ago; 22years old, not a cent to my name and still dancing for money. I just pray Vinnie doesn't give a shit that I'm gone, cause if he wants to find me, I'm sure he will, and I don't even want to think of what will happen then.

Ariel suggested a disguise to make me feel more comfortable, so I'm wearing a lolly-pink bobbed wig and Barbie-pink lippy, the best I could do to disguise myself with hardly any cash to splash on an outfit.

I run my hands seductively over the red sequined outfit I have on. I can't help but snap out of my thoughts when one of the guys from the party takes a seat directly in front of me. He's easy to dance for, young, maybe mid-20s and cute, longish, sandy-blond hair with a curl to it and a sexy-as-fuck simile with dimples. He's dressed in black jeans, a white t-shirt, and a leather jacket. He looks good enough to eat. But it's his kind blue eyes that keep me focusing on him, and my first-day jitters disappear.

There are plenty of other girls dancing here tonight, but he hasn't taken his eyes off me. They're a piercing blue, gorgeous, the kind of eyes you could get lost in. He's seriously dreamy. The type of guy that would never look at me twice unless I was on a pole.

And there it is, that slap back to reality. I know who I

am, and I wouldn't normally be worth his time of day. Yet he watches my every move tonight.

My group's turn on the stage is done, and it's time for us to make the rounds, offering lap dances. I sway my way over to him, hips moving to the music. "Hello, handsome." I purr, placing my hand on his shoulder. Faking every bit of confidence I don't have.

Close up, he smells divine. He is so good I'm thinking this must all be just a figment of my imagination, some sort of mirage I have made up to get me through my shift—or maybe those shots of tequila were stronger than I thought.

He relaxes back in his chair, getting comfortable as I move around him. That smile, man, he's something else.

"What's your name, gorgeous?" he asks, his deep voice making my insides somersault. He reaches out playing with the tassels on my outfit, his hungry eyes roaming down my body, starting with my breasts, then all the way down my legs.

I'm surprised by his question; most guys don't care what my name is. "I'm Bambi," I say, batting my eyelashes. It's the most ridiculous name, but all the girls here have names from either Disney films or children's stories. Weird, but it's fitting for me, I guess.

"Of course that's your name." He smirks.

I move around him, dropping to my knees then slowly running my hands up his legs. As I stand, my breasts are just millimetres from his face. "Named after the beloved childhood character, because I too am an orphan." Why did I just tell him that? It's his eyes, they have me under a spell. He asks a question and I want to tell him everything, but I really need to shut the fuck up.

His face drops as he takes me in, his gaze questioning. "Oh, that's a sad story."

"Least that's what I was told anyway. I have no idea what happened to my parents, really." Why am I telling him my sob story? Because I secretly want to be saved by a gorgeous man like him. Rescued like a stray cat, taken home and cared for, loved. I really have hit an all-time low when all a handsome man like this has to do is ask me a few questions and I'm ready to go home with him. You'd think I would be more wary after the last situation and where that got me, but nope, still hoping for a saviour.

"That's awful!" I see the pity in his eyes, and I need to change the subject, get his eyes back on my body, not looking so sad. The poor man is here to be entertained, but he's going to go home feeling as depressed as I am.

"I guess, it was a long time ago now." I shrug, lifting one leg over his lap so I'm standing but straddling him. I run my hands up my body, starting with my tummy, until I reach my breasts. I squeeze them together and his attention is back where it should be, my tits. Good. I was blessed with amazing breasts, totally out of proportion to my thin frame. They've gotten me every job so far.

I roll my hips towards his cock. He is hard and massive, I can feel it through his jeans.

"What's your real name?" he asks.

I laugh at his question. "You know I can't tell you that. What's yours?"

"Drew." He pauses, watching me. "Tell me, what's a lovely girl like you doing dancing in a strip club, anyway?"

I turn away from him, so I'm almost sitting on his lap, my arse rubbing up against his hardened length. My head falls back, resting on his shoulder as I move on his lap. He is so chatty.

"Why do you assume this isn't what I want to be doing?

There's a lot of girls that love this job, and we make a shit-load of cash."

"I don't know, I just don't see it for you. You seem smart," he whispers, and I'm so close to him when he talks, I can feel his warm breath on my neck.

It's confusing. Being so close to his body has me thinking all sorts of naughty thoughts that I don't normally have while doing this job. But his words are pissing me off. Who does this guy think he is, sitting here, all judgemental about my life choices? Bet he has never had to struggle a day in his life.

"Thanks, guess I should take that as a compliment," I say, the sarcasm dripping from my every word.

"Sorry, I didn't mean to offend you or anything. You just don't look that happy to be here."

Oh, he's just trying to be nice. "Don't worry about it. I guess you're right, it's not my life ambition to strip forever. It's just a placeholder until something better comes along."

I turn back to him again, facing him. "You could try something else," he suggests.

"Not that simple. I just moved here and no one else is hiring. I've tried. Why do you care, anyway? Most guys I give a lap dance to just want to ogle my body, not give me career advice."

"I don't know. I was watching you up on the stage earlier. You just seem like you're going to be someone important in my life, and I want to help you."

My heart kicks up a beat. He wants to help me. What a strange thing for him to say. I take a step back from him, not quite knowing how to react. Am I being pranked or something? Can he read my thoughts that scream help me? I'm one more bad mistake away from ending it all. Or have I just got to the point where the deep depression I'm in is written all over my face, even when I'm trying to plaster on my best smile? And to say I'm going to be someone important in his life? I doubt that!

"You got all that from watching me dance for you? I must be better than I thought. What, has it been a while since you got laid or something, you getting desperate? There are girls here who will help you out with that if you need," I offer sweetly.

He pulls me back towards him, our faces so close. "I don't have any trouble getting laid, sweetheart, trust me."

"Okay, if you say so, handsome." Over his shoulder, I get the nod from my manager. I need to move on to someone else. "As lovely as it's been dancing for you, Drew, I'm being told I need to continue on. Enjoy your night," I whisper into his ear.

As I try to slip away, but he grabs my wrist. "I'm not finished with you yet," he protests, his voice low and growly. I glance back to the guard watching me and smile so he knows I'm okay.

"If you're lucky, I might come back." I give him a wink and pull out of his grip, sauntering away before security causes a scene. I can feel Drew's eyes on me the whole time I do. I would have liked to keep talking to him, it was nice to have a conversation, but I move on to the next guy, doing my routine.

I try to black out the way Drew just made me feel. What was that? I'm so used to being treated like shit that some good-looking guy says a few nice things to me and I go all mushy again, ready to make another mistake. I need to get my head together, toughen up a bit. I can't afford any more bad decisions.

This next guy I dance for is younger, but he couldn't care less about my life, and he's handsy, digging his fingers into my arse. I take a step back, glaring a warning at him. I need to keep my distance for this guy. I scope the room for that security guy and notice he's watching. He nods to Ariel, and she grabs my hand, and I dance with her, keeping our distance from the guy.

As we dance, I can't help but glance in Drew's direction. He's now talking with two other guys about his age, and they're all looking back at me. I feel a little uneasy. Something about the way one of them is looking at me isn't right. Has Vinnie worked out where I am already? No, he couldn't have. I'm just being paranoid.

Drew smiles over to me. "Bambi." He gestures with a wave for me to come over to where he's standing with his group. "Come meet my friends."

I wonder what they want. I whisper to Ariel, "Come and save me if I give you the signal."

"No worries, hunny." She takes over with Mr Handsy.

I sway my hips as I walk towards them. I twirl a strand of my wig around playfully, my eyes never leaving the three of them. They're all tall and handsome, the other two in suits. They look like they have money, intimidating standing as a group. One has dark hair and is unshaven, the other is more clean-cut looking with light brown hair—he's the one I don't like the look of. The way he assesses me makes my palms sweaty.

Drew introduces the other two. "This is Fraser and Blake. They're here for the buck's party as well; it's one of their business partners that's getting married."

I nod, standing back from them a little. "Nice to meet you, boys." I'm still wondering why I've been called over.

"Drew tells us you're new to the area," says Blake, the one who scares the shit out of me.

I play with the fringing on my costume, trying to look

away from his steely gaze. "Yeah, just been here a few weeks." What's it to him, anyway? I'm really regretting saying anything to Drew. What if it was some sort of a trap?

"You on the run from your boyfriend or something?" Blake asks.

My eyes dart to him then to Drew. What does he know? I suddenly get the urge to run, but where am I going to go? If Vinnie has sent a guy to find me, there will be nothing I can do. I look back at Drew, but he looks uncertain of what his friend is talking about. "Ah, why would you ask that?" I can feel my hands start to tremble. I don't like where this is going at all.

"Because my dad is Max Donovan, and he sent me to find you," he says, and the fear I felt when he first looked at me all makes sense. I can see it now, the family resemblance is there. He is fucking Mr Donovan's son—I'm so screwed.

I need to get out of here. I take a step back and bump into Drew. With the three of them all standing so close to me, I have no chance to run. I look over to security. He can see my discomfort and is on his way over. I give him a wave and the best smile I can muster to say I'm fine. I don't need to draw any more attention to myself. I have to talk myself out of this somehow.

"W... why? I'm not who you think I am, sorry. I have no idea who that is, you must have the wrong girl."

Drew's eyes flick to Blake. He looks confused, and I get the feeling he has no idea what's going on. "What are you talking about, Blake? Who's your dad?" Drew asks.

Blake ignores Drew, keeping his attention on me. "Why do you seem like you're about to run then?"

"Blake, stop it, you're scaring her," says Drew. I like how he sticks up for me against this arsehole. It's not going to save me if Vinnie gets a hold of me, though.

And he's right, I am scared. If they take me back to him, I have no idea what he will do to me. I have seen too much and then run from him; he is going to be beyond furious. I can feel tears pricking in my eyes as they dart between Blake and Drew. What do I say so they believe me and let me go? I try and look as calm and happy as I can. I don't want them to know how they are affecting me. "I'm just confused. I don't know who you're talking about," I mutter.

Blake's face softens a little. "Bambi, I'm not going to tell them where you are. I don't work for my dad. I'm nothing like him. But I just wanted you to know, they're searching the town for you. You're not safe working somewhere like this. They'll find you here. It's only a matter of time, my dad knows everyone in this line of business." He has a warmth to his eyes, I see it now. Something tells me I can trust him, but I'm scared to trust anyone at this point. I have been wrong so many times in the past.

I can hear my pulse pounding in my ears; it's making it hard to think. They're looking for me here? I don't have anywhere else to go. I can't hold the tears back any longer, and I can feel the trickle as the first escapes down my cheek. I wipe it away. "You don't understand. I don't have any choice. I have to. I need the money. No one else is hiring, and this is all I know. What am I supposed to do?" I spit at Blake. Someone like him would never understand. He would have had all the money in the world when he grew up, with a dad like his.

"We can help you find you something different," he offers with total sincerity. "You can't work here." I want to believe him.

But I don't know if I can even trust any of them. He could be pretending to help me, to lure me into a trap. But I have no one else, and I'm so frightened right now I can't even think straight. The way Drew looks at me, I feel like he's a decent guy. I fucking hope I'm right. "You can't let him find me. I don't want to go back to him. He's dangerous. I... I saw things. I can't go back. Please don't tell him where I am."

"I won't, *we* won't, you can trust us," Blake says.

"How do I know that? I don't know you," I cry.

"Man." The other guy, I think his name was Fraser, knocks Blake on the arm, tilting his head towards the door. "Is that your dad?" he whispers, but I hear him, and I follow his line of sight.

Fuck, it's Mr Donovan. I'm screwed.

"You have to be fucking kidding me," chokes out Blake. "Drew, your jacket, get it on her now. Cover her up and get her out of here."

I need to run away from all of them. "I can't go with him. I don't know any of you, I'm not going anywhere. Besides, security wont just let me slip out of here with you, it's going to cause a whole big scene," I protest. They can't tell me who I'm leaving here with, I don't even know if I can trust them.

Blake rests his hand on my shoulder, and I flinch. "We have to get you out of here. Seriously, if you don't want him to find you tonight, you need to get out of here now. We will deal with security."

Before I can plead my case again, Drew wraps his jacket around me, then takes my hands. I look up into those gorgeous eyes. I want to believe I can trust him, that he will save me from this living hell I'm in. "Come with me. You can come back to my place. My dad and brother are both cops in this town. I promise you can trust me. I will keep you safe. You can't stay here," Drew begs me.

I have no other choice. I have to trust him.

I glance between the guys in front of me and over to the

door, where Mr Donovan and now Vinnie—oh fuck, he's here as well, and they're talking to the bouncer. I'm out of here, it really is the only option. I look back to Drew. "Okay, Drew, I trust you." He takes me by the hand.

"Is there a back door?" Blake asks, and I nod. "Take her home, Drew. I--"

Those are the last words I hear from Blake as I'm ushered farther down the back of the club by Drew, and their words are drowned out by the music.

We make our way past the changing rooms, and I remember I need to grab my stuff. "Wait, I need my bag." I don't want to come back here again, so I need to get it now.

"Be quick," says Drew nervously. He waits by the dressing room door as I run through as quickly as I can and grab my bag and the dress I came in, throwing it over my head. Ariel comes running through the door.

"What's going on?"

"I'm sorry, I have to go. That guy out there talking to the bouncer, he's the one after me."

"Okay, you get out of here, I'll see you at my place later." She hugs me.

"I'll let you know."

I rush back to Drew, and we sprint for the back door, pushing it open into the cool night air and the back alley of the club.

Outside, it's eerily quiet in comparison to the blaring music. We hurry down the darkened street. My body is shaking, and he notices.

"You're cold. Here, let me warm you up until I can get you home. It's just a short walk to my parents' place." He puts his arm around me, and I let him. I'm wearing next to nothing, even with my dress over the top, and I'm freezing—or maybe it's the shock of it all. How did Vinnie find me so quickly? I knew this would happen. I'm never going to be safe from him.

We stop walking when we arrive in front of a beautiful Queenslander-style home; this must be his parents' house. "Are your parents home?" I ask tentatively. I don't have the energy for dealing with parents tonight.

"Yeah, but it's late, they'll be in bed." He tucks a strand of my wig behind my ear.

The wig—what use would this have been, anyway. I tug it off and let my hair out. It's long and falls down my back. "I should just keep walking to my apartment."

He takes me by the hands. "You're not going anywhere by yourself tonight. Those guys Blake was taking about, they might have your address. You're staying with me until I know your place is safe for you to return."

"I don't know about that, Drew, I don't want to impose. This is your parents' house, and you don't even know me."

"I know enough. You can stay in my bed tonight, I'll take the couch, and in the morning my dad will be able to help you. We can work out a plan so they don't find you. I promise I won't let anything happen to you. You will be safe here with us."

He rubs his hands up and down my arms, trying to comfort me. He is so kind to want to help me, and I have no idea why. I look up at him. "Why are you helping me?"

"Because you need a hand. I would do the same for anyone if they were as down on their luck as you. It's the way I have been brought up, and my parents would kill me if I didn't. It's what us Walkers do." He cups my face, running his finger over my lip. It sends a thrill right though my body. His touch is electric, energising, and I don't know if it's the adrenaline rush, but I want this man so badly I can taste it.

I bite the inside of my mouth to stop myself from acting on my impulse and just kissing him. He lowers his hands from my arms and laces our fingers together. "And I told you earlier, you're someone important to me, I know it already."

"Drew Walker, you might just be the sweetest guy there ever was."

He grins. "What's your real name? I can't introduce you to my parents in the morning as Bambi."

"It's Jenna, Jenna West."

He smiles and pulls me into his chest, and I let him. I need to feel the comfort of another human. After everything I have been through, the warmth of his body and the small gesture of a hug and knowing someone in this fucked-up world actually cares enough to go out of their way for me, it means everything.

While we stand in his parents' front yard, his arms wrapped around me, I go over his words in my head. 'You're *someone important to me.*' Such a strange thing for him to say when we have literally just met, but I can feel it too. He's going to be someone important in my life as well.

ALSO BY A K STEEL

Always Fraser — Broken Point book 1
http://mybook.to/alwaysfraser

Eventually Blake — Broken Point book 2
http://mybook.to/eventuallyblake

Only Theo — Broken Point book 3

Forever Drew — Broken Point book 4 (Coming soon)

If you enjoyed Only Theo, please leave me a review. Reviews really do make such a difference. Even a short one-liner is a big help. Thank you.

ABOUT THE AUTHOR

About A. K. Steel

I'm a contemporary romance author of books with swoony men, twists and turns, and always a happily ever after.

I'm a busy mother of three pre-teens, who lives on the beautiful South Coast of New South Wales, Australia. I have always been a creative soul, with a background in fashion design, interior decoration, and floristry. I currently run a business as a wedding florist and stylist but have always had a love for reading romance novels. There's just something about how the story can transport you to another world entirely.

So, in 2020, I decided to jot down some of my own ideas for romance stories—always with a happily ever after, of course—and from that came my debut novel, *Always Fraser*. From that moment, I haven't looked back. Writing has become a part of me. I have a long list of stories plotted, and I look forward to being able to share them all with you soon. I hope you enjoy reading them as much as I loved writing them.

XX

For all the news on upcoming books, visit A.K. Steel at:
Facebook: https://www.facebook.com/a.k.steelauthor
Instagram: @aksteelauthor
www.aksteelauthor.com

ACKNOWLEDGMENTS

My partner, Kiel, you have changed my life in so many wonderful ways. Thank you for pushing me to start writing. Without your encouragement and love, I never would have put pen to paper and started this fantastic journey in the first place. I feel like I found myself this year, and I'm finally where I'm supposed to be. Without you, this never would have happened.

My amazing mum, Kay, thank you for your constant love and support. You read every word I write and have always been my number-one fan. You put up with my meltdowns and endless questions, you are my best friend, and I'm grateful every day to have you in my life.

My dad, it's been seven long years since you left us, but the outlook you had on life still inspires me every day. It's the reason I believe that if you work hard enough, you can achieve any dream, no matter how impossible it seems.

My kids—Hamish, Marley, and Quinn—thank you for looking at me like I'm amazing and can do anything, even when I don't feel like I can. Everything I do is for you. And I hope I have shown you that with a bit of determination and hard work, your dreams really can come true.

Karen, my friend and mentor, you made this dream feel possible. Every time I thought I couldn't do it, you encouraged me to keep on going. I couldn't have done any of this without your knowledge and friendship.

T. L. Swan and the girls from the Cygnet Inkers group, I'm loving being on this journey with you all. You girls keep me positive and motivated, and I love you for it.

Lindsay, my editor, thank you for your patience with a new author. Your knowledge and expertise have made this book what it is.

Sarah, for my gorgeous cover design, and your patience with my indecisiveness. I love the cover you created for me.

My beta readers—Elise, Shelly, Kirstie, Bek, Francesca, Jemma, Patricia, Tobie and Anita—thank you for your time, honesty, and support. Without you lovely ladies I wouldn't have had the courage to publish and share my story.

My proofreader Kay, thank you for double and triple-checking every word.

To my friends and family who have been so supportive along this journey—you have all been so amazing—thank you.

And lastly to my readers, thank you for taking the time to give a new author a chance, and making my dreams become a reality.

Printed in Great Britain
by Amazon